Best Wishes,

Linda!

A. Leh[illegible]

Hamlet

The Novel

Alan W. Lehmann

ISBN: 978-1-4834-2867-3 (sc)
ISBN: 978-1-4834-2866-6 (e)

Library of Congress Control Number: 2015906119

Lulu Publishing Services rev. date: 04/20/2015

Dedication

To William Shakespeare, whose unparalleled imagination, human sensibility, and expressive brilliance command our respect and admiration.

Preface

I have always admired Shakespeare's plays, particularly the tragedies, and even more particularly, *Hamlet.* Centered as the story is around the character of a young man who is presented as a historical prince of Denmark, the play's complex, interwoven themes draw the reader or viewer into a world that is at once familiar and foreign.

Foreign? Few of us are princes or privy to grand wealth and power. The story is set in a European kingdom half a millennium ago in a culture riven by religious tension and driven by struggles for power. In addition, the Elizabethan English in which Shakespeare's play is presented creates a linguistic burden for many if not most contemporary playgoers. These factors combine to create the play's exotic strangeness.

Familiar? Each of us spends a sizeable portion of his or her early decades struggling to make sense of the world and to find a suitable fit in it. At one time or another, many of us become significantly overwhelmed by life's challenges. Although he is a prince, Hamlet (like us) must wrestle with the moral and practical trials of his youth and station. So, for that matter, do other characters: Ophelia, Laertes, Fortinbras and Horatio. It is this factor that makes Hamlet, as well as the others, resonate so with readers and playgoers of nearly all ages.

The play embodies and revisits several critical themes that may be most effectively posed as questions. What are the roles and responsibilities of kingship (or leadership), and how are these best exhibited in the fluctuating dynamic relationship between a king (leader) and his subjects? What is justice, and how should it be obtained and administered? (How should it differ from revenge?) How might madness moderate our expectations of responsibility in and for those who have been thus afflicted? How does moral corruption spread from single acts by isolated individuals to a general pattern of behavior within a polity, to the point where corruption becomes the rule and honest behavior the exception? In what kinds of situations may we be forgiven our dishonesties? How do love, fear and ambition play off one another in the minds and actions of people at all levels of society? Do we have free will, that is, can we choose our loyalties and values or are they the product of a conditioning or fate that we only vaguely apprehend? And finally, what of that concept fate: is there any ultimate purpose to our lives? None of these questions is thoroughly answered by *Hamlet*, yet each is drawn into focus for the percipient reader or viewer.

As a young student I was lucky enough to have a number of teachers and professors who were able to transmit to me through their insights, and through our required reading of Shakespeare's plays, that there exist important questions in life, and that drama can bring these questions into focus. Thus, in my own career as a teacher I felt it important that my students be given a basic exposure to Shakespeare (and particularly to *Hamlet*). Still, the obstacles of distance in language and history are formidable for many youngsters who may fail to understand that in their own lives they are grappling with issues similar to those so dramatically presented by the characters in *Hamlet*.

Consider the numerous pains and injustices that riddle our contemporary society: absurd forms of inequality, dysfunctional families, "disprized" love, and the maddening conclusion to which too many of our youth arrive, that none of us matters, that life is meaningless, and that there are few values worth pursuing or defending save perhaps the pleasures of the moment. If exposure to *Hamlet* (Shakespeare's matchless original or my adaptation) creates any useful perspective from which youth may conclude that they are not alone, and that life is a challenging puzzle for the best *and* the worst of us, then this novel has done its job.

I wrote *Hamlet: the Novel* to make that exposure a more accessible experience, one that may create a motivational space from which those unaccustomed to Shakespeare's genius may step to more challenging works.

Al Lehmann
November, 2014

Contents

Prologue

First Causes

"It has been argued that everything has a cause, but that in trying to discern the causes of things, one must eventually find oneself back at a first cause. The saint named Aquinas called this first cause 'God.' We puny mortals will likely never gain an understanding sufficient to comprehend the intricate chains and webs of power and influence that create and sustain or direct our world. Perhaps that is why philosophers and priests ultimately fail to explain them.

Despite all these uncertainties, felt so intimately by us, God's creatures, I am certain of one imperative truth. Past events do affect the present, and through it, the future. The ghosts of men and women long dead still circulate among us, touch us, whisper to us, and though we may not always listen to them, or even sense their presence directly, we succumb to their influence, playing a role long written into the scripts of our lives, even while imagining we are free."

–from one of Prince Hamlet's
papers found among his effects after his death.

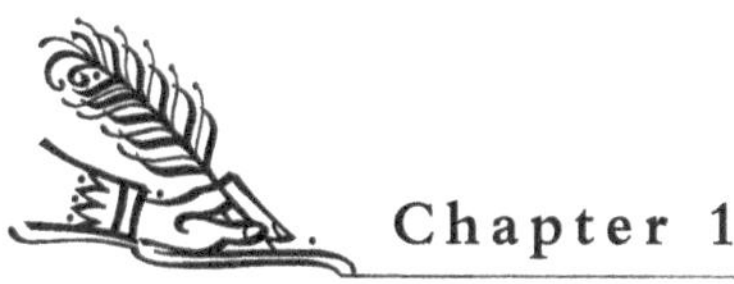

Chapter 1

Dark Beginnings

The castle stood silent, its massive crenellated walls and sentry platforms a dark outline against an only slightly lighter sky. Masses of cloud hooded the thin crescent of the moon, and in the few gaps of clarity only a few stars shed any light below. An uneasy wind gusted in fits off the salty reaches of the Oresund, the offshore expanse of salt water to the northeast. Along Elsinore's harbor, fishing vessels creaked at their moorings. Occasionally a dog barked, only to be answered by others farther off. The town was dark, too. It was late. A torch belonging to the watch at the castle gate lent a flickering, smoky light over the approach. Although the watch stood alertly beside his shelter, no one else was about. He stamped impatiently to warm himself, turned his back to the charcoal brazier that glowed behind him and forced himself guiltily to maintain his attention.

It was late but not so late that the bakers were yet awake, readying the great ovens for the day's breads and the other more delicate creations a king might wish for. But another person besides the watch, was still awake. In a third floor window of the castle's main building, beside one of the great towers that made up the castle's defensive design, a candle glowed.

Within the room a lightly bearded man in his early thirties sat unmoving, hunched at a wooden writing table. On the wooden surface beside his frayed elbow slept a white cat, stretched luxuriantly on a velvet cushion. A few papers lay on the table and the man held a quill, which he hesitantly dipped into a pot of ink. Then he bent forward and began to write.

It is dark outside my casement window. From the little drafts that periodically twist the candle flame beside me as I write, and from the stiffness in my knees, I can tell that it is getting cold. My hand is stiff, too, and though my quill is sharp and ink in good supply, I linger as I write. I begin to tell my tale, and then begin again, for what I write is far too strange, far too important to tell it wrong. Brother Henrik scowled when I asked him for paper, but the importance of these writings makes his disapproval irrelevant. I shall have to ask him for more paper soon. The new king Fortinbras is prodding me to hurry, and kings are to be obeyed. What am I, if not loyal and obedient?

It is less than a week since the great burial. Ah, the funeral! There has not been a funeral like that in Elsinore in all of history! A king, a queen, and a prince (the queen's son)—all buried together, along with young Laertes, son of the king's senior councilor. (Even in such a simple enumeration the tangle of things begins to show!)

The great church was filled to overflowing with people—sad people, uneasy people. Yet even with their fear, or perhaps because of it, they came. Women cried. Some men held whispered conversations. Others remained quietly aloof, the wilderness of insecurity in their eyes. The priest was brief in his homily, a lesson based on the inevitability of death, as in Genesis it is prescribed to all of sinful mankind. But to his credit, he also included reference to our hopes for the life to come with our Savior for all righteous souls. God save us all.

The writer lowered his quill a moment and crossed himself reverently. He bowed his head for a moment, as if in prayer. Then he took up the quill, dipped it into the ink, and continued to write.

Despite great King Fortinbras's regular queries, though, this account of Prince Hamlet and his untimely death will take time to write, for the story is complicated by numerous and thorny factors: many people are involved, from all classes of the world; some are liars and thieves, some merely ingenuous victims; some are of royal blood, others simple commoners. Levels of deception overlap, numerous plots collide, and chance, as always, plays its deceitful role. And behind all of that, chanting his mournful tunes and grinning his rictal smile stands Fate, wearing the robe of Death, who, as the priest reminded us, shall come for us all one day. I know only part of the story, but I am determined to record what I know faithfully.

Of course, it is understandable, I can tell *only* what I know, though the King Fortinbras (and any other readers) may conclude that I have embellished events, or perhaps left essential features out. It is well known that Prince Hamlet was my friend and I his vassal. It might be suspected that the story I tell is only partly true, that I have polished the metal of my friend or exaggerated his enemies. They will have to come to their own conclusions. But I hope that when *I* am gone, the essence of this story will remain, that people who read it will understand Hamlet's fundamental nobility, and that they will be forced to mourn his loss as I have, for only his early death has prevented his greatness from becoming truly manifest.

As the Scriptures record, David slew Goliath the giant, a lesson that illustrates how the advantages of power and greatness do not always defeat apparent weakness, but are rather defeated by virtue and by the favor of our Lord God. Hamlet lacked power, but he clung to virtue. Can it be true that he lacked God's favor? For though his enemies were ultimately vanquished, Hamlet never became king as did David, nor did he fulfill his potential greatness. Yet I am getting far ahead of myself.

I was close to Hamlet, closer than to any other man (or woman, for that matter). Within the embrace of his confidence I learned much of how this strange tale unfolded. Thus, I was positioned well to gather in the details that led to the Danish court's catastrophic destruction on that fateful October day, at least as Hamlet understood them. I experienced many of them. Further, I was present at a number of other relevant events and occurrences that, although they may have seemed innocent, or at most, unusual at the times of their unfolding, on reflection may be seen as critical parts of the whole story.

I have also been made privy to important documents. Upon the deaths of Polonius (and later the rest of his family) the family's belongings were stored for a time in the cellars of the castle, many documents and papers among them. Polonius was, after all, a minister of state, and he had many private papers. Both Laertes and Ophelia were able writers, and Ophelia's diary and letters are exceptionally revealing. Further, Hamlet himself left extended notes addressed to me, as if he knew his death were imminent (as it was, alas!) and he intended that I should understand events through his eyes. May he rest in everlasting peace! I loved him greatly and shall miss him always.

Knowing exactly where to start such a tale requires judgment. As the great philosopher Aristotle once wrote in his *Poetics*, every story has a beginning, a middle, and an end. Though we know the end with violent clarity, choosing the beginning must be done more prudently. (Some of my fellow students in Wittenberg, sophisticates as they imagined themselves to be, would have taken me all the way back to Genesis to the serpent in the Garden, and although they would doubtless have been smiling over their cups of ale or wine while delivering these pronouncements, there is more truth to their amusement than they realize. But I'm getting ahead of myself.) As for the middle, what is to be included is a recollection clawed for, even cried for, sometimes missed, but finally, it is to be hoped, composed as a reliable narrative.

I have chosen to begin the tale more than thirty years ago on a fertile island northwest of Elsinore. If stories have violent ends, why should they not have vicious beginnings? And this beginning certainly was vicious.

As some may know (and anyone who claims himself a Dane *should* know), the Denmark we know today was not always ours. True, we *claimed* much of it, through all the laws of heraldry and primogeniture, but many of the same areas—shorelines, islands, rolling plains--were claimed at times by Sweden, at times by Norway, and even by those arrogant Germans to the south. Parts of Denmark, and especially the island in the dispute I am about to recount, have changed hands many times, usually through violence. This was one of those times, and the Norwegians were our foes.

Oddly enough, it was our own king Fortinbras' father, a Norwegian king (now long gone to God or to Valhalla, who knows which?) who was instrumental to the events. He and now so-called 'Old Hamlet,' Hamlet's father, had long contended over two of the islands off Denmark's shore not more than half a day's sail from where I write. On the nearer of those islands the blood was spilled, and through that day's butchery, Denmark came to control them. I was less than a year old at the time, no doubt tugging at my nurse's dug, when these events unfolded. But years later I questioned my father about these events, events praised by the priest who taught me my letters (Father Kristian, God rest his now departed soul).

My father told this part of the tale in his own, characteristic way. We were sitting before the hearth in his modest cottage near Elsinore's docks, sharing some dark and bitter ale while the wind blew outside. He coughed once into his sleeve and gazed into the low flames licking the peat fuel. Then he began.

"It was a surprisingly pretty day," he murmured, the irony evident in his tone. "The oak leaves of the nearby forest had darkened from their fresh spring color into their summer green. Birds were trilling, and the air had that seaborne freshness that stimulates the blood. Of course, our blood was up anyway. We were with Hamlet, our king, marshaling our ranks across a green meadow split by a narrow creek that spilled gurgling into the bay where we had disembarked." He coughed again, a rough cough that suggested the infirmity of age, then drank. He continued.

"At first the meadow was empty, except for an ill-clad cowherd and the three brindled cows he was hurrying up the slope and onto a path into the woods. Then one of our ranks noticed that, about half a league away on the other side of the meadow, three horsemen emerged from the forest and pulled up short. Norwegian swine! One could tell that they weren't comfortable on horseback, but their leader straightened up and pointed our way with his lance, and the others craned to look. They seemed to exchange some words, then wheeled their horses and turned back into the forest."

"Only a few of our men saw them before they disappeared, but a low muttering began to spread through our ranks. King Hamlet, who had observed their appearance and rapid departure, raised his hand. He had been standing with the Lords Bjorn and Alfred, as well as Brother Karol (as bloodthirsty a priest as has ever lived, I assure you), but now he faced us men. We scrambled into some form of order, beneath our banners and with our households."

My father took another swig of ale and wiped his beard on his sleeve. He smiled to himself, as if reaching deeply within himself to the place where vivid memories lie like buried gold or grave goods, the true values that show a man's worth. He continued.

"'Noble Danes!' Hamlet cried out to us. 'Today God has brought us forth to defend our lands. Our ignoble brother Norway claims this island, as well as Feylas Rock Isle that we can see from here across the sound to the east. But we know it is God's will that these lands be ruled by us, justly, fairly, and with God's holy wisdom. The Norse king, a dog's arse if there ever was one, is on this island with his army.' Hamlet paused. 'He needs a good whipping!'"

"The men raised their shields and cheered, a rousing sound from a thousand throats. Then they banged their spears on their shields in a powerful rhythm, at first erratic, but soon a forceful repetitive drumming like the marching of thousands of nailed boots, a sound that never fails to fire the blood. Hamlet raised his hand after a short interval, and the men settled back into a respectful silence, sullied only by the odd cough or murmur."

"Just then, one of Hamlet's lords addressed his king, and they both looked back toward where the Norwegians had disappeared. A long file of armed men was entering the meadow, led by a tall, powerful man on horseback, obviously the Norwegian king, flanked by two priests in rough robes. We watched carefully as several hundred men began to form up into shield lines."

"Then, two of the horsemen we had seen before spurred their mounts into a slow trot toward us. They wove past a few rocks or stumps hidden in the long grass, splashed across the creek at the low point in the meadow, and moved purposefully toward us, pulling their horses to a halt about twenty yards away from King Hamlet and his lords. All was silent save for the breathing of the horses and some birdsong quivering from the woods. Then one of the Norwegians spoke in that overly sing-song accent of theirs, but with serviceable Danish."

"'My lord king Fortinbras II, paragon of virtue and power, and ruler of these lands through God's will and the precedence of antiquity, commands that the Danes he sees before him leave his land.' He paused, seemingly satisfied with the ceremonious tone of his message. Then he added, 'Or, if they will swear fealty to the lord Fortinbras as rightful king of these islands, some may remain and settle with all the rights and privileges, as well as duties, beholden to such fealty. The land is fertile and spacious, with room for many, but the land belongs to Norway and will remain in our kingdom. So says my lord King Fortinbras.'"

"A murmur rather like a growl began to swell among our men. One of the Norwegian horses nickered softly. His rider patted it gently on the neck, holding the horse back carefully. King Hamlet, now facing the Norwegians, raised his hand indicating the need for silence. Our murmur subsided. He spoke to their embassy in a strong, clear voice, nearly loud enough to be heard as far away as the Norwegian lines. I knew his speech was for us as much as it was for the Norse. *Their* army was now deployed, two triple-lined wedges with their king and his officers between them. They stood still, watching us intently."

My father glanced at me slyly, as if to measure the impact of his narrative—the old rascal! But I know the lure of a good story, and truth be told, I was hooked! Noting my interest with a small smile, he turned back to the fire, drank once more, then went on.

"Our great King Hamlet replied, 'Your king is a liar and a fool. These islands are clearly deeded to Denmark, as recorded in the land count parchments in St. Gustav's Cathedral in Elsinore. If your king has sufficient stamina, he might brave our company and come to Elsinore to learn the truth.' He paused. 'Or, perhaps he lacks the courage for such a journey.' He paused again, as if warming to his theme. Then he continued more forcefully, drawing himself up in such a way that for a moment we thought the Norwegian emissaries cringed. Then, in a surprisingly calm but resonant voice, he said, 'We have come with our soldiers to show your king our resolve that these rights enjoyed by our predecessors will not be ceded to any ragtag claimant who can flaunt a few shields in his service. These lands belong to Denmark and will remain with us. Tell your master so.'"

"Our men grumbled their approval, but the Norse rider colored, visibly angered. He raised himself on the stirrups, perhaps stretching to get a better view of our numbers. Then, muttering something to his comrade, he wheeled his horse around; his comrade followed, and without another word they trotted back to the Norwegian lines. There they conversed with their king and other Norwegian officers, who frequently turned their heads toward us."

"A soft breeze began to ruffle the trees and grass, and the sun was approaching its zenith. The incoming tide lapped at the gravel beach to our right. We stood at ease, awaiting our king's command. For his part, he stretched, and I couldn't but be impressed by his muscular size. He seemed to exude confidence and strength. He was a king not to be forgotten."

"We waited for more than an hour. Some among our number were permitted to rest in the shade at the edge of the wood, where our pickets reconnoitered to ensure that the deceitful Norwegian was not sending troops to our rear. But all was quiet. Some of the men ate of the meager provisions from the leather bag each man had tied to his waste. The king's guard, twenty or so strapping soldiers in light armor, remained alert, stationed in a regular perimeter around the king and his advisors."

"At last, a party from the Norwegian lines detached itself from the main body of their troops. Their king, another massive man like our Hamlet, with torcs of gold around each bulging arm, led them. Picking their way carefully, the riders made their way down to a shallow but fairly level depression on their side of the creek. There they dismounted, all save one rider and a priest, who pressed on toward our lines. It was the same messenger who had come previously. When the two of them came near enough to be heard, they stopped, and with a coarse shout, invited two from our Hamlet's party to parley. They held up their hands to indicate they were unarmed."

"'See what they want,' Hamlet instructed Harold, one of his officers, curtly. 'Take Ravik with you. No weapons.'"

"Harold and Ravik unbuckled their broadswords and laid them on the turf near the king's feet. They unsheathed their knives and laid them upon the scabbards of their broadswords. Each bowed to the king. Then, after a quick glance at one another, they walked down to the parley, hands raised palms outward to show that they had no weapons."

"We men watched with interest, and those who had been eating got to their feet, eager to know what was happening. Harold and Ravik quietly greeted the Norse embassy. Then the four men began to talk. Their voices, always indistinct, rose and fell with the breeze. The Norwegian priest held a scroll, which he unrolled and showed to Harold, while Ravik and the Norwegian soldier eyed each other warily. Harold glanced back toward our king with wide eyes. Then he accepted the scroll, touched Ravik on the shoulder, and both turned back toward our lines. The Norwegian soldier impassively watched them return to us."

"Harold and King Hamlet separated themselves from the king's party a few paces, and Harold unrolled the scroll before him. Hamlet read it carefully, or seemed to, for he looked it over for a considerable time, five minutes or more, glancing every so often toward the Norwegian king, as if taking his measure. We in the lines waited, for the most part patiently, although I could tell that many of the men were bursting to know what was happening."

My father paused and looked at me intently, as if to fathom some mystery I might be hiding, or to find the words he needed to warn me of some unclear danger. When he continued, he lowered his eyes to the fire and murmured, "Trying to overmaster curiosity is not a natural instinct for man. We are curious as cats, as my old tutor once said, a trait particularly strong in my friend Polonius, an ambitious soldier if there ever was one. But that's another story." He stared once more into the fire and prodded a log with a fire iron. The log flared up, and a fountain of crackling sparks rose into the chimney. Then he went on, more quietly, more seriously.

"Finally King Hamlet looked up at Harold, nodded, and they returned to the others, where the king and his advisors spoke at length in hushed tones. More than one looked fearfully at the king, and one officer shook his head vigorously as if in disagreement, and seemed as if he would take the king by the shoulder. But the king raised his hand and now nearly shouted, 'No. I will do this.' He looked the man in the eye until the man turned away.

"Then, the king turned and walked toward our troops, who again murmured apprehensively among themselves. He began to speak.

"'Their turd king has dropped his glove before me in challenge! He offers to fight me, the two of us alone, yonder on the greensward. He who kills the other may claim the disputed lands in perpetuity for his heirs and lineage.' Hamlet paused and took a deep breath. 'I will do this. In the Holy Gospels, God may speak through signs and wonders, but in our world He most often molds our fates through the arms of his kings. I intend to be God's right arm, to fight for His honor and glory and for the pride of Denmark.'"

"He briefly knelt, crossing himself, and at his example we crossed ourselves as well. Standing, he drew his broadsword, which glittered in the noonday sunshine. He flourished it above his head. Then he turned and began to walk down the grassy slope to a flat area within a bend of the creek."

"A thrill of pride and terror coursed through me. A babble of conversations rose to a rumble among our ranks. Harold and the king's guards made to accompany Hamlet, but he turned fiercely and waved them back. Across the meadow I could see the Norwegian king making his way, alone, toward the flat."

"Each man wore light armor: greaves on their shins and leather breastplates, as well as metal helms. They were like Achilles and Hektor, going to meet their fate beneath the walls of Troy! Oh, that our Hamlet would be Achilles, and show his wrath!"

"Hamlet had not sheathed his sword, and Fortinbras drew his own, which glinted fearsomely in the sunlight. He trotted confidently toward the flat, an area perhaps twenty or twenty-five paces on each irregular side. At the edge on his side of the square, he squatted and then stood again, rolling his massive shoulders, stretching out his muscles. Hamlet reached the flat moments later and stretched his great arms over his head. He took his sword by the blade in his gloved hand and raised it like a cross toward heaven. He kissed the hilts, then tossed it lightly up, only to catch its handle as surely as he might grasp a cup of wine."

"The Norwegian ranks raised a great cheer for their king, and we did the same for ours. Our priests were crossing themselves nervously. I could see that Lord Harold was nearly bursting with pride or anxiety, I could not be sure which. The kings faced each other, alone."

My father turned to me. I had been staring at him, rapt in his account. He mused softly, "It's curious how some great events are colored by memories of inconsequential things. I remember swatting a fly away from my face, which was wet with nervous sweat! A kingdom at stake, and I remember a fly!" He paused and drank, then wiped some foam from his moustache.

"The whole event was finished nearly as soon as it began, again contrary to what we might have expected. One imagines that a battle of two such great warriors would be a drawn out affair, and to speak true, both men drew blood. But their fight can't have lasted more than three or four minutes. Fortinbras gave a great shout and began to move toward Hamlet, who raised his sword in readiness."

"The clashing of their blades rang throughout the meadow. I imagined the sound echoing off Elsinore's sturdy walls! Minutes into the contest, I vividly remember Fortinbras's sword point's nicking across the front of Hamlet's thigh, flicking crimson across the grass. A great, terrified groan burst from our ranks and the Norwegians cheered."

"Fortinbras closed to make a more killing blow, as Hamlet seemed to slip almost down onto one knee. Fortinbras violently swung his great sword, but our king rolled to one side, allowing his foe's point to pass harmlessly into the turf. Hamlet swiftly ran his own blade across Fortinbras's exposed forearm and sawed back. Fortinbras screamed and dropped the blade."

"Before he could react further, Hamlet was on his feet. Fortinbras shuddered in terror as Hamlet swung his great blade! He struck Fortinbras a massive blow to the neck. A gout of blood erupted into the sunshine. Fortinbras' head toppled to one side. Hamlet pulled the sword back, even as Fortinbras dropped to his knees. Hamlet swung again, decapitating the Norwegian king."

I felt my gorge rise at his description. I crossed myself and drank. Unmoved, or if anything, proud of his gruesome recollection, my father continued.

"As you might imagine, a howl of anguish rose from the Norwegian ranks, even as our soldiers raised a tremendous cheer. Hamlet stood still a moment, panting with his exertion. Then he knelt and unclasped the helmet from Fortinbras' head. Getting to his feet, he held up his arms, gripping the head by the hair in his left hand and raising his stained sword high over his head in his right."

"Our troops cheered again. Harold and two other nobles rushed forward to stand by our king. Hamlet then turned to face the Norwegian line. 'Come get your king,' he shouted in his loudest voice. 'Then leave this island.'"

My father drained the last of his ale and then looked from the fire to me, a smile quivering at the corners of his mouth. I am told that the memories of our youth, no matter how shocking or difficult the time might have been, are precious to us in our years of age. *My* hand trembled as I lifted my cup and drank with him. Then another pair of thoughts occurred to me in rapid succession.

"Was Claudius, the king's brother, present at this great fight?" I asked. "And what did the queen say when she received news?"

My father snorted. "You imagine I am privy to the movement or conversations of royalty? How would I know what the queen said?"

Then, "As for Claudius, he was not there. Claudius was never one for risk, at least not in my memory. He was never a warrior such as Hamlet was. Who knows what he thought...?"

His voice trailed off for a moment, but then he added in a cynical tone, "Given subsequent events—Old Hamlet's poisoning, to be precise—he must more recently have approved his brother's heroism; after all, he became the ultimate beneficiary, did he not? Of course, that benefit did not last long, did it?" He looked sideways at me with a gruff chuckle. Then he returned to watching the flames.

Within days, the Norwegians had left the island. My father explained that a battalion of Danish infantry remained stationed in the village beyond the woods, and our engineers built a fortified camp from which to establish our sovereignty. It was a great day, a heroic achievement in my father's eyes, an extraordinary event. Unfortunately, the Norwegians retained their own memories of these events.

I allowed my own imagination to play back over what I truly knew about the insight in my father's speculations. I felt a whiff of pride at the old man's judgment, but said nothing. As the fire burnt down we finished our drinks. I said my good nights and made my way back to my quarters in the palace, reviewing in my own mind the initial results of this epic combat. This great contest, happy as it was for Denmark, had its own darker side. Paradoxically enough, this great victory seemed the seed of many evils, yet perhaps other blessings, to come. If I have learned anything from trying to reconstruct these events, it is that the threads of fate are tangled and long.

The bearded young man looked up from his writing. He lay the quill down, blew on the final parchment where the ink was still wet, and examined the page thoughtfully. Pale light could be seen through the grimy window. He picked up the quill, dipped it in the inkwell, and wrote once more at the base of the page: Horatio Stenmark.

Chapter 2

Old Hamlet's Court

Horatio gently patted the cat (he had named it Cleopatra, for the great Egyptian queen). It flicked its tail and purred briefly, looking inscrutably at Horatio. He smiled.

Then, with a thoughtful expression, he dipped his pen in the ink and began to write.

> I find myself relying on many people of the older generation, that is, the generation of Old Hamlet (the king, Hamlet's father, rest his soul), for the background I feel I must provide. Brother Henrik has been less disapproving with his distribution of paper tonight. In fact, he smiled when he saw Cleopatra, my feline companion. When he tried to stroke her, though, she hissed at him, a response that may diminish tomorrow's portion.
>
> I feel I must find some explanation or description of who these victims were, beyond their royal titles. With the permission of Fortinbras' chamberlain, a sour-faced Norwegian with limited understanding of either Danish speech or manners, I managed to arrange to meet and talk with Old Hamlet's chamberlain, a man clearly down at heart now that he lacks gainful employment. We

talked for several hours today in a private room above the grain exchange.

(I only hope that my remuneration for taking on this task will suffice to pay the debts I am accumulating in the process. I had to offer the chamberlain three copper pieces for his insights, and the grain exchange wanted one piece for the use of the room. I must adjust my expenditures soon or I will lack the funds to carry out his majesty's order.)

The chamberlain, a man called Jacob Nordstrom, was surprisingly voluble and well spoken. We sat at an oak table, sharing a small pot of stew (he had a surprising alacrity for pulling out the most succulent morsels) and a pitcher of ale. When I asked him about the previous royal household, he was quite forthcoming. Here, roughly remembered, is what he told me—if not word for word, reasonably close to it.

"There was no denying it: Her majesty Queen Gertrude was a beautiful woman. Not only was she physically alluring—her ready smile, her golden hair, her well-proportioned figure—but she was also gracious, and charming. Her insight and wit illumined any conversation in which she participated. In good-natured debate one might imagine her comments to be harmless or frivolous, only to find that it was she who had cut to the core of the matter (often through the metaphorical neck of her interlocutor). Her words were precise and well chosen. She did not abide fools readily. Perhaps she thought me one of those, from time to time."

He sighed, speared a chunk of meat, inserted it in his mouth and chewed thoughtfully, as if the meat somehow contained the words he needed. I sipped my ale and waited for him to continue.

"She could often see *right through* others, in the sense that her ability to judge character knew no match. It was *she*, not Old Hamlet, who understood the duplicity of the Polish king in the dispute in northern Prussia, now years past, but dramatic and dangerous at the time. Oh, I know, all credit goes to the king, and it's true, her husband's tactics dispatched the enemy army in short order, but had he not enjoyed the advantage of her thinking he might have missed his chance."

He paused, chewing vigorously. Then he tugged a well-worked piece of gristle from beside his molars and tossed it off into a corner.

"It was obvious that our great King Hamlet loved her beyond measure. For her part, as far as I could judge, she showed every joy in their union, especially her devotion to young Hamlet, upon whom she doted through his childhood."

"The king finally sent Hamlet away to school to 'temper his metal/mettle.' (The king was always fond of puns.) But once Hamlet had departed to Wittenberg, a city known for its university of higher learning, even the king himself admitted to the inner court that he missed Hamlet. His choice of Wittenberg was especially puzzling to me, because Wittenberg is a protestant university town."

Jacob took a sip of ale and frowned, considering. "King Hamlet may have been protestant, but he still had Roman Catholic leanings," he said. "He told me later that every man who imagines himself to have a mind should be challenged by what may or may not be judged as heresy at one time or another—when better than when young and vigorous? I found it hard to agree, but a king's judgment is a king's judgment. Final."

Jacob drank again and lifted his cup, indicating to me that he would like another. I sighed inwardly and signaled to the servant standing near the doorway apart. He bowed slightly and turned to his errand. Hans continued.

"Young Hamlet was a puzzling child. He did grow up learning to fight, as his father so devoutly wished. When training with his fencing tutor, Hamlet adapted fast and fought well, but there was a part of him that was almost absent. Swordplay came so naturally to him that he managed its physical exertions seemingly thoughtlessly. He was one of only a few fighters I have seen who despite sweating copiously with the exertion of the match, nonetheless manages to make his actions appear effortless."

"I recall once watching one of his learning sessions. When his tutor gave him some rather extended advice on how to parry a particular kind of attack, Hamlet merely laughed and said, 'If I have to think such moves through, I'll be cut to pieces before I react! Am I not countering well?'"

"His tutor scowled, then laughed his grudging acknowledgement that Hamlet was, indeed, fighting well. I supposed the man felt an overpowering loyalty and obligation to the king, and determined to turn the young man into the best swordsman Denmark might produce. Certainly Hamlet's reactions were exceptionally quick, as if he understood the pattern of his opponent's blows even before a sequence began. When the king came to see Hamlet in training, one could see that the father was very proud of his son's ability."

"Hamlet's problem (or so the king thought) was that when he wasn't fencing, he was *always* thinking. There was a devilish curiosity to him. He would ask the most vexing and peculiar questions, such as, 'Can God, if he is all-powerful, create a boulder so heavy that even He cannot lift it?' Where is the end of everything? How does God make the sun shine so brightly?'"

Jacob laughed, an almost childlike chuckle, one of fondness.

"Despite these idiosyncrasies, he seemed a happy youngster, and even Old Hamlet, strict as he was, must have hoped and believed that his son would make a great king one day, perhaps even outshining his own performance as monarch. All the more reason, or so he judged, that his son should learn from the best (even though he had some suspicions about "philosophy" and the strange ideas that might come from priestly lectures)."

"Young Hamlet made his mother proud, too, (though mothers are usually easier to please than fathers, an observation about human nature that most elders can attest to). Perhaps Hamlet got his peculiar curiosity from his mother. She was no regular woman. Her intelligence and grace aside, there always seemed to be a mystery to her."

"True, she must have been a willing lover and was always a devoted mother, and yet, once, when Old Hamlet inquired as to her welfare or happiness (I remember the afternoon quite well—there was a storm beyond the ramparts, discharging lightning that frightened the servants) she was unable to answer immediately, as if to do so would be to admit some unpardonable offence. She stared for several moments out the window at the lightning flashes—perhaps God Himself was testing us all that day. Then I recall her kissing him dutifully and asking in return, 'Whatever could be the matter?' There was at times an invisible yet impenetrable wall around herself that it seemed no one had access to."

"One of the queen's personal servants once told me that Old Hamlet seemed to have gotten the impression that perhaps his brother Claudius had a kind of inside track to understand her. When he observed Claudius and Gertrude conversing there was a characteristic ease to their conversation, a pleasant sort of comfort to their exchanges and polite banter. When our king somewhat circuitously questioned his brother as to his understanding of Gertrude, all Claudius would say was, 'She seems a fine but private lady, my liege, truly one worthy of a king, but not one whom I would profess to understand beyond my conviction of her absolute loyalty and devotion to you, which is as it should be, of course.' Such answer made our late king believe that Claudius was no more fathomable than Gertrude!"

Jacob leaned back, stretching his boots toward the fire. Curious now, I squirmed a little impatiently and he went on.

"Claudius, too, was a mystery. Hamlet had loved Claudius since he was old enough to understand that Claudius was his brother, or so I think. Hamlet was the older brother, but only by eleven months. And Claudius was a bright child, one who by the time they were young men was essentially Hamlet's equal in most qualities to be prized in princes."

"They had sat through the same tutors together as children, and had explored the castle hand in hand. As youngsters they had ridden through the parks together and wagered on their respective hawks!"

"Two years before Hamlet's ascension to the throne, the two young men (hardly more than boys) had noticed young Gertrude at one of the castle balls, a gathering of nobles and their kind held twice a year at Elsinore. Her beauty was breathtaking, and both of them were struck by it. Between the two of them, it was Hamlet who screwed up his courage to ask her to dance first. Of course, she must have known that he was the prince-elect, the king-to-be. Perhaps at that realization her fate was sealed."

(Knowing what I now know, I raised my eyes at this remark. *The invisible Claudius*, I thought to myself. *And his queen*...)

The old chamberlain sighed, and he selected another chunk of lamb from the pot. He chewed it reflectively, swallowed, and wiped his mouth with a coarse linen kerchief. Then he went on.

"The fate that, through birth, selects one man to be a king and another not is a mysterious force, for truth be told, it sometimes seemed to an onlooker that Claudius coveted naked power more than Hamlet, who must have simply assumed it was his due. Once Old Hamlet became our king a kind of polite distance developed between him and his brother. Although Hamlet valued his brother's advice, they were less often together."

"Some affairs of state, of course, were for Hamlet alone, and he certainly had no desire to share the throne with Claudius, whom he may have judged shrewd, but perhaps not wise enough in his assessments to be frequently relied upon. Claudius became a sort of shadow, frequently in the background of things, too like Hamlet for his own good."

When I asked about Polonius and his noble children, Laertes and Ophelia, Jacob was less charitable.

"They were an ambitious family." He spat into the sawdust beside his chair. "The mother, rest her soul, died when Ophelia was very young. It must have been a shock to Polonius, who relied on his wife implicitly to look after young Laertes. But, Polonius hired a nurse from among the court maidens, a young slut who had lost an ill-bred child of her own. I was surprised the girl was still at court, given the power of the church here in Denmark. However, she proved a diligent servant, and with her dutiful care of his children Polonius managed to raise them into decent youngsters despite his royal obligations."

"After his career in the army, Polonius became one of Old Hamlet's chief councilors, especially with respect to matters of diplomacy and foreign relations. He knew his law well, as far as I could judge, but he had the ear of the king less often than he might have wanted. The council as a whole was dominated, aside from the king, by a man named Valentin (but he later died after being afflicted by a strange tumor in his neck). I always felt that Polonius had an eye on better things, and truth be told, he was a close confidant of the king's brother, Claudius--and your father, I believe..."

He gazed upward toward the rafters as if reading some obscure text there. "The offspring were predictably similar," he asserted, and looked back at me. "Young Laertes was given the best tutors available, and it was apparent that he would be sent to one of the foreign universities when he came of age."

"Ophelia was a pleasant girl, not too intelligent but bright enough to know how to aim for the main chance. She was a pretty thing, pleasant of face, but prone to giggling a little too much, especially when she was around young Hamlet. I couldn't help but think that there was design in her humor, perhaps a design enforced into her behavior by her father..." He paused, staring into the darkness for a moment.

"In any case, you know full well how the family's fortune improved upon the death of King Hamlet. Was this bounty an accident? I think not."

This was the essence of Old Jacob's narrative. I was a little shocked by his final speculation, although on retrospect, it's clear that he was nobody's fool. In fact, he seemed surprisingly astute, but then again, it's probably rather foolish, the way we sometimes assume civil servants to be simple, obedient dolts rather than the shrewd observers upon whom crowned heads rely.

(As for the new king's chamberlain appointed by lord Fortinbras, though, he has a rather limited view of the king, whom he sees simply as God's appointed, a holy figure to whom he owes utter allegiance. In most ways, this is as it should be.)

For myself, I suppose it would be nearly as foolish to try to understand a king as to try to understand God Himself, although as students in Wittenberg many of us were hubristic enough to try!

Ah, Wittenberg. Would that we could go back to such simpler days! If youth is a folly, it was, at least for me, a joyous one--for a time, at least.

Horatio paused in his writing, lowering the quill to the tabletop. The cat rolled sideways, and she pawed desultorily at the feather. Horatio pushed her paw away and massaged the back of his own neck. He had been rather tense while writing, although he wasn't sure why.

He blew the ink on his last sheet lightly to dry it, then stacked the sheets carefully. But looking back at the sheets in his hand, he withdrew the last one once more and placed it on the desk. He took up the quill once more, and in careful letters wrote at the bottom of the sheet, Horatio Stenmark,

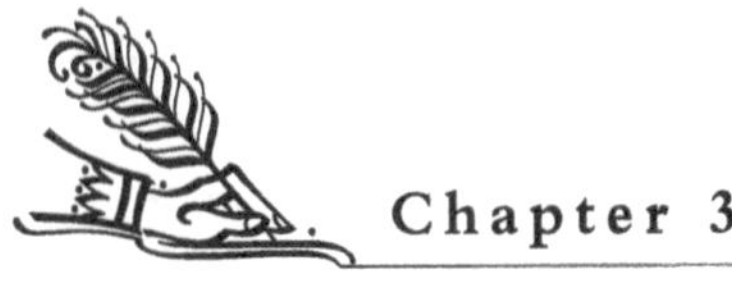

Chapter 3

The Hazards of Royalty

Midafternoon sunshine flooded through the tall windows of the west hall of the palace, lending a mellow aspect to the interior. The oak parquet shone golden in the light, and the crimson drapes that had been drawn back from the glass were blood brilliant beside each tall pane. They matched a crimson-cushioned seat beneath each window. Hamlet sat upon one of these, gazing out the window, thinking, or perhaps dreaming. Such terms are almost interchangeable when speaking of young people whose lives stretch and spread before them as an array of endless possibilities.

Earlier in the day, Old Hamlet had spent two hours with his son, introducing him to some of the finer points of dealing diplomatically with other powers in the world, both foreign and domestic, either of which might pose a threat or offer considerable benefit.

"Consider, now," Old Hamlet had begun. "Denmark has been at war at least three times since I assumed sovereignty: once with Norway, once with Sweden, and once with Poland." He tapped the map, a large pale lambskin featuring a fantastic drawing providing the basic outline of the Baltic Sea, with royal red shading Denmark and its island holdings, Norway's sculpted coastline in green, Sweden's irregular shape in yellow, and the northern European mainland south of the Baltic in grey.

"All of these powers have access to the sea. Indeed, each needs it both for food and for trade." He pointed at the narrow passages between the islands over which Elsinore and the Danish crown held control. "However, we control the trade between the great sea to our northeast and the greater sea to our northwest. Ships who wish to pass our position need to pay a tax. That tax is a source of a great deal of our income."

He smiled in satisfaction, and then continued. "While the sea to the northeast is rich and wide, it is not boundless, and it can often become a venue for conflict. After all, now and then we experience a poor fishing year. Then the pressure is on all our countries' monarchs to guarantee access to good fishing grounds. In bad years we have our tax revenue from shipping, but we must retain our fishing rights as well."

Young Hamlet examined the map critically under the approving eye of his father. He noted the narrow, island-studded gap between the peninsula on which Norway and Sweden are found and the islands, currently controlled by Denmark, north of the Danish mainland.

"Is that where you killed Old Fortinbras?" he asked, pointing to one of them.

Old Hamlet let out a short sigh that might have been taken for impatience. "Yes," he replied. His eyes flicked upward, remembering. "Yes," he said again, then looked at Hamlet seriously. "It was an ugly business, but the duel probably saved many lives. It goes to show that the responsibilities of kingship often include great risk."

Young Hamlet grimaced. "You might have been killed," he finally said.

His father smiled. "Suppose he *had* killed me? Then where would *you* be now? Or I, for that matter..."

While speaking, he had gestured with his open right hand. Now he squeezed it into a fist, as if it held some secret mystery, and then, snapping the fingers open, watched the air as if some invisible bird were being released to escape into nothingness. He smiled again, and then chuckled almost grimly.

Hamlet smiled weakly in response, but did not laugh. To him death was a great evil and a greater mystery. The idea of losing his father, or of any death for that matter, was abhorrent to him, even though his training in swordsmanship was purposed specifically to killing—quickly, efficiently, and effectively.

He had seen a number of real, dead bodies. His mother's father had died just three years ago, or so. Hamlet remembered gazing at the old man on his bier, hands folded on his chest, eyes blankly closed, a faint smell of incense and candle wax in the air. Hamlet had wondered then about where his grandfather had gone. Heaven? Hell? He knew his grandfather had been an angry man, one prone to torrents of rage at times, and greedy, as well. Without priestly absolution Hamlet knew, either or both of those sins may well have been denied the old man his salvation. But it seemed sinful to try to second-guess God.

Then there was the old servant Michael who served the wine at table. He had simply keeled over one winter night, dropping the crystal decanter onto the flagstones to shatter in a shower of glass and a blood-like spray of French wine. He had fallen limply with one leg kicked out absurdly. His eyes had gazed vacantly at the head table where Old Hamlet and Gertrude stared back in amazement before the noble Polonius had snapped his fingers to another servant who had taken charge of the body, lifting it clumsily and carrying it out of the banquet hall through a side entrance. A serving maid hastily brought rags and carefully sopped up the wine and glass. Prince Hamlet had nearly vomited his meat pie.

It was astonishing, really. One moment there had been a man, smiling, gesturing, speaking; the next there was a convoluted lump of muscle, bone, and guts...but no man. Perhaps the priests were correct in their explanations of the immortality of the soul. But it was certain to Hamlet then that there is no immortality of the body. *It rots too fast,*

Hamlet thought. *The man leaves the house, and the house falls down.* He smiled wanly at his analogy.

"Now," Old Hamlet went on, "consider our own nobility. Who among them is trustworthy? True, they all swear allegiance to me as rightfully anointed king. But who among them wouldn't replace me if he could, if he dared?"

Hamlet looked at his father uneasily. He knew that his father sometimes feared for his crown, not from the common people, who seemed to love him, but from any of a dozen or so nobles who in his own mind might feel more worthy of kingship or more greedy for its perquisites than Hamlet the Dane.

"Polonius?" Hamlet suggested.

His father stared at him blankly for a moment. Then he roared with laughter. Tears even sprang to his eyes. He finally ceased laughing, snorted a breath, and then laughed again. Hamlet felt a bit embarrassed, perhaps even a little ashamed. What had he missed?

When his father finally quieted and gathered his breath, he said quietly, "No. Not Polonius. He probably has his own designs...agenda the clerics call it, if you will." He breathed deeply once more. "I sometimes believe he thinks I don't see what is directly before my face." He snickered once more. "Polonius is loyal. I'd stake my life on it."

A knock at the door interrupted their speculation.

"Come," ordered the king. A youthful page entered the room, bowed deeply, and approached.

"My lord, I have been sent by the lord Polonius to inform you that a number of matters of state require your royal judgment. He is with Lord Secretary Willesen in the library. He will wait there with the relevant documents or attend you with them wherever you see fit."

Hamlet raised his eyes and glanced at his father, who looked frankly at the youth and answered. "Tell lord Polonius I will come to the library by and by. He will wait until I come."

"I shall, my liege," the young man replied, bowed again (nodding graciously to young Hamlet), and left the room.

The king smiled again at Hamlet. "As I said, Polonius usually has his own designs."

He took up the map, rolled it carefully, and fastened a scarlet ribbon around it, then stood it upright in a large box that contained other similar rolls. Hamlet appeared a little disappointed.

"It wouldn't hurt to let him wait a bit," his father said, "but I fear matters are every bit as urgent as the boy reported. We will talk again soon," he said to his son, and he strode out of the room.

Now Hamlet sat in the window sunshine, thinking about power, thinking about his father. He knew as eldest son he would one day be expected to take his father's place (though that didn't bear thinking about—he loved his father too much to wish to consider Old Hamlet's death), and he was determined to have the judgment and knowledge to rule effectively, in essence, to be as royal as his paternal exemplar.

He wondered if he would ever have to fight a duel such as that between his father and the Norwegian, and whether or not he would prevail. He wasn't afraid of such a fight; in fact, he sometimes craved the action, that thrill of focus that crystallizes when the body and the mind seem one, when life is balanced as if on the edge of a cliff or the edge of a knife.

He smiled at his own imaginings, the new young "King Hamlet" returning to the palace, victorious over some enemy: a Polish prince, perhaps, or a German.

Just then a door opened at the far end of the hall. Through it came three elegantly dressed young women. One of them laughed boldly at something another had said. Then a slender, dark-haired one caught sight of Hamlet, and she motioned the others to be quiet. But they continued to approach together.

Hamlet set down the book he had with him and gave them a look of frank appraisal. He recognized the dark one as Ophelia, Polonius' daughter. She was startlingly lovely, a slim woman with very dark hair and bright, alert eyes. The others were two of her maids.

When they had approached Ophelia curtsied, and her maids followed suit.

"How does my lord Hamlet this fine day?" she inquired politely and looked confidently into his face. Hamlet felt a slight suspension of his breath.

"Better for your inquiry, lady Ophelia, thank you," he replied, smiling faintly at her. One of the maids raised her hand to her mouth and stifled a giggle that sounded a little like a cough. The other watched expectantly.

"Will my lord be attending the feast this evening? The whole court has noticed that in your absence events and conversation turn to dullness despite the fare, and we have missed you of late."

That she might speak for 'the whole court' was transparently flattering, but Hamlet was not opposed to flattery from a beauty such as Ophelia. He framed his answer carefully.

"I have been preparing for my imminent return to Wittenberg for another extended session. The king has instructed me to complete my studies there, despite the prayers of my mother, who I fear would rather retain me here in Elsinore."

A shadow of dismay passed across Ophelia's face, although she smiled quickly again and said, "Perhaps the more reason for you to enjoy the company of your countrymen—and women—here at home. Surely the German monks cannot provide the quality of intercourse your family and loving subjects provide?" Eyes lowered, she smiled once more.

Hamlet too smiled at the ambiguity of 'intercourse.'

"Sometimes one must go far afield to seek knowledge and forms of understanding unlikely to be found at home. But I will have Danish company of my own." He warmed to his own theme. "As in the past, Horatio will be there with me, and the lords Rosencrantz and Guildenstern, all three men of trust and of high reputation."

He smiled again. Although he was a trifle shy, he was not intimidated by her beauty. He liked her—her ready wit, her conversation, even her scent, a faint violet fragrance.

He said gently, "However, to answer your question, yes, I will be at the feast this evening and am counting on the pleasure of your conversation at table...and perhaps afterward."

Unwilling to titter at the obvious suggestions, the maids smiled knowingly and looked at their feet. Ophelia smiled at Hamlet.

"My lord, we will take our leave of you until this evening, then." The three women curtsied, and Hamlet, having risen to his feet, nodded pleasantly. The women turned almost as one and moved off down the long hall, their shadows pacing beside them in the late sun. Hamlet watched them go, their characteristic feminine gait. A light laugh echoed down the hallway. He felt the stirrings of desire, and he wondered briefly about other designs.

Chapter 4

From the Diary of Ophelia

Cleopatra stared at Horatio expectantly from her cushion. Horatio reached out and absently stroked the cat's head. The cat lifted its head toward his hand and emitted an appreciative purr. Horatio scratched it gently under the chin, then turned back to the pages he had been studying. He held one that was only partly covered in text up in his left hand to better catch the light, and examined it briefly. In his right he held his quill, poised to write. Then he laid the sheet back onto the table and began.

> I long had difficulty fully understanding the importance of Ophelia to this story. Of course, Hamlet loved her. He said so, although perhaps that revelation is left better to later in the story. But I was certain that there must have been more to things than a young man's romantic desire, heartfelt as he expressed it. Some of that obscurity has been lifted through my access to Polonius' family's papers, including Ophelia's diary. The attached entry, which will be placed within my broader report, reveals that Ophelia truly was a remarkable young woman, someone far more astute and clever than her maidenly behavior in the palace revealed.

To begin with, she was literate, and truth be told, her writing was as good or better than that of many a Wittenberg student whose words I have chanced to peruse. In fact, on more than one occasion she wrote poetry, and if some readers might argue it is not very good, I would like to see their own to compare to it.

(It is true that writing poetry is an art and a craft, and like many another requires apprenticeship and application to produce its finest evocations, but it may also be argued that sometimes poetic form is the most suitable expressive structure for presenting and defining any strongly felt ideas. Sometimes to write is to feel, and to feel is to write. Might poesy simply be a form of that compulsion?)

Further, she was a young woman raised without a motherly example. Given that her mother died giving birth to infant Ophelia, Hamlet's lady needed considerable wit and resolve to grow into her role at court. True, the fact that Polonius had already opened the door deserves some mention. And it is also true that the example of her older brother Laertes, who shone with many skills, must have encouraged her sibling competitiveness. But all my experience of Ophelia, even when things went...badly...showed me that Hamlet's choice of paramour was a natural direction for his love. Hamlet was a shrewd judge of character, and if her nearly unnatural beauty stimulated his manhood, I for one, certainly understood.

Horatio again retrieved the sheet he had been examining and began to read Ophelia's words.

I saw Prince Hamlet again today, sitting in the window of the great west hall. He seems to spend much time alone, as if the world has placed some great puzzle before him, one that he alone can master or solve. (I say "alone" with two meanings: he is the only one who can solve it, and it is a solution that he will come to more easily without the presence of others to disturb him.)

This is a perfect sample of her insight at work, that ability to distinguish subtle differences of meaning within the same term. She is almost philosophic.

Horatio looked once more at the page.

I am always struck by his singular handsomeness—his easy smile, one that I vainly imagine he saves solely for me. (How foolish I seem to myself sometimes.) Yet he stirs my heart, and despite the presumption I irregularly feel when I allow myself to admire (dare I say love?) him so unreservedly, I cannot but wish he would show me some sign that he feels at least somewhat the same for me.

My maids and I were traversing the west hall to meet Mother Agnes at the chapel, there to pray briefly before going to continue our work on a larger arras for the west wall of the throne room. (When Queen Gertrude offered the work to Mother Agnes and Mother Agnes inquired whether I, as well as my maids, would assist I was enormously gratified. The hanging is to feature a great coat of arms of the king's family! The needlework will be immensely challenging.) There was Hamlet in the window seat, alone as usual, thinking of God alone knows what...

Father too knows of my affection for the lord Hamlet, although he pretends not. I cannot as yet be certain whether or not he approves. On the one hand, were Hamlet truly to love me, it would enhance our family's reputation and influence enormously. However, like trying to leap across a creek or messy puddle, to overestimate one's ability to jump can lead to some wet and dirty consequences. (I have yet a small scar on my knee from just such an effort!) And surely Father knows that it would be all too easy for the king to interpret my love for Hamlet as nothing more than an expression of my father's ambition. Such an understanding, however mistaken, could lead to much unpleasantness.

Today Hamlet was polite, as usual, and though we spoke of little of significance, I once more felt that he understands my feelings. I try to indicate my esteem for him without falling into the dreadful error of gushing like a simple farm girl. For his part, he seems somehow simultaneously affectionate and aloof, capable of perfect intimacy yet somehow as if he is locked behind a cloudy pane of glass that only he knows how to remove. May God grant that he might remove it, for it divides us in a manner that pains me greatly.

Hamlet informed us that he is once again going to Wittenberg for the an extended academic year. I am dejected at the thought of his absence, yet I am resolved that I will wait for his return. Surely he understands, without my saying so directly, that I love him?

Do you see? Hamlet was my prince, closer to my heart than any other man. I knew what he felt for Ophelia, beneath his princely rectitude. It is only on reading the diary that I comprehend more fully how taken Ophelia was with Hamlet, as well. I understand now too, as did Ophelia then, some of the potential obstacles to their love. I always suspected the presence of their mutual attraction, and in the privacy of my own soul I wished them the best. They seemed ideally suited to me.

But I may be leaping ahead, as Ophelia so descriptively put it in her diary. It would be easy to get things out of order. From my own conversations with Hamlet, it was clear to me that he loved Ophelia long before we left for Wittenberg that fateful summer. But *then* all things seemed possible, and a great, unburdened future stretched before us.

Although the party of us headed for Wittenberg did not speak of these things out of respect for the prince, Rosencrantz, Guildenstern, and even young Yedric understood Hamlet's affection for Ophelia. Rosencrantz had his own cynical view of things (he always did), one always attuned to the sinister vagaries of lust and ambition. The rest of us were perhaps more naïve, but I would wager the meager contents of my purse also happier.

Of course, when Bartholomew came to Wittenberg later that summer, everything changed.

Chapter 5

Wittenberg

The sun had set less than half an hour ago, and although the northern sky was still its summer pale, it was dark indoors.

It was a good night in the Grey Goose Inn. At least twenty-five men and a few women were in small groups around the large public room, occupied with what men do late on a late summer evening—drinking and planning their whoring mostly, and gambling. Scents of cooked meats and breads along with wood smoke pervaded the air. Fish oil lamps spread uneven illumination over the tables, and large candles burned in sconces on the walls. It was noisy.

Noise in a public house is a common thing, and a good thing if you are a publican. No matter what the sounds, behind them is always the 'chink' of coins! Tonight a small but healthy fire blazed and crackled in the huge hearth on the far wall.

A group of bearded young men, students by the style of their black gowns, was singing a Latin song at a table near the kitchen entrance, something about fate, the publican thought. (His Latin was very simple, limited to a few words and phrases he had gleaned from the many students who frequented his premises from year to year.) One of the students had a particularly melodious voice, surprisingly pleasing, even if it was difficult to hear over the shouting and cursing from the dice game in the opposite corner.

Laughter periodically erupted from a table near the door where Gottfried, the town's voluble butcher, was telling his usual salacious stories to a group of drunken hangers on. Henrietta, the buxom kitchen maid, thumped two more tankards of ale down on their table and laughingly bent to listen.

In the nearer corner was a quieter group, though, decidedly not drunk (although a flagon of wine stood like a proud cock in the center of the table). Five well dressed students, including the Danish Prince Hamlet (who resided in a pair of the better rooms upstairs) were in serious conversation. Occasionally one would sip from his goblet. But these men were not here to get drunk.

The prince raised his hand to interrupt whoever was speaking and laughed, then became serious again. The publican listened. He liked to listen.

"Go on, Horatio. Tell us in other words, with no juggling of meanings or puzzling paradoxes. What is God's interest in the world?"

It was a powerful question. Certainly the publican didn't know the answer, and although he had never thought much about it in such a precise way before, he was interested. The youngish man across from the prince drew a lank of dark hair away from his eyes, glanced away to think for a moment, and then replied.

"Lord Hamlet, it would be presumptuous for *anyone* to claim to *know*. But as you have asked, and as I introduced the idea with my oath, I feel I must reply with what limited means I have."

The prince smiled, as did his other companions. It never seemed too presumptuous for the *priests* to claim to know God's will. But with his interests in morality and philosophy, in many ways Horatio was something like a priest. If anything he was better educated, but in the paradoxical way in which the nuances of knowledge sometimes erode confidence, Horatio was considerably more modest.

The man to Hamlet's left looked up intently. He was a dark-complexioned student of laws named Rosencrantz, a sharp, ambitious young man of means from southern Denmark. He was well dressed, nearly as well as the prince, with a velvet doublet and smooth kid gloves that lay on the table next to his untouched wine.

Next to him sat Guildenstern, his constant companion (and some thought bum boy, although Hamlet did not sully his concern with such things). Guildenstern was pale and blond, with a wispy moustache over a wide mouth that often featured a generous smile. His demeanor was calm and accommodating, friendly and sanguine.

Opposite Hamlet beside Horatio was a sleepy youth named Yedric, a somewhat lesser light among his fellow students, but one loyal to God and to his prince—after all, he was Hamlet's personal servant. He smiled admiringly at Hamlet and sipped some ale, then looked at Horatio, obviously curious as to what he might say.

Recognized by his fellow students as the most intellectual of them all, Horatio had read Plato and Aristotle, Boethius and Augustine (not to mention Aquinas), and he was able to quote liberally from his readings, especially when trying to address some of the challenging questions raised in their classes. But he was no mere parrot of empty academic rhetoric; he had a fine mind with its own merits. He despised sophistry whether from priest or pedant, though he understood and occasionally used its rhetorical strategies.

Horatio was Hamlet's best friend. The two of them spent many late evenings in discussion about philosophical subjects—moral philosophy, religion, and of course young Hamlet's preoccupations with policy and governance. After all, Hamlet could expect to be king one day in the event of his father's death. Hamlet deeply admired his father and the methods of his rule, and he strove with his studies to prepare himself, to make himself worthy of the crown when it should fall to him.

To the other three, being admitted to these discussions was at least as interesting as Brother Carl's lectures, or those of Father Stephen, which were always heavily larded with religious texts and stories of the saints that all the students were well familiar with. Horatio continued.

"My lord, do you enjoy the garden at Elsinore?"

Hamlet squinted at him critically, then smiled. "Horatio, I detect a kind of evasion here. What might the garden have to do with my question? And by the way, despite whatever its flaws may be, I *do* love the garden at Elsinore!"

"Bear with my circuitous thinking for a moment please, my lord, and I beg you, answer me this. How do the various parts of the garden function together? For example, in the garden we find beautiful flowers, fruits of field and tree, many extraordinary insects, and so on. We see birds and lizards--even sometimes snakes!"

The thought of snakes seemed to make him pause. Then he added, "Mice scurry among the plants. Moles burrow underground. Birds nest in the trees, adding the beauty of their songs and plumage to the place. And so on. It seems to me that each of these beings has a place, a perfect role in the garden's society, if you will. And yet, how does each get that role? How do the actions of each one cumulatively serve to create the garden as a whole? I believe that this wonderful pattern of life is the work of God, whose miracle of design makes the garden what it is."

"Now," he said, and paused to sip abstemiously from a small glass of wine before him. Guildenstern picked up the flagon and poured more for Horatio, after, of course, offering some to the prince, which he declined with a curt wave of his hand. Hamlet stared at Horatio. Horatio wiped his lips with a linen handkerchief and continued.

"Consider these wonderful beings, enacting their purposes much as I imagine occurred in the original Eden! Of course, Eden would not have had weeds," he added with a chuckle. Hamlet smiled.

"God is the invisible gardener," Horatio stated conclusively. "His is the hand that moves all beings, that generates the beauty that we all enjoy and the bounty upon which we all depend." He paused. "Of course, our *earthly* gardens also contain evil. Satan has worked in gardens since the beginning. The scriptures tell us so, and so I believe."

"So do I," exclaimed Guildenstern, rather loudly. "Well stated, Horatio."

Horatio smiled, but Hamlet pressed on.

"But why would God concern himself with these many *tiny* things, wondrous and beautiful as they may be? Surely God has *large* things with which to contend! Satan, for one, as you have reminded us. Our world features wars, famines, and other catastrophes! I have even read that whole mountains can explode in smoke and fire. These are events of a magnitude to interest a God. But—worms? Falling leaves?"

Hamlet sounded almost impatient. He was young, after all, thought the publican, as were all the students. He shifted a little closer to the conversation.

"My lord, surely God's purposes are beyond man's comprehension," suggested Guildenstern, somewhat obsequiously. Hamlet frowned.

"Perhaps so, good sir, but may not a prince, a chosen one of God, query these things?" Hamlet raised his wine and finally drank.

Rosencrantz frowned. He sometimes found Guildenstern to be too accepting of authority, whether in the form of lecturer, priest *or* prince. He also had difficulty reconciling his frequent, unstated disagreements with Hamlet to the passions with which he felt them. Hamlet went on.

"After all, God's creation is a huge thing, unimaginably huge and complex. Why would He concern himself with small things—a hawk's taking a mouse, for example, or even a man's picking a flower for his favorite maid? Why would he not simply create His perfect world—and then let it run like some great machine? Surely the infinite spheres *beyond* our little world, wonderful as it is, require His attention!"

Horatio thought a moment, and then answered. "God is a being whose limits (if there be such) and purposes, are so far beyond mortal understanding that I feel somewhat foolish even pretending to understand them. But I believe that God is always with us, is always concerned with our lives, our goodness, and our fortune. It is our lifelong duty to follow His commandments as Moses recorded them and thereby to deserve the love and care that God gives us. So I believe."

The publican scratched his head and turned to fill another stein with ale. These students were so filled with self-importance! Imagine trying to understand God! What fools, even the prince (although he would never have said so).

"Let me come at the problem from another angle, then," argued Hamlet. "Suppose, as we are meant to believe that God ultimately determines everything on earth, as you suggest. Such determination must then include us, as well, being part of his creation as we are. But if God determines everything, what becomes of our freedom?"

He paused, eying Horatio calmly. Horatio lifted his hand and looked away from Hamlet, as if to gather his thoughts. Hamlet pressed on. "We *seem* to act of our own free will. You lift your hand; you turn back to me. Rosencrantz here drinks or does not as he wishes."

At this comment Rosencrantz hesitated, as he had been just about to take a sip of wine. He blinked.

"Yet if we are truly free," Hamlet said seriously, "then at least one part of the world escapes God's control. If God be all powerful, how can He not control our freedom, too?"

"It is in God's power to grant us our freedom," replied Horatio. "He has done so, as the Church assures us, in order that we might love Him freely, as beings made in the image of God, who loves us freely."

Yedric eyed Hamlet uncertainly, and Guildenstern, having just swallowed some wine, let out a long sigh.

At that moment the door of the inn was pushed open from outside and three well-dressed strangers, two of them wearing cuirasses and carrying short lances, entered the room. Candles flickered in the draft, the singers stopped unevenly, and even the gamblers looked up from their table. The publican gestured, and the maid, Henrietta, hurried back to the kitchen behind him. The tallest of the three men scanned the room, and spying Hamlet and his fellows, strode quickly to their table and bowed deeply. One of the other two men swung the door shut, and the two stationed themselves to either side, erect and watchful.

"Bartholomew," Hamlet greeted the newcomer in a warm voice. "What brings you to Wittenberg? One hopes no news of tragedy or harm. Guildenstern, give the man a drink, can't you? Where are your manners?"

Coloring noticeably, Guildenstern hastily poured the man a small draft and offered it to him. But Bartholomew did not take it. Instead, he addressed Hamlet in a low voice.

"My lord, I have private news for your ears alone. If in your wisdom you choose to share it afterward, that is for you to decide. May we speak privately?"

Hamlet appraised him curiously. A man at the end of a day's journey did not usually refuse a glass of wine. In a less jovial tone, he said, "By all means. Yedric, be so kind as to ensure that the men at the door are offered food and drink. Bartholomew, bring your wine. My student quarters are above, as you may guess that the university lodgings are insufficient to my needs. Let us repair to my rooms, that you may deliver your message in confidence and privacy."

He turned to Horatio and the others. "Gentlemen, we will return as soon as time, or God, permits." He smiled at his own small joke. Horatio smiled as well. Rosencrantz snorted and smirked at Guildenstern, who appeared to have missed the joke.

Hamlet rose and the men followed suit, each nodding to Hamlet in a slight bow. Bartholomew clasped his wine and followed Hamlet toward the oak staircase along the wall. The publican watched them expectantly and hastily dispatched Henrietta to light lamps above, then turned, smiling in gratitude, as Yedric approached him, opening his purse.

Hamlet and Bartholomew ascended the staircase behind Henrietta, out of sight onto the upper floor, and the normal noise and activity quickly resumed below.

Henrietta paced quickly along the upper corridor with more tapers for the prince's rooms in her left hand. "With your permission, lord," she said to Hamlet, indicating with a gesture of her lit candle her intention to enter. Hamlet nodded, and wordlessly watched as she unlatched the door. The two men followed her inside, where she quickly lit candles in wall sconces and placed a pair of small, fresh candles on Hamlet's desk.

The initially shadowy interior gradually revealed itself in the candlelight. It was a corner room featuring a small fireplace on one of the exterior walls faced by two leather armchairs. A window, now shuttered, would normally shed daylight onto a large table, now somewhat littered with papers, some quills and ink, and two or three leather-bound volumes.

As the two men waited impatiently Henrietta kindled a small fire in the grate. It smoked for a moment or two and then flared up, the draft sucking the smoke up the stone chimney. Nodding in satisfaction she asked Hamlet politely, "Will there be anything else, sir?"

"Not at present. You may go."

"At your service, my lord," she said softly, and curtsied.

Henrietta let herself through the door into the corridor and closed it securely behind her. Then she walked thoughtfully toward the light and sound spilling up the staircase from below.

Hamlet sat at his table, gathered a few of his papers into a semblance of order, and placed them beside the books. Then he turned to Bartholomew. To his shock, Bartholomew had tears in his eyes.

"Please, sit," said Hamlet gently, indicating a second chair alongside the table, but Bartholomew remained standing, head lowered toward the prince. He dabbed at his eyes with a glove.

"My lord," Bartholomew began, "I have the worst of all bad news." He hesitated, seeing Hamlet's apprehensive expression. "My lord, the king, your father, is dead."

The words struck Hamlet like a blow to the solar plexus. He exhaled sharply and looked at Bartholomew for a long moment. "Dead?"

"My lord, it is nearly three weeks since he was found in the royal garden at Elsinore. We have been riding nearly without pause to bring you the news." He paused and looked at the floor. In a quieter voice he added, "It was not an ordinary death."

Hamlet felt a chill pass through him, a sensation of uncertainty, of express evil. He crossed himself.

"Not ordinary?" he asked.

Bartholomew finally took a drink from his goblet, set it onto the table with a soft 'clunk' and breathed deeply. "You know how your father customarily took a short sleep in the afternoon in the garden? He and your mother used to walk there after their midday meal. Then she would leave him and he would work or rest in the shelter between the two great oaks."

"And?" Hamlet asked.

"Polonius found him there, alone. The servant who would normally be in attendance was nowhere to be found. I beg your liege's pardon, but it was a terrible sight. Your father's body had red, scaling scars over the visible parts of his skin. He had a terrible expression on his face, one of absolute horror, as if he had seen Satan himself!" Bartholomew crossed himself.

"Polonius claimed to have seen a serpent slipping away through the grass, and it was he who reported that your father must have been stung by that same serpent. It would seem a reasonable supposition," he added, nearly as an afterthought. He swallowed audibly.

With a fixed expression, pale-faced, Hamlet stared at him. Feelings churned within him—fear, anger, disappointment, and an aching sadness, as if some fearful poison were already at work in his own body.

"That's not all the news, is it?" he asked, in a voice whose calm belied the emotional maelstrom behind it.

"No, my lord," Bartholomew answered. He looked away into the shadowed corners of the room, and once again addressed his prince. "Your uncle Claudius, the king's brother, has taken the crown of

Denmark. As the new king, my lord." He paused again. "He has married your mother."

"My mother?" Hamlet exclaimed. "My mother!" He turned toward the fire, now grown to a crackling blaze from the flickering kindling Henrietta had left. "Oh, my God, help me," he groaned, as if suffering some great pain deep within.

Bartholomew didn't know what to say. He had imagined this moment a hundred times since he had departed Elsinore three weeks earlier, how controlled in feeling and bearing he would solemnly inform the prince of these uncertain truths, ready to prove his strength and support. Instead he had cried like a boy. He felt a shadow of shame cross his heart, and yet his pain was real.

He looked at Hamlet, a man moments before cheerful and controlled, one now ashen-faced and grief-stricken.

"My-my lord," he finally stammered, and then stopped. Hamlet was also crying. Tears were sliding ineluctably down his cheeks.

"Leave us," Hamlet finally croaked.

Bartholomew got to his feet, bowed clumsily, and let himself out of the chamber.

Hamlet let out a great sob. Then he stood as if to face some horrible intruding attacker, only to sit down again. He shivered, and hugging himself he struggled to gather his thoughts. He would have to go home. The conclusion rang through his consciousness like some great bell tolling out a command—come, come, come, come. He needed to see his mother. He felt as if some irrevocable fate itself was beckoning him. He knew it was time to go home.

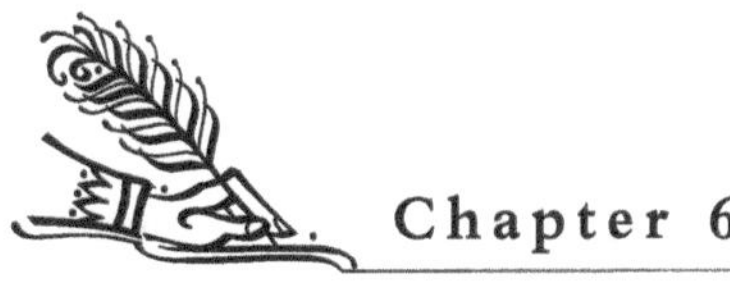

Chapter 6

The Snake in the Garden

The garden at Elsinore was beautiful. An enclosed space of about 150 acres, the king's private garden featured high, stone walls, one of which contained a lockable gate that led directly into the palace. Three other gates led to outer, wilder areas beyond the royal precincts. There the Royal park extended for several miles west from the castle area, with gravel strand and the sea to the north, and increasingly dense forest to the south beyond the cultured park.

Within the walls, the king's private area was a summer riot of blossoms and scent, but the box hedges that formed its internal geometric design, and the tall evergreens that marked its external boundaries (just inside the garden walls) gave it a measured stateliness, an order fitted to the geometries of rule.

King Hamlet loved the garden, a place where he felt secure and happy, strong, comforted by its symmetries. Even as king he understood that above all, nature rules. But thus, when his gardeners were able to mold and tame nature into patterns to please, the king himself felt augmented and sanctified.

Between two great oaks about a hundred yards from the palace gate, an earlier king had ordered built a roofed enclosure, open between the low walls of its surround and the pitched slates that made up the roof. Inside were two long tables with accompanying chairs, a large grated fireplace whose chimney rose up the end wall through the slates, and several wicker sofas, padded in season with large leather cushions embossed with the Danish royal crest. More than one of the king's deer had been roasted in that fireplace for outdoor feasts over the years! Beside the fireplace was a small door leading to a covered exterior kitchen, mostly disused, but functional when needed.

"My lord?" said Gertrude in an inquiring tone. She sat on one of the sofas with her embroidery, a scene featuring hounds and hunting. Hamlet looked up from where he was seated at one of the tables, examining a document. "Although it is summer, it feels cool, Hamlet. I think it may rain. Shall we not go inside?"

A raven sailed down to perch on the half wall. It cocked its eye at the king. He looked intently at it and waved his hand dismissively, as if it were one of his lesser subjects; it flapped its wings abruptly and croaked noisily, pushing itself up and out of sight beyond the roof.

"*You* appear cold, my love. Go inside, if you will, and warm yourself." There *was* a cool breeze, almost a wind, from the seaward side of the garden. He paused thoughtfully, and then added, "I have my cloak should I need it. I will finish this business first. Anders will attend you." Anders, one of the household servants who had been standing unobtrusively beside the enclosure's entrance, stepped forward and bowed to the queen.

Gertrude regarded him quizzically. "All right," she said. "But please come in soon. And remember, as well, the Swedish ambassador will be with us for dinner, along with two northern traders from Russia who wish to dazzle us with their furs! Some of the ermine they brought two years ago was extraordinarily fine," she added, memory exciting her desire.

The king yawned, covering his mouth politely. "I'll be in when I'm finished," he repeated. He looked at her appraisingly. She was still beautiful—stately and charming. He smiled at her.

"You go along," he suggested again. "I'll be in soon. Does that trader have nothing but ermine?" he asked as an afterthought, but Gertrude had already turned to go, Anders slightly behind her and to her left.

King Hamlet watched her walk away down the path, Anders like a dog at heel. Then she turned through an opening in the hedge, and the two of them disappeared. The raven emitted a strange gurgle, this time from one of the nearby firs. Hamlet turned once again to his papers.

The news was not good, but was it ever? Again there was conflict with the Polacks to do with the grain trade. How much fish could they want for their corn, anyway? It was less than a decade since their war, no, less than nine years! Surely the Danes had taught those peasants their manners.

Hamlet hated having to mistrust his neighbors, and yet it seemed to be the only safe strategy for a king. After all, he had killed their crown prince, the leader of their army, on a frozen lake not far from Cracow. Over two thousand Danish souls had died in that battle. *It had to be done*, he thought to himself. The Polish had been trying to ally with the Teutonic knights, and who else but Denmark had stood firm, bulwark against their planned confederacy, a union which would have threatened their domination of the whole northern European plain, including its coastal riches? Now, if agreement could not be reached in the corn trade, violence would threaten again.

Then there were the Swedes, an untrustworthy lot if ever there was one. Fortunately, they were occupied, and had been for three years, in an extended, if small, war with the Finns.

Finally he had to think about the Norwegians, another gang of cutthroats and pirates. Again, Fortuna had smiled. Old Fortinbras' brother Olav, the man who had taken power after Hamlet had forced them to give up the islands, was taken ill with dropsy, or so the diplomats told him. It was unlikely that these Norse would cause problems in the near term, but given their seafaring capabilities, Hamlet felt it necessary to monitor their actions.

Hamlet yawned again, a deep, cavernous yawn. Perhaps just a short sleep, and then he would finish. He stretched, stood, and removing his cloak from the back of the chair where he had been working, he moved over to one of the couches where he stretched his great frame out on the cushions. He shook the cloak out over himself and rested his head on his arm. He yawned. Then he slept.

In the kitchen, one of the servants who had served lunch to the king and queen glanced into the lodge. The king, who was breathing deeply, lay stretched supine; then, he turned onto his side. The servant watched the king's body lift and fall with his deep, regular breaths.

After a moment, the servant slipped quietly out the back of the kitchen, away from the king's enclosure. He stood very still for a moment, as if thinking. Then, facing down the length of the garden, he lifted his right arm and waved it once, from right to left. He paused, then hurried quietly down a side path toward the gate that led to the palace.

About two hundred feet away from the kitchen entrance, a figure emerged from between two heavy shrubs. He watched the servant make his departure. When the gate had closed behind the servant, the newcomer began to make his way quietly *beside* the gravel path, footsteps silent in the lush grass. He took his time.

The person was well dressed, perhaps wealthy from the quality of the clothing. The left hand held a small, dark bottle, and the right a fine handkerchief. The figure paused at the entrance to the king's enclosure, waiting, watching.

It started silently once, when the shadow of the raven raced past on the grass, the raven winging by overhead. It croaked once, a hollow, empty sound. Moments later the raven had gone.

Old Hamlet moaned softly in his sleep, stirring slightly. Then he slept on. His watcher moved quietly to the king's side, and looked for a moment at his profile. Then, silently removing the stopper from the bottle, and bent carefully over the king's head, the intruder gently and steadily poured a cloudy liquid into the sleeping man's ear.

The king groaned. Opening his eyes slowly, he raised his hand to try to brush away the liquid. As he did so, he emitted another groan, this time a questioning groan, one of pain. His eyes widened, and he tried to sit up, but he seemed to have lost control of his muscles.

He attempted to speak, but all that would come out of his mouth was a grunt of surprise, as if his tongue were too thickened to articulate. The muscles on his neck stood out in cords, and his head jerked forward, then back. Spittle began to drain from the corner of his mouth.

Then he lost control of his bowels, emitting a stench from which his attacker recoiled. His whole body twitching, king Hamlet sagged back onto the sofa, an expression of absolute terror and dismay distorting his features.

The assassin watched him die. The whole process took about a minute and a half. Hamlet's body trembled, and his face went white with exertion, sweat breaking out across his forehead. His mouth foamed again. Then his body went into a great spasm for four or five seconds, and finally sank into stillness.

The killer replaced the stopper in the bottle and wrapped it in the handkerchief, taking especial care not to touch the spill stain beside the monogram stitched into its corner. Frowning at the dead man, who stank from his fouled breeches, the intruder thought, *even a king's shit stinks.*

Placing an ear close to the king's mouth the assailant could sense no movement, no air. The figure straightened quickly, looked around carefully, and walked purposefully back along the path the way it had come. In another few moments the garden was silent, save for the drowsing of bees and the occasional call of a thrush from one of the trees in the orchard across the garden.

About forty minutes later, a middle-aged man entered the garden from the palace gate. He, too, was well dressed, wearing a silk-lined cloak with a fur collar. He carried two leather folders secured with scarlet ribbon. He appeared in a hurry. He walked quickly toward the king's lodge.

"My lord?" he called. "Are you here, my lord?"

As he paced along he jerked himself to a stop. The grass not five feet away to the left of the path parted, and a dark serpent about four feet long slid out onto the gravel. It raised its head a foot or so off the gravel, weaving slightly as if to examine Polonius, who stood rigidly, heart pounding. Then the serpent seemed to whip itself into the grass beside a flowering shrub and slipped away into some undergrowth. Polonius crossed himself, and putting his hand on his heart, willed himself to go forward again.

"My lord?"

When he reached the enclosure, he paused momentarily to straighten his doublet. The king appeared to be sleeping. This was not unusual. Polonius had found him thus at least three times over the past fortnight. *This Polish business,* he thought to himself.

Polonius moved toward the king. He hated to wake his majesty, but it was only a little over an hour until dinner with the Norse traders, and he also desired the sovereign's advice on a personal matter, one to do with his son, Laertes.

He looked more closely at Hamlet as he approached. Then he gasped. The king's eyes were open. Two flies were walking on the king's cheek. One lifted, buzzing furiously, then landed on the king's ear. Hamlet's face appeared locked in a manifestation of absolute horror. His lips were peeled back, revealing a rictus of pain and anger.

Dropping the leather folders, Polonius fell to his knees and crossed himself repeatedly. Moving forward on his knees to the king's side, he moved his hands to Hamlet's face, touching the forehead briefly, and finally closing Hamlet's eyes. Then, heart pounding and tears running down his cheeks, he made the sign of the cross over his dead king.

After a moment, he scrambled awkwardly to his feet. He reflexively bowed to the body, which seemed to be silently snarling at some unseen assailant. The leather folders lay unopened on the slate flooring. Polonius turned, hastened from the enclosure, and broke into an awkward run toward the palace.

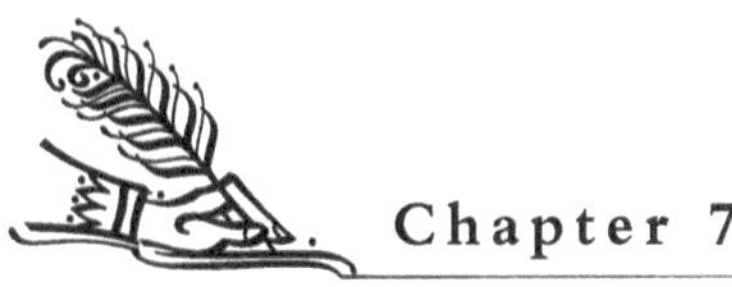

Chapter 7

Hamlet's Return

It was morning, only just, and it was raining. Heavy drops rattled on the coach's leather roof, nearly drowning out the sucking sounds of the wheels pulling through mud and the panting of the horses, audible even through the canvas window shade. It seemed as if it had always been raining. Even the air inside was wet, and now, along the coast of the main island, it smelt of salt. Groggy but awake, Hamlet huddled beneath his cloak in the corner of the lurching carriage, trying to ignore the snapping of the driver's whip and his continuous cries to the horses. He shuddered from cold. He shuddered too from apprehension, from his imaginings of what he would find in Elsinore.

Too long had passed since Bartholomew had given him the ugly news in Wittenberg—interminable days of verminous roadside inns with their bad food, of being shaken in the coach, of cold, and of cold imaginings. The short voyage to the island on which Elsinore was situated had been rough, too. Hamlet felt nauseous simply remembering the ferry's floundering movements under a dark sky illuminated only by lightning flashes.

Across from Hamlet Yedric snored lightly under a woolen blanket, seemingly immune to the jolting and the noise. The coach tilted ominously as one wheel surmounted a large rock in the road; then it settled and continued on.

Hamlet felt somehow smaller. His money was running low. He had no idea what precisely awaited him. He pulled his cloak more closely about his shoulders. He could see his breath. He closed his eyes in a futile attempt to sleep once more, but his thoughts were whirling, as if he had drunk too much wine. What had his mother done! Had his father been buried? Had Claudius provided a suitable funeral with all the necessary rites? How could his father have died? Claudius? His uncle? Married to his mother? It was almost unthinkable.

The coach lurched again. There seemed to be more noise in the distance. Hamlet heard a bell tolling and hoofbeats as the coach seemed to rise onto a cobbled surface. He leaned forward and swept the window shade aside. Rain slashed through the opening, but he could see grey surf falling on a gravel shingle a hundred or so paces to his right, and he knew immediately that they were approaching the seaward eastern gate of Elsinore. He shook Yedric by the knee, startling him awake.

"We're here," Hamlet said tersely. Yedric rubbed his eyes and he shook himself briefly, tugging the blanket closer about his shoulders. Then he yawned, awkwardly covering his mouth. He looked expectantly at Hamlet, who stared implacably back at him.

At that moment, the coach slowed, then halted. It rocked on its hard springs for a moment or two. Hamlet heard a shouted cry from the driver and a muted response from the city walls. Massive hinges squealed and the familiar gate rumbled open. The coach jerked into motion again and Hamlet watched as smoking torches still lit from the night flared into view and then disappeared behind the coach as it creaked into the central square. The driver knew his business, rattling the coach over the cobbles and up the low hill toward the royal enclosure. Again, shouts of identification were exchanged. Three minutes later the coach halted. Someone tugged open the coach door and a low voice murmured, "Prince Hamlet. Welcome home."

The speaker, one of the household servants named Gersen, straightened from his bow, and Hamlet looked at him. Gersen extended his gloved hand, but Hamlet grasped the edge of the coach instead and vaulted lightly to the ground. Yedric followed.

"Yedric, see that my quarters are prepared. Ensure that there is some food and wine."

Hamlet eyed Gersen again, who flushed slightly. The rain had let up to a fine mist, but water still gurgled in the gutters. Hamlet brushed a few drops of water from his brow. There extended an uncertain moment.

"Well," said Hamlet finally. "Take us in."

Gersen stepped aside, managing a hurried bow as he did so, and indicated with an outstretched hand the obvious way into the palace.

"Go," Hamlet said to Yedric, with some impatience, and Yedric fairly bounded into the palace entry and disappeared inside. Hamlet stepped toward the entrance at a lesser pace, and Gersen, once again straightened from his bow, made to follow. Before he had managed a step, however, Hamlet had turned to face him, blocking his way.

"I would like to take you at your word Gersen, to feel truly welcome to this place." Hamlet's voice was low but intense. The word 'welcome' came out slowly, emphatically. "You are a comrade of Bartholomew, are you not?"

Gersen paused a moment, then replied, "I am, my lord."

"Given the heartfelt nature of your *words*, I should like to speak with you privately at length before the evening is out. Come to my quarters after dinner but before the ninth evening hour. I will receive you then. Let no one know your errand. Do not..." He emphasized the importance of the word. "Do not *fail* me."

"I will come before the ninth hour, lord," Gersen replied evenly. He lowered his eyes, and then said, "By your leave, I should attend other duties until then." He bowed. When he straightened, Hamlet gently waved him away, and he turned and crossed the courtyard in another direction.

Hamlet turned to the arched entryway and strode through it into a spacious hallway. A hound that had been sleeping beside a bench looked up at him and blinked. A servant who had been at attention beside the door took his cloak. Hamlet straightened and was rubbing his cold hands when through one of the interior doorways came his mother followed by two maids.

"My dear Hamlet," she said, and moving to him took him by the hands he had involuntarily extended.

"God save you, Mother," he said, appraising her coolly. She kissed him on both cheeks but he remained cautious, stiff.

"We are grateful to have you home once more, among family and countrymen. Welcome," she said, and kissed him again. He allowed himself to hold her close briefly, then stepped back.

"I am told you are married, Mother." His words held no menace and did not betray the bitterness he felt. His mother turned her eyes aside, and then as if recovering her confidence, returned his frank gaze.

"I am queen, and the country is under a firm hand." She, too, could be frank. She stared at him with the kind of innate authority only a mother can have over her son. Then she continued. "But let us speak of these things in more detail later. You look tired, and sweaty from your journey. I am informed that Yedric is with you and has gone to prepare your quarters, which are as you left them. Go. Bathe. Regain your composure and your energies. Tomorrow we will dine together. Come to us then."

Hamlet bristled internally at her use of 'us;' did 'us' mean royal queen or royal couple? He couldn't tell.

"We will dine at the sixth hour," she informed him. "In the west dining room."

She squeezed his hand impulsively and turned to leave. She swept past the curtseying maids.

"Mother?" he said, almost plaintively.

She stopped and turned to him, contemplating him questioningly.

He paused, as if trying to find an adequate word or phrase. Finally he said, "Thank you, Mother. I will see you then. We will speak then." He wasn't sure who 'you' would be, precisely, but he would find out. His mother smiled faintly, then left the room followed by her maids.

Yedric emerged through a different entrance. "Your rooms are ready, my lord."

"No snakes?" Hamlet asked with a bitter little smile.

"Snakes?"

"No, of course not," Hamlet said. "Not yet, at any rate," he added as a kind of afterthought. "Is a bath prepared?"

"Soon, my lord; servants below are heating water as we speak."

"Good," said Hamlet. "I feel not quite clean…"

Hamlet walked purposefully through the doorway, fingering the hilt of his dagger with his left hand as he walked. Yedric followed. As they crossed the great hall toward the family apartments, a woman with long black hair, on a balcony high above watched intently from the shadows. When Hamlet and Yedric passed through another arched entry and out of sight, she paused, then turned and disappeared.

The tap on his quarters' door was just sufficient to draw Hamlet alertly out of his speculations. He looked pointedly at Yedric, who had bounded to his feet out of a light doze on the sofa beside the door. Yedric shook his head lightly, then turned to the door which emitted another soft rap. He opened it.

Outside Gersen stood wrapped in his best cloak (not fine, mind you—a servant could not afford fine). Yedric stepped aside and indicated he should enter.

Hamlet, who had been seated across the room, stood and said, "I am pleased you are a man of your word. Come in and warm yourself at the fire." He gestured to a low flame in the apartment's grate.

Gersen bowed, a gesture of the head more than anything, and removing his cloak, handed it to Yedric, who laid it gently on the arm of the sofa where he had been sleeping. Gersen moved further into the room where the prince waited, and at Hamlet's indication, seated himself on the sofa only a few feet from the cushion where the prince settled. He looked at Hamlet.

"You will appreciate, sir," Hamlet began, "that I lack information."

Gersen's brows raised slightly, but he did not speak.

"Precisely," Hamlet went on, "I wish to know about my father's death."

Gersen lowered his eyes for a moment or two, seeming to take an obscure interest in the embroidery pattern on the arm of the sofa. Then he spoke.

"I cannot account for many, or truly even any, of the events surrounding the death of your royal father. The explanation of that dreadful occurrence seems to hinge upon the testimony of Sir Polonius, whom you know to have been your father's chief councilor, and who, as we speak, is now the chief councilor to his majesty king Claudius."

Hamlet bristled somewhat at this characterization, but allowed Gersen, who was not looking at him, to continue without interruption.

"Polonius explained to the other trusted councilors of the king that he had seen a dangerous serpent on the garden walk, and that when he reached his sovereign lord to speak to him, he found to his shock and dismay that the king was dead. He presumed that your father was bitten by the snake." Gersen looked up to meet Hamlet's gaze.

Hamlet stared at him a moment, then asked, "And where was my mother when these events, unsavory as they are, unfolded?"

"In the royal apartments, my lord. Indeed, I was present on a household matter (we were preparing for the visit of some traders, I believe, at the time) when the news of your father's death was delivered to her. She seemed horrified, and she turned for comfort to your uncle, who was also present, comfort which he readily provided."

Gersen paused a moment, selecting his words carefully. He needed to be accurate, but neither accusatory nor exculpatory. "Your uncle held her close about the shoulders, allowing her to spend her tears on his doublet. After a period, he gently pushed her from his bosom and helped her to sit, whereupon they seemed to share their unhappy shock."

"Indeed," said Hamlet.

"In sooth, my prince, it was as I have described."

"And how was it that my uncle should suddenly have been called upon to lift the royal scepter and to don the crown of my father?" Hamlet's voice had now increased in volume, and his facial expression was one of mystified irritation.

"My lord," Gersen continued, "it was put about by Sir Polonius that the barons of Denmark would meet within a fortnight to determine the nation's course." Gersen frowned. "Some at this meeting raised the question of your rights of primogeniture, but these were waived off as being of secondary importance to the security of the realm, particularly as Denmark has received threats from a vagabond prince of Norway, threats that may yet come to require military action."

Hamlet straightened at this latter bit of news. War against Norway? It wasn't impossible, he knew.

"And my mother?" he said. Here was the nub of the issue. Both Hamlet and Yedric eyed Gersen intently.

"My lord, neither I, nor any of the servants, is privy to the reasoning of royal men and women," he answered. He bowed his head again.

Hamlet glared at the bowed head. "And?" he said, suggesting further inquiry.

After a lengthy pause, Gersen spoke once more. "My lord, your mother has always shown great favor to your father's brother. How could it be otherwise? He was, aside from you, your father's nearest. With such favor comes a kind of comfort, of intimacy. As your father was gone to God, it was not surprising to those at court that the queen might find comfort with those closest in mind and family. I am sure you were paramount in her heart and mind once it was clear that your father, the king, had fallen. But time and distance contain imperatives of their own, do they not?"

Hamlet hated imagining his family's intimacies discussed by servants, and yet he could not expect otherwise. Further, he could not fault Gersen for his discretion, but he felt equally frustrated by what he felt certain was a kind of polite evasion.

"We will speak again," he finally said. "I am grateful for your candor." He nodded at Yedric, who retrieved a coin from a purse he kept under the hem of his doublet. Gersen rose, bowed gently, and moved to the door, where Yedric passed him a coin and let him out quietly. Gersen nodded his thanks.

For his part, Hamlet gazed vacantly at the low fire, whose coals popped lightly and hissed, much as the audience at one of Elsinore's public theater presentations might have done.

Chapter 8

A Division of Sympathies

"Well? Have you seen him?"

Claudius looked at Gertrude, and although she appeared mildly chastened, a smile also played at the corner of her mouth, like that of a child who has been caught lying, but who has managed to cover up the most serious part of her dishonesty.

"Of course I've seen him, my lord. He is my son and only child. Do you imagine I could ignore him?" Her voice held an edge of irritation, and her eyes flashed with unmistakable annoyance. Gertrude could hold her own. Claudius may have been her *new* husband and now her king, but Gertrude had internal reserves of strength that gave her the confidence to speak candidly. She looked at Claudius expectantly.

He glanced down as if chastened himself, and then, as if recovering his role as sovereign and master, he demanded, "Well? What did he say?"

She lowered her voice and replied, "We scarcely exchanged a dozen words." She paused and picked up a silver pitcher of wine from the sideboard. She carried it carefully to where Claudius sat, wine cup in hand. She gestured with the pitcher toward his cup, and he held it out. She poured.

Placing the pitcher back on the sideboard, she gathered her wits, as he sipped it thoughtfully and waited.

"Forsooth, I am astonished at how rapidly he has come home to Elsinore," she said softly. "But I am glad he is here. He is my son." Raising her brow slightly, she added, "He appears well but troubled." And then, eyes watering very slightly, she said softly, "In my own travails and selfishness, I had almost forgotten how much I care for him."

Claudius frowned and set down his cup. He rose to his feet and crossed the room to where Gertrude stood nearly lost in absent contemplation. He placed his forefinger under her chin and she raised her head to meet his gaze.

"I know," he said. And then, almost as an afterthought, he added, "I care for him too, you know. He is my nephew, my brother's only son, and now," he added with a thoughtful pause, "our son."

He spoke almost tentatively, and he looked carefully into Gertrude's eyes as if somehow there existed some kind of clue to her inner being there. Indeed, he almost hoped he would find some clue to his *own* inner self there. He had never considered himself a father, or even imagined its eventuality. Might he actually fulfill such a role for Hamlet, despite his new son's full adulthood, and be a completely fulfilling husband to Gertrude?

He slid an arm behind her waist and drew her to his embrace. He kissed her gently and lovingly, and he could feel her heart begin to race slightly against his chest. He gazed carefully into her face once more.

"I cannot but think that he must be very disappointed, perhaps even angry," he said. "After all, he has every expectation of kingship, and he must see me as an impediment to his own arguably legitimate ambitions."

Gertrude stiffened, despite her long-practiced self-control. She knew what he was thinking, and she knew that he knew. Hamlet could be trouble.

"Hamlet was never a violent child," she protested softly. "Or an ambitious one. He was always more interested in metaphysics and morality than in the military. He is no threat. As for his ambitions, time can always allow for their fruition, can it not? Neither you nor I will live forever."

She wondered whether or not Claudius would believe this softening of Hamlet's rougher edges, but a mother must protect her child.

Stepping back slightly, but not releasing her, he raised his voice in protest. "I do not suspect Hamlet as some kind of threat! And I am no threat to him. I only hope that I may serve to expand his possibilities, to lubricate his future into the monarchy he will one day have grown to deserve through skill and merit rather than simple and unpredictable primogeniture. I care for him. May I not consider him my own son now? I am now his legitimate father (if we discount the fastidious disapproval of Father Jacob, who is old and a little silly now, anyway), and we are man and wife."

He wondered whether or not she truly accepted this characterization. After all, how well did he really know this woman? How well does any man know any woman?

"What about this?" he suggested after a moment. "In a few days' time, in front of all the court, I will name him my successor, all as part of a public expression of my love for my deceased brother, his father, for you as my wife, and for him. Surely that will mollify any angry misgivings he may hold?"

Gertrude thought carefully. If Hamlet were anything like his real father such promises would never be enough. Old Hamlet had loved nothing so much as his crown, not even his queen *or* his son. Still, young Hamlet was a bit of an unknown, a bit of an enigma, and who knows what foolishness he had picked up from the monks in Wittenberg? But although he was a large, strapping young man, much like his father, he had never shown much interest in future rule except when Old Hamlet had demanded his companionship and attention. And what child could resist the demands of a father he loved, particularly a man (and a king) like Hamlet?

Her own heart trembled as she remembered her previous husband. He may have ignored her for days on end when busy with matters of state, but when he came to her as a lover he had been wonderful—attentive to her needs, tender, strong and powerful.

As a proud princess she had at first been offended by his inconsistent attentions, but whenever she was with him she had felt a thrill that seemed to renew itself and strengthen as the years went on, even as she had felt herself succumbing to the more easy-going yet smooth and consistent charms of Claudius, the king's brother. It was odd, she thought, how even within the confines of her clear-eyed religious faith she had never felt ashamed of her secret desire for Claudius, particularly when King Hamlet had left her alone. And there had always been sufficient nurses and servant companions to mind young Hamlet.

A woman has desires beyond days filled with served meals and needlepoint, does she not? So when during the brief struggle against Norway for the northern islands she had found herself alone with Claudius on several occasions she knew that neither of them had been surprised to find themselves rutting enthusiastically together in her private chamber. Still, she missed her husband Hamlet, a man of strength and contradiction, of humor and romance, of both power and tenderness.

"Gertrude?" Claudius prompted.

She looked up at him blankly for a moment, then said, "You are my husband and my king. If you feel my Hamlet will best suit Denmark as your successor, then you must nominate him. And of course such action cannot harm your relations with him as both sovereign and as 'father,' although you know how much he adored your brother…" Her voice died away a bit, as her memory once again slid to her deceased husband.

Claudius pulled her to him once more, and she felt his breath on her cheek and the caress of his beard. He kissed her beneath her ear and said, "We will try it. He is a fine and suitable young man who has suffered a grave loss. We must try to make it up to him as we can."

Then, he continued in another direction. "Meanwhile, we must deal with this new Norwegian business. Young Fortinbras continues to pester us with threats of war, although it's hard to imagine that that young pup has the strength to follow through in any meaningful way. Still, forewarned is forearmed, at least to some degree, and it's not as though he lacks motive. Thus, it is important that we prepare."

"Are you meeting with the ambassadors this evening, my lord?"

"I am. I will have no formal dinner tonight, but let us have an official welcome for young Hamlet tomorrow. Perhaps Ophelia can be there along with her brother and father. You know that Hamlet always had an eye for her."

"Ah, yes, that minx." Gertrude could be curt and judgmental when it suited her. "Still, she's a sweet girl in many ways. Yes, let us plan for that. I will have the appropriate invitations issued and preparations made."

Claudius kissed her cheek again and made to depart.

"Your majesty," Gertrude said, and made a half curtsey. Claudius chuckled slightly and turned to go. As he strode from the room he suddenly thought that he couldn't believe his fortune, despite how long he had dreamed of it, how long he had acted the part of a loving brother and obedient prince, how long he had lusted for a woman he could not have. Now he had it all: queen, crown, and fortune. He would never let it go, he thought to himself. Never.

Gertrude watched him out the portal. She, too, felt her fortune. When the snake had killed Old Hamlet she had imagined she would never recover, despite her illicit love for Claudius. Now she was queen again. Again! How many women, no matter how royal, could claim that?

Then she thought of Hamlet and of her plans for the dinner. It promised to be an interesting meal.

Chapter 9

The Camp of Young Fortinbras

Although it was early evening, the summer sun was still relatively high and very bright. The effulgence glinted off the waters of the fjord, and the big firs growing up the steep Norwegian mountainsides were a brilliant summer green. A glacial stream gurgled and splashed down the slope from the forest and emptied noisily into the fjord a hundred yards or so to the north.

At the head of the fjord was an open field, crowded with tents and a few wooden structures—a barn and three small houses. From beyond the tents up the mountainside could be heard the irregular crack of axes, and every so often the ripping sound of a great tree falling among its neighbors. Smoke rose from a dozen open fires, and men bustled everywhere. Although birdsong rang from the forest, it was nearly drowned out by the uneven ringing percussion of blacksmiths' hammers. The air was redolent of summer flowers and wood smoke, as well as roasting meat.

Only three long ships were drawn up on the gravel strand nearest the settlement, sails folded away safely, but a fleet of twenty or so was anchored just offshore in four orderly rows. On the strand, a contingent of well-muscled men, bare to the waste, was working on plugging ships' seams with a mix of pitch and grass.

A fourth ship cruised smoothly up to the simple dock, oars shipped in response to a snapped order from a tall young man, perhaps thirty-five years old, standing in the stern. He had thick blond hair and a ruddy complexion. A large sword hung at his side, partially hidden by a smart cloak that was thrown back from his heavily muscled shoulders.

As an oarsman secured the ship to the dock, the young man jumped purposefully from the ship and approvingly surveyed the activity. He quickly thumped along the dock's planking and set off along the strand, boots crunching in the gravel.

He stopped to exchange a few words with one of the men absorbed in waterproofing. The man looked up, laughed briefly and turned back to his work. Then the young man from the ship turned and trudged up the slope toward the farm buildings. The oarsmen from his ship clambered onto the dock and began to follow toward the encampment.

On a rough stool near one of the settlement fires another young man glanced up from the leather armor he was mending. Seeing the cloaked figure approaching, he hastily set down his work and rose to his feet.

"Lord Fortinbras!" he called excitedly, and moved down the slope to meet the young man.

"Lars," responded Fortinbras warmly. He glanced around. "Preparations appear to be going well." He clasped Lars by the hand. Lars gave a half bow and smiled.

"Yes. Four more ships with eighty-four more men joined us this morning. They've brought weapons with them, although they will need to be provisioned with food. And silver, of course."

Fortinbras frowned, then smiled wryly. "Well, when we've taken our islands back from those Danish dogs there'll be plenty of booty to go around. Until then, they'll have to be patient."

He gazed up toward the smiths, who were hammering blades in an uneven, clanging rhythm. He smiled again, then went on.

"The men know how these affairs proceed. If any of them has the courage to do some killing and attracts a little luck, he'll go home to his village a wealthy man. For those who die fighting, Heaven awaits with feasting aplenty and tales to last forever."

He looked around once more, then back at Lars, and asked more seriously, "Tell me, when will the last of the ships be ready?"

Lars calculated for a moment. "The ships will be ready within another two, perhaps three weeks, give or take a few days. However, if our campaign is to last more than a few days we need to acquire more food provisions. Although we may hope to take what we need from Danish peasants on the islands, our security may rely on our having plenty of food in reserve, at least enough for two weeks for all our men."

He scratched his neck, then added, "I have four agents traversing the back country to purchase the needed items. However, there is always some resistance from the peasantry when it comes to parting with their food, even when it is only surplus to their needs. If we need, we might use a little more forceful persuasion to generate their co-operation. *Promises* of silver don't go far in this country."

"We want to sail in clement weather," Fortinbras stated matter-of-factly. "We need to be ready soon."

"We can do it, my lord," Lars answered. "We are making all possible efforts."

Fortinbras looked back at the ships. Behind them the lowering sun threw the shadows of their spars toward the shore, like lances driving into the breast of the beach. He sighed.

He thought momentarily of the new Danish king, Claudius. Although he knew little specific about the man, he had learned from the captain of a local trading vessel that the previous king, Hamlet, had died under mysterious conditions. *That* evil man, the killer of Fortinbras' father, had been a warrior to fear. Claudius was an unknown. Perhaps he would prove a weakling, physically or morally. God knew that Norway had a right to those islands. Surely He had allowed the Danes to take them only to test the strength, faith and resolve of Norway.

Then he thought of Norway itself. His uncle Olav, the present king, was already greying. He had been a fierce man in his youth, had even contested Old Fortinbras for the Norwegian crown. But Fortinbras knew that his uncle king would never gather the ambition to challenge the Danes again. *It has to be done,* he thought to himself. *I will do it. I will.*

He turned to Lars once more. "Let us find some ale and eat," he said. "We have much planning left to do."

Lars bowed slightly again and indicated that Fortinbras should precede him toward the largest of the farm's houses, a heavily thatched log structure with a stone foundation. The two men crossed the beaten-down grass between two groups of tents and approached the house. A soldier at the door straightened visibly as the two men approached. He bent to open the door, and the two men entered.

Shadows continued to lengthen as the sun dipped toward the northwestern mountain slopes. It would be night soon enough.

Chapter 10

Guards and Ghosts

Although it was at first unusual, Horatio was now beginning to write in the afternoon. One of the king's servants had seen to that.

"King Fortinbras is adamant. You must work harder on your report. He is not convinced that you are telling all you know, and he has expressly stated in my presence that he believes that you are working so slowly because you are struggling to find more effective ways of hiding the truth."

The servant, a middle-aged man obviously unaccustomed to the livery of the court (probably an ex-soldier) glared at Horatio.

For his part, Horatio glared back. He may have feared Fortinbras, but he was not pleased to have some Norwegian bumpkin chastise him. He gathered his thoughts, then spoke.

"Please, please. I have sworn my life to lord Fortinbras as my true sovereign. I have agreed, most willingly, to try to explain the events leading to the 'havoc,' as he calls it. I am writing for several hours each night, sometimes until after midnight." He paused. "I have every motive to find and record the truth. I have sworn to try, both for his majesty, to whom I owe my ongoing allegiance, and to my former sovereign prince Hamlet (rest his soul)."

The servant scowled. Horatio continued. "I would happily forward to the king my record of events so far, although I have only one copy and would feel more secure if he might influence our local abbot to assign a monk to create a second copy from my original."

"The king wishes you to work faster, and so you must. As to your request for a monk's assistance, I can bring the issue to the king's attention and we will see whether or not he will see fit to agree. Meanwhile, you are to begin to work on this during the day, as well as write in the evening. Your readings from the university in Wittenberg may be of interest to you, but your duty to the king must come first."

The servant bowed and swept imperiously out of the room. For his part, Horatio nearly laughed, for the man clearly had little familiarity with the manners of court, and Horatio had never been bowed to in his life. Still, the assignment was clear. He would have to think harder and write faster. Brother Henrik would have to find more writing materials, and soon.

Horatio set aside the remains of his dinner. With luck, the serving girl Petronilla would forgive his haste and might even straighten up his room. He stood and collected his cloak from the peg by the doorway. Securing it over his shoulders, he left the room through the same doorway the servant had used. He slipped the bolt home, then turned and walked slowly down the corridor toward the back staircases that ascended to the tower room where he had been writing.

He hoped Henrik had obeyed his injunction not to disturb his papers. "Forbid us things, and they become what we desire," tended to be an accurate description of human motives, however, and it wouldn't have surprised him if Henrik had snooped, despite his sworn pledge to obey Horatio's wishes.

After climbing past two floors of apartments, Horatio reached a gallery from which his writing room could be reached. He looked behind him, a bit wearily, but as he approached the door of the room he seemed to gather his energies. This always seemed to happen, he thought to himself. As soon as he began to think, to remember, the story seemed to reform before his eyes, almost like one of the stage plays Hamlet had so loved.

He unlatched the door of the writing room. From the small window a band of afternoon sunlight lit a narrow patch of floor and a corner of his writing table.

Good, he thought to himself. Henrik had brought more writing paper and ink. He peered closely at his group of finished papers. The hair he had laid carefully against the side of the small pile was undisturbed. Maybe there was more to the faith of the church than he was generally ready to credit, or at least to that of Brother Henrik, despite his taciturn and grouchy nature.

He felt something rub his leg. He absently bent down and rubbed the cat gently behind the ears, then picked it up. It resisted briefly, then allowed Horatio to set it on the table next to its cushion. It looked at Horatio, one of those impenetrable cat gazes that suggest some impossible question.

"Yes, I have to work," Horatio said to the cat. As the cat circled the cushion and then settled itself upon it, Horatio pulled up his chair and sat. He selected a quill, tested its point briefly, and drew the pot of ink toward him. He removed its stopper, and selected a clean sheet from the pile Henrik had left him. He thought for a moment or two, stroked the cat again with his left hand, then, as if he had been commanded by the cat, bent forward and began to write.

I didn't believe Marcellus when he first approached me with his story, for I've never believed in ghosts. Oh, yes, I know, we're meant to believe in the Holy Ghost, that member of the Holy Trinity that seems somehow to permeate the Godhead between Father and Son. And I do believe. I do. But the existence of God's spirit throughout His creation and the existence of ethereal doomed souls that wander the Earth as conscious spirits after death are two different things. The Kingdom of God is of necessity obscure, mysterious, for who can fathom the depths of His creation? But

I had always been at least somewhat skeptical of human ghosts, despite popular imaginings and reports.

I must admit that Marcellus seemed convinced himself that he had in fact seen the ghost. And in truth, he didn't show any of that evasiveness of the eyes that seems to mark even the most accomplished liar. Further, I knew of no reason why Marcellus would lie about such a thing.

I did not know Marcellus by name at first, although I had encountered him as part of the Elsinore military staff several years before while on an excursion with my own father. Marcellus had immediately seemed to me a sound man, insofar as one judges these things in strangers.

He came to me one midmorning about a week after Hamlet returned from Wittenberg. I was still unpacking my own few belongings from my recent arrival when I heard a sharp rap on my door. Marcellus had sought me out personally through one of the lesser palace servants, as though he knew me, either personally or by reputation. He had no real reason to remember me.

I had not yet gathered the will to go to see Hamlet. I know that Hamlet did not realize at the time that I would follow him from Wittenberg, but what could I do? I admired him beyond words; he was my fellow student, my friend, and above all, my prince. I had to keep myself where I could serve him, should the need arise.

That morning, I was hoping to sit down to read some of the more challenging passages from *The Confessions* for an hour, once I was finished unpacking. (I have always been fascinated by St. Augustine.)

Marcellus seemed troubled before he even opened his mouth. "Please pardon my intrusion," he said, as I once more took my seat. He was polite for a soldier, I thought.

"My name is Marcellus," he went on. "I hoped I might speak with you in private."

Now I *was* curious. A soldier? Wanting to speak to me? In private?

"Your humble servant," I replied (with perhaps more courtesy than necessary). I indicated that he should sit opposite me beside the small fire that burned in the grate. I waved the servant away, and he bowed and went out the door, closing it behind him. "May I offer you tea?" I said, indicating the simple pot on the small table beside me.

"Thank you, my lord, no." He paused as if to gather his thoughts, and ideas martialed, began.

"My lord, I have need of your services. Of course, I realize that I have no right to request your help. But at this time I believe that you are the only man who can help." He looked at me earnestly. My curiosity was tingling.

He coughed politely. I waited. "It is not for me alone that I request your assistance," he finally went on. "I believe the matter may be very important, perhaps even of significance to Denmark itself."

This *was* unsettling. I reached for my mug of tea, then left it and leaned toward Marcellus.

"And why would you bring this matter to *me*? As you know, I am a simple scholar and have little influence on large matters." Of course, I was flattered inside, although I don't think I showed it. The idea that my assistance might alter the affairs of Denmark was intriguing, nearly infatuating.

"It is your scholarship, your understanding that I require, sir," he said, his round open eyes gazing frankly into mine.

He was so candid and so serious I could hardly decline.

"I am at your service," I said after a moment. "How can I help you?"

Marcellus pulled his military cloak more closely about his shoulders, a gesture that at the time seemed absurd, given the warmth of the morning fire. After looking around a moment he gazed at me again, as if judging my worth. Then he said almost secretively, "I have seen a ghost."

At first I laughed. The sound of my voice was so sharp that even I immediately felt chastened for having done so, for Marcellus frowned darkly and clenched his fist around a bunch of his cloak.

"Please," I said. "I am sorry," though I was still smiling. "Tell me."

"It was the ghost of the king that's dead—King Hamlet," he said in a low voice.

I felt a quiver around my spine, a kind of shiver. My smile quite died.

"King Hamlet?"

"Yes."

"Where did this occur? When?" I asked.

"Last night—on the guard platform on the northwest corner tower of the castle's seaward fortification. Another soldier, Bernardo, was with me. He can vouch for my words. He is not with me, but I told him that I intended to speak to you about this matter. He did not wish me to reveal these things, but he is young—inexperienced—I overruled his anxiety."

"What did this ghost do?" I asked, more gently now.

Marcellus took a deep breath, as if gathering his resolve.

"It was an hour or more after midnight. You know how the fog swirls in off the sea at night. Bernardo and I had completed the first period of our watch and had begun to brew tea when it appeared."

He thought a moment. "At first it was no more than a lighter part of the fog itself, as if a candle or two were burning behind a heavy veil, more than a dozen paces from where we sat. Bernardo saw it first, although he will deny this. He gaped past me as though he were frightened by something behind my back. When I turned to look, a dim form seemed to materialize from the fog itself."

He stopped a moment. "I will have some of that tea after all, sir, if you don't mind."

"The tea is cold," I said. But I got up and instead poured Marcellus a drink from the sherry decanter I keep on the sideboard for winter nights. "Here," I said. "Try this."

Marcellus accepted the cup, sniffed it gingerly and took a swallow.

"What was this form?" I asked, somewhat impatiently.

Marcellus drank again, wiped his beard while looking at the floor (as if there might be some mnemonic feature in the stone flags), and then spoke again, his voice low to the point where I could hardly hear it.

"It was a man in armor. He held no weapons, but the visor of his helmet was up. It was the king as I have seen him in life. I swear it. He looked at us with an expression of great sorrow, or perhaps of great anger. We could not tell. Bernardo threw himself onto his knees before it and begged it to speak to us, but it raised its head haughtily and turned away. Then it stalked away into the fog." Marcellus crossed himself and drank again.

"I don't believe it," I said firmly. "No. You were drinking," I said accusingly.

"I swear not, sir!" he said, anger just beneath the surface. "It was the king."

I thought for a long moment. The scents of tea and wine lingered in the air. I looked at Marcellus again, a long appraisal.

"All right. *I* believe that *you* believe you saw the king. Now what? What do you want from me?"

"I believe he, it, will appear again, sir. I want you to watch with us. Tonight. If you will, sir." He thought, briefly. "I know you do not believe it. *I* could hardly believe it at first. But to whom should I have gone with this story? Who would not have reacted as you just did, blaming the foolish, drunken soldier?"

His point was clear. What fool *would* believe such nonsense? Still, he did not seem in any way a fool, aside from the wildness of his tale.

"So?" I asked.

"Would you watch with us tonight, sir? If it does not appear, then perhaps we *were* fooled. Fog and torchlight can create strange appearances in the night. But I have stood watch at this castle for over fifteen years, and I have never seen what we saw last night. Will you, sir?"

I gathered my resolve a moment to say 'No,' but his earnestness prevented such hardness.

"All right," I answered. "When shall I come to you?"

"Bernardo will fetch you at the eleventh hour." Then, belatedly, "I am most grateful, sir. You are a scholar. Who else is there among us that might speak with a ghost?"

Who, indeed? I thought, but did not say aloud.

"I will be here," I said.

Marcellus rose swiftly, bowed briefly, and said, "My lord, I thank you." He turned and let himself out the door.

Of course, even then I did not believe a word of it. But then words are easily doubted. It is facts and events that are much harder to dismiss.

I had almost forgotten Marcellus' visit by the time I had laid out my evening meal. I had spent much of the day arguing with one of the king's minor functionaries about whether or not I should continue to be allowed rooms in the great castle. My previous rooms had been authorized by young Hamlet himself (to my great and lasting gratitude), but given intervening events—the king's death, the new marriage, and so on—everything was uncertain.

The servant of king Claudius' royal accounts keeper came to my room early, not more than a half hour after daylight. His imperious hammering on the door might have been that of the king himself! When he recited his errand I simply laughed (truly, he had no more incentive than that of ingratiating himself with his superiors by saving the royal treasury a few coins). He smiled shyly then and asked if he might come in.

We spoke for the better part of an hour, sharing our uncertain views of the new royal household. By the time he was ready to leave we had already enjoyed two glasses of sherry together, rather an unusual breakfast, but ultimately a pleasure! He took his leave with the express intention of explaining the importance and necessity of my presence in Elsinore to his master (although I was not yet sure myself what that might be).

I spent the afternoon reading more than one section of *The Confessions*, an astonishing work. I had never believed that such a senior father of our holy Catholic Church could have allowed himself to express such blasphemies! "O, Lord, give me chastity, but not yet," will resound through the centuries, I am sure of it.

Yes, chastity. Perhaps fate would have turned in a different way had chastity been a greater priority for Hamlet—or for Ophelia. But we are what we are, sinners all, and will account for our acts one day.

I was eating some cheese and bread for my supper when once more I heard a knock. I knew immediately who it must be, and a kind of dread began to gnaw at my guts. The man at the door was a stranger, a soldier.

"My name is Bernardo," he said. "Marcellus requested that I escort you to our watch platform."

I looked at him. He seemed unbearably young, but then I was only in my late twenties myself.

"Will you accompany me, my lord?" he asked earnestly. "It is after the tenth hour, and I am required to watch with him after the eleventh."

I turned to the candle on my desk, which had burned far further than I expected. Truly, St. Augustine is a compelling thinker and a veritable man of God. I looked back at Bernardo.

"Allow me to fetch my cloak," I responded.

He waited patiently while I swallowed another gulp of wine and gathered my cloak, a heavy woolen garment, from the hook behind the door. I blew out the candle, almost startled by the relative dimness of the light from the torch down the corridor.

"Lead on," I said to him, and I bolted the door behind me.

We walked down a number of corridors, each of which led to a new staircase, climbing always upward.

When we reached the battlements, it was another cold night, but brilliantly clear. I gazed for a moment at the half moon glowing above the sea. Stars were dazzling overhead, a visual celebration of God's majesty. I shivered, both with cold and with exaltation, not to mention with a small anxiety that nibbled at my entrails.

Bernardo led me along a long gallery flanked on one side by a crenellated wall and on the other by a drop into an elevated courtyard. We ascended a staircase to a circular tower, whose interior stair led to the guard platform. We circled up the tower, listening to our own breathing, which steamed into the darkness before us. Had it not been for the star and moonlight coming through the arrow slits we would have been unable to see anything.

"Who's there?" a nervous voice called out. From its tenor, I thought I recognized the tones of Marcellus.

"Friends to this ground," answered Bernardo, "and liegemen to the Dane."

"Bernardo?" the voice said again. We stepped through the small doorway onto the platform where Marcellus waited.

"He," Bernardo replied.

A small brazier flared briefly, illuminating Marcellus' face momentarily. It must have lit mine too, for he said, "Welcome good Horatio. I was uncertain whether or not you would accompany Bernardo."

I sniffed as though to indicate I felt somewhat insulted, but in truth, he was right. Had Bernardo not appeared I would probably have been comfortably asleep. However, I did my best to smile, and answered a bit irritably, "Well, where's this ghost?"

Bernardo crossed himself seriously, and Marcellus said, "Last night it appeared just after the first bell. If it should come again, I warrant it will be near the same time."

Bernardo approached the brazier and extended his hands to warm them. Then he turned to Marcellus and me and asked, "Tell me. Why are we doing this?" We looked at him a bit stupidly for a moment. "I mean," he added, "what is the reason for the doubling of our watch, among all the other military preparations that seem to be proceeding apace? Have you not noticed? Shipwrights and their workers are at their work seven days a week. Young men from the countryside are arriving daily in the town and being provided the best of weapons. Is war afoot?"

I glanced around uneasily. Of course, I knew that war might be imminent. It is amazing how quickly rumors spread, and even before I was within the castle precincts one of the grooms attending the coach horses had breathlessly alerted me to the new war preparations. War seemed as if it might be inevitable. I felt somewhat uncomfortable that these brave men were so uncertain, so ignorant of events, despite the gossip, yet these were the kind of courageous souls who have always defended the kingdom. Perhaps their officers had ordered them to ignore common talk, but the evidence was everywhere to be seen, as Bernardo had observed.

"I can tell you a little of that," I said, somewhat uncertain of how much they should be allowed to know. Of course, all that I knew came from the groom, and then from servants in the king's hall, and who knows how reliable they might be? "The rumor is that young Fortinbras of Norway is eager to prove himself by regaining the islands lost by his father to our former King Hamlet. Do you know the story?"

Marcellus nodded, and Bernardo grunted assent.

Horatio continued. "Young Fortinbras has sent letters to King Claudius demanding he relinquish those same islands to Norwegian control or be prepared to defend them by force of arms."

Marcellus looked at him speculatively. "Perhaps these events are the subject of the ghost's appearance," he marveled. "Ghosts are known to provide warning of evil events."

Although I had not truly considered this, I had to admit, if the ghost were real, such might be possible. Before I could continue my thoughts, however, Bernardo hissed with great vehemence, "Look where it comes again!"

I turned and immediately fell to my knees as if struck by a hammer! By my living breath, it was the king! He gazed at us imperiously yet wildly, as if astonished by some bizarre event. I crossed myself repeatedly. I felt as if I might heave up my dinner. I was terrified.

"Is it not like the king?" whispered Marcellus, on his own knees at my side.

The pale light emanating from the vision seemed to throb and pulse, brightening and dimming like some great visual heartbeat. The ghost lowered his gaze and turned away as if to leave.

From some reservoir of strength within me, I heard my own voice. "Stay, illusion!"

The light rose again slightly and the figure gazed briefly and piteously at me.

"If thou hast any business with us humble mortals that may do good to Denmark and her people, speak to me."

It glared at me as if offended.

I tried again. "If thy presence and gracious manner can in any way be construed a message to our royal court and to thy royal son, speak to me."

This time it raised its armored hand and slowly made the sign of the cross. Then, head lowered, it turned and began to move away.

"Speak, O royal ghost, I charge thee, speak!"

"Shall I stop it?" Marcellus asked, raising his spear anxiously. But he was too late. The figure paced deliberately away from us into a fog that had materialized out of nowhere. The light of his presence dimmed, and then he disappeared.

Bernardo, too, was on his knees. He had vomited in terror and appeared utterly spent. The stink of his puke stained the night air. Marcellus placed his gloved hand on Bernardo's shoulder and said, "Come on, son. A bit of water will set this right," and he unscrewed his flask and handed it to Bernardo, who drank greedily, spat, and drank again. He shook a little, whether with fear or cold I could not tell.

Marcellus turned to me. "Well," he said. "Was it not like the king?"

I looked around apprehensively before answering. Then somewhat guiltily I admitted, "I did not believe you. I am ashamed. I believe you now." I shivered and pulled my cloak instinctively closer around my shoulders. I *was* ashamed that I had doubted these good, honest men.

"We must tell young Hamlet," I said.

The two looked at me stupidly. "He is here in Elsinore," I said. "We must tell him. Tomorrow. Tonight is a royal banquet in honor of his return."

Marcellus nodded. "I will accompany you," he said thoughtfully. "We both will, he added, speaking for Bernardo, who continued to stare blankly off into the fog where the ghost had disappeared. Then, as if the breath of some capricious god had blown it, the fog lifted and the stars blazed forth as before. There was no sign of the ghost, only the sound of the ocean breakers smashing on the rocks at the foot of the castle and the lonely hoot of a night owl on the hunt.

Chapter 11

A Royal Dinner

The west dining hall was bustling with activity. Smells of roasting meats and fresh pastries permeated the air. A young lute player sang softly from his velvet cushion on the floor near the royal table, something about a courageous knight and true love's faith. A large hound padded through the entrance to the singer's side, where at first it sat, then lay facing the king's table.

Nobles with a variety of consorts or accompanying family members were already seated at long tables along the north and south walls, facing the large open interior of the room. Near the head table and also facing the room's open interior and the great west windows was the kitchen entrance, in the east wall. King Claudius was seated with the lord Polonius at the head table at the east wall, in casual if low-voiced conversation.

Although no hint of it could be seen in his manner, at least at first, Claudius was ill at ease. Since his own ascension to the throne he had not seen young Hamlet. He was unsure how the young man would react at this meeting—to events, to fate as it had played out. True, it was predictable that Hamlet would feel strongly the loss of his father. How strongly he would feel resentment against Claudius for his assumption of royal power was another matter, even though the nobles called to court had judiciously approved.

Claudius lifted his wine cup and took a healthy swallow, ignoring Polonius' last remark, but Polonius, looking left to a side entrance, had already stopped in mid-sentence. Gertrude swept in followed by two of her maids to the head table. She eyed Claudius critically. Polonius hastily stood and bowed. "Your majesty," he greeted her.

"Lord Polonius," she replied automatically.

Claudius drank again, enjoying the warmth of the wine in his breast and the confidence it brought him. He set the cup down and rose to welcome Gertrude.

"My queen," he said, taking her hands and seating her gently to his left beside him. He kissed her softly on the cheek she offered him. He sat once more, wondering oddly which of the royal cooks had prepared this evening's repast. He was hungry *and* anxious, but pleased that Gertrude had joined him.

"Polonius was just advising me on the Norwegian issue," he said to her. "He says that his agents report young Fortinbras to be a serious threat."

"Fortinbras is young, and we are strong," Gertrude replied. She had little patience for weakness of any sort. "My lord Polonius," she said more loudly, addressing him past her husband, "we are not uncertain of our position regarding that young upstart, are we?"

"Good gracious, no, my lady," he answered. "But it is prudent policy ever to be prepared for the worst. In the event of any outright hostilities I am sure our Danish forces will prevail."

Gertrude appraised him uncertainly, eyebrows raised. She had never completely trusted this man. Claudius looked at her and said, "Well?"

At that moment a page at the main entrance snapped erect and clearly announced to the room, "The royal prince Hamlet!"

The lute player broke off in mid-phrase, and as he had upon the entrance of the queen, set his instrument aside against a table leg and rose to his feet. The dog yawned, and lowered its jaw to its paws. Servants stopped their motions and bowed toward the entrance, where

Hamlet walked in cautiously, stopping and looking around, eying the guests.

He was dressed completely in black, including a crow's feather in the hat he doffed as he approached and bowed to the head table.

"Your majesties," he said, without even a hint of irony.

An excited buzz had risen from the tables at his entrance, but it as quickly died. All eyes were on Hamlet and the king's party.

"Hamlet!" Claudius exclaimed. "We are overjoyed to find you once again at home, especially at this time of both mourning and celebration."

Hamlet eyed the king.

"Should we celebrate that we mourn, or mourn that we celebrate?" he asked.

This was precisely the aspect of Hamlet's irritable personality that Claudius had always despised—his ironic ambiguity. Gertrude hid a small smile behind her napkin.

"Should we not all celebrate any morning that follows a dark night?" the king replied, glancing to his right and left for approval, trying to keep the conversation light. A few guests chuckled quietly, but most remained silent, watching.

"Might not a dark knight create many a cause for mourning?" Hamlet responded. Claudius frowned and reached once more for his cup. Gertrude laid her hand on his arm, for just at this moment Ophelia and one of her maids entered through a north entrance, the new arrival again capturing everyone's attention. She curtsied gracefully and smiling, looked directly at Hamlet.

She was dressed in a beautiful grey gown, low-cut after the current fashion, her black hair framing her soft face, hanging forward along her elegant neck and down to the swell of her bosom.

"Welcome, Ophelia," said the queen with a smile, and Claudius nodded his agreement. The audience was quiet, everyone's attention on Polonius' beautiful daughter. After a moment's silence, Ophelia said, “My lord Hamlet, we are both gratified and honored that you have come back to us.”

Hamlet returned her gaze seriously. She continued. “Would I be too forward to request the honor of being seated at your right hand?”

Nodding, he walked along the table to join her. “I would have it no other way,” he offered in a low voice. He looked from Ophelia to his mother, then to the king. Then, ostentatiously and with a low bow, he took her hand and kissed it.

“It appears the dark night is followed by the dawn,” he said. Ophelia smiled radiantly. The queen observed them, pleased and fascinated. Claudius’ lip curled upward slightly, and he lifted his cup.

A pair of servants hastened forward to seat them. The maid stood behind them against the wall.

Claudius turned questioningly toward Gertrude, while Polonius, smiling obscurely, fiddled with a napkin. Gertrude simply smiled at the king and quietly remarked, “Well, wasn’t that instructive?”

Polonius then whispered to the king, “Perhaps it would be wise to say something further.” Claudius looked momentarily lost, then nodded and rose to his feet. Those assembled at table immediately rose in near concert—except Hamlet, who rose to his feet only after a few meaningful seconds’ delay.

Claudius began to speak. “Hamlet, we are only too mindful of the special relationship that events have thrust upon us. From our vantage of the throne of Denmark we wish to extend to you our most heartfelt love and generous regard. As you may imagine, we heartily miss your father, our dear departed brother.”

He paused, and then looked up meaningfully at Hamlet. “We have humbly accepted the responsibility of kingship with gratitude and remorse linked by both chance and duty—the ugly hazard of the serpent’s sting that so evilly took our brother’s life, and our duty to ensure the vigor and survival of his estate. In our acceptance of this sacred role we have assumed responsibility for the welfare of Denmark and for the continued health and prosperity of our brother’s family.

Hence, with the support and approval of the noble families, under the impetus of my own heart and the acquiescence of your mother's will, I have taken Gertrude, your mother, to wife."

He paused again to examine Hamlet for some response, who rather than return the king's gaze, looked down at the table before him.

"We married, trusting in our familial bonds to seal your consent to this union, wherein by law and custom our roles, mine as king, and yours as prince, become as much those of father and son as of uncle and nephew. Allow me, if you will, to extend to you the love and care of both a king and father."

He raised his cup and glanced around the room expectantly. The assembled diners quickly found and raised their cups in imitation of their liege. Claudius waited a judicious moment, then called out clearly, "The king and his country drink to Hamlet."

"To Hamlet," the assembly dutifully intoned, and they drank.

Hamlet colored noticeably, but at first said nothing. Ophelia glanced at Hamlet, who looked around at the assembled nobles as if memorizing their faces. For their part, they returned his gaze, all, it seemed, waiting for some sign, some princely response. Finally Hamlet spoke.

"A prince must lack both nobility and conscience if he misunderstand either responsibility or duty, particularly duty of family." He eyed his mother closely. "How say you, Mother? Has duty been done?"

Gertrude blushed slightly but responded quickly enough. "Denmark is safe and well, and the queen shares the general confidence in the state of affairs. As for other duties, these are rather of a more private nature."

She smiled and watched as the assembly emitted a few scattered chuckles at her wit, rather more bawdy than might have been expected. Hamlet scowled.

Polonius coughed to break the tension, as a group of six or seven servants strode into the hall through the kitchen entrance bearing platters of roast boar and venison, steaming pots of stew, large pies redolent of vegetable, plates of cheese, and a great bowl of dried fruit. Two other servants followed, carrying additional large pitchers of wine.

Claudius sat and drank, and the assembled group relaxed into their seats, resuming a number of animated conversations. Claudius and Gertrude accepted a selection of viands from the foods initially offered, and following their service, those carrying platters and pitchers fanned out to the other tables.

"My lord," Ophelia began. Hamlet tilted his head toward her as the general buzz of conversation continued to increase in volume. "Although the time is never right for such messages, please allow me to express my condolences to you for the untimely loss of your father, king Hamlet." She raised her eyes to his, as if seeking some kind of assurance.

Hamlet looked at her, an inquisitive, penetrating look, almost a dark look. The glow drained from her face in reaction, and she broke her gaze away to stare at her plate.

He finally spoke, but rather than recognize her polite comment, said, "You will find the cheese and leek pie particularly delicious, if the cook can live up to his former achievement as I remember it. And the dead bits are particularly fine!"

She glanced back up at him, expression uneasy.

"As for my sadness and my need of condolence, speak not of it. For what blackened mood cannot be lightened by time and forgetting? Besides, the diced formality of raw words lacks flavor compared to the stirred disorder of well-cooked experience. Who knows what smoky deeds and overripe intentions have led the world of Denmark to the table where we dine? Mourning may be a kind of hunger that no dish can satisfy. But I note your loving care and I thank you."

"I fear I do not quite follow your reply, my lord."

Ophelia blushed. Had she offended him? Perhaps her dress was too informal given his mournful sensitivities. She had chosen her evening's costume with care, the soft grey dress embroidered with gold thread, gathered to accentuate her bust. Her maids had helped her dress and arrange her hair, all three complimenting the beauty of the arrangement. She looked again at Hamlet, allowing her eyes to rest momentarily on the sheen of his black silk doublet.

Hamlet felt an immense weariness and a kind of disgust for the whole occasion. Despite his longing for Ophelia--her beauty, her charm, and her general joy in life--his mood was overpowered by his anger at his mother and his repugnant uncle.

"I am finding it difficult to eat," Hamlet said to her quietly. "The animals are quite dead and prepared to perfection, and yet the thought of eating them repels me."

Ophelia examined him warily.

He continued almost in a parody of philosophy. "The digestion of death is a chore we all must face, some with greater cheer than others."

"Will you not eat?" he asked, lifting her plate toward her face, even as she recoiled noticeably from his unexpected gesture. "No?" he said. He put the plate back on the table in front of her.

"For my part, I believe I'll drink," he finally said. He clasped his goblet, lifted it to his lips and drained four or five swallows. Then he rose stiffly to his feet and leaning on the table addressed his mother.

"Madam," he called out. "Queen!" And even more loudly, "Mother!"

She turned from the conversation she had been sharing with the noble to her left and looked at him.

"I must take my leave, Mother," he said. Standing abruptly, he gave the merest hint of a bow, kicked the chair behind him backwards where a servant moved swiftly to grasp it before it might fall, and turning, walked quickly out through the north entrance.

Claudius looked to his right to Polonius, who was staring at Ophelia as if to ask, "What have you done now?"

"My, didn't that go well?" Gertrude said ironically to Claudius, who grunted.

Nobles who had noticed the exchange in sufficient time to stand seemed to be wondering whether or not it would be suitably polite to sit again. Ophelia had stood when Hamlet did, and her eyes, now filling with tears, turned toward the wall and her maid. She turned to look at her father, then again at her maid, to whom she nodded. Gathering her long skirt, she hastened along the table to the main west entrance and left, her maid rushing to follow. Conversation erupted around the room.

Polonius snapped his fingers at the lute player, who strummed an opening chord and began to sing once more.

In the west hallway Ophelia stood uncertainly in shadow, tears running down her cheeks. This was not at all the way the evening was supposed to unfold. Her maid held her hand and awkwardly tried to comfort her.

As he walked down the other hallway toward his quarters, Hamlet felt himself color with rage and shame. Each time he saw his Uncle Claudius he found himself feeling angrier, cheated of his rightful position. His mother was too happy by half. And he felt shamed by how he had allowed his anger to flow into his treatment of Ophelia. He could scarcely believe his own behavior. He picked up his pace.

About thirty minutes later, a knock sounded at the door to Hamlet's quarters. Yedric allowed Gersen to enter, took his hat, and led him into Hamlet's sitting room, where the prince was gazing distractedly into a small fire. He acknowledged Gersen's bow with a soft wave and indicated that he should sit. Gersen settled onto a chair opposite Hamlet and waited.

"I would speak with you further, Gersen."

Gersen nodded, acknowledging his acquiescence to Hamlet's summons.

"Have you ever been married?" Hamlet finally said after a long moment.

"No, my lord."

"In love?"

"I am unsure, my lord." He struggled a moment for words, as Hamlet stared at him. "I have deeply admired several women, my lord."

"And bedded them?"

Gersen coughed into his gloved hand gently. "On one or two occasions, my lord."

Hamlet looked back to the fire and sighed softly, almost a quiet snort. Then he asked, "Did you attend my mother's wedding?"

"I served as part of the king's—your uncle's—retinue." He lowered his gaze the floor. "I was commanded to organize the wedding feast—food, music, and so on."

"Ah, yes. I imagine it was a fine affair," said Hamlet.

"The king and queen were pleased."

"Would you say that the queen was happy with her new alliance, as it were? Did she express any reserve, any reluctance? Did she smile? When the priest pronounced their estate, did she kiss the king?"

Gersen coughed gently into his glove once more while he gathered his thoughts. "I would have to say that the queen appeared contented with her choice. Her actions were not those of an unhappy woman." He paused. More slowly, he added, "She did kiss the king."

"Your honesty becomes you," Hamlet said softly. Standing at the doorway to the chamber, Yedric had a worried guise etched on his face. "My uncle is a convincing king, is he not?"

Gersen appeared as if he would rather be anywhere else. He rubbed his brow softly with the back of his hand. "He is the king, my lord," he finally said.

"Yes, isn't he?" said Hamlet more to himself and to the fire than to Gersen. "Tell me, if you please, how did the assembled nobles react to the new 'arrangement?'" Hamlet laid especial stress on 'arrangement.'

"My lord, they did what prudent men do in the realm of power."

Hamlet raised his eyes directly at Gersen, who went on.

"They accepted the reality of the new situation. I am sure that many of them mourn deeply the loss of your father, king Hamlet;

however, ideals, which may often glow like burnished copper, are soft, and often give way to the polished and hardened brass of events. The nobles in court and at the wedding seem loyal to the new king. Forgive me if I judge too easily, but I feel I am reporting only what I have seen and experienced."

"Of course, of course."

Hamlet was being exceedingly generous. He finally said, "Please forgive my directness. I know you must answer and as a servant you must obey, but sometimes in this world it becomes a question of *whom* to obey, and *how*, and *when*, does it not?"

Gersen looked at Hamlet and nodded mutely.

"I would be most grateful if you would not mention our conversations to anyone else. You do understand, do you not?"

"Yes, my lord," Gersen answered.

Hamlet waved him away and looked back at the fire. Gersen got uncertainly to his feet. He retrieved his hat from Yedric, who led him out.

The fire was low, and it flickered irresolutely. For a few moments Hamlet distracted himself by trying to predict where the next significant flame would arise, only to die down once more.

"Fire as metaphor," he mused to himself. He extended his hands to warm them. "Perhaps hell isn't as horrifying as the priests tell us," he thought. He closed his eyes and imagined hell's flames. After a while he dreamed.

When Yedric returned, Hamlet was already sleeping, half reclined on the sofa where he had been seated, his head cushioned on the crook of his arm. Yedric watched him for a moment or two. Finally he sat on the stool beside the door where he was charged with managing the entry and being ready for any conceivable errand a prince might require. Soon he too slept.

Chapter 12

Hamlet and his Father

Horatio sat in his familiar chair. The late afternoon sun had gradually surrendered to some heavy cloud racing in off the sea, and it was gloomy in the room. He would have to light a candle soon. He dipped his quill and held it a moment.

The cat rubbed against his calf, and Horatio absently reached down to caress it, waiting for its purred response, but also thinking of the ghost, and of Hamlet. Horatio began to write.

> Fathers are mysterious characters at the best of times. We know they are close to us, by blood at least, but they can also be frustratingly distant. They seem to own us, to have us in their hearts by some virtue we cannot adequately name, and they often sit in judgment over us, their prisoners of the heart.
>
> At first, as young children we simply see a father as a familiar giant male, emitting his recognizable smells, reaching for us with the ease with which he might grasp his cup or his pipe. We hear his laughter and his sighs. We sense his appraising eye upon us and blush internally, suddenly inexplicably wanting to please. He fondles our mother, who caresses him back, actions that we find both shocking and reassuring.

Later we see a man, paradoxically frail and strong, foolish and wise, loving and mistrustful. Sometimes we hate him and fear him. We wish to like him and to be like him. Mostly we desire his approval and fear he will withhold it. It may be true that we *always* look to our mothers, and only sometimes to our fathers. Yet when we look to him, it is with a special regard.

This conundrum is even fiercer for a prince. After all, how many among us might expect to have a king for a father? I think Hamlet never knew quite what to make of his father, although I am surmising, for I saw them together only after I came to court, and then infrequently.

This advantage of coming to court deserves a brief explanation. For reasons that as a small boy I did not understand, my mother was invited to come to court to attend Queen Gertrude. My father was in the army and did not accompany us. Hamlet and I met, and we got on well together. I was lost in a sort of hero-worship—he was my prince, after all—and he seemed to trust me. He talked to me in a way he addressed no others around, as if I were his brother or a priest of the church. This trust was of enormous value to me, and I resolved at once never to let him down or disappoint him, if I could prevent it.

When Hamlet grew older he began vaguely to understand the impact of my family's separation, but I seldom missed my father. Hamlet arranged with his mother that at court, I would be his fellow student and sometime companion.

Until she died of a fever in my thirteenth year, my mother remained as a senior maid within the queen's retinue of attendants. Gertrude then arranged, with Hamlet's connivance, that I be given rooms not far from the royal apartments. I live there still. At first, coping on my own was something of an adjustment, but my life was filled with tutors and with Hamlet, and for several years servants of the royal household handled my needs for food and clothing.

I am relieved that my own father still lives here in Elsinore where I can see him from time to time, although we are not particularly close. I think when I first came to the palace I began to drift away from him emotionally (although every so often I would miss him fiercely), and for his part, he preferred to remain with his military companions and preoccupations.

As for the royal family, even at court I rarely saw Hamlet with his father. King Hamlet was far too busy with affairs of state to spend much time with his son, although on odd occasions we sensed his attention: when weather was clement a servant would sometimes inform us that we would be riding to the hunt that day in the king's party; on more than one occasion the king's supervisor of the household took us with him out buying in the town, showing us how to choose the freshest fish or the finest cuts of beef and venison.

Once I was privileged to play a card game with Hamlet and his royal father! I was terrified that I would play out of turn or that I might make some offensive gesture or remark (even though I can't imagine what either might have been). I watched the play carefully, and I think the king allowed Hamlet to win, but not without some careful and thoughtful decisions.

Hamlet appeared to love his father unreservedly. Hamlet always carried himself as a prince and was rarely, if ever vulgar. He did not show himself as needy or weak in seeking his father's attention. Yet despite this apparent attitude, somehow it was clear that he craved his father's approval, signs of which were evident to me but which one more anxious to please might miss—the odd smile which might be taken for an ironic criticism, or a gesture that might equally mean celebration or impatience. But beneath every gesture, every comment, every facial expression of both of them lurked love. Ah, yes, I know that "lurked" is an odd word. But what other best fits the presence of something hidden by design, part of the ongoing action yet somehow unacknowledged, or present but unperceived due to the ignorance of those present? It is this love that made it imperative that Hamlet be informed of the ghost.

I knew where most likely to find him that particular day. Hamlet made a habit of walking in the morning. He seemed to be made for movement—energetic gestures that expressed his feelings, as well as necessary exercise for his athletic body.

Sometimes he would walk in the royal park, but since his father's untimely death young Hamlet had avoided it. (He later told me that on his return to Elsinore he had briefly visited the site of his father's death. Here he had experienced a marked depression and horror as if the reaper himself were waiting there for him, too.)

Occasionally he would quit the royal enclosure altogether and walk down through the town, refusing the offer of company from any of the palace guards. "If I am not to be safe in my own country, wherever in the world might I be?" he had asked the guard captain impatiently. I suspect that Polonius had arranged for one or two ununiformed soldiers to follow unobtrusively at a distance, and Hamlet probably knew who they were. He became resigned to such a guard provided he remained unhindered. Now, instead of such excursions he had developed the custom of pacing the long lobby near the royal chapel, up and down, again and again, often seemingly lost in thought.

Marcellus, Bernardo and I hoped to find him there, and we accepted our good fortune of seeing him just a few dozen paces away when we entered at the west end.

"Hail to your lordship!" I called, and he stopped his pacing and looked up.

"Horatio!" he replied, and smiled, an expression I had longed to see. "What make you at Elsinore?"

I had no ready answer, but suspected he already understood that I was simply there for him, for duty and for friendship, and for whatever he might need.

He approached, and gripped and shook my hand. "Let me think," he said in the tone I had long become used to hearing when he was about to say something sarcastic. "My father's funeral. No, that can't be it...hmm...ah, my mother's wedding!"

I colored momentarily and replied, "It did follow rather soon, my lord."

"Thrift, thrift, Horatio. The funeral's baked meats were probably still warm when the servants forked them onto the platters for the wedding feast. No?"

I might have laughed were it not so depressingly true (although the wedding was long past).

"My lord," I said to him, and he appraised me with a friendly but cool eye. "This brave soldier, Marcellus, and I have important news for you." I took a deep breath. "My lord, last night I think we saw your father."

"My father?" He stared at me incredulously and perhaps bitterly bemused. "My father is dead."

"I beg you, Hamlet, listen to Marcellus. He will explain."

Turning to Marcellus, Hamlet said, "Well, then, sir, explain."

Marcellus bowed low, as Hamlet was nearly scowling at this stage. But with courage and with clear language (I wish our Wittenberg tutors had been as plain-spoken) he told our prince the story of our encounter with the ghost.

Hamlet became increasingly agitated as Marcellus recounted our experience. He turned to me and asked, "Is this true? You saw him? Just as he says?"

"Yes, my lord," I replied.

"Was he bearded?"

"A salt-and-pepper beard, as it was the last time I saw him."

"Did he appear angry?"

"More sorrowful than angry, yet there may have been some anger in his aspect."

"How long did he stay?"

"The time it might take to count a hundred—perhaps a hundred and fifty."

"Longer!" Bernardo interjected.

"Not when I saw it," I corrected him.

Hamlet looked from one of us to the other, and back again.

"I will watch with you tonight. Perhaps he will come again."

"I warrant it will," Marcellus said.

I nodded agreement. *It*? I thought to myself.

But oblivious to this slight, Hamlet turned and gazed out one of the windows along the lobby toward where one could see a ship under construction in the distant harbor. The laborers were pounding and sawing, although no sound reached us. They appeared as if they were some kind of absurd pantomime. Sunlight glittered on the water beyond.

"I will come to you between 11:00 and midnight," Hamlet said. "If, as you say, my father's ghost walks the earth, perchance he has some message, some message of import that we must heed. I must hear it. I must see *him!*"

"I will escort you to the guard's station myself," I offered. Hamlet nodded again. He stood, arms akimbo, tapping his foot distractedly. Marcellus bowed low, as did Bernardo, once more like a pair of mimes in tandem.

"We will take our leave, my lord," he said softly, and Hamlet waved them away politely. They paused briefly and looked at me, once more at Hamlet, and then turned and walked quietly down the corridor, Bernardo whispering urgently in Marcellus' ear.

"My quarters at half-past ten," Hamlet said gently, looking me in the eye.

"I will be there, my lord."

Hamlet gripped my hand briefly, hard, then released it and turned to go. Turning back, he said, "One more thing. No one else knows of this?"

"Only these two men from the watch."

"See that no one speaks of this," Hamlet said softly. "It would not do to unnerve the palace, after all." He gazed at me earnestly. "It is important that no one else know."

"I will follow them immediately and stress unto both of them your will in this matter," I replied.

Upon hearing this agreeable reply, Hamlet turned and walked away down the lobby. I turned the other way to catch up to the two soldiers, who had just exited at the far end.

Horatio lifted the sheet and blew lightly on the ink. Cleopatra blinked at him. Horatio began to reread the entry from the first sheet, but almost immediately he picked up his pen again and wrote at the end of the last sheet.

Why might a father, a kingly father, appear at such a time? I have never imagined the return or appearance of my mother, ghost or in the flesh. My prince, however, was faced with not merely its imagined presence, but with the apparition I had already once seen. I knew even then that something critical was at hand. For all our sakes, and especially for that of Hamlet, I felt I must gather my courage and my strength, for who knew at the time where this might lead?

Horatio stared for a few moments at the last bit he had written. Then he gathered the pages into a small sheaf and placed them carefully beneath his small stack of previous writings. I have only begun, he thought to himself mournfully. Fortinbras, the king, will be impatient...yet I must get it right. He must know how these things came about. I cannot deceive a king, and there is so much more to tell.

He then reached for the smaller, leather-bound notebook that contained Ophelia's diary. He remembered cautiously removing it from her quarters the night after her death. He turned to a page whose corner had been turned down and began to read.

I have dismissed my maid for the night, and now I am alone. I know not how to understand my state, although my lord Hamlet is at the center of its provenance.

I cannot fathom his behavior to me, at one moment solicitous and admiring, and the next once again distant and, dare I say, unkind. He graciously allowed my immediate company at tonight's banquet, a charming permission that caused my heart to race. Yet I had not been seated at Hamlet's hand for more than a few minutes when his conversation took on the most puzzling tone, that of a man condescending and petulant.

He was dressed all in black, as if his father's funeral had been that afternoon rather than over seven weeks ago. (Of course, he was unable to attend the funeral, or his mother's wedding, for that matter.) I made an effort to express my condolences on his loss, but he spurned my sympathy, as if I were some stupid child that might need instruction.

His majesty the king spoke to Hamlet of the recent accession to the crown and of the marriage to Hamlet's mother, in general terms, of course. For his part Hamlet seemed to mock the king and queen—not in so many words, but certainly in tone. I felt both frightened and personally insulted. I couldn't understand him! I feel both hurt and angry, although I can never express these responses to him. And I know that underneath these obscurities and irritations there still exists the man I love, the man who I hope still loves me.

I left the banquet in tears, although I did my best to hide them from the assembled diners.

I don't know what to do.

I am further troubled that my brother is to return to school in Paris soon. He and my father must see the king, who will almost certainly grant permission for Laertes' departure. I felt Laertes' previous absence deeply, for he is my only truly sympathetic confidant. I know that he's a bit of a rake, for the gossip of the palace girls often reaches my ears, but he understands the world from a perspective I am denied, and I have no doubt but that he is devoted to me as his sister and friend. I must speak to him at least once more before he leaves, for my troubles concerning Hamlet remain unresolved, and I cannot speak of this to my father.

Horatio lifted his eyes from the page and stared at the candle, now guttering near its base. He felt a gnawing sympathy in his chest. He turned the page and continued to read. The next page seemed to be a future entry.

Laertes has given me his best advice on Hamlet. How did he put it? He abjured me to think of Hamlet's 'affections' as merely a 'trifle,' the interest of a man desiring little more than carnal satisfaction. I was offended by Laertes' judgment of this matter, and I told him so, at which point he mellowed his characterization this way, as best I can remember.

"Perhaps he truly loves you even now," he finally said. "But consider. Hamlet is a prince, and his marriage will be made for dynastic reasons, not for those of personal preference. A future queen of Denmark will be selected from royalty, probably some foreign power. Then consider how your heart will ache should you accede to his protestations of 'affection' as you call it. Suppose you allow him now fully to express his 'love,' providing him full access to your chaste self. Then, when he must marry another, it will crush your heart, and your fitness for other marriage will be besmirched in ways no nobleman could forgive. I say this so bluntly only because you are my only sister, conjoined to my heart through sibling obligation and natural care."

Well, those words pierced right through me. Father had already warned me to be careful of Hamlet, to be polite but distant, as it were.

> *Of course, fathers are notoriously distrustful of daughters at the best of times, but I have been wary despite my powerful attraction to Hamlet, whose very presence makes my heart race and my spirits lift...at least until now.*

Horatio looked up again, as if considering some puzzle. He finally closed the small volume and set it aside. Gently, he lowered his head to the cushion of his arms on the tabletop. *Just a moment of rest,* he thought to himself. *I need to find something here,* he thought. But his thinking led merely to dreaming, and he slept the sleep of the just.

Chapter 13

On the Guard Platform

The following day, Horatio approached his writing room feeling all the gloom of the day's weather. For two days a gusty rain had tormented the skies over Elsinore, threatening to turn to snow. He guarded his candle with his free hand, uncovering it only to allow himself to open the door. The candle guttered wildly, then steadied.

"Like my thoughts," Horatio imagined, "flickering hither and yon like ghosts in a graveyard."

He shoved the door shut behind him and moved to the table, where he lit two more candles that were standing fresh beside his writing materials. "Bless Brother Henrik," he thought to himself. For some reason the cat was missing. He looked about for it briefly, then dismissed its absence.

He wished there were a fire, but that was, perhaps, too much to hope for. He blew on his hands as he seated himself. He left his cloak partly wrapped about himself. Taking a quill from a clay jar, he checked its point visually. Then he drew a fresh sheet of paper from the now generous supply that for some reason Henrik had left for him, pulled the stopper from his ink well, dipped the pen, and began to write.

One might have thought our second meeting with the ghost could be anti-climactic, but the presence of Hamlet made events even more dramatic. His presence created even more mystery than the ghost had alone. True to my word the previous day, I escorted Hamlet up the circuitous route to the guard platform.

For his part Hamlet was strangely silent. He followed oddly like some faithful dog, even though I should have been the hound to his commands. He would look at me every so often as if about to speak, perhaps some youthful confidence or comment, but then would turn again to our path—the corridor, the stairs, the passageways, and finally the parapet walkway.

Marcellus was waiting, polite and watchful as always.

"Well?" Hamlet asked him.

It's instructive how a simple interrogative expression can convey so much concern and power. Marcellus himself knelt when he heard it, only to be pulled gently to his feet by his prince. "Now, now," Hamlet said. "We shall be friends, shall we not?"

"I have seen only darkness, and felt only cold, my lord," Marcellus said, eyes cast toward his feet, but finally looking at his prince with more confidence. "But I am sure it will appear." He led us around a corner of the parapet where Barnardo was warming his hands before a small brazier that flared up intermittently.

"Yes," Hamlet said gently, again only a single word, potent, filled with unexpressed presentiment.

Marcellus produced a flask of brandy, and although he appeared embarrassed to offer it to a prince without a silver cup, he lifted it toward Hamlet, who smiled finally, took it and drank.

"Ah, drink," Hamlet said reflectively. "We should not be so eager to embrace its benefices."

Still, after having paused, he sipped again, and then handed the flask on to me. "You know," he said to us both, "other Europeans think predominantly of us as drunkards. Our reputation for 'quaffing' leads them to a rather low opinion of the Danish."

He turned to warm his hands at the fire. "I heard such comments on more than one occasion in Wittenberg."

I sipped, allowing the warmth of the brandy to spread into my gut.

"It's odd," Hamlet added. "Despite all the accomplishments of our countrymen, our explorations, our fulsome trade, our artistic achievements—these are ignored, and we are known instead only for our love of drink."

"It's sometimes so with individual people, as well," he went on, turning to share his thoughts with us. "A man might be pure as grace, a loving husband, a loyal subject, and yet, having some single fault, such as a stammer or a tendency to be quick to anger, for example, be condemned for this one minor flaw, whatever his virtues. We seem to look always for the evil, never the good, to expect the worst, even to demand it, and to forget that man is at least partly angel."

Hamlet was rarely more impressive than when grappling with some philosophical problem, some dilemma or moral issue. It was as if we were momentarily in the pub in Wittenberg. He smiled at me over the brazier's low flame, a weary smile that held both amusement and sadness intermingled. I bravely smiled back.

It was cold, as Marcellus had commented, and I clutched my cloak more closely about me. A dog barked somewhere in the darkness below the wall, then howled plaintively. Another closely answered him and there was momentary snarling from below. Then it was silent again.

I was about to ask Marcellus for more brandy when I felt a familiar prickle, the sensation of being watched. I turned to where moments before a sea of starlight had hung in the western darkness. Now all was mist and swirling movement. I heard Marcellus' swift intake of breath.

"My lords!" he whispered hoarsely. A faint light strengthened within the fog, a light that coalesced into a human form as it moved, slowly and steadily, toward us. It was old Hamlet, the king!

I looked to Hamlet where I had always found the reassurance of power. But Hamlet's power seemed to have melted away. For my part, I felt even more terrified than during my first experience. Aside from seeing the apparition materialize from the mist, we could actually hear the rattle of his armor. My very blood ran cold!

When the royal apparition approached he seemed to see Hamlet, and emitted a groan that sounded like the terror and despair of a whole nation. Hamlet was shaking and quivering, and sweat silvered his forehead, even though we felt the iciness of the night gnawing at our entrails.

The ghost waved to Hamlet to come to him, but from his knees where he had fallen, Hamlet called out.

"Oh, Father! Royal Dane! I am here." The ghost simply stared at him, then beckoned once more. Hamlet paused and looked up at me where I had drawn back against the stony wall of the parapet. "What should we do?" he said.

The ghost waved at him again, more impatiently this time, it seemed to me. I shuddered at its imperious gesture. What could be more unnerving than the combination of a ghost *and* a king?

"My father needs me," Hamlet said, and he got unsteadily to his feet. The ghost beckoned again.

"Do not accompany it, my lord!" said Marcellus.

"By no means!" I added, grasping him by the arm. Hamlet shook his arm free. He took a deep breath, as if to steady himself.

"What is to fear?" he asked rhetorically, standing more firmly. "He is my father. He beckons. That is all I need to know."

But I could tell at least part of him was convincing himself and not speaking to me.

In a stronger voice he said, "My life isn't worth a pin to me, so what of any value might he take? I have already been squeezed like a grape in the press by my uncle and spat like its seeds by my mother. How can my father hurt me further?"

It was only with this brief comment that I understood clearly how deeply he had already suffered, and his grief shook me.

"What if it is *not* your father?" I asked wildly, grasping at his arm again. "Think of it! Suppose this apparition is some messenger of Satan, sent to draw aside your reason and shift you into madness! Think of it!"

Hamlet turned and looked me in the eye, an expression on his face that melted my resolve even as he hardened his own.

"I will go with him!" he said.

He pushed me aside. The ghost turned and strode into the mist, disappearing almost immediately. Hamlet followed.

Marcellus turned to me. I have never seen a seasoned soldier seem so beaten, yet still he said to me, "We must pursue the prince. Surely we must protect him!" He exhaled and breathed deeply once more.

I recall looking at his wild-eyed terror. He almost bleated anxiously, "Something is rotten in the state of Denmark." I shuddered, then plunged into the mist with Marcellus right behind.

Horatio paused to think for a few moments. He scanned the last page briefly, and wished he had a tankard of ale.

He was somewhat unhappy with his style—too wordy, he thought. He would have to write more carefully, and yet he knew, once he was in the grip of his memory, the words simply came—he didn't think much about them. It was as if the story had a spirit of its own and was writing itself, through him. He sighed.

Chapter 14

A Filial Promise

Hamlet was flooded with terror, spiked by a contrary determination. He felt cold tendrils of fog wetly caress his exposed face and neck as he struggled to follow the apparition of his father. It seemed to glide as much as to walk, its glow nearly disappearing into the fog like moonlight behind thickening cloud.

Hamlet called to him.

"Oh Father, do not torture me with doubt and fear. Speak to me."

But though it hesitated briefly, the ghost merely swung a heavy arm to indicate that Hamlet must continue to follow.

Hamlet found himself climbing yet another stone staircase, panting in the wet air, nearly slipping on the damp surface. Finally he found himself within a curved turret surrounded by a crenellated wall. Somewhere an owl shrieked. At the far wall of the turret the ghost turned and stared piteously at Hamlet.

"Mark me," he said, and raised his hand to indicate that Hamlet should not approach too near. Hamlet backed against the cold stone of the wall and felt with his left hand for its rough support. Then he sank to his knees.

"Father?"

The ghost gave him a long, appraising look.

"I find thee apt," he finally said. "Yes. I am your father's spirit, doomed for a time to fast in purgatorial fires by day, and to walk the cold night, while my earthly sin is purged away, for you must know, I died unshriven."

Hamlet sobbed softly.

"My torment is a living portrait of all horrors. With all faith in one true God, and with the prayers of my family and people, I may yet be saved. But earthly justice, kingly justice must yet be served. To that end you must mark me."

"I will," Hamlet replied.

"You must avenge my foul murder."

"Murder!"

"Murder most foul and unnatural. The rumor of my death given out by Polonius and others was that during my habitual afternoon sleep in the garden a serpent stung me. But know thou noble youth, the serpent that did steal thy father's life now wears his crown."

Hamlet gasped. "Oh, my prophetic soul—my uncle!"

"Aye. That deceitful, treasonous beast! In my secure hour he stole upon me, and while I slept poured cursed hebona from a vial into my ear. Its effects coursed all through the natural gates and alleys of the body, compressing my organs and thrusting the cold finger of death into the chambers of my heart. My outer body became crusted over with scars and scabs, toad-like and ugly."

"Oh, horrible, most horrible," Hamlet muttered.

"Then, using the witchcraft of his wits, this adulterate satyr seduced the will of my once faithful queen." He grimaced. "If you have honor, courage and pride, let not the royal bed of Denmark become a nest of luxury and incest. Avenge my murder. You must kill Claudius."

Hamlet continued to sob softly. Then he straightened his shoulders.

"I am your royal son. I will do as you command," he said. He felt a kind of unnatural rage course through him, and he placed his hand on the hilts of his sword, as if in his imagination Claudius were even now before him, cowering in guilty fear.

"But Hamlet," the ghost said.

Hamlet gazed at him with longing and anxiety.

"Do not hurt your mother, the queen. Leave her to God and to her conscience. Allow the thorns of guilt that nudge her heart to prick and sting her. Her sins will find her out."

Hamlet frowned in concentration. In his mind's eye he saw two alternating images: the mother he had loved so long with his now deceased father, smiling and laughing, only to be replaced by her and Claudius touching and conversing at dinner only nights ago. A huge wave of hatred and disgust for her washed through him.

He looked up. It seemed as if his father were fading before his eyes. The fading image spoke even as it was disappearing. "Remember me, Hamlet. Remember me."

Hamlet's eyes blurred with tears. He reached up with a free hand to wipe them away, and even as he did so his father was gone.

Remember thee, he thought. *Remember thee? Aye, poor ghost. In the compendium of all human knowledge, what is more worthy of memory?*

Then he thought, *As to my uncle, it's only fitting that I write it down, in bold, black ink the stark truth: a man may smile, and smile, and be a villain! At least I'm sure it may be so in Denmark. Aye, remember thee…*

At that moment, he heard the loud calls from below the parapet, the voices of Horatio and Marcellus. "Hamlet! Lord Hamlet! Illo-ho-ho my lord! Hamlet!"

As if responding to a favorite piece of music, he took a deep breath and nearly smiled a little. He slowly got to his feet and carefully descended the stairs through the fog. And though he was still shaken by the encounter with his father, by the time he was half way down the staircase he had begun to laugh lightly, a snicker as if at some private joke

Then, in response to Horatio's calls, he raised his own voice in reply.

Chapter 15

"Swear!"

Horatio shook his head as if to clear his memory. Then once again he began to write.

I know not how Hamlet escaped our search for so long. As a famous playwright once noted to describe the disappearance of some demonic witches, "The air has bubbles, and this is one." It was as if Hamlet and the ghost had disappeared into nothingness.

Marcellus and I searched the length of the parapet twice. At one point Marcellus held me by his belt wrapped around my waist so that I could hang out over the wall in the event Hamlet had somehow fallen. Even if he had I could not have seen him in the darkness below. All I could hear was the heavy sighing of the wind through the wall's crenellations and the crashing of waves far below.

It was only on the third pass, calling out Hamlet's name, that I heard a shrill whistle and his laughing reply, "Ho ho ho, Horatio! Come, bird!" as if I were some lost falcon.

I rushed to his side and forgetting myself, clasped his arm. "My lord Hamlet!" I said in relief, looking him up and down as if to reassure myself as to his reality. He only laughed, a strange, giddy laugh that made me examine his face once more for some clue as to his state. I let go his arm, and murmured once more, "Oh, my lord. Tell us what has occurred."

Hamlet abruptly ceased laughing.

"No. You'll reveal it."

He turned and gazed out over the parapet once more into a darkness no longer clotted with fog, although swirls of it remained, shifting past in the irregular breeze off the harbor. Stars seemed to wheel overhead as if spun with a great wind. An owl hooted somewhere.

"Faith, no, my lord! You have my word, in faith."

I glanced at Marcellus, who as if on cue, agreed. "My lord Hamlet, by my faith, I will be secret."

Hamlet looked us both up and down as if assessing some casual yet costly purchase in the local market.

"The ghost is real, that I can tell you, but life is but a thread and death but a shears, and to link the two what better than trust in God's will and hope for a tomorrow that stretches toward our common eternity?"

He paused, then asked in a serious voice, "Have you no business?" He looked from me to Marcellus and then back. "Surely you have. Every man has business. I believe that my best business just now is to go pray. Yes, pray."

"These are wild, whirling words, my lord," I stammered.

"Do I offend you?" he asked, and snorted another laugh and then glared at me. I drew back.

"There's no offence, my lord. Surely you know that you cannot offend me."

"Ah, but you are mistaken," he stated flatly. He stared out over the parapet. Marcellus and I exchanged bewildered glances. "There is *much* offence," Hamlet finally stated. Then, gripping us each with one hand he drew us near. "You must do me one significant service."

"We will, my lord," Marcellus immediately replied, and I nodded.

"Swear that you will not reveal to anyone what you have seen and heard tonight."

"We will not, my lord," I said softly.

"In faith, I will reveal nothing," said Marcellus.

Hamlet backed away from us and looked away again. Then he drew his sword. The harsh whisper of blade against scabbard startled me. He clasped the sword blade in his gloved hand and raised it before him like a cross in the hand of some mad priest.

"Swear on my sword," he commanded.

Marcellus protested in bewilderment, "We have sworn, my lord, already."

Then came the strangest moment of all. From deep beneath the stone battlement at our feet sounded a low groan, and then a dark voice that I recognized at once as that of Hamlet the old king imperiously echoed, "Swear on his sword..."

His demand so reinforced, Hamlet advanced again toward us. "You hear this fellow from beneath the battlements...swear on my sword."

"Day and night but this is wondrous strange!" I involuntarily exclaimed.

"Then as you would a stranger, give it welcome," Hamlet replied matter-of-factly. As if reprimanding me over some failed argument at school he added, "There are more things in Heaven and Earth than are dreamed of in your philosophy, Horatio."

Once more the voice from below, a low, grating whisper, uttered, "Swear."

"Put your hands on my sword and swear," Hamlet ordered firmly again, "not to speak of anything you have seen or heard tonight."

"We will not, my lord," Marcellus replied. I, too, nodded. But Hamlet looked askance at us and led us further down the platform along the crenellated wall. The owl hooted once more from further off. Hamlet beckoned us close, still holding his sword by the blade, the cross of the handle swinging slightly, glinting silver and black in the moonlight.

"And even one more thing," Hamlet then said, as if in afterthought, choosing his words very carefully. He gazed at me, as if he would plumb the very depths of my honesty.

"I may not be the man you think you know in future. As we sometimes think it fit to dress in different ways to reflect different moods or to signify occasion, I may find it needful to present my soul in ways you have hitherto not seen. My dispositions and my moods may quiver and color in various ways."

He looked at us meaningfully, then chirped a giggle all out of character. He winked at me and grinned what one might have interpreted as a drunken grin, then appeared utterly sober again the next instant. I recoiled briefly from the incongruity.

"By your oath, swear to me before God you will never admit to anyone, no matter the charge, that anything you have experienced here with me might somehow be the root cause of my behavior."

Again, the voice below echoed, "Swear."

I placed my hand on the cold metal and felt the rough callouses of Marcellus' palm close over mine. "I swear," we said, nearly in unison.

Hamlet placed his own gloved palm over ours and closing his eyes, took a deep breath. When he opened his eyes, he released our hands. He turned his sword and returned it to its sheath. Then he said, "Well. Let us go in and take some wine. The day will break soon and we have yet to sleep, but as is true for friends *and* scholars, to drink together is to bind our souls in faith and friendship. Though daylight may kindle in the east, we may rest assured that darkness will return as well." Thoughtfully, he added, "What better way to prepare for darkness than with friendship?"

It was many days later that I remembered this rhetorical comment, and I considered it often as subsequent events unfolded. This became especially true when Hamlet later explained to me, privately and in more detail, why he had changed, and the nature of his father's command, "Remember me!"

But as usual, my ideas are racing ahead. There was much more to occur (and now to be told) before the implications of that command became clear. And it's odd how time and events repeat themselves. It's almost as though Hamlet is speaking to *me* from beyond his grave and saying, "Remember me." Remember. Ay, my poor prince, *my* poor ghost.

Horatio felt something rub his leg. Cleopatra had returned from wherever she had been sleeping. She emitted a soft purr as Horatio scratched her head.

Gathering his papers together carefully, Horatio placed the writings in a leather portfolio he had brought for the purpose of taking them back to his own quarters. He needed to review them, he felt.

A pale light could be seen through the window glass. "Daylight may kindle in the east," he quoted to himself, almost hearing Hamet's voice as he spoke the words in his imagination. He yawned. Standing, he threw his cloak over his shoulders, clasped the portfolio under his arm, and left the scriptorium once more for his own quarters.

Chapter 16

Hamlet and Ophelia

Hamlet was gazing into the fire from his favorite chair when Yedric informed him of Ophelia's arrival.

"The lady Ophelia," he stated carefully, as if reciting catechism.

Hamlet glanced up hurriedly, then rose to his feet. "Show her in," he instructed. The servant left the room.

Hamlet brushed his doublet of any crumbs that might remain from his evening meal, then stood beside his chair, hand on its back, as if nonchalant. Yedric and Ophelia entered, and she curtsied, lowering her eyes to the floor for a moment as she did so.

She wore a dark velvet cloak, which she unfastened and held out behind her to the servant, who took it and folded it over his arm. Her gown was a simple dark blue, and she stood on heeled shoes that made her appear slightly taller than he knew her to be, although her head was still lowered, and she did not look directly at him.

"Lady Ophelia," he finally said softly. "To what good fortune do I owe your visit here, in the heart of my…privacy?" He moved his hand abruptly as if brushing aside some unpleasant insect, and Yedric bowed and left the room.

"You are not happy to see me, my lord?" she inquired, looking up at him.

"On the contrary, my lady, my evening was dissolving into a fog of foolish speculation. Your presence makes the sun emerge once more." ("An idiotic metaphor!" he thought to himself.) Ophelia allowed herself a small smile.

"My lord, forgive my forward inquiry, but I must ask whether or not I might have offended your dignity in some manner. If I have, I feel compelled to offer my sincerest apology." She paused glancing down again with bated breath.

Hamlet looked at her. He could scarcely contain the thumping of his heart. She was exquisitely beautiful, an erotic saint.

"My lady," he finally offered lamely. "I presume you refer to our abrupt parting from the king's banquet." He frowned at the wall, not meeting her eye.

He turned to her once more, but paused before going on more slowly as she looked up at him.

"Please, Ophelia, my departure had nothing to do with our converse. Indeed, had not other, contrastingly unpleasant aspects to the evening intervened, I would have been contented to enjoy your company for much, much longer. It is for me to request your indulgence for my curt and no doubt unexpected behavior."

He reached out and took her by the hand, leading her to a leather sofa beneath a dark window. She allowed herself to be led. He felt the tension in her fingers through the leather of her kid glove. They sat side-by-side, a full moon floating in the darkness behind them. He let go of her hand.

Despite his smooth language, Hamlet felt somewhat ill at ease. He rubbed briefly at a tension in the back of his neck. He had long been aware of his status among the court's eligible women (and some of the ineligible ones). He knew that virtually any of them would come to his bed for the asking, indeed, from the summons of one of his servants.

He remembered only too well his initiation into the amatory arts, arranged by his mother and two of his servants. It had been an initiation he had enjoyed, once he had overcome his adolescent anxiety, followed by astonishment. The soft-breasted kitchen maid had allowed him to spill seed all over her belly long before any true congress had occurred. The young woman still smiled at him in a knowing way on the infrequent occasion he might see her. A few weeks later, a rather beautiful prostitute employed by the queen's brother had given him lessons in both enjoying and pleasing a woman.

But Ophelia was different. He considered her someone integral to him, somehow connected to him, not simply as some happy physical accident like finding a particularly pleasing beer.

She pursued her original line of thought, though. "Then I am forgiven?" she inquired softly, finally looking into his eyes.

"If you forgive *me*, then, yes," he said. "Ophelia, I have told you before how I care for you. I thought of you often in Wittenberg."

"Oh, yes, Rosencrantz has told me of your preoccupations there—your 'philosophical' inquiries and evening 'conversations.'"

"Ah, Rosencrantz! He too is returned?"

"He and Guildenstern are about the court, trying to appear useful and loyal. I believe my father refers to them as puppies, but if such they be they have their canine teeth." She looked about, then back at Hamlet, who stared unabashedly back at her, a small smile twitching at the corner of his mouth.

"My lady, do not torture me with indirection," he finally said. "This visit is not about Rosencrantz and Guildenstern *or* Wittenberg." He looked at her, as if in momentary pain. Then he took her arm and pulled her closer to him, her face only inches from his. She stiffened slightly and blushed, but when he kissed her she did not resist.

"My God, Ophelia," he said when their mouths parted, "after all that has been between us, do you doubt that I love you?"

She turned more directly to him and sought his mouth once more, pulling his face to hers with her gloved hand. "Oh, Hamlet," she murmured, and kissed his face again and again. Tears coursed down her cheeks. He tried clumsily to brush them away, but she simply kissed him more in response. Her heart hammered in her chest.

After a few moments she pulled back slightly and dabbed at her wet cheeks with the silk kerchief he hastily offered her. "What can we do?" she finally asked. She took his hand and held it to her mouth.

Hamlet finally pulled away himself and got to his feet.

"My lady," he finally said. "I must see you again, soon."

She nodded her agreement. "It can be...arranged." Her heart was beating very quickly, she thought.

"But," he went on, "Not all the world is as it seems. Perhaps it never has been. If at any time you imagine my love to be unreal and that imagining prove to be the case, may God strike me. But if you perceive unkindness in my demeanor, think it no more than cloudy weather or a winter's fever, an inopportune ague acting out his role and not the real me at all."

He looked at the alarm in her eyes. "Please, my lady, believe me. The times to come are as apt to test *you* as they are me. As our Savior instructed us to build our house upon a rock and not upon sand, think of me as your rock, no matter how the currents may wash us this way and that."

She lowered her eyes, then extended her hand, and he helped her to her feet.

"I must go," she said. "My father will return from his duties before the ninth hour."

Hamlet kissed her cheek and she flashed him a winning smile, then looked toward the entrance. He escorted her through the anteroom where Yedric was busying himself with papers of some kind at a side table. He did not watch them pass, but he scented the light fragrance of violet.

At the hallway entrance to his apartments Hamlet opened the door. One of Ophelia's maids waiting in the hallway curtsied carefully to them both. Hamlet kissed Ophelia's gloved hand and murmured, "God by you."

Ophelia, too, gave a slight curtsey, then turned, and with her maid, walked away. Hamlet watched them go.

"She seems truly to love you, my lord," Yedric said from his seat at the table without glancing up.

Hamlet looked at him. "Finish sorting my papers," he finally said, and returned through to the inner room where the very air still held her presence. Hamlet gazed at his reflection in the window over the sofa, beyond which there was now only blackness. The candle on its sill wavered slightly. His image from the window glass wrinkled in the heated air from the candle, insubstantial as a ghost.

Chapter 17

Queen Mates King

Polonius eyed the pieces on the board. Although he controlled a pawn fewer than Claudius did, he held a distinct positional advantage. Claudius had taken his bait, moved his queen to king's knight six to capture a bishop Polonius had been willing to sacrifice, and now Polonius' plan was nearly in place. Moving his castle aside two files to place Claudius in check would free a diagonal for his queen to sweep in and finalize the game. He examined the board again more closely. Had he missed something?

Claudius leaned back once more against his chair's arm, and placed his chin on his hand, eying his opponent rather than the board. He smiled at Polonius' indecision. He straightened up and reached for his wine cup.

"You have several moves available, I think," he said genially. He sipped some wine. "The castle move would be most effective, perhaps, although you might have something else in mind?"

Claudius enjoyed routinely defeating Polonius at chess, although sometimes he felt Polonius was throwing the match. He looked closely at his councilor for some clue.

Polonius glanced deferentially up at Claudius. "My liege," he said politely, "I am ever seeking a master's move but rarely finding one other than that of a simple servant." He smiled at the king. "I think it more astute of me to concede, as I fear your queen will compound her mischief in the next few moves, and my forces will be reduced to dust and ashes."

Before the king could reply, a servant entered and politely announced, "My lords, the queen."

Immediately upon his announcement, Gertrude entered. She wore a simple yet elegant gown of soft brown wool, but the dull gleam of the gold band around her forehead would have left no doubt to any casual observer that this was the queen.

Polonius hastily got to his feet and bowed deeply. "Your majesty," he said deferentially. He turned to Claudius and bowing once more said, "I will take my leave of you, my liege. Should you require anything from me, Alexis here will know my whereabouts. I have remaining matters to complete to do with the Norwegian business that I should be about."

Claudius nodded. As Polonius and the servant left the room, Claudius, too, rose and went to Gertrude.

"My love," he said to her gently, taking her hands and looking into her eyes. Raising herself on her toes, she kissed his cheek softly, then sought his mouth. He kissed her deeply, pulling her close, but she pulled back. He released her and stepped back slightly.

"My lord," she said to him, suddenly turning away. "I am worried. About Hamlet."

Claudius frowned. *"Hamlet, Hamlet, Hamlet,"* he thought. "What is it now?" he asked.

"I may have some wine?" she asked.

Claudius moved to the tray on a side table, hefted the clay flagon decorated with the Danish coat of arms, and poured a healthy measure of the brilliant red liquid into a silver cup. He placed the stopper back in the flagon and brought her the cup. Gertrude lifted it and drank daintily a sip or two.

"Thank you, my lord," she said. Then, looking directly into Claudius' face she said, "I fear my son—our son—may be going mad." Claudius raised his eyes, an expression of mingled curiosity, concern and alarm.

"'Mad' is a strong term," he finally replied.

"You know how oddly he has been behaving." She put down her cup and rubbed her hands together. "Remember when he insisted that the fowl for Tuesday's dinner be killed, cleaned and plucked at table, all in the name of some incomprehensible concept of justice? And the day before that when he had the screaming tantrum at Father Mark after mass—all that nonsense about purgatory and prayer. He still wears black everywhere, every day. And today he's done something even more bizarre." She lifted her cup and drank again, more deeply this time.

The king sighed. "What now?"

"He's been singing dirges in the main lobby of the castle. He strides up and down, occasionally shouting strange oaths. Then suddenly he'll approach one of the guards and strike up a conversation about fencing, often with some kind of perverse sexual humor to do with swords and scabbards. They hardly know how to behave around him, and their discomfort seems only to fuel his strange behavior."

Claudius raised his eyebrows. "Does Polonius know of this? You know how Ophelia dotes on the prince."

"How can he not know?" she answered. "The servants all report to him." In a quieter tone she added, "Ophelia has been foolish enough to encourage Hamlet on other occasions. Polonius has instructed her to refuse his attentions."

Claudius looked at Gertrude, a softness in his eyes, but also a cautionary shrewdness. In a low voice he said, "He is not the prince and student of Wittenberg we have known and loved, that is certain. Something is troubling him deeply."

"I don't understand it," she said. "We both knew there would be some kind of adjustment needed for him to adapt to your accession. It was to be expected. And I suppose our marriage came as something of a shock. But these reactions are more than we imagined or anticipated."

"We knew there could be *trouble*," Claudius said pointedly. It had to be said. It had to be out in the open. He knew it. He thought Gertrude should know it.

Gertrude looked up at him and her voice flared a little with anger, or perhaps merely frustration.

"Yes, yes, of course, we have spoken before of all of this. But Hamlet is of my flesh. It frightens and affronts me that he might suffer from some malady for which I might realistically be deemed the cause."

She sat on the stool recently vacated by Polonius and absently toyed with one of the chess pieces. "Or *any* malady, for that matter," she went on more quietly. She tapped the knight on the board, then let it fall over with a soft clunk and raised her eyes once more to Claudius.

"Gertrude, your son is a man. It is only fitting that he feel the depth of his father's loss, as do I, and that he suitably mourn it, but as the son of a king he must accept and understand that fate does not always work in one's favor, and that the hazards life throws on one's path are obstacles to be overcome, not enemies we allow to defeat us. Hamlet is a prince, and he must become, nay, live his role—that, or be tossed aside by history and chance."

Claudius' heart quickened as he watched Gertrude cringe at his words. He could hardly bear her pain and hated to see her suffer.

Is this love, he wondered to himself, *this ongoing psychic binding I feel, connecting my very being to her every mood?*

"Gertrude, you know I love him, as do you. We will find out the cause of his distemper, truly. Perhaps in our management of state we have been remiss and have not included him in our affairs in a manner sufficient unto his talents and ambition."

Gertrude regarded him, her expression softened by love and respect, by hope.

Claudius looked away from her for a moment. He gazed at the window, where sunlight spangled dust motes hung in the air. Then he turned back to her. He moved again to her side and taking her hand, raised her again to face him. He kissed her once more, deeply, and she responded by rounding his neck with her arm, pulling his mouth to hers.

There was no more need for words. Their mouths parted, and he stared into her eyes, speechless for a moment or two. Then he said, "Come," and led her through a side entrance toward the royal apartments. He had at least an hour before he had to address himself once more to the Fortinbras problem. Gertrude allowed herself to be led, through the sitting room where frequently they would break fast together, and into the bed chamber, where the huge bed had only hours before been made up. She quickened her pace to follow him.

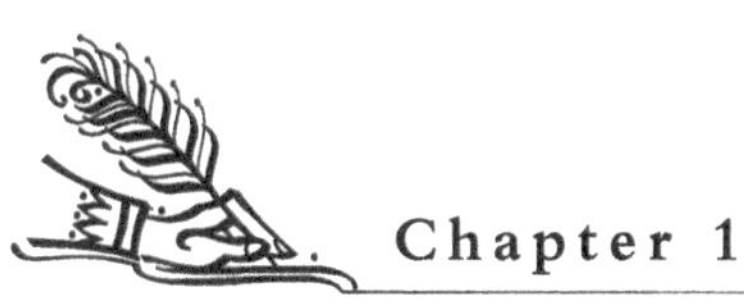

Chapter 18

Sin and Forgiveness

Horatio seemed oblivious to the hubbub of the castle—the incessant movement of servants (especially those speaking Norwegian!), the construction workers who had been recruited to redesign the royal quarters. Bricklayers and plasterers were as likely to be seen in the castle hallways as chamberlains and maidservants. He walked, head down, apparently lost in thought, toward the scriptorium.

It was late afternoon, and sun slanted through the narrow windows in the upper hall, illuminating the black and white tile on the corridor floor. Black—and white—as if the world could be divided—chop!—into two distinct sections. Black and white. Good and evil. The strange artificiality of this division distracted Horatio's attention.

Were it only so easy! he thought to himself as he turned a corner toward the rooms at the outer wall. It was still cold, though, and he tugged his cloak more closely about himself, hoping vainly that Brother Henrik had put some coal on the fire, or at least some aromatic apple wood.

He reached the scriptorium door and tugged it open impatiently. The cat was waiting on the table, as usual. It blinked at him. Two fresh candles stood in sticks beside a small pile of clean paper. Horatio smiled. *Henrik is learning*, he thought. He closed the door behind him and moved purposefully to the table. There was no fire in the grate, however, and he kept his cloak wrapped round his shoulders.

Cleopatra yawned, stood and stretched. Cats are imperious, Horatio thought. Furry little queens and kings. He smiled again.

He sat, selected a quill, and as Cleopatra returned to her cushion, he selected a new sheet, and dipping the quill in the inkwell, moved it to the page and began to write.

Much has been said about Hamlet's so-called "madness." I choose to say more.

True, Hamlet's behavior began to seem rather extraordinary in the days following our encounter with the ghost of his father. Yet in truth, did he not warn Marcellus, Bernardo, and me of this very possibility? How did he put it? 'I may find it needful to present my soul in ways you have hitherto not seen. My dispositions and my moods may quiver and color in various ways.' How apt that description was!

I had the opportunity to speak to Ophelia only days after the ghost's final appearance. Her eyes were dark, her expression morose, and she did not, at first, wish to speak to me. I have known her since we were children, however, and she knew, at least, that I was no threat to her.

(Truth be told, I always loved her a little, although I knew she was destined for Hamlet. And I loved him more.)

We met in the main chapel, found near the royal apartments in the castle precincts. True to her faith, she was kneeling at prayer as I entered. I could hear monks chanting in the nave. Candles guttered fitfully before her, as if her words or thoughts might be blowing the flames around.

"My lady," I whispered to her in order not to surprise her at prayer, but she reacted as if she had been expecting me. She crossed herself before the silver crucifix, muttering to herself (or to God), and only then, after a few seconds, rose to her feet and peered at me in the dim light.

I could hear the rising and falling of chanted syllables: 'In nomine patris, et filii, et spiritus sancti, amen.' Then we listened in silence as half a dozen monks who were responsible for observance of the hours filed past, bare feet pattering and shuffling on the stone flags. Finally she spoke.

"Horatio," she said simply. She looked at me expectantly, as though I might have some secret to impart or some gossip to share.

"My lady, I understand you have had an unpleasant encounter with the prince." Not 'my prince' or 'Hamlet.' It was as if I were seeking distance or perspective.

She brushed past me and indicated that I should follow. Once outside the chapel she led me to a bench beside the entrance. She seated herself gracefully. At her gesture I sat beside her.

"No encounter with the prince can be 'unpleasant,' Horatio, you know that equally well as I." Only then did I notice her lady-in-waiting standing silently beside a statue of St. Andrew, still as a stone.

"Lady Ophelia, please do not mistake my meaning. I am not here to mince words or quibble over definitions. I had enough of that in Wittenberg." I recall sighing rather deeply. "My lord Hamlet has been, well, unpredictable in many ways recently. Might you help *me* to understand why?"

I peered at her face closely. She did not look at me, but tugged impatiently at her sleeve and frowned. Her servant coughed softly. I did not look away. After a moment or two I discerned a tear slowly sliding down Ophelia's cheek.

"My lady," I said softly, and I extended to her my linen handkerchief, which she took and dabbed at her cheek.

"Why do we come to church, Horatio?" she asked me earnestly.

I backed away slightly and thought a moment.

"We come to share our faith," I said finally, rather weakly. "Here we feel safe, in God's hands, and we express, alone or together, our gratitude for God's bounty."

"And what of sin?" she asked guilelessly and clasped my arm momentarily. "Do we not come to church to seek forgiveness?"

"That, too," I agreed, but felt myself to be on less certain ground.

Ophelia stretched out her hand and placed my now damp linen into my palm. I felt a great desire to comfort her physically, to put my arm about her frail shoulders, but I refrained. She sniffed softly, then spoke again.

"Although it is not my place to say, I worry, nay, I fear that Prince Hamlet may have become inhabited by a curious, reckless madness. I wish not to compromise your confidences, Horatio, those with the prince or with anyone else. However, you have asked, and I shall answer. Our Hamlet's conversation and behavior seem ever more erratic and unusual. He frightens me, for he seems to suffer some kind of ugly misery. Whether or not I am at fault in bringing about this affliction I cannot say, although I would be most horrified if, in fact, I were. My father, too, is very concerned, and has warned me to keep the prince at a distance."

This last sentence was said as if her father's judgment was to be simply the last word on things. *Surely young women are not so foolish*, I thought to myself. Yet Hamlet's behavior of late—his odd singing, his peculiar demands at table, his improbable laughter at completely obscure events—was indeed unsettling.

"My lady, do not trouble yourself personally over these uncertainties." My voice sounded hollow and insincere, at least to myself. "Royalty commands itself to be unique, unusual, a state that reflects its extraordinary role in the world. For us to judge the prince with simple terms, terms freighted with dangerous meanings, would be foolish in the extreme."

I felt better at this last equivocation, and why not? Truth be told, I had enough personal experience with the prince to lend full credence to Polonius' judgment, but equally significant experience to suggest that Hamlet's behavior was (and was continuing to be) all an act for his own obscure purposes.

I looked at Ophelia again, and she looked up into my eyes. There was no evasion in her face, at least. I spoke again.

"Do you feel in need of forgiveness?" I finally asked, and I pressed her hand.

She looked down again and said nothing for a moment or two. Then, providing a simple paraphrase from scripture, said, "Have we not all sinned and fallen short of the glory of God?"

I knew then that she was not going to reveal herself further, yet that in a sense, she had revealed all. I let go her hand and drew back. She glanced away once more, as if to relieve me of any responsibility in the matter. I briefly gathered my thoughts.

Finally I said, "My lady, I am expected at court and need to attend. The king is to speak about the Norwegian threat. But do not mistake me. I am your friend, and lord Hamlet's loyal servant. If you are in need, particularly with respect to our prince, come to me. I will help, if I can."

She gave me another long glance of appraisal. Then she said, "I would have thought no less of you, Horatio. Go with God. We must all go with God."

"Amen," I said, and nodded, although my faith has always been far from finished.

Ophelia stood unsteadily. Her maidservant moved swiftly to her side. Ophelia took her arm, and the two turned to leave.

I sat for a moment, thinking about the many possible acts that can occur between a prince and a lady. I felt myself color.

When I looked up, the two women were gone. I too stood, and I followed them until they headed toward the entrance to the castle's many apartments. I watched them go, the afternoon sun casting their shadows beside them. Then I turned toward the main castle hall where I knew courtiers would be gathering in anticipation of the king's latest public plans. *The business of the kingdom must continue,* I thought lamely to myself, and I made my way toward the entrance.

Chapter 19

A Royal Audience

A gabble of increasingly loud conversation greeted me as I made my way down the busy hallway to the main castle hall. When I entered, nobles and servants were milling about, talking and listening to one another. Near the thrones, which occupied a dais in front of a scarlet velvet arras, Polonius was speaking softly to his son, Laertes, Ophelia's brother. Laertes was nodding in reply, a nervous expression twitching the muscles of his face. Hamlet too was there, dressed in his usual black, leaning back against a wall and eating an apple.

Just then a page dressed in white and blue silk entered the chamber from behind the thrones. In a strong voice, he called dramatically, "Ladies and gentlemen, the king and queen!"

The assembly hastened into a ragged order along the carpeted walkway leading from the hall entrance to the thrones. The king, with Gertrude on his arm, entered the chamber, smiling his greeting to us. We all bowed low (the women curtsied), and a hush came over the room. Even Hamlet bowed (after tossing his half-eaten apple toward a passing servant, who had to scramble to catch it). Hamlet wiped his lip with a soft kerchief that he then stuffed into his sleeve, and moved toward Polonius and the royal couple. The king frowned at him.

"My lord," Polonius began seriously. "I have the latest documents to do with the Norwegian challenge, as you instructed."

"Ah, yes," Claudius responded. "Are the ambassadors present?"

Two well-dressed gentlemen stepped forward and bowed once more.

"Voltemand! I might have known Polonius would entrust you with this task. You are a worthy choice, sir."

Voltemand nodded in acknowledgement at the compliment and smiled at his king.

"Cornelius, too, I see. Well."

Claudius turned to the assembly and, raising his voice, began to address the issue we had come to hear about: the Norwegian threat.

"As many of you are aware, and within whatever circle of gossip or rumor you may have traveled, a young prince of Norway, Fortinbras (as was named his father, slain by our noble brother many years ago) has threatened our kingdom with aggressive claims, intent upon reclaiming those lands lost by his royal progenitor. No doubt he has heard of our great loss, the death of our dear brother, and thinking our kingdom to be unprepared, is intent upon using his mercenary forces to enforce his will. However, it is equally apparent to us that Norway's legitimate king, his uncle Olav of the wealthy Oslo region, is unaware of his nephew's levies or his purposes. We have decided to send our two trusted ambassadors, Cornelius and Voltemand, to send our greetings, and also our warning, to Olav, that this young man's demands will not be tolerated, and that any issue of violence from him or his troops will evoke the strongest response from us in Denmark. Voltemand, you have the documents?"

"I do, my lord."

"Then haste you and Cornelius on this important journey. We are certain that Olav will rein in his hothead nephew and that all will be well. However, it is important that we be prepared in case events outrun speech; hence the military preparations you have nervously been observing. Let all in my kingdom know that we are ready to repel any threat from whatever quarter."

Relieved applause resounded throughout the hall, and Claudius smiled at this tribute. Voltemand and Cornelius bowed, turned, and exited the hall amid hushed exchanges in the audience.

Gertrude had seated herself on the queen's throne, and catching the king's eye, she smiled, obviously approving.

"Now," Claudius went on, turning back to the audience. "Laertes, I understand *you* have some suit."

Laertes stepped forward and bowed low, but did not speak.

"Understand, Laertes, your father is my good right hand, as statesman for Denmark and councilor to me, my other self, as it were. In recognition, know you can scarcely ask something that will not be my immediate offer, for my debt to your father knows few boundaries. How can I help?"

Laertes finally found his voice. "My lord, I came home to Denmark from France to fulfill my duty and respect in your coronation and marriage. That duty completed, I wish to return to university in Paris to complete my studies there, the better to contribute to your kingdom on my future return. I beg your approval and permission for this venture."

"Polonius? What say you? Do you approve this young man's imminent departure? Are his plans sound?"

Polonius bowed slightly and said, "My lord, Laertes is a student of the laws in Paris, and as such has learned much in the art of rhetoric and persuasion. I have agreed that, with your permission, he should return to Paris to complete his formal learning. As you might guess, we both hope he may one day serve his king as well or better than I have served mine."

"Well bethought!" Claudius replied.

He smiled broadly, for nothing feels better to a man than the opportunity and the means to appear generous at little cost to oneself.

"Laertes, return to Paris as you will. Expand your life there, comporting yourself that you may exemplify the better parts of Denmark to our European neighbor, and return to fulfill a life here of both benefit and enrichment. Spend your legacy of time with caution and industry, as you would any valued bequest, to credit both yourself and your country. But also live your life there with pleasure, ensuring that you place yourself to glean what riches of personal observation may serve us all in the future."

He smiled broadly at Laertes, almost as if he wished Laertes were his son rather than my less tractable friend, Hamlet.

"Go with my blessing."

Laertes bowed once more and took his leave.

"Thank you, my lord," said Polonius. The audience dutifully applauded the king's generosity and foresight, and he smiled again. Then he scanned the audience, looking for someone.

At this moment I felt a tug on my sleeve. It was Hamlet, who, during the proceedings, had made his way to my side, almost hidden behind me. I turned to whisper to him, but he raised his eyebrows, winked, and put his finger to his lips.

Finally spotting him, Claudius said more soberly, "Ah, Hamlet, our nephew, our kinsman, and our son. Come forward."

I felt Hamlet stiffen at my side. He whispered to me from the side of his mouth, "A little more than kin, and less than kind."

It was an acid comment, to be sure, and it shocked me a little, although I'm sure I was the only one to hear it. I sensed his tension, but he breathed deeply and pulled himself more erect, and the audience parted to allow him to move forward. Two paces from the king he bowed low, sweeping the floor in front of him with his black hat, and greeted the king ostentatiously. "Your royal, puissant majesty!" he said in a somewhat husky and breathless voice (although it sounded almost like piss-ant).

"Hamlet," Claudius continued, "We know the loss of our dear brother, your father, to have been a grief and shock beyond mere words. It does you credit to exhibit this loss with mourning attire. But as time progresses we the living must accommodate our loss, accept its verdict as God's and nature's will. This accommodation allows, nay, commands us to resume life's flow as worthy subjects both to God and crown." He thought a moment.

"You must recognize, your father too lost his father, and that father his own. It is the way of nature that each generation should succeed the next. And we who remain behind give recognition and heartfelt love to the departed through our mourning, and then proceed to live as God ordains, in loving pursuit of His will and of the good of our fellow man."

He softened his tone somewhat, but his message grew harder. "Your obstinate condolement begins to stale the message that mourning is meant to send. It is...it is unmanly."

Hamlet snorted at this, half sniff, half swallowed exclamation.

I couldn't fathom yet why the king would raise such issues in public, before the court. Lords and ladies exchanged puzzled and ominous glances, but remained attentive. My heart went out to the prince.

Gertrude finally interjected, "My son, why are you putting on this 'show,' this exhibition of a grief that long before should have mellowed to a dull and disappearing ache of recognized loss? Why do you continue to seem so unhappy?"

Hamlet suddenly seemed angry. "I know not 'seem' Mother! My suits of black, my dark expression, my gloominess of speech and aspect—these are things a man might simply *act*. We know that many people harbor pretense and exhibit selves quite other than their true souls. How many opportunities we have to dissemble, both to mock and to deceive." He glanced at Claudius, but spoke on. "*I* am not acting! Time is no balm to my unhappiness. Not this time."

As quickly as it had risen, his anger seemed to subside. He lowered his eyes and frowned at the floor, as if trying to discern some explanatory meaning there.

Claudius began again. "Hamlet, a deeper purpose for this gathering is to reinforce our royal decree that you shall be inheritor of this throne after me."

A flutter of hushed conversation flowed through the crowd, followed by generous and sustained applause. This was truly an assembly to remember, eventful, contradictory and strange. Hamlet's unusual behavior was well known about the court. Some said he was mad! Surely the king would not entrust the kingdom to a madman! Yet Hamlet's replies were cogent and reasonable. Most of the audience had cause to love him, as he had been very popular about the court ever since his year of confirmation had placed him in the forefront of all the youthful nobles.

Claudius raised his hands and the hush returned. I couldn't fathom what Hamlet might be thinking.

"To that end, Hamlet, the queen and I have determined that since your studies were so untimely interrupted, rather than go back to Wittenberg you should remain here with us, participate in greater measure in our deliberations, and learn the way of kings from a second source in the absence of your first father."

"Stay with us Hamlet," Gertrude pleaded. "We need your presence, and with God's will, your cheer about the court."

"I will in all my best obey *you*, Mother," Hamlet replied after a moment.

Although I knew what Hamlet meant, that he was not inclined to obey the king unless necessary, Claudius cheerfully exclaimed, "It is a loving and a fair reply! Be as ourself in Denmark." He winked. "Our court contains multitudes—tasks and distractions to suit the most eclectic taste—not to mention the most beauteous maids to be found the world round." He appeared pleased with himself, as if he had completed some great achievement or revealed some remarkable discovery. He looked at Polonius and nodded.

Polonius, stepped slightly forward and proclaimed, "Long live the king."

"Long live the king," responded the audience.

Hamlet merely stared about him, as if at some bedlam occasion that no sane man can fathom, but whose meaning and proceedings are evident and of comfort to all the *mad*men present.

Gertrude stood and took Claudius' hand. He raised her hand and kissed it, and smiling at one another, they exited the way they had come in. Hamlet rolled his shoulders as if to release intense stiffness and looked around him.

The audience began to intermingle once more, chatting much as they had earlier, exchanging opinions, no doubt, on the day's events. They drifted out of the hall in two's and three's until only Hamlet and I remained.

Hamlet watched them go, an inscrutable expression on his face. Then he turned to me. "Horatio, your loyal friendship is sometimes all I have," he said, and a shiver of pride and apprehension both ran through me. "I tell you," Hamlet said, "we'll remember these events in days to come with bitter amusement."

He moved forward and settled wearily onto the dais below the thrones and stroked the leg of the queen's chair.

"This foolish woman is wanton and weak. She has knit herself into a package of power and pre-eminence to suit her ongoing ambition, and I'm certain she cannot tolerate its unraveling. As for her reaction to the death of my father, a horse would have mourned longer. What *can* be the appeal of these incestuous sheets, I wonder?"

I was shocked at his angry candor. Yet I understood.

"It cannot, and it will not come to good," he said finally. He pushed himself up, then added, "But I must be more cautious. I am in the belly of the beast. Will events digest me, or vomit me up? Time will tell."

He clasped me by the hand and said, "Until later," and he turned and walked quickly out of the room, not looking back.

Horatio paused in his writing and laid down his quill. He had been writing for six hours. At some point the cat had gone, and the candles were burnt nearly to extinction. He stood and rubbed his lower back. Then he collected his papers, blew out the remaining candle, and left the chamber, into the waiting darkness.

Chapter 20

Fatherly Advice, Fatherly Care

Laertes' travel belongings were already aboard ship. In another half hour the tide would shift and she would weigh anchor. A stiff breeze snapped the rigging and whipped the Danish insignia at the stern.

Laertes looked respectfully across the table at his father Polonius. They were sharing a simple lunch of herring, bread and wine in a small inn near the harbor. It was a humble establishment, although Laertes had checked it out in person to see that the food was worthy of his father. Polonius had been positively cheered by the quality of the wine. Through the open window the shouts of dockworkers and the rattle of wheeled vehicles on cobbles could be heard above the sighing of the wind.

"Laertes, I wish you to know you have all of my support for your ventures in Paris. The opportunity to study is a great gift for a young man." Polonius paused and briefly eyed his oily fingers. He rubbed them clean with a grey napkin, then went on. "As I said, a great gift. I would not have you squander it."

Polonius looked meaningfully at Laertes, who blushed. Laertes knew that ever since he was a boy he had been a bit of a hothead, even though he had always exhibited a sly intelligence and true family loyalty. He nodded. Polonius' meaning was clear enough.

"To that end," Polonius continued, "I want you to remember a few principles. We may have spoken of some of them before, but they are worth repeating."

Here we go again, thought Laertes, but he looked his father in the eye to indicate his attention.

"It is easy as a young man to be too critical, and too loud in voicing one's criticisms. Therefore, think before you speak, and don't act until you have carefully considered the possible consequences of your actions." Polonius raised his finger as if to emphasize his point.

"Let others judge you, but reserve your own opinions. If you lessen your own obtrusiveness you remain a smaller target for the arrow of those companions who may be (or may become) your opponents, while they, revealing all, are outlined like great and simple targets." This was sound strategy. Laertes knew it.

Polonius raised another finger, as if he were counting off the points he was determined to make.

"Be selective in the company you keep. If you are lucky enough to make true friends, their friendship tested, clasp them to you with hoops of steel. Friendship is the gold of social intercourse, while indiscrete and indiscriminate socializing is the dross."

"I am at one with this advice, Father," Laertes replied, but Polonius was not finished.

"Don't allow yourself to be easily drawn into a quarrel. I know you fancy yourself Denmark's finest swordsman (and truth be told, you have a fine aptitude for swordplay), but however appealing your inner voice's crying for vengeance might be, violence should be the last resort for determining the resolution of disagreements." Polonius burped, wiped his lips, and then added, "That being said, if fighting should become unavoidable, make sure it is the other man who bleeds and not yourself."

Laertes straightened his shoulders and smiled. He had few doubts on this score, at least.

Polonius scratched his beard briefly and went on in a less strident tone. "Do not hesitate to spend your money on fashionable, high-quality clothes and boots. But the key here is quality more than vogue. As the French often argue, 'Clothes can make the man,' but they can as easily unmake him, if he is perceived as simply gaudy and showy, the sartorial habits of the simple-minded."

Laertes glanced down at the fabric of the royal blue cloak that hung from his left shoulder. It seemed fine to him. He looked at Polonius, who nodded at him as if in agreement, and then continued.

"Don't borrow or lend money! Friends may seem needy, but if you allow them to borrow you'll be more likely to lose both the money and the friend. And if *you* borrow the temptation to spend extravagantly may overcome your thrift. I haven't taught you to be careful with money for nothing. You can be sure that I'll send you adequate money for your station, no more, and I expect you to manage it."

Laertes nodded glumly. He was thinking of those fine French wines, among the other expensive pleasures that Paris had to offer.

Polonius softened his tone somewhat and smiled. "This above all," he said. "Be true to yourself, to your inner self, for it follows as the night the day, that such a habit of personal perspective will make you true to your friends, your family, and your nation."

Polonius clasped Laertes' hands between his own. "There," he said. "My blessing with thee."

Laertes bowed his head to his father. "Thank you, my Father," he said. "I will in all things struggle to live up to your trust."

"I doubt it not." Polonius released Laertes' hands and gestured toward the door. "Now go. Your servants are waiting aboard ship, even as we speak, and the tide is full." Even as he said this, a large gull squawked outside their window and winged up into the steady breeze where it seemed to sail suspended from some invisible heavenly string.

Laertes nodded and stood. He picked up a small bag from the floor beside his seat. Then he said, "Good-bye, Father." He walked to the door without looking back.

Polonius watched him go, then got to his feet himself. He dropped a few coins on the table, left the inn, and turned toward the palace grounds.

But on his return to the palace quarters his recent equanimity upon his son's parting was quickly dashed.

He was shocked, taken aback by Ophelia's report. "The prince was here?" he asked incredulously. "Half undressed?"

"My father, I did not encourage him." She peered apprehensively at Polonius as if unable to determine whether he would embrace her supportively or strike her in anger. Her eyes were red from crying, and she dabbed her cheeks once more with her silk handkerchief.

Polonius stared at her in amazement, eyes shifting from her pained expression to examine the room for evidence of improper dalliance, should there have been any. But the room was in order, aside from the faint scent of sweat, and the fragrance of lavender from the spray in a small vase on the mantle.

"Your brother was right," he finally said. He raised his voice. "Laertes was correct to warn you. He warned you, did he not?"

Sniffing, Ophelia nodded.

"And did I not forbid you to see the prince?"

Ophelia nodded miserably. "I did not invite him," she replied in her own defense, and turned her eyes aside.

"You're a young fool!" Polonius hissed. "Do you not realize the untenable position you have placed me—us—in? You have no business consorting with the prince! You'll make me seem ambitious, when all I wish is to serve my king and country. Don't look away!"

Ophelia turned back to him and looked up at him from under lowered brows. She cowered under the lash of his voice. She began to weep once more.

"Oh, stop it, stop it," Polonius finally murmured. He moved to Ophelia, took her by the shoulders and drew her to him. "What did he say that upset you so?"

Ophelia drew the handkerchief from her sleeve and dabbed her eyes once more.

"Oh, Father, he didn't *say* anything. He stared at me for several long moments. In my surprise, I stabbed my finger with my needle." She showed him the dark dot on her fingertip. "Then he approached me and grasped my arm, pulling me toward him. But he would not speak. I was terrified. He seemed to study my face, his eyes wild. Finally he let me go and backed out of my room, staring at me all the while." She sobbed softly again and gazed at her father uncertainly.

"He didn't speak?"

"No, my lord."

"Half undressed?!"

"His doublet was loose, my lord, and one of his stockings was twisted around his ankle! No hat on his head. I've never seen him in such a state. Truly, I fear he may be mad!"

"Mad!" Polonius thought a moment. "Mad for thy love, if anything."

Ophelia blushed.

"My lord, I repelled his letters, as you commanded more than a week ago. But something is terribly wrong. I fear not only for me, but for Hamlet as well." She blew her nose softly and wiped her upper lip, which quivered.

As if seeing something new and clear for the first time, Polonius drew himself up.

"I must tell the king! Hamlet is mad for thy love. *This* is the cause of his recent, unusual behavior."

He paused and then, grasping Ophelia lightly under her chin he looked her in the eye. "I'm sorry," he said to her more softly. "Truly, it is the way of us older folk to imagine we know everything, much as it is the characteristic vice of youth to suffer from their own naïve foolishness. I thought he might hurt us—you."

He turned away, thinking a moment. "Yes," he said, as if to reinforce his own decision. "I must tell the king."

Polonius released his daughter and turned to the door. Before going out, he added, "Lock the door. I have a key."

Ophelia nodded abjectly and watched him, her familiar but now somehow strange father, closing the door, leaving her alone.

Chapter 21

Loyalty Reordered

It had finally stopped raining. For four days and some hours the sky had been emitting water, as if some great angel were emptying his gigantic pitcher on Fortinbras' camp. The roofs had rattled (when they didn't leak), and the wooden troughs below the eaves had gurgled. Occasionally lightning had split the sky above the mountain to the east. Men observed these flashes nervously and some fingered amulets, for though Christian, they often thought back to Thor when the thunder rumbled. Now, though, the clouds were lifting, and patches of blue could be seen through rifts in the grey.

The men in tents had not grumbled, at least openly, but Fortinbras and Lars, his second-in-command, knew they were cold and wet. Already men could be seen emerging from the tents, wringing out wet things and checking out the western sky.

"We must do something to cheer them," Fortinbras said. "How is our supply of salt beef? And especially ale?"

"Better!" Lars said cheerfully. "Just before the rains came, two herdsmen brought thirty mixed cattle to exchange for silver. I knew they didn't want to take the cattle back again, not all the way across the pass to their high pastures in the next valley. We got them for a good price. I think we should slaughter two or three and feast the men—hot food and good drink go a long way to dispel cold and discomfort. The cattle are penned only a mile up the slope in the small meadow just off the trail, the one where the falls tumble down the canyon wall at the far end. It will take more than a week to butcher the remaining cows and salt and pack the meat."

"Order it done. And break open a cask or two. We're not yet ready to embark for Denmark, not for another week, at least. And let's have some competition—wrestling, perhaps, on the flat just above the beach. We need to keep the men active."

Fortinbras pulled a large golden ring sporting a blood-red stone from the index finger of his left hand. "This prize to the winner." He handed it to Lars, who cheerfully clasped it and held it up to the light.

"This will get their spirits up," he commented, and pocketed the ring. He looked from their viewpoint outside their headquarters down to the fjord.

Sunlight now spangled the water. The tide was coming in. "At least the ships are ready," Lars added. All along the gravel strand, for several hundred yards, long ships were pulled up with their dragon prows on shore. Then he straightened up and shielding his eyes from the sun, gazed further down the fjord. "My lord," he said, somewhat more urgently.

Fortinbras had been occupied mending the heel of one of his boots. He glanced up quickly, then stood and followed Lars' gaze.

Far off down the fjord were three long ships, powering toward the camp. Even at a distance Fortinbras could see the rhythmic sweep of the banks of oars. And each ship, under full sail bellied out by the western breeze, featured the royal coat of arms of Norway.

"King Olav!" Fortinbras said sharply. "How did he even know where we were?"

Lars did not reply. Now some of the men below in the camp were pointing down the fjord, as well.

Within fifteen minutes the three ships had swept into shore. Four burly warriors wearing heavy red cloaks trimmed with otter fur and carrying short battle axes leaped from the prow of the largest ship and planted themselves strategically, ready to fend off any unwelcome violence. Although Fortinbras' fleet numbered some thirty-odd ships, these royal emissaries seemed utterly calm.

"Go tell the ships' captains—no violence. Now." Lars nodded and trotted down the short trail among the tents.

Fortinbras returned inside the headquarters for a few moments. He washed his face and beard in a basin on a shelf by the wall. He opened a trunk beside his cot and removed his best cloak, which he swiftly donned. He considered wearing his sword, but then thought better of it. It was the king, after all.

When he came out again he noticed that his men were gathered in small groups of twenty or so around their captains, who could be seen gesturing as they spoke to the men. Lars had done as commanded.

Fortinbras straightened his shoulders, and looking as manly as he could, picked his way down the gravel path to where his uncle, the king Olav waited, seated on a leather three-legged stool. Around him were five or six gigantic men, all armed with axes. When he got to within ten paces of the king's party he knelt onto one knee and lowered his head.

"Lord king Olav," he said reverently.

No one spoke for a long ten or twelve seconds.

"I see at least *you* are dry," Olav finally said. "Your men seem to have seen better days."

Fortinbras raised his eyes and peered at his king, who was frowning at him.

Olav was a big man, with large arms and shoulders and long, grey hair that hung in two thick braids down onto his chest. Only the expensive fabric of his tunic and the wealth of gold chain around his neck betrayed his noble stature.

"They are good men, lord king," Fortinbras finally said.

"No doubt, no doubt," Olav remarked. "But they seem to have nothing to do." He pointed up the slope to where Fortinbras' men stood in groups, staring curiously at the new arrivals.

Olav suddenly stood up, and Fortinbras made to get up as well, but Olav said quickly, "Did you hear me say 'rise'?"

"No, lord king." Fortinbras colored. He did not like being made to look weak in front of his men.

"I have received a letter, brought by two ambassadors from Elsinore." Sarcastically now, he said, "No doubt you've heard of Elsinore."

"Yes, lord king."

Voice like flint, Olav went on. "Apparently some young puppy has been pestering the Danish court with threats of violence. A puppy named Fortinbras." He nearly hissed out this last line.

Fortinbras flushed even darker. "Lord king, I sought only to win your approval and blessing by achieving something great for Norway."

He paused a moment, weighing his thoughts. Then more softly he said, "I wish to regain the islands lost by my father many years ago." He looked up at Olav once more. "You know that it is customary, nay, it is necessary for a prince to prove himself. I sought to do so; I still seek to do so."

Olav thought for a few moments. Finally he said, "Rise."

Fortinbras got to his feet and looked directly at his king.

"Come aboard my ship," Olav commanded. He turned, and signaling to his guards, headed back to the largest of the three boats. Without assistance and despite his age, he clasped a rope loop hanging off the gunwale, and placing his boot on an external rib on a plank on the ship's side, swung himself aboard. Fortinbras followed uncertainly. By the time he reached the ship's deck, the king was already disappearing into a small cabin just aft of the mast. Two more husky guards armed with axes stood alertly at the entry. Fortinbras approached them gingerly, nodded, and passed the two men, who simply looked at him expressionlessly. He stooped and entered the cabin.

Olav had already seated himself alongside a small writing table where a scribe, a young man wearing monk's robes, was waiting. The scribe's fingers were ink-stained, but he held a long quill poised just above a brass inkpot. Outside a gull squawked, and a rope slapped irregularly against the mast. Fortinbras peered toward his king, adjusting to the relative gloom. Olav gestured to a bench against the wall, and Fortinbras stepped over and sat as directed.

"How many men have you recruited to your cause?" Olav asked.

"Four hundred and twelve," Fortinbras replied.

Olav raised his eyes appraisingly. Fortinbras glanced at the table where the scribe began laboriously to write. "You're very precise, aren't you? Four hundred and twelve …" His voice died off thoughtfully. "And just when did you imagine you would inform me of your plans?"

Fortinbras inhaled deeply, then answered. "I wanted to surprise you, to gift the islands to you and to the honor of the family. If all had gone to plan, we would have been finished before any leaves had fallen."

Olav crashed his fist down onto the tabletop with a great thump. Fortinbras's heart raced momentarily, but he remained still. The scribe glanced up in surprise at his king and at Fortenbras, then turned back to his writing. "A king does not like surprises!" Olav shouted. "I do not like surprises."

Fortinbras winced and hung his head. After a long moment he looked up again at Olav, who continued, more moderately.

"Your father, too, was a fool. Oh, yes, I can see by the flash in your eyes that you resent my comment and doubt my judgment. But I knew him. You were still tugging at your nurse's dug when my brother so foolishly pulled the Danish king's beard by trying to claim those islands. He threw away his life in a contemptible exhibition of pride and ambition. I saw it happen. The priests brought me his head," he said slowly, and he stared at the cabin wall for a moment. Then he snapped his fingers and pointed at Fortinbras. "Now you threaten to repeat that stupidity!"

"But don't you see," argued Fortinbras, "with the Danish king's death, surely they lack the organization and readiness to repel a rapid attack. It is said that the new king Claudius lacks the strength and foresight that characterized his brother, and the prince, Hamlet, is a mere student." He said this last word with marked disdain.

Olav frowned at Fortinbras, then spat to one side. "One must never underestimate the Danes. They may be great drunkards and seem to play the fool. But they are a force *not* to be trifled with. You and your 'four hundred and twelve' are like biting fleas and Denmark a very big dog, one that would likely scratch you into the gutter. However, . . ."

Here he paused and waited for Fortinbras to look at him. When Fortinbras once more raised his eyes Olav continued. "*I* have a plan. If you will obey me as a true prince must, then you may make use of your men yet. There is blood and plunder to be taken, all right. But not from the Danes. Not yet, at any rate. Now listen."

Fortinbras straightened his back and gave Olav his full attention.

"On the Polish coast is an isolated village called Dashtov. It contains ample plunder and is a suitable challenge for a prince's first military command. I have already replied to the Danes' King Claudius to arrange safe passage for you and your men through Danish waters. Take Dashtov, if you can. Then we will see where your ambition might take you from there."

He nodded toward the cabin door.

Fortinbras considered a moment, then replied, "I will not disappoint you." He stood, perhaps anticipating more instruction, but Olav merely stared at him. Finally he bowed to Olav, and left the cabin.

Chapter 22

Madness Explained

The Danish king's main reception room was a dignified room, large enough to befit a sovereign, and yet small enough to allow for the kinds of intimate intercourse that are essential to diplomatic conversation. It was richly furnished. To one side stood a large polished table at which Polonius usually sat with his notes and documents, the king's seal, writing implements, and other odds and ends. Two slightly elevated thrones sat facing the room to the left of the table, at right angles to Polonius's position. Again to their left, along the wall was a long cushioned bench for petitioners. Sconces for torches were anchored to the walls every few feet, although light from these was simply not needed due to the sunlight flooding the area from clerestory windows behind the thrones. The floor was flagged in large, black and white tiles, although a crimson carpet led from the door nearly to the dais on which the thrones sat.

Gertrude occupied the smaller throne to the king's left, where she sat as if occupied in private thought. Next to her on the larger throne to her right Claudius listened to a young man who spoke earnestly though quietly in his ear, showing him a document. Polonius hastened into the room through a door in the wall behind his table, papers in his hands, as usual.

"Polonius?" Claudius said. He motioned for the young man beside him to leave, but kept the document in his hand. The young man bowed and walked quickly down the aisle out of the room. "You wished to speak to me?"

Polonius deposited his papers on the table and rounded it to approach the king. He carried a slim sheet from among the papers he had brought in with him.

Gertrude lifted herself from the half slouch she had been in and watched the two intently.

Claudius looked at him.

"My lord," Polonius asked gently, "I need to speak to you about Hamlet. I have a confession of a sort to make."

Claudius raised his eyes. Gertrude straightened even more and bent toward Claudius and Polonius. "A confession? Go on," Claudius said.

"My lord, first I must ask you, what do you think of *me*?"

"You have been a faithful and honorable servant," Claudius answered. "At least until now," he added with a bit of a smirk to Gertrude, who also smiled. But turning back to Polonius, he could see that the older man was serious. "Go ahead," Claudius said.

"My lord, I hold my first duty, even above that of family, to my country and my sovereign. Thus, I know I am bound to explain to you the following."

Now he had the full attention of both Claudius and Gertrude.

"My lord, we here are all aware of Hamlet's…transformation…his, well, shall we, for lack of a better term, call it madness?"

Gertrude straightened and raised her eyebrows at Polonius, but before she could say anything Claudius raised his hand toward her, and continuing to observe Polonius, said, "And?"

"I believe I know what has led to his lamentable condition."

"Truly? *That* his mother and I have both longed to understand. Explain."

"You both know, of course, of my daughter Ophelia. Only a week or two ago I became aware that something of a courtship was occurring between her and Hamlet. Now, had I turned a blind eye to this affair, had I pretended that only the simple workings of youth and its natural attractions were at work here, I would have been doing your majesties a serious disservice, as well as these two young people. I took my young mistress aside and I warned her, nay, commanded her that she should not accept Hamlet's attentions. 'He is a prince, a man beyond your class, a star whose sphere is quite separate from yours,' I told her. 'You must not expect or even hope for his love, for he is circumscribed by his birth, his obligations to the king and his mother the queen, and to Denmark itself.' I instructed her to return his gifts and letters and to lock herself from his resort. It was the only loyal action for me to take."

Claudius examined Polonius carefully. He knew there was more to Polonius's concerns than this particular class distinction. However, he nodded his approval, and Polonius continued.

"Now, as part of her duty to me, Ophelia gave me this letter, one of the letters from Hamlet to her. If you will, shall I read it for you?"

"Yes. Do so."

Polonius squinted through his eyeglasses at the paper and proceeded.

Oh, My Dear and Beautiful Ophelia,

It is both my joy and (apparently) my fate to find that Cupid has cast his amorous dart with your image on it into the farthest recesses of my heart. I am caught in the spell of your shape and perfume, and your very voice commands my notice and my deepest affection.

Although I lack words properly to express my love to you, I scrawl these lines in the hope that you will apprehend and approve the intensity of my desire and believe the nobility of my purpose.

Know above all that I love thee best.

He that thou knowest thine,
Hamlet

"Hamlet sent this to her?" Gertrude asked.

"Indeed, Madam," Polonius answered. "You know yourself the vagaries of the heart and the hazards of...uh, young love. Is not love a whirlwind that twists our very being at the best of times? And when it is refused, does not such a painful outcome drive us to distraction? I believe that her refusal has done precisely this and confounded his reason."

"Do you think it is this?" Claudius asked Gertrude.

"It may be," she said, not wholly convinced. "Though I think it more likely to be his father's death. And perhaps..." Her voice trailed off.

"I am certain that neglected love has taken him from himself," Polonius asserted. He passed the letter to Gertrude, who reread it silently to herself.

"How might we test this...theory?" Claudius asked.

"Well, you know how Hamlet often walks in the lobby just outside this very room for hours at a time, deep in concentrated thought. Sometimes he reads; sometimes he talks to himself. Suppose we arrange for him to meet Ophelia there, by 'accident,' as it were? You and I can be hidden behind an arras nearby, listen to their exchange, and hear for ourselves the nature of their affections."

Gertrude frowned at this proposal, but just at just that moment, Hamlet slipped his head in the door from the lobby entrance thirty feet away. He laughed aloud, to himself it seemed, and disappeared equally quickly.

Claudius looked in frustration at the empty doorway.

"Let him go," Polonius whispered urgently. "I'll go speak to him. Later I'll tell you what I find out."

Claudius and Gertrude exchanged a long glance. Claudius waved Polonius toward the entrance where Hamlet had been only moments before. Polonius gave a low bow and hurried after Hamlet.

Chapter 23

An Enigmatic Conversation

In the hallway Polonius had to hurry to catch up to Hamlet, who was striding down the lobby, the one where it seemed only months ago he had encountered Ophelia and her maids on a sunlit afternoon. At least the sun still shone.

"Do you know me, my lord?" Polonius asked Hamlet, still from three or four strides behind the prince. Hamlet stopped and rounded on Polonius, who stopped abruptly. He gazed at Polonius, as if trying to remember something. Then he snapped his fingers as if with successful recall, and he cheerfully said, "Excellent well! You are a fishmonger! Why only last week the salmon in your basket…"

"Oh, no, not I, my lord.

"Well, I wish you were as honest as a fishmonger, then. They, at least, give true value and are honest in their dealings."

"Honest, my lord?"

"Of course, of course! Don't you know? To be honest is to be one man in ten thousand, one diamond in a beach of sand."

"That's very true, my lord. And although I could never claim to the status of diamond, I like to think that I am as honest as the next man."

Hamlet stared at him, a shrewd smile on his face. "Precisely my point," he said.

Polonius frowned, looked aside for a moment, then, turning back, noticed the book Hamlet was carrying.

"What is it that you read, my lord?"

Hamlet reopened the text and riffled through some pages as if checking something. Then he looked up and smiled ingenuously at Polonius. "Words, I think." He looked again. "Yes, they're words all right. Words." He waited.

After a pause of eight or nine seconds Polonius tried again. "What is the matter, my lord?"

"Between whom?"

"No, I mean the matter that you read. What is it that you read?"

"Ah," Hamlet said meaningfully. He peered once more into the text, running his finger along a couple of lines. "Well, this author, probably another man something less than honest, argues that old men are wrinkled, short-sighted, and rather foolish, a feature especially to be noted in their conversation. Of course, I hold this all to be simply another prevarication, but to what end I cannot tell." He looked at Polonius again. "How's your eyesight? Are those not spectacles you're clutching in your left hand?"

Polonius looked at them stupidly for a moment, then transferred them into a pocket of his gown.

"Did you know," Hamlet asked, "that the sun can breed maggots in a dead dog?"

"I have heard of such a tale, my lord."

"Ah, but not just the tail, all through the body—the heart, the liver, the spleen…the womb. By the way," Hamlet went on. "I mean not to be nosy in the manner of a busybody (as there are far too many such men and women these days), but I am curious…have you a daughter?"

Polonius stiffened at the non sequitur, then smiled gently and answered, "I do my lord."

"Let her not walk in the sun! We conceive of many things, but as your daughter may conceive…well, we couldn't have that, could we?"

Polonius's eyes flicked back and forth. He looked at Hamlet again, an inquiring, pained expression on his face. Finally he spoke again.

"My lord, with your permission I'll take my leave."

"Oh, please, please, there's nothing I would give away more readily," he said grandly, and he opened his arms toward Polonius as if he would embrace the old man in parting.

Polonius shrank back involuntarily, for Hamlet was grinning wildly at him, and in his hand he held an open dagger. Then Hamlet backed a few feet to the wall where he sat heavily onto a bench. He tapped the open blade against his own throat, and while staring at Polonius said simply, "Except my life." As if to drive home the point, he said once more, "Except my life."

Polonius shuddered and backed away, bowing slightly every few steps. "Fare you well, my lord," he finally said, and turned and hastened away.

Hamlet looked at him and snorted in derision. *Fool!* he thought. He felt momentarily unclean. Then he got once more to his feet, sheathed his dagger, and walked off in the other direction.

Chapter 24

A Lesson in Deceit

Three hours later, Polonius sat almost idly, fingering his seal of office, the large medallion hanging around his neck that signified his position as chief councilor to the king, advisor, confidant, and if need be, spokesperson. On the desk stood a half-empty carafe of wine and a glass into which he had poured another portion. He fingered his recently completed letter to Laertes, his third in as many days to confirm paternal support while his son adjusted to the foreign culture in Paris.

The letter contained little more than family greetings and further parental advice. Laertes was much too young to be entrusted with state secrets, and given that Polonius spent most of his waking hours in service to the king, what else did he have to talk about? And he did not want to seem too obvious in his desire to know the reception his son had received in Paris. After all, Laertes was a handsome young man, dashing in appearance and manner, an obvious catch for an ambitious foreign girl. Polonius' lack of knowledge of Laertes' successes and failures, indeed, of his very happiness, was frustrating, and he worried about how his son might fare in the French capital.

Fatherhood can be such a chore, he thought. He felt he needed to devise some method of learning Laertes' activities in Paris—his son's accomplishments, Polonius supposed, as well as the predictable lapses in judgment.

In the letter he did, however, mention the strangeness of Prince Hamlet, particularly that exhibited this afternoon—his odd irrationality and his ill-mannered, conversational irregularity, his strange dress and stranger habits. Polonius couched all of this, of course, in politic terms. One never knew for *sure* who might be an agent of the king, someone who might read others' letters, and it would never do to offend his majesty.

A lit candle stood on his desk even though it was broad daylight. He needed hot wax to seal his letter. Having folded the letter, which also mentioned his worries about Ophelia (whom he knew Laertes loved dearly), he tilted the candle and poured a thick glob of white wax onto the letter's final edge to make a seal, and he impressed it with the family's signet, a broad relief showing a scholar holding a sheaf of papers in one hand and a falcon in the other. The scholar exhibited the posture and expression of a man standing strangely proud in a manner that suggested knowledge, power and authority. Then, after blowing on the wax to help it harden into place, Polonius picked up a small bell from the desktop and tinkled it gently.

A moment later a well-dressed servant entered the room and bowed to Polonius, who was smiling as if he had just thought of something very clever.

"My lord?" the servant asked politely.

"Reynaldo. How old are you now, and how long have you served me?"

Reynaldo's eyes rolled briefly toward the ceiling, then, looking back at Polonius, he answered, "Fourteen years, if it please you. I had my 37th birthday last May, sir."

"Marry yes, it pleases me, indeed," answered Polonius. "I remember that Ophelia was very tiny when her sainted mother died, so tiny we feared for her life, as well. You came to me when your own parents passed away only weeks after." Polonius mused a moment. "Remember Laertes then? What a young rascal he was?"

"Oh, indeed, sir. He has become quite, quite grown up now, has he not?"

"Indeed, indeed." Polonius reminisced a moment longer, drumming his fingers idly on his desktop. Then he said, "Reynaldo, I need you to go to Paris for me."

"To see young Laertes, sir?"

"Yes, to deliver some letters and money. But it is important that you follow my instructions carefully, and carry them out *before* you visit my son."

Reynaldo appeared mystified. "What shall I do?"

"When you reach Paris, before visiting Laertes, I wish you to try to familiarize yourself with the Danish community in the city, doing so at times when Laertes himself is otherwise occupied and not present. Yes?"

"I understand. But to what end?"

"In your conversation with these Danes, I would like you to pretend a somewhat distant knowledge of my son, saying perhaps that you have heard of his prowess as a swordsman (a skill in which he does shine, as you know)."

Reynaldo nodded. He knew perfectly well of Laertes' skill with a rapier. He was among the top swordsmen in Denmark.

"If any of these gentlemen admits any knowledge of Laertes," Polonius went on, "I wish you to describe his reputation from Denmark in somewhat *less* than flattering social terms. You might comment on his notoriety as a drinker, or a gambler, his preference for evenings in the public houses rather than for pursuit of his studies; you might even comment on his reputation as a bit of a libertine, a man unafraid of sowing a few wild oats in a brothel."

Reynaldo frowned. "Would not such a tale dishonor your son, my lord?"

"Not if you describe these errant ways merely as the common actions of one whose youth and liberty have allowed him more license than a man of more considered judgment might act upon. 'Boys will be boys,' they say, and the distance between boyhood and manhood can sometimes be rather slight, do you not agree?"

"Of course, that is true, but it seems odd that you, of all people, might wish to sully your son's reputation, particularly in a foreign clime."

Polonius smiled and tapped a finger gently on his temple. "Ah, but there is a method to this seeming madness. Imagine yourself branding my son with one of these common offences of youth's foolishness. Suppose, then, that your interlocutor knows Laertes, either personally or by reputation. He may, on the one hand, express surprise and indignation, because Laertes' behavior in Paris has been, in his experience, exemplary. Such is to be hoped, of course."

Polonius looked across the room as he began to appreciate his own scheme even more.

He continued in a slightly less sanguine tone, "Or, he might answer, 'Ah, yes, Laertes. He *is* a wild one. I saw him just the other night in a rather serious quarrel with a Florentine,' or, 'I believe the man to whom you refer has a taste for too much Burgundy wine,' or some such response. Then your bait of falsehood will have captured a carp of truth."

Polonius paused and over his spectacles peered at Reynaldo inquiringly. "You understand now?" he asked.

Reynaldo was nearly speechless with admiration for the plan. He smiled at Polonius. The old man really was quite devious. Reynaldo supposed that this was one of the skills a king's councilor must have in abundance, along with many others. "Yes, very good, my lord. I *do* understand," he said.

Polonius handed him the latest letter along with a purse of ducats. "Make sure he receives this money, Reynaldo, when you finally make your visit to him. And the letters, as well."

"I shall, my lord."

"And Reynaldo, even though we who have seen longer days may find some of his behavior a bit wild or somewhat juvenile, refer to him any corrective advice in such a way as to sympathize with his motives. Give him understanding, not direction. It is only through freedom that a man truly comes to himself, and if his honesty looks both inward and into the world at large, he can only ultimately thrive. Do you not agree?"

"I do, my lord."

"Good. Then, be on your way."

"I shall leave on the next available ship, my lord."

Reynaldo placed the letter and money into a satchel that hung from his shoulder. He gave another short bow to Polonius, then turned and left the room. Polonius looked after him briefly, before turning back to his desk.

He strove to recall what he was supposed to be doing before this clever plan had inspired him. He smiled.

Chapter 25

Recruitment of Spies

Not far away, Gertrude and Claudius sat side by side in one of their more cozy parlors.

"So, we are agreed then?"

Gertrude nodded glumly. She could not disagree in any diametric way with the king in any case. But she did speak up for Hamlet.

"My lord, I know Hamlet has been out of sorts. His father's death was a terrible blow to him." She raised her hand to indicate that Claudius should not interrupt.

"To us all, of course. He was your brother. He was my husband. We loved him. But it is in the nature of sons not merely to love, but to idolize their fathers, and Hamlet did his. As for Rosencrantz and Guildenstern, our enlisting their aid is all well and good, but why do we not ask Horatio? He has been much closer to Hamlet than they ever were."

Claudius grunted. "Horatio's too pure by half. We might convince him to act in what we, and he, might see to be Hamlet's best interests. But the man has no ambition. And he's certainly no actor—just a silly academic, lost in his 'philosophy.' Hamlet may trust him, but we dare not. And if Hamlet were to get even a whiff of dishonesty from his best friend he might go completely out of his wits. None of us wants that, surely?" He raised his eyes plaintively to Gertrude.

"I will defer to you in this, as I do in all things, of course. I merely worry for my son." Gertrude sighed.

"As do we all." Claudius called sharply. "Chamberlain! Bring us Rosencrantz and Guildenstern."

A man in the livery of a king's trusted servant slipped in and bowed. "At once, your majesty," he stated deferentially, and he bowed once more. He exited smoothly and was not gone more than a minute and a half before he returned, with Rosencrantz and Guildenstern just behind him. Guildenstern appeared worried, Rosencrantz merely pleased. Both of them bowed low.

"Rosencrantz! Guildenstern! We are grateful for your attendance, for we have imminent need of your service."

"Indeed, we are at your service, to be commanded," replied Rosencrantz somewhat breathlessly. Guildenstern merely nodded.

The king paused to choose his words.

"You must know, as gossip permeates the court, and news flies from perch to nest like finches to their nestlings, that Hamlet, your fellow student and friend, has fallen on a sore distraction. He is not the man he was." This last statement was delivered with solemn intonation, slowly and deliberately.

Guildenstern finally found the nerve to speak. "Your majesty, it is true that we have heard distressing news of the prince."

The king went on. "Her majesty the queen and we who love him cannot adequately fathom the source of his unhappy nervousness. As you have been his trusted friends, both in Elsinore and in Wittenberg, you might have access, through worldly conversation and collegial intercourse, to the fount of his unhappiness. If it be in our power to address his coarser cares we should like to do so. We would like you two, in the manner of friends, to try to ascertain the origin of his troubles and to report back to us, that we might use our sovereign power to act in his and all our best interests."

He paused. Rosencrantz and Guildenstern exchanged glances. "You have me, do you not?" asked the king.

Gertrude added, "I am sure there are no men living to whom he more adheres than to you, his friends from childhood and from the university. Will you not work on our behalf?"

"My liege, we lay our service at your feet." Rosencrantz was emphatic on this point. Then he added, "My lord, my lady queen, if there be any means through which we can be of assistance, we shall employ it with all diligence."

"Thank you, gentlemen. We were sure we could rely upon your love and discretion," the king stated.

He clapped Guildenstern on the shoulder and added, "I'm confident that young men such as yourselves and our son have shared many an adventure in Germany, and surely your mutual trust will enable your efforts, for us and for him. Think you not?"

Claudius laughed knowingly, as if sharing his knowledge of some youthful misdemeanor or indiscretion these two men and Hamlet might have committed in their freer lives in Wittenberg. It felt a kind of artificial bonhomie to Rosencrantz, and yet he understood at once that this was potentially a wonderful opportunity. Any direct service for the king holds out the prospect of advancement. This was just the sort of chance that Rosencrantz had been longing for. Why else had he done everything he could to join Hamlet in Wittenberg? Further, he knew he could rely on Guildenstern to do what he was told.

"We will serve your majesty in all due faith," said Rosencrantz, and Guildenstern nodded in breathless agreement.

"Well, then, at your earliest opportunity make contact with our son. You need not mention our request, of course. You understand."

Gertrude raised her eyes at her husband but said nothing. The two young men merely bowed deeply, and having noticed that the king had already turned away from them, made to leave.

"Do not fail us," the king said over his shoulder, as he picked up a silver wine goblet from the side table.

The two men hastily bowed again, and quietly turned and left the room. In his overconfidence, failure was the last consideration to enter the mind of Rosencrantz.

Chapter 26

Deceit and Credulity

"The king has directed that I inquire as to the progress of your report."

Horatio started, and turned to look over his shoulder. Osric stood just inside the door of the scriptorium, holding his hat in his hand, much as he had when inviting Hamlet to the fencing match. He smiled knowingly at Horatio, who turned his back to him once more and lifted his quill to continue writing.

"The king has never been known for his patience," Osric added in a low voice.

"Tell King Fortinbras that I am making progress, then," answered Horatio somewhat sharply. Then, in a more accommodating tone, he added, "These events were complex. They included many people. And even though I was near the center of events, there are some mysteries to their unfolding that even *I* can only conjecture about. But I am working hard on this report, as you may see," he said, pointing at a pile of completed manuscript.

Osric stepped toward the table and reached for a page, startling Cleopatra, who arched her back and hissed at him. Osric stepped back withdrawing his hand, even as Horatio placed his own hand on the large glass paperweight that held the manuscripts in place on the corner of the table.

"Oh, no," Horatio said. "These are as yet unedited. The final version will appear in good time. Please explain to his majesty that due to the importance of his request, unless he commands otherwise, I can release the report only when I am sure it is in its final, most accurate form. Surely he wishes the truth, insofar as it may be found?"

He paused, then adjusted his chair so that he might look more directly at Osric and said, "Wait. Before you go…you delivered the challenge to Hamlet…remember?"

Osric drew an audible breath, then answered, "Yes. I remember."

"I will have occasion to speak further with you about that affair. You can manage that, I suppose?" Horatio asked.

Osric lowered his head, then looked at Horatio. "Yes. I'm sure you can find me."

"Yes, I'm sure I can," said Horatio, and he turned once more to his writing. Osric turned quietly, opened the door, and stepped softly into the passage. He closed the door behind him.

Horatio held his quill over the page, listened as the door latched. Then he bent his head and began to write.

Lying, bearing false witness, is a sin. So the priests tell us, and so it is written in the Old Testament. Yet lying seems to come so easily. Expedience directs human affairs, and in its amoral name truth slips away to a dusty corner where it is forgotten or ignored.

I remember arguing with Hamlet in Wittenberg about the value of truth. He was mightily concerned about how his future kingship might *require* that he sin by telling untruths, that he might find himself compelled to lie in order to protect the kingdom. I tried to convince him that to deceive and to lie are not quite the same, that deception requires the participation of the deceived, either through their making unwarranted assumptions or through simply misperceiving what should be an obvious truth and interpreting events in another way entirely, a way perhaps more beneficial to the deceiver, and usually more appealing to the deceived.

It is certainly true that Hamlet intended to deceive—the king, his mother, Polonius, and (perhaps for her protection) Ophelia. He may even have deceived me, although it pains me to consider the possibility.

Hamlet was also very fond of the theater, the success of whose devices depends upon deception, and upon a willingness to be deceived. I often found the contrivances of actors to be too far from real life for me to have any confidence in the worth of their stories. But Hamlet was certain that there is a marvelous, almost magical value in acting that approximates euphoria. He once called it a means of transcending the ordinary mundaneness of our daily lives.

When he first told me of these ideas, I had to agree. Actors in a cast co-operate in their deceptions to the end of making us see our world in a new and more significant way. Imagine, however, that the actors are *not* co-operating, but trying to deceive one another! There you would have *real* theater! That is what was happening in Elsinore under Claudius!

Of course, competing deceptions in life rather than in art make events even more complex than they really are, until one might begin to believe that real truth cannot be found, only its approximations. There were many competing deceptions in this story.

The actions of Rosencrantz and Guildenstern form part of this net of lies and semi-truths. Hamlet saw quite through their petty dissimulations nearly immediately upon their return to Denmark. It was easy work for a man such as Hamlet.

First, they had no reason to return when they did. Rosencrantz needed to complete his reading of the law, and could not possibly have finished his university work by the time he suddenly reappeared in court with Guildenstern.

Second, these two were not personal servants to Hamlet, nor truth be told, all that close to the prince or to me, though they were often companions of an evening.

Third, the initially aimless style of their conversation when they made their presence known to Hamlet here in Elsinore struck Hamlet as insincere and motivated by forces quite other than the friendship they professed.

I had been reading in the lobby. Hamlet had been sitting in a bay window opposite, absently rubbing some flaw in the glass and staring either outside or at his own reflection when Rosencrantz and Guildenstern appeared at the door. Hamlet rose and greeted them with initial warmth.

"My friends! Rosencrantz. Guildenstern. How do you, lads?"

"As the indifferent children of the Earth," answered Guildenstern, first for a change. "We're hardly the button on Fortune's cap."

"Neither are we trodden under her heavy shoes," added Rosencrantz. They both looked at me, but I merely raised my hand in greeting, smiling at what I knew was coming.

"Ah, then you're in the *middle* of her favors?" queried Hamlet. It was a well-known straight line.

"Faith, her privates, we," the two said in unison. Guildenstern smirked, Rosencrantz chuckled, and even Hamlet permitted himself a light snicker at the old joke. I went back to my book, but my concentration was pure pretense. I was more interested in the unfolding conversation.

"But why are you here in Elsinore?" Hamlet asked.

"To visit you. No other occasion," Guildenstern answered hastily. Rosencrantz glanced warily at Guildenstern, who looked back at him as if checking his lines.

Hamlet became immediately suspicious.

"Were you not sent for?"

"My lord?" replied Rosencrantz.

"Please, please. Be direct with me. Did not the king and queen send for you?"

When Rosencrantz and Guildenstern shared a guilty expression Hamlet knew his suspicions were correct. (As Hamlet said that night on the guard platform, how odd that we seem compelled to search for the flaws in people rather than for their virtues. For in most ways, at least in the beginning, Rosencrantz and Guildenstern were virtuous men. But Hamlet was exquisitely attuned to their flaws.)

"Never mind. Say nothing. I see by the confession in your looks that you were sent for."

He stepped away from them and crossed the gallery to pour some wine for himself. He turned, and after sipping, stated matter-of-factly, "I will tell you why, in the event that the king and queen have commanded you to keep secret. When you report to the king, you will have revealed nothing that I do not already know."

He drank again, then began to laugh quite heartily, a laugh that went on for thirty or forty seconds. Then abruptly he stopped and became quite serious. He waved one of his arms about as if searching for words or phrases. Then he walked to the window once more sighing deeply. Finally he turned back to us and grinned. His abrupt transformations were quite disconcerting.

"Over the past weeks I have become a transformed man." He sniffed peevishly, as if someone had cheated him at cards or dice. He pulled a handkerchief from his sleeve and gently patted his brow. Then he folded his arms and grimaced at them. He looked at them as if he had never seen anything so disappointing. He sniffed again.

"I've lost my very desire for life," he finally went on. Rosencrantz and Guildenstern exchanged glances.

Hamlet pointed at the window and said, "Although the world contains the same wonders and beauties it always has, it seems nothing more to me than a sterile platform, a dusty stage in a run-down theater, lacking any sort of stimulus that might stir the heart or energize the sinews." He gave them a mournful stare. "I've lost my mirth. I have difficulty finding purpose or delight—in anything."

"Consider a man, one like you yourselves, like me. We contain all the human graces and qualities that enhance experience and that mark us as quasi-holy beings: reason, feeling, and apprehension nearly like that of God Himself! Yet for all our goodness I find it difficult to find anything to like. I care not for men—or women, for that matter. We're all dissembling fools, are we not? We crawl between Earth and heaven, chasing shadows, desiring this bauble or that trinket, when it all ends in the same dismal plot of earth."

Rosencrantz and Guildenstern looked at one another, obviously curious where this was going. Hamlet continued.

"The king and queen would like to know what's wrong with me. What's *wrong*. With *me.* The *prince of Denmark*." He drank again, then said with a peculiar grin, "Well, I'm a bit mad. Quite a bit mad, if you will. But you *can* inform my uncle-father and aunt-mother of this."

At this moment he set down his cup, and approaching the two of them, curled his arms over their shoulders. They appeared quite discomfited, but Hamlet ignored their tension. He whispered to them, as if releasing some amazing secret, "I am but mad north by northwest." He giggled, a long erratic titter. Then he looked Guildenstern in the eye and muttered, "When the wind is southerly, I know a hawk from a heron." He winked extravagantly.

Guildenstern stared at him for a long moment, then giggled. "Well, of course, my lord. Everyone knows that, though."

Rosencrantz coughed politely and stared at Guildenstern darkly. Hamlet merely smirked. "Then I'd be a fool not to know it, wouldn't I? More to the point, wouldn't the king?" Hamlet added seriously. Guildenstern's expression became much more serious.

"My lord," Rosencrantz said quickly, "If I may change the subject, I felt it important to inform you that the Tragedians of the City are here in Elsinore. I know how much you appreciate and understand dramatic performance, and I am sure they would endeavor to produce their best work were you to grant them audience."

Hamlet's demeanor became immediately more serious, and simultaneously more upbeat. He raised his eyebrows.

"The Tragedians of the City?" he asked.

"Indeed, my lord. We passed them on the road as we were approaching Elsinore ourselves and spoke with them briefly. Not so, Guildenstern?"

"Yes, yes indeed," Guildenstern affirmed.

"Well, make them welcome! I would love to see them perform again. Remember their performance of speeches from Oedipus Rex in Wittenberg last September? They were marvelous! I, for one, shall never forget."

"My lord, may we speak in your name?" asked Rosencrantz.

"Not in the name of the king?" asked Hamlet, a bit disingenuously.

Rosencrantz coughed into his gloved hand softly, then raised his eyes to Hamlet. "We are yours to command, my lord," he said.

"I think it better for your health that you obey the king," said Hamlet. He smiled. "But you may use my name. Bring them to me as soon as possible, tomorrow at the latest."

"We will, my lord," answered Guildenstern. "And so, may we take our leave? It has been a long journey."

"Of course, of course," answered Hamlet. "And you will want to report to the king and queen ere you go to bed," he added.

> Rosencrantz exchanged a look with Guildenstern. Then the two of them bowed to Hamlet, who reiterated, "Tomorrow," and then waved them off. They straightened, as if they were a combination of nobility and chastened children, turned, and fumbled their way out of the room.
>
> Hamlet later explained to me that by then he had no great hopes for the two of them. After all, the king has the offices, the power, the money. Where else would any ambitious man turn for favor and affection? And even I had always seen Rosencrantz's ambition, not to mention the slavish way Guildenstern followed his lead. As usual, Hamlet's judgment was insight itself.

Horatio straightened and rubbed the small of his back. Once more the candle had burnt down near to guttering out. Cleopatra slept peacefully on her cushion.

Horatio blew the ink dry on his last page and gathered the night's writings into a careful, ordered collection. He added them meticulously to the pages under the paperweight. He wished he had a glass of wine. Rubbing his eyes, he got quietly to his feet, lifted his cloak from the peg by the door, blew out the candle, and allowed his eyes to adjust to the moonlight streaming in through the narrow window. Without disturbing the cat, he let himself silently out of the room.

Chapter 27

Love and Loss

Ophelia looked up from her needlepoint. Her father had entered her chamber and stood silently beside the door looking intently at her.

"My father?" she said.

Polonius started, as if from some minor trance. When he spoke it was as if he were wrestling with some dilemma. However, he did not pause further, and said, "Ophelia, the king has requested our assistance."

Ophelia raised her eyebrows questioningly. "*Our*?" she asked.

"Come with me," Polonius went on, ignoring her question. He beckoned with some urgency.

Ophelia set her work down and got to her feet. "Am I appropriately attired?" she asked softly. She straightened her hair.

"Yes, yes," Polonius said with a little impatience. "Come."

Ophelia selected a short cloak from her armoire, slipped it over her shoulders, and followed her father out of their apartments and into the castle hallway leading toward the royal quarters. As they walked, he spoke again.

"Ophelia, the king and I wish you to converse with Hamlet."

Ophelia slowed her pace momentarily, but her father grasped her by the arm to pull her along and said, "Hurry. We mustn't keep the king waiting."

"Will the king be there?" asked Ophelia.

"Yes. Well, no." He stopped and held her by the arm. "Listen, Ophelia. His majesty wishes to hear the prince in conversation with you. You know how Hamlet often uses the lobby outside the throne room, where he walks, and sometimes talks to himself. We wish you to meet Hamlet there, as it were, by 'accident.' His majesty and I will be hidden behind one of the tapestries, a vantage point from which we may overhear your conversation."

Ophelia freed her arm from her father's grasp and looked at him fiercely. "Oh, Father, do not ask me to do this! Not after demanding that I refuse his tenders and invitations!"

"Ophelia, I know that this may be difficult for you. But the king commands it. And we must obey. *You* must obey."

Ophelia felt a kind of nausea chew at her innards. She felt panicky and angry.

"Now, come," Polonius said again.

Ophelia again began to move forward with him, her mind whirling with images and feelings, her heart thudding heavily. They passed through a series of lesser chambers and entered the lobby. Claudius stood beside another entrance, talking softly to one of the servants. On seeing Ophelia and Polonius he gestured to the servant, who bowed quickly and left the room. Claudius approached them.

Ophelia curtsied deeply, and Polonius bowed. When she glanced up at the king, she felt somehow reassured, for he appeared neither impatient nor upset.

"Does she understand?" Claudius asked Polonius.

"Yes, my liege." Polonius handed Ophelia a small book. "Now look you, Ophelia. Simply sit on this bench, reading." He pointed to a small bench against the wall of the lobby. "It will demonstrate, at least a little, how lonely you are." He pointed to a pair of floor-length tapestries featuring hunting scenes that hung between two great windows. "The king and I will be there. Do your best to lead Hamlet near the tapestries so that we may clearly hear him. Do you understand?"

Ophelia looked once more at Claudius, who smiled reassuringly at her. "I understand, my lord." She opened the book, entitled *The Hart's Struggle*. Smiling inside, she mused that Hamlet would have to be an idiot to think she would ever choose that reading material.

"Let us secrete ourselves, my liege," Polonius said to Claudius. The two of them moved to the tapestries and slipped behind them, which quivered for a moment or two, and then hung still. Ophelia stepped over to the bench, arranged herself amid her skirts, and opened the book. The first few lines, read,

Hunters rarely feel sympathy for the game they seek, yet when one sees the terror in the eyes of a wounded deer, one sometimes wonders at mankind's capacity for violence. The wild hart, victim of the chase...

but at that moment Hamlet entered the hallway about twenty paces away. He looked at her and gave a long sigh, then approached. He stopped in front of her.

"Lady Ophelia," he finally said.

"My lord, how goes it with you?" she asked politely.

Hamlet looked at her fiercely, as if determining what response would be adequate to explain his inner turmoil. He finally muttered, "Oh, well, well...well, I think." He turned from her as if to leave.

"My lord, on our infrequent encounters you have seemed preoccupied of late, perhaps in ways one such as I might only imagine. I trust I have not, in any way, been instrumental to any unpleasing thoughts or states of mind." She tried to give him a small smile, and she squeezed the book in her hands.

Hamlet snorted at her, then gave a loud guffaw. "Instrumental?" he spat. "And just what music do you imagine to have played? A dirge, perhaps? A 'totentanz?'" He pointed his finger at her and grinned. "I know. A tarantella, the only dance fitting for a spider."

"My lord?" she gasped.

Hamlet grabbed her by the wrist and yanked her to her feet. He pushed his face close to hers and said, clearly and slowly, "I loved you once."

Ophelia pulled slightly away, straightening her posture and trying to maintain some dignity. She stared into his eyes a moment, her expression blank. Finally she said, "You made me believe so."

"Ah, yes, but even to profess so much is to open oneself to the accusation of lying. Perhaps I didn't really love you at all. It is possible I merely pretended. We are all actors and actresses, are we not?" She did not answer, but turned her eyes away.

He pushed Ophelia back onto the bench, then seated himself beside her. She shifted herself away from him and looked at him. He spoke again.

"Well, tell me then. Are you honest?" He gazed at her inquisitorially.

"My lord, do you doubt me?"

Hamlet snickered. "Doubt? How could I doubt *you?*" He looked away a moment, then back at her. "Well, then, are you beautiful?"

"Surely, my lord, it is not a woman's place to remark upon her own physical charms."

She glanced away, allowing herself briefly to scan the arras behind which, she knew, the king and her father stood listening. "Why do you ask me these things?"

"Beauty and honesty do not make good companions," Hamlet said to her. He eyed her challengingly, as if she had some puzzle to solve.

"What better companions might there be within a soul?"

"Ah, within, without—are these not one and the same? Besides," Hamlet continued, "beauty corrupts honesty."

Ophelia turned away.

"Oh, yes," he continued, "beauty will turn honesty into a whore before honesty can transform beauty into *his* likeness. Paradox? Yes.

But the times give it proof. All that shines may not be gold. And we are all deceivers and deceived."

"My lord, do you suggest that I have lied to you?"

"*Have* you lied to me?" Hamlet stared at her with visible intensity. She looked away again, and picked at some loose lace at her wrist.

"Lady Ophelia," he said at last. "I have a useful suggestion. Why don't you enter a nunnery? God will cleanse you and spare you from temptation. Why would you be a breeder of sinners?" He laughed momentarily. "Look at me! I think I am indifferent honest and yet… and yet, I could accuse me of such sins it would be better *my* mother had not borne me. What *should* such fellows as I do crawling between Earth and heaven? I have more sins to confess than I have time to enumerate them, define them. My sins cling to me!"

He raised his voice until he was nearly shouting. "I am proud! Vengeful! Ambitious! What son of woman is not? So," he said with a softer finality. "Get thee to a nunnery. Free thy soul. Find some purity if you have it not." Hamlet got up and started to walk away.

"Oh, my lord Hamlet," Ophelia stammered, and then she started to cry softly. He turned and stared at her a moment.

"Oh, here we go," he heard himself say. He returned to her and tugged her roughly to her feet once more. She pulled herself back wildly and tried to wipe away her tears with one hand.

"Don't play the hurt one with me," he shouted at her. "You think we men don't know how you play us for fools? You and your kind play the coquette, flutter your eyes and expose your bosom (oh, I know, it's the fashion), twitch your behinds in subtle invitation! You make up your face, hiding the countenance God gave you in order to tug at the Satan in us."

Once again he was nearly yelling. "Beauty! Honesty? Hah!" Then he stopped suddenly as if inspired. A long moment passed as he stared at her. Under his withering gaze she finally looked away. "Where's your father?" he asked suddenly.

Ophelia took a sharp breath. He released her and she dropped to the bench as if exhausted. She looked down and away, and then said, "At home, my lord."

"What? Not nearby? Well, you'd best sidle off and tell him that a fool is best found in his own house, for the world is filled with the foolers and the fooled."

He stood and began to walk away. Then he returned to lecture her once more.

"I tell you, if I were king there would be no more marriages. After all, only a married man may play the cuckold. Those who are married now, all (but one) shall live. The rest should keep as they are, happy and free, like you and me."

He repeated these lines in a sing-song fashion. "Happy and free, like you and me."

Then, serious to the core, "Get thee to a nunnery, you pretty fool. For your own safety. For the good of mankind. To a nunnery—go!"

At his, Hamlet stood impetuously, shook off her restraining hand, and paced away. Ophelia, all in tears, watched him disappear through the door at the end of the lobby. She lowered her head to her hands and sobbed heavily.

Polonius and the king emerged from behind the tapestries.

"Love?" said Claudius. "His feelings seem not like love to me. And as for madness, though his speech seemed illogical at times, it was not like madness."

He turned to Polonius, who was occupied comforting Ophelia, who for her part continued to sob quietly. When Polonius looked up, Claudius added, "There is something else--a sleeping snake within his mind, that once disturbed, could with its poison cause us a staggering collapse."

Polonius turned back to Ophelia. He patted her back and said softly to her, "You need not repeat what he said. We heard it all." Then, turning to the king, he objected lamely, "I still believe his unhappy state to be the result of neglected love."

Claudius regarded him skeptically, but rather than argue with the old man said decisively, "I shall send him to England for the demand of our neglected tribute. Perhaps the change will sort him out—new people, new challenges. There he can forget his unhappy preoccupations, and should fortune support us all, return renewed and himself once more."

Ophelia looked at him, an expression of despair. Polonius said, "You must do what you think best." He paused a moment, then said, "Might his mother not talk with him? You know it is said, 'An ounce of mother is worth a ton of priest.' Surely she might be round with him in the subtler ways in which mothers speak to sons."

"We shall see," Claudius answered. With that equivocal remark, he turned and paced away down the lobby.

"Come, Ophelia," Polonius said softly to her. "You have done your duty. No one could ask more of you." He dabbed at her cheeks with a silk handkerchief. She took it from him and blew her nose softly, but the tears continued to run.

Finally Ophelia stood in a labored fashion and eyes lowered, followed her father, who offered his arm protectively, back toward their quarters.

Chapter 28

Theater of the Absurd

The music was dreadful—loud and inharmonious. Along the walls stood an assortment of Danish nobles, clapping and stamping time. They leered at one another and laughed as if party to some obscene joke.

On the dance floor Hamlet was dancing with his mother. Nearby Ophelia was dancing with the king, who was grinning lecherously while he caressed her rump, to her obvious pleasure. Then, for some unknown reason, the queen broke off with Hamlet and slapped him, hard. Hamlet grasped her by the wrist and slipped his dagger out of its sheath with his other hand. He raised it over her face as if to strike, and she cowered away.

The nobles laughed and cheered. "Get the bitch!" shouted one of them, who seemed to be wearing a Greek thespian's comic mask. But then he pulled the mask away, revealing himself—Laertes! Laertes' ugly expression softened and he began to cry, at first sobbing silently as tears coursed down his cheeks, then loudly. Hamlet looked at Laertes in bewilderment. Then he looked at Horatio, an expression of such longing that Horatio thought his heart might break.

Horatio woke with a start. His own eyes were damp with tears. He lifted his head from the pillow and looked around in the half-light. It was very early. He wiped his eyes with the edge of his bedclothes.

It was a dream, he told himself silently. He raised himself onto his elbows and breathed heavily, then sank back onto his pillow. He pulled his blanket tightly about him. *A dream*, he concluded, and closed his eyes once more, only once more to see in all its vividness the fantastic scene—Hamlet standing, his dagger raised over his mother while Claudius lecherously caressed Ophelia, who giggled uncontrollably.

Finally Horatio lifted himself out of bed, shivering in the morning chill. The coal fire had long burnt out. He gathered a robe to him from a chair beside the bed, wrapped himself, and stepped hastily to a table under the pale window, where he poured water from a pewter ewer into a tin basin. He splashed water over his face and beard and scrubbed hard until he felt completely awake.

Horatio thought of the theater, of how actors could create and recreate simulations of the world that could capture our emotions and ideas. He remembered the Tragedians of the City, who had spent the night before the play in some guest quarters in the south wing of the palace. Hamlet was responsible for this rather fine accommodation, for when Polonius had offered them servant space, Hamlet had overruled him.

"I shall use them according to their deserts," Polonius had asserted in his typical bureaucratic fashion.

"God's blood, man!" Hamlet had replied. "Use every man according to his desert and who shall escape a whipping!"

He had softened his tone, then, but was still instructive. "Use them after your own honor and dignity. The less they deserve, the more merit can be seen in your, in our, generosity! Take them in."

Grudgingly, Polonius did so. Thus, rather than on moldy straw above the stables, the actors had slept in feather beds in the south wing. Horatio smiled. At the time he had thought to himself, *I wonder what Hamlet has in mind for these players…*

He slipped on his boots and wrapped his robe more tightly about himself. He opened a small cupboard above the table and removed some sausage and bread. Then from his meager bookshelf he selected a small volume of Aristotle's *Poetics* (*appropriate for drama*, he thought to himself) and settled himself in the chair under the window, which had now lightened considerably, to read and eat his breakfast. He opened a page at random (it was a well-thumbed volume) and began to read.

Since the objects of imitation are men in action, and these men must be either of a higher or a lower type (for moral character mainly answers to these divisions, goodness and badness being the distinguishing marks of moral differences), it follows that we must represent men either as better than in real life, or as worse, or as they are.

How true, Horatio thought to himself. *How might one ever, except due to the events that unfolded, have seen the king or the queen except as characters of a higher type. And Polonius...* Horatio sniggered to himself, but rapidly sobered. He chewed a morsel of sausage and read on.

Whether tragedy has as yet perfected its proper types or not, and whether it is to be judged in itself, or in relation also to the audience--this raises another question. Be that as it may, tragedy--as also comedy--was at first mere improvisation.

Improvisation--there was a key word, he thought. *What were Hamlet's best efforts through all these struggles, except a desperate form of improvisation? I will need to use that word in my report. But the players were certainly not improvising.* But he was getting ahead of himself.

Horatio crammed the last bit of bread into his mouth and got to his feet, leaving the volume of Aristotle on his table. Still chewing, he returned his sleeping robe to a hook on the wall, swallowed, and began to dress carefully in his court clothing. When he was satisfied that however inadequate his wardrobe might be, that he had done his best, he left his quarters and headed for the scriptorium, the word 'improvisation' reverberating in his mind. He had a lot more writing to do.

Once in the scriptorium, Horatio prepared his materials rapidly. Before settling down to write he slipped Cleopatra a few carefully sliced morsels of his breakfast sausage. The cat chewed it greedily, its head and jaws jerking slightly as it gnawed a bit of gristle.

"Would you eat another cat?" Horatio mused half aloud, watching the cat eat. *It may be only metaphor, but we humans certainly 'eat' each other,* he thought fatalistically.

The cat licked its paw and methodically cleaned its whiskers. It stared a moment at Horatio, then moved to him to receive his expected caress. Horatio stroked it repeatedly, enjoying its pleasure as if he were purring himself. Then he picked it up and set it on its cushion, where still purring, it pricked and released the cushion's surface with its claws, as if plumping the pillow but with a kind of repressed violence. Finally the cat settled itself, looked once more at Horatio, and then settled into a doze.

Horatio wiped his greasy fingers on a handkerchief, dipped his quill in the inkpot and began to write.

Hamlet was excited, and very pleased, to meet the Tragedians of the City once again. The oldest of the company, a man who had assumed the name of 'Thespis,' was a particular favorite of the prince. When they were escorted into the hall, Hamlet went to each in turn, shaking their hands and greeting each warmly by name. It was obvious that they, too, remembered Hamlet or their ability to feign friendship was so ingrained in them that, had Hamlet been merely a merchant, they would have shown him similar happy gratitude and deference.

"You, gentlemen," said Hamlet, "will save my benighted soul!"

Hamlet was always able to express some hyperbolic sentiment when it suited him.

"I say, these pedestrian bodies that inhabit my world leave me excited as dust at the roadside when there's been no traffic for three weeks!" He winked at me, as if to say 'Of course I don't mean you,' but I was already smiling. He turned then to Thespis, and said, "A speech, a speech, we must have a speech!"

Thespis frowned (or perhaps feigned a frown—who knows?) and said, "Is there a particular speech, my lord?"

"You recited a speech once recounting the murder of Priam—it was from Aeneus' *Tale to Dido*. Please, please, do you remember? It began something like this."

Hamlet proceeded to recite an opening line of some merit, iambic syllables bounding with energy, but the old man shook his head.

"'Tis not so?" asked Hamlet. "It begins with Pyrrhus, no?" Thespis nodded. Hamlet tried again.

The rugged Pyrrhus, he, whose sable arms,

Black as his purpose did the night resemble.

The old man smiled and continued with a three-minute monologue recounting the horrors of Pyrrhus' intrusion into the royal chambers of Ilium, how Pyrrhus ignored the screaming protests of Hecuba, Priam's wife, and with his great bronze sword skewered Priam before her very eyes, thence proceeding to cut him to pieces.

The remarkable thing about Thespis' performance was that at the end of it the old actor was actually crying in sympathy with the tears of Hecuba, and the elicited tears of the gods, who were supposed to be crying along with her.

Polonius, who had come in with the actors, groaned aloud and protested that the scene was wildly overdone. But Hamlet ignored his protests and clasped the hands of old Thespis in admiration.

"Ignore him," he said to Thespis of Polonius. "He's only interested in bawdy jokes or some silly dancing. Or he sleeps."

Polonius frowned at Hamlet's characterization of him (although this accurate depiction of Polonius' foibles amused me).

When Hamlet had instructed Polonius on how to house the actors, and Polonius, somewhat chastened, was leading them away, Hamlet held old Thespis back for a moment. I stood at Hamlet's side. He looked at me briefly, and then, as if making up his mind, turned again to Thespis.

"Listen, old friend. Can your company still perform *The Murder of Gonzago*, you know, the Italian play in which Gonzago's brother kills him in order to steal his fortune and his wife?"

"Oh, yes, my lord, we played it just weeks ago in Bremen."

"I'd like you and your company to perform it here before the court, tomorrow, or perhaps the night after. You could do that, could you not?"

"Yes, my lord."

"And if I were to ask you to insert a few dozen extra lines into the play, your players could memorize them and make them a more or less natural part of the story?"

"Of course, my lord. We are actors. It is our trade and, dare I say, our profession?"

Hamlet smiled knowingly. "I will deliver them to you this very evening."

He pointed at the doorway, through which even now the last of the players was following Polonius. "Well, best follow along, then, no? I am delighted that you are here in Elsinore."

"The pleasure is ours, sir. And if we can be of any further service?" Hamlet shook his head. The old man smiled at Hamlet, bowed, turned, and followed.

Hamlet turned to me, and, perhaps in response to my raised eyebrows, said somewhat curtly, "Oh, don't ask yet. I will provide you with ample explanation in due time." He smiled shrewdly, then declaimed dramatically, with gestures and all,

"Besides, the winds in the forest and the waves on the sea,
All beat their times, do you not agree?
And when time's beaten rocks into sand on the shore,
Then the truth comes stealing through a hidden door."

He smirked at his own rhyming. "Really!" he added, then turned away from me and left the room.

I stood there, suddenly a bit paralyzed with apprehension, as if that hidden door were already swinging open to reveal something terrible but true. It was only two nights later that the truth truly blazed out before us, although perhaps only Hamlet and I were fully aware of its import.

At this point, Horatio laid his pen aside. He felt hungry, but also a bit tired. He had been sleeping poorly of late, and Osric's recent message of King Fortinbras' impatience had set him on edge. He decided to lay his head down on his arms on the table, just briefly, to rest his eyes.

As his eyes closed he caught once again his dream vision of Claudius dancing with Ophelia. His heart raced momentarily in disgust. Then he slept, dreamlessly.

Chapter 29

To Be, or Not to Be?

When Horatio awoke, it was to the smell of hot food. He sat up and rubbed his eyes. The light was low in the window, and to his left was a plate containing two wedges of liver pie and some cooked carrots. He looked around him, but no one was there. Beside the plate, written in a strange hand on some of his own paper, was a note.

Horatio

Your work is far too important to have you lack nourishment. I have taken it on myself to provide you with some supper in the hope that you will continue your work. I read the first few pages...

At this point Horatio snapped awake and reached for the paperweight that covered his draft. He could immediately see that it had been moved, but when he picked up the first few sheets he saw that they had not been tampered with.

...but I did not remove anything. I can see why the king might wish a clear report of events. Enjoy your dinner, but please, make haste with your writing.

Osric

Horatio's heart rate gradually steadied. *I must do something about the security of my report*, he thought. Although he didn't much like Osric, he didn't fear him. Yet this work was too important to have servants pawing through it at their leisure. He resolved to remove the work to his own quarters when not writing, even though that might entail some inconvenience, and perhaps even a little danger.

He slipped the knife from his belt, and using the wooden spoon provided by Osric (*how peasant-like*, he thought), he dug into the pie. *There is no ale*, he grumbled to himself, but then, as if bidden like a servant, his thoughts shifted to what he had to write about next: Hamlet's darkest contemplations.

It is only fitting that I reveal some more of Hamlet's state of mind at this point in my history. Indeed, if the mind of man matter at all in the outcome of things, surely the mind of a prince matters more than most. And Hamlet had an extraordinary mind.

It was a few nights after Hamlet's encounter with the ghost of his father, old King Hamlet. The prince had called me to his rooms (young Yedric had fetched me), and indicated that he wished to talk.

(This was very like some of our habits at Wittenberg. We would usually study the required texts on our own, but in the manner of Socrates, Hamlet often sought me out to question me. It was a process he used to clarify his own thinking, and I was grateful for its benefits to my own understanding. Sometimes he would extemporize his own thoughts at length, as well. In Wittenberg, however, our colloquies were usually thrilling and exploratory, not gloomy and conclusive.)

Frowning, he directed me to a chair across the table from him. There were wine and goblets on the table between us, but he offered me none, and he had obviously had little or nothing to drink himself. He sat facing me, his chin in his hands initially, and he rolled his eyes a little as if trying to recollect something. Then he straightened up and raised his hand. He even pointed at me for a moment, and then let his hand drop to the table.

"Why do we live, Horatio?" he asked in exasperation.

I looked at him, wondering whether or not he wished a response. In true rhetorical fashion he went on.

"I can tell you," he said fatalistically. "It's because until our life is removed we have little choice."

Here he paused, as if to gather force for his gloomy contemplation.

"Oh, I know. We're supposed to be able to choose freely. But given the constraints life throws up around us—the boundaries of parentage, class, language, church—I cannot but think that our choices are determined from the day we are born." He sighed.

"Tell me truly," he demanded softly. His voice was less conjectural and his expression much more serious. "Have you never considered taking your own life? After all, do we not love to sleep? And is death not simply a universal, extended sleep?"

"But my lord," I stammered. "Surely it is against God's law." I shivered, but he looked up at me and gave a wan smile, then diverted his conversation to another subject.

"I know I have not been forthcoming about my own encounter with the ghost of my father. I propose now to tell you what happened. I do so because you, among all the court, are the only man I can trust. Do you understand? I am willing to place my fate into your hands, and insofar as knowledge can lead inevitably to danger (as Adam and Eve both found, to their dismay and profound disillusionment), this telling may put you, too, in danger."

He looked at me steadily. I could see the reflection of the candle's flame in his steady eye. "Will you hear?" he asked.

My heart was thudding in my chest. I swallowed and after only a brief pause, nodded.

"The ghost, my father, told me a story, an ugly story, the story of his murder."

I bent toward Hamlet, as my chest continued to thump. "Murder!" I exclaimed.

"He told me, in no uncertain terms and some detail, that the story of his death we have all been provided, the 'death by snakebite', was a fabrication. He told me the true story in great detail, some of which I will spare you here. The location of the death was accurate—in the orchard. However, as my father put it, the snake who stole my father's life now wears his crown."

I must have gasped audibly, for Hamlet raised his hand as if to quiet me. Then he went on.

"My uncle poisoned my father by pouring a distillation of the juice of hebona into his ear while he was sleeping. In subsequent days Claudius went on to seduce my mother, another sordid chapter to the story."

I shuddered involuntarily.

Hamlet touched my arm and sighed. "My father—his apparition, perhaps his soul—is now in Purgatory awaiting God's fate—unshriven, unannealed, suffering away his sin sufficiently, it is to be hoped, that he yet be granted God's mercy for eternal life."

I crossed myself, and Hamlet nodded at the expression of my piety.

"There's something further," he added.

"What, more?" I asked, already appalled.

"As the morning air approached, my father's spirit gave me his last command: to avenge his murder."

I gazed at him, my consciousness grappling as if with air to find some word of solace, of advice, that might mean something to my prince...my friend.

"What will you do?" I finally asked, for I understood all too plainly that a family murder demands revenge. Yet regicide?! It was beyond imagining. All the same, here it was, the final straw, the key to unlock so many mysteries—Hamlet's irritability, his unpredictability, his...madness.

"I swore to the ghost to avenge my father," he finally said. "To tell you true, I *was* at first maddened beyond all imagining at the idea of Claudius' perfidy. My mind whirled with images of cutting my uncle to pieces—before my mother!" Hamlet grinned, then winced.

"Now I am not so sure," he finally said. "I cannot be certain whether or not, as you warned me on the night in question, the ghost is real, or that his story is real. And yet," and here he grinned again, as if at some private knowledge, "since I was old enough to count I was consistently unsure of Claudius' loyalty to my father. I've always disliked the man. Perhaps even more now that..."

He once again changed subject suddenly.

"You know that Ophelia will no longer see me," he said matter-of-factly.

"My lord, I had no such knowledge until now."

"Yes, well, it seems her foolish father holds me in suspicion as some rake intent upon staining her virgin chastity. God's blood, the pestilence of such prudish paternity makes my blood boil. But she has gone along with his instruction that my courtship, such as it is, be repelled, and that, as they say, is that."

My mind was racing. I had always known that Hamlet held a special fondness for Ophelia, and she was indisputably a beauty that held the promise of happiness. I was unsure what would upset Hamlet more—the insulting mistrust of Polonius or the loss of access to young Ophelia.

"Well," Hamlet went on, "'Tis all one, as they say." He sighed heavily once more.

"Listen," he finally said. "I need you to consider something with me, the subject of my initial question. Why do we live?" He looked at me in true puzzlement, and there was something in his voice that once again nagged painfully at me, pricking me with anxiety. I began to feel some real alarm. But there was familiarity to his posture that told me that now was not the time to interrupt.

"Is that not the real question for all of us?" he continued. "To be or not to be? After all, what is it to die? Is it not like sleep—an endless sleep? And who among us does not take refuge nightly in his own land of dreams? For if death is really nothing more than sleep, a balmy satisfaction from the day's endless cares and frictions, who would not willingly seek it out? Today? This minute? We could all our own comfort create with a bare blade."

He fingered the handle of his dagger suggestively, and then drew it out of its sheathe. He tested its edge on the meat of his thumb. I wanted to reach across and snatch it away, but I sat, paralyzed with fascination.

"But sleep, there...there's the real problem," he continued. "Because what dreams may come when we enter that sleep of death? That must make us pause and think. For surely the pangs and irritations that make up even the most tranquil life are sufficient to make one long for death."

I looked at him in incredulity.

"No?" he said innocently. "Come on. The officiousness of bureaucratic necessity, the scorn of one's peers, the idiocy of our entertainments, the evanescence of our pleasures..." his voice trailed off, then added in a near whisper, "the pain of disprized love...are these not enough to drive one to desperation?" He lowered his eyes momentarily.

"What is death," he finally asked, "but an undiscovered country from which no one ever returns?" And as if to answer himself, he added, "And so, we bear our current miseries as best we can, unwilling to risk an unknown eternal future. *That* concern alone, I would contend, is what generates this extended misery we call a life. And meanwhile, those desires and obligations we deem important lose all their luster, and our motivations wither like autumn stalks." He crossed himself. I, too, did so once again.

"So, let us drink," he said decisively, and poured out two goblets of wine. He passed me one, and without awaiting his cue, I swallowed some greedily. He merely smiled, and raised his own goblet to his lips.

"I will need your assistance soon," he said, after we had drunk.

"Whatever I can do, I am yours," I replied.

"I am grateful. Tomorrow night the Tragedians of the City will be performing before the court. They will play *The Murder of Gonzago.*"

I took a deep breath and let it out. I knew the play.

"Within it is a scene coming near the murder of my father by my uncle. Observe the king carefully." He looked at me intently.

"It is said that guilty people who have seen their own crimes enacted in a play have been so struck with remorse that they have confessed their personal evils. Might the king not react to this story in a telling fashion? He may blush or blanche, he may startle. Who knows? I am as certain of this as I am of anything, though, that this play may be just the thing to catch the conscience of the king."

And so I was committed. We would watch the play the next night.

At this point Horatio raised his head. His neck ached. He couldn't remember when he had lit the candle, but it, too, was burning down. Cleopatra was softly and industriously licking the last greasy morsels of pie from Horatio's plate. She looked up. Horatio put down his pen and gently removed the cat to its cushion. He blew the ink on his last sheet, gathered the evening's work together, and placed it at the bottom of the pile.

He stacked it and all his previous writings together. From a drawer he withdrew a length of ribbon, with which he tied the manuscripts into a large bundle, securely held. Tucking it under his arm, he blew out the candle, and in the dim light from the window, opened the door and left the room. The cat watched him inscrutably, then lowered its head onto its paws and closed its eyes.

Chapter 30

Halfway to Reassurance

Polonius' apartments in the castle were comparatively spacious, featuring a large office area devoted to his work as counselor, servants' quarters, a small cooking area (well tended by Sven, Polonius' Swedish cook), a comfortable parlor with a large fireplace, and bedrooms for each of the family. The smallest of these was Ophelia's room, a cozy chamber featuring a large wardrobe, her own washing table, an area under the window where she could write, a loom to one side where she often whiled away an afternoon weaving, and of course, a comfortable bed suited to a maiden of gentry.

It was early afternoon on a grey overcast day, and dim indoors. Ophelia sat at her writing desk, tempted to light a candle but conscious that such extravagance, even for her family, would not meet with her father's approval. Polonius was elsewhere in the castle on royal business. Ophelia had just read Laertes' letter, a private missive to her alone. At least Reynaldo had been sensible enough not to deliver Laertes' letter to her through her father. He was a decent man for a servant, she thought. Supposedly he was leaving for Paris himself, soon. She cast her eyes over the letter again.

Dear Sister,

The unhappiness you reported in your letter is precisely the kind of difficulty I warned you of prior to my departure. Did I not tell you that Hamlet's affections are not his to give? Did I not suggest that the loss of his love, for whatever reason, could cause you grief? And so, at the hands of our father, it has happened. But more than the harshness of a father's hand is to blame here. Surely you cannot blame him for Hamlet's madness, or your lack of judgment, for that matter.

Your description of Hamlet's various behaviors seems to me nothing less than the description of a madman. Then can you not see, and with some gratitude at that, that our father's instructions have been for the best, by providing for your safety? For to have knit your soul too closely to Hamlet's could have left you indissolubly tied to a man who might cause you nothing but even more heartache than you have recently expressed to me.

It is important above all that you remember the fourth commandment from your catechism (which I know you review with all faith): "Honor thy father." Has our father not cared for us, granted us the material basis of a wealthy and hopeful life? Then how can we question his regulation of our desires? He loves us and has shown his love in all ways, even though his discipline is sometimes initially painful.

Remember though, sister, that I hold your happiness and affections as key to my own fulfillment. We are of one blood, and as you suffer, so suffer I. Therefore be of good cheer, and even though it may go hard for you for some time, my thoughts are with you, always.

Remember, too, that God spared us even as he took our mother from us. Although this loss undoubtedly changed the management of our own upbringing, and would probably be felt as a greater loss had we not been so young at her passing, we must surely understand that as God granted us our very breath and life, He intends for us greater things. Then with what ingratitude and impiety would we spurn Him were we to disobey our father and to hold our personal miseries as more important than the direction God must hold for our lives within the purview of our father's direction?

I hold your image in my heart and wish you only the satisfaction of ultimate happiness, my dear sister. Therefore gather your courage and fortitude and fend off these feelings of despair whose demons you say trouble your sleep and your waking. In the fullness of time God will grant you the happiness you deserve, I am sure of it. Until then, know that I remain your loving and supportive brother,

Laertes

Ophelia sighed. She laid the letter back down on her desk, then picked it up again and placed it in a drawer, underneath other writing materials. She did not want her father to see Laertes' letters. It seemed at the moment that Laertes' words were all that sustained her, but even they weren't very helpful.

She got to her feet and moved to the small altar featuring a statue of the Holy Mother of God. She knelt on the cushion in front of it and began to pray.

In the castle lobby leading to the royal chambers, Rosencrantz and Guildenstern stood in low-voiced conference. The gloomy light through the window merely highlighted Rosencrantz's mood.

"Well, what will we tell him?" Guildenstern asked urgently.

Rosencrantz thought a moment. He replied slowly. "The prince was kind enough to keep our secret, so why should we reveal it? Surely we have learned enough of the legal profession in our time in Wittenberg to enable us to report little or nothing in plenty of superfluous words that nonetheless seem revealing and significant. Simply follow my lead."

Guildenstern looked at Rosencrantz doubtfully, but at that moment a servant popped his head out the door of the king's chambers and indicated to them that they were wanted. The two men followed him inside, where they bowed low to the king and queen. Polonius, too, was present, but he remained seated to one side, watching. Gertrude nodded to them absently, but Claudius approached them energetically and said, "Well, what have you learned? Rosencrantz? You say." Gertrude examined them uneasily from her sofa.

"My liege, in our single meeting so far we spoke at length with the prince."

"And? How did he receive you?"

"Most like a gentleman," Rosencrantz answered, and Guildenstern nodded energetically beside him. "He even shared a joke with us, although it was out of keeping with his general mood, which is decidedly morose."

Claudius frowned. "What did you discuss?" he asked.

Rosencrantz coughed gently behind a gloved hand. "He talked much of honesty, sir, although the drift of his meaning was sometimes a bit obscure."

At this moment Polonius came to life. "Ah, honesty, yes," he added. "He told *me* that an honest man is to be a single diamond to be found on a beach of sand, like one man picked out of ten thousand. Terribly pessimistic, I would say, would you not agree? One in a hundred, maybe, if one were mildly disappointed in life..." He broke off as Claudius gave him a disapproving look.

Guildenstern decided to help. "He seemed suspicious and at the same time, completely indifferent to the world and its ways in some regards, but also immensely disappointed by life, as if a heavy weight pressed upon him. He welcomed us, though, especially when we told him of the players."

"The players?" Claudius asked.

"Yes, my liege," intervened Polonius. "A company of players has arrived and is here about the court, and Hamlet has engaged them to perform for the court tomorrow evening. In fact, he has pressed me to ensure that your majesties be invited to attend."

"Is this true?" Claudius asked Rosencrantz.

"Indeed, my lord."

"Well then, by all means, encourage these delights. Anything—that it might pull the prince out of his dreamy despair! And of course, Gertrude and I will attend. See to the arrangements, Polonius." Claudius gestured imperiously, and Polonius nodded.

Gertrude rose from the sofa and joined the gentlemen. "We thank you for your efforts on behalf of us and of the prince. Please, be at home here at the court. We shall eagerly await the play, whatever it may be, and will attend with pleasure, especially if it might help our son."

"I am sure I speak for Guildenstern as well as myself when I say that we are yours to command." Rosencrantz bowed once more, and Guildenstern followed his lead.

The king looked at Gertrude a moment, then nodded at the two men. "You may go, then," he said with some finality, and after bowing once more, the two turned and left the room.

"I remember being an actor in the university myself, when I was a youth," Polonius said wistfully.

Claudius shot him an impatient glance, then turned back to Gertrude. "Well," he said. "The two gentlemen--were we expecting anything more?"

"Sometimes it seems as if *we* are in some giant play," Gertrude responded. "But I don't know my lines."

Polonius smiled politely.

"Polonius," Gertrude added, "please ensure that everything needed for this entertainment is provided in a timely manner. Anything we can do to bring Hamlet up from his depressed state is a line of action we must pursue."

Polonius nodded, gave a short bow, and left the chamber. Claudius touched Gertrude's hand, then walked to the window and gazed out. "How often it is that the things we see are not what we see," he finally said. "Do you not think?"

Weighing his words, Gertrude merely looked at him.

Chapter 31

The Play's the Thing

Horatio sat uncomfortably on the oak seat in the scriptorium. The cat was nowhere to be seen, but the table was well lit with two candles this evening. (Horatio had found them when he first entered the chamber. Osric had left them with an encouraging note that said: *Write, write.*)

He dipped his quill in the open ink and then paused again, thinking of the cavity under the floorboard in his quarters where he had hidden the rest of the manuscript. He didn't know how much power Osric might wield in the palace, but he wanted the opportunity to re-examine, at least once, all that he had written, before Osric might place it before king Fortinbras.

He dipped the quill again and began to write.

In the evening, when I arrived in the hall (redesigned by the players to serve as a theatre), Hamlet was busy with Thespis. I could not but overhear some of their conversation.

"I know you are an actor, Thespis, and one of the finest I have met," Hamlet was saying. "But I need to be sure of these scenes. Look you now, it is important that your company's performance be more natural than..." gesturing futilely, he sought how to finish, then said, "...than nature herself."

Thespis frowned, stared a moment at the floor, then looked back at the prince.

"Ah, yes, I know that's an impossibility," Hamlet continued. "But it's the goal that any actor must aim at, to hold a mirror up to nature, to create the forms and attitudes of real life in such fashion that any observer would take them for truth were he not *aware* that he was being fooled. You know how so many second-rate actors are: exaggerating, clumsy, absurd! I'd rather the town crier called out my lines than have them blustered by some inadequate player."

Thespis nodded, a rueful expression on his face. "I am forced by my own experience to agree, my lord. But I think you will find our company up to the task you envisage."

But Hamlet was not finished.

"Further," he said, "you know how immature, nay, silly, many *audiences* are, how they hope for foolish lapses and clumsiness that might serve as farce or weak comedy, but that in the case of any serious drama simply appeal to the uninitiated and ignorant." He thought a moment, then said, "Polonius might sometimes be an example of such, although he did act in university as a young man..."

Thespis smiled. He got the message, although had anyone lectured him like this, aside from Hamlet, he would probably have walked away. But from Hamlet, it seemed, any criticism was worth Thespis' hearing. Hamlet cleared his throat and spoke again.

"Too many people simply misunderstand the importance of the theatre. They see it merely as a pleasant way to pass the time, a bit of diversion. Those of us who truly know the theatre, *we* comprehend its mystery and its true function: to show us ourselves."

Hamlet smiled at the older man. "Enough of this, though," he said, and Thespis nodded. Hamlet clapped him on the shoulder and said, "Ensure that the players be ready, will you?"

Thespis nodded again. "We will be ready anon," he said, and moved toward the dressing area where presumably the players were donning costumes and make-up, the magical trappings of the illusion they would so soon create. It was only then that Hamlet came to me, and when he spoke, he seemed to make the dross of my unworthy life glow golden.

"Horatio," he said.

"My lord?"

"I've never told you adequately just how much you mean to me."

I smiled, both pleased and wary.

"You are my best, and indeed, my only friend, Horatio." He must have seen my surprised frown, for he hastened to say, "It is not some foolish impulse speaking, or some flattering attempt to draw more loyalty from you that causes me to say so." He smiled at me in a way I had not seen for weeks, a visual expression of what must have been momentary good cheer.

"Besides," he continued, "what point would there be for me to flatter you? All you have is your basic nature and goodness to feed and clothe you. But I need you to know that your even-handed virtues, your acceptance of life as it is without allowing its pains and rewards to undermine your judgment, these make you the man that my soul has chosen for her friend. These traits are truly enviable, and further, your nearby embodiment and expression of these habits of attitude create a foundation of safety for my own...lapses." And here he frowned once more.

I am sure that my eyes must have watered momentarily at this point. He looked away, yet I know that he could see the fathomless gratitude I felt.

"You always knew this, though, did you not?" he said as he turned away, probably to spare me the indignity of seeing my tears, although he saw Polonius entering the far end of the hall. I squeezed down my feelings, and he turned back to me, speaking even more softly.

"You know the details I have since told you of my experience of my father's ghost. You know the accusations made against my uncle by this otherworldly tale." He breathed deeply. "This play will create a scene much like the scene in which the ghost claimed that he, my father, died. Watch my uncle. Watch him closely. I am sure that if he be guilty he will recognize the event and that he will react in some revealing way." Hamlet looked at me closely. I nodded.

"I will, my lord."

"I have never doubted that I may rely upon you," he concluded.

Polonius had made his way toward us, even as many of the younger nobles of the court (escorting young women, of course) and other hangers on were entering the hall. Hamlet greeted him deferentially (although I could tell his attitude was all in irony).

"My lord, my lord, you were once an actor, were you not?"

Polonius looked at Hamlet as if unsure just what to expect, then he seemed to preen himself slightly and smilingly replied.

"I played Caesar in a play about the murder of Julius Caesar. Brutus killed me in the Capitol."

"What a 'brutus' thing to do!" exclaimed Hamlet, and smirked. Polonius could only smile at this wordplay, but when Hamlet peremptorily ordered him to prepare the players, he frowned once more. Still, he hastened to do it. Hamlet *was* the prince, and to be obeyed.

Only moments later a herald entered and blew a customary phrase on his trumpet. "Their royal highnesses Claudius and Gertrude!" he announced. Those of us in the hall quickly knelt, and the king, with the queen on his arm, entered the room. Claudius glanced around as if pleased with himself. He smiled and indicated that we should rise, and then approached Hamlet who looked at him inscrutably.

"How fare you, prince Hamlet?" the king asked.

"Oh, excellent well! I eat the air that nourishes every living thing! Although chickens prefer grain and pigs their swill."

"This answer puzzles me, Hamlet. I can't quite take hold of these words."

"Ah, but they've already flown away, sailed on the wind of speech, gone, gone..." Hamlet trailed off. Then he said, "But, well, there will be many words tonight! In the play! The forthcoming play! You will be amazed!" He gazed off into the sky painted onto the backdrop, silky clouds on a cerulean firmament. "These tragedians are truly the makers of fine illusion, so fine we think it real," he said, and looked intently at Claudius.

"Do you know the story?" asked Gertrude.

"Ah, that would be telling," said Hamlet to her. "But since you've asked, I *can* tell you that it's a story of murder and knavery, one to make your very spine quiver. Oh, yes."

The queen looked sideways at him, but Claudius tugged her elbow and guided her to the two elegant chairs that had been brought at Polonius' instruction to serve as theatre thrones for the two of them.

Gertrude turned her head and asked, "Will you sit with me, Hamlet?"

"No, Mother," he said, catching sight of Ophelia. "That shining magnet you see yonder," and he pointed at Ophelia, "pulls my very metal." He walked toward Ophelia, who, upon seeing Hamlet's approach, lowered her eyes, and then dipped in a graceful curtsy. She gathered her skirts and sat carefully on one of the low cushioned benches that had been arranged for the audience.

"My lady, may I lie in your lap?" Hamlet inquired.

Ophelia put her hand on her bosom and said, as if insulted, "*No*, my lord." Even the queen raised her eyebrows at his gross importunity.

"I merely meant my head upon your lap." He eyed her for her reaction, then added, "Did you think I meant country matters?"

The sly pun on 'country' was not lost on Ophelia, and she flushed. She opened and closed her mouth twice before managing to say, "I did not think so, no. Of course, you may put your head in my lap if you're going to sit on the floor beside me." She looked at him as if to challenge him, as if to say, I can play along if necessary. But Hamlet took it further.

"You know, that *is* a fair thought to put between a maid's legs..."

"*What* my lord?"

"Well..." He paused a moment, then shook his head guilelessly and mouthed, "Nothing. No thing. Not one thing." His voice dying away now. "Nothing."

Ophelia looked away, but Hamlet had already reclined beside her and was about to lay his head down when one of the players came forward to announce, rather by rote, I thought, "For us and for our tragedy, we beg your hearing patiently."

"Is this a prologue, or a prayer?" Hamlet asked rudely.

"It *is* brief, my lord," Ophelia interjected.

Hamlet turned and gazed at her intently for a moment. "As woman's love," he said, and then he turned to look at his mother.

Gertrude frowned, but did not meet his eye. The king looked at him sharply and asked, "Do you know the play, Hamlet? Have you heard the plot? Surely there is no offence in it?"

"No offence in the world!" Hamlet exclaimed. "The play is called *The Mousetrap*. In it there *is* a murder, but it comes off rather as a jest. The story recounts the murder, by his brother, of a duke named Gonzago. It's a knavish piece of work, enough to make a criminal shudder. But your majesty and we who have free souls need not worry over such ugliness. Later the brother gains the love of Gonzago's wife. The play was originally published in Italian, a very choice composition, but it has been well adapted to the Danish tongue, as you shall see. Ah, there are Baptista, Gonzago's wife, and the duke now..." His voice trailed off as a distinctly royal couple came onstage. Servants on all sides of the audience extinguished their torches, to the expectant 'ahs' of the audience. The stage leapt brilliantly to life, the only lit area in the hall.

"You are as good as a chorus, my lord," whispered Ophelia.

"Ssshh!" whispered Hamlet in return.

I was standing to one side in the audience. Fortunately the king and queen were seated at the very front, and there was sufficient light from the stage to allow me to observe their reactions. I watched carefully, although I was continually distracted by the story unfolding on stage.

The duke wore a kind of coronet and a heavy cloak over his other finery. The duchess wore a long scarlet silk dress, accented by a blue scarf. She appeared younger than her lord. He was first to speak. He took her by the hands and gazed into her face.

"My love, we've lived within our marriage vows,
Like birds, anest, upon some supple boughs;
And through the many years we've happ'ly thrived
With what both we, and Fortune, have contrived.
But now, as age has put me in decline,
Like withered leaves upon some autumn vine,
I know my death will likely make us part;
And so I hope that you can give your heart
To one as kind as I..."

At this the duchess interrupted him.

"Oh confound the rest!

Such hope would be pure treason in my breast!
In second love I'd surely be accursed:
None wed the second but who killed the first.
A second time I kill my husband dead,
When second husband kisses me in bed.
To try to love another would be wrong,
And I would feel its evil before long.
So if a wife might need to feel new care
Or find another, fresher life to share,
God's justice would soon mark how she betrays
And number ever shorter her life's days.
Her motives, wind in sail, might rest on thrift,
But love's light craft would float away adrift,
And leave her cast away upon life's shore,
Bereft of others, lonely ever more.
I will not ever render such a sin,
For gaming such with life one cannot win.
May God provide me everlasting strife,
If once a widow, ever I be wife.

The duke tried gamely to convince her, realistically, I thought.

I do believe you think what now you speak,
But what we do determine oft we break.
Purpose is but the slave to memory,
Of violent birth, but poor validity.
Which now, the fruits unripe, stick on the tree,
But fall unshaken when they mellow be.
What to ourselves in passion we propose,
The passion ending doth the purpose lose.
The world is not for aye, nor 'tis not strange
That e'en our loves should with our fortunes change.
For 'tis a question left us yet to prove,

Does love lead fortune, or fortune love?
But orderly to end where I begun,
Our wills and fates do so contrary run
That our devices still are overthrown:
Our thoughts are ours, their ends none of our own.
So think thou wilt no second husband wed,
But die thy thoughts when thy first lord is dead.

The duchess was adamant, however, swearing that she would never marry again, no matter the circumstances. How did she say it?

...pursue me lasting strife
If once a widow ever I be wife!

Of course, Hamlet couldn't let this opportunity pass. He called over to Gertrude, "Mother, how do you like this play?" I didn't know whether or not he was smiling. Was it his bitterness speaking?

"The lady doth protest too much, methinks," Gertrude answered gamely.

"Oh, but she'll keep *her* word!" Hamlet turned again to the play, and I couldn't but think that the queen must have been annoyed nearly beyond measure. She kept glancing over at Hamlet, an expression of deep anxiety flickering across her face. She grasped Claudius' hand. He patted it but kept his attention on the play's action.

By this time the duchess had left the stage, and the duke was lying on some cushions in a contrived garden, sleeping. At this moment the character Lucianus, brother to the duke, entered and began reciting how he had collected his poison, a murky mixture in a green vial, which he held up for the audience. He then knelt beside the duke, and with one hand very lightly caressing the duke's coronet, he began to pour the fluid into the duke's ear.

"The king rises!" exclaimed Ophelia, and the audience members clambered raggedly to their feet. Hamlet was already up, moving swiftly to Claudius, who stood staring in shock and surprise at the actors.

"He poisoned him in the garden for his estate," Hamlet nearly shouted at the king, who paused, then turned and advanced deliberately toward him.

"Give me some light," Claudius commanded in a hoarse voice.

"Light, light," shouted Polonius, who was moving to join them. Gertrude was standing, gazing at the scene in shock. Both Lucianus *and* the duke had scrambled to their feet, and the musicians who had been accompanying the action had ceased to play. The king stood staring at Hamlet, who simply smirked at him.

"What, frighted with false fire?" he said to the Claudius.

Claudius stared at him with a palpable fury. But he was obviously uncertain how to proceed. "Away!" Claudius finally said to the assembled group, and he turned, walked to Gertrude (whom he took by the arm) and exited the theatre, followed by the buzzing crowd. All except me.

"Well, Horatio, you must have seen."

"I noted him very well my lord."

"On the scene of the poisoning?"

"Yes, my lord. He was very upset." I thought of the king's flushed face, his angered countenance.

"Ah, let the stricken deer go weep! How does the verse go?"

I provided the last couplet for him. "For some must watch while some must sleep, thus runs the world away."

"Indeed," said Hamlet. "Indeed. Thus runs the world away..."

For a few moments the theatre was silent. Even the players had scampered off to some hidey hole. Then, before we could even get our breath from all the excitement, Rosencrantz returned, followed by Guildenstern. One might have thought they were joined at the hip. Hamlet had picked up one of the musicians' recorders from where it had been dropped. He tooted on it annoyingly.

The two men approached, and when they had Hamlet's attention, they bowed. Upon resuming his upright posture, Rosencrantz ventured, "My lord, may we have a word with you?"

Hamlet removed the recorder from his lips and gave Rosencrantz a generous grin. "A whole history, if you wish," he said.

"My lord, the king, in his retirement, is in extreme distemper."

"With drink?" asked Hamlet, and once more tooted on the small flute.

Rosencrantz frowned, and moved once again before Hamlet, who had turned away. "No, my lord, with choler. His anger is clear for any to see."

"You might more profitably inform his doctor. Purgation is a useful remedy, but such purgation as *I* might give him might produce only more choler." He turned to Guildenstern. "You. Guildenstern. You love music, do you not?"

Guildenstern shrugged, guiltily it seemed to me. "Indifferent well, my lord."

Hamlet moved to him and pushed the recorder toward him. "Will you play upon this flute?"

"I cannot, my lord."

"Oh, please, you are too, too modest. These are the stops here. You blow in the end here and produce most eloquent music." He pushed the flute at Guildenstern again, who looked at Rosencrantz as if for help.

"I know no touch of it, my lord," Guildenstern finally said.

Hamlet grasped him by the arm and spun him to pull him face to face. But even then Guildenstern could not face his eye.

"It is as easy as lying," Hamlet shouted. "You fool. You would play upon *me*. You want to know *my* stops. And truth be told," he said, pointing to himself, "there is much music in this little organ. But you cannot make *me* speak, either."

Rosencrantz stared at the two, Guildenstern struggling to escape Hamlet's grip, still looking at the floor. Hamlet finally let him go.

At that moment Polonius entered, and Hamlet deliberately walked in the other direction, tooting on the recorder for all he was worth. Guildenstern moved to Rosencrantz, as if for comfort.

"My prince, may I have a word?" asked Polonius disingenuously. He caught up to Hamlet, who now was leaning on a pillar, examining the recorder.

"Which word would you like?" Hamlet asked.

"May I..." Polonius began, when Hamlet interrupted him by tapping him with the flute impertinently on the shoulder, then pointing with it at some clouds painted on the theater scenery.

"Do you see yonder cloud? Is it not camel-shaped?"

Polonius turned to where Hamlet pointed. "It has a hump shape like a camel," he finally conceded.

"Methinks it is like a weasel," Hamlet then pronounced.

Polonius looked again. "It is backed like a weasel," he finally agreed.

"And very like a whale," Hamlet went on, smiling roguishly at me as he did so. Immediately came the *non sequitur*. "By the way, what did you want?"

Polonius straightened. "The queen, your *mother*, would like to speak to you before you go to bed. She will await you in her apartments at the eleventh hour."

Hamlet paced away to the far wall and stood looking at the perspective of the painted sky, tapping his recorder on his thigh. Then he paced back smiling. "Well, who can disobey a mother?" Hamlet asked rhetorically. "Tell her I shall come 'by and by.'"

"I will inform her so," Polonius answered.

"'By and by' is easily said," Hamlet remarked, and winked at me. I recall smiling, actually doing everything I could not to laugh.

Polonius moved away again toward, the door, turned once and looked at Hamlet carefully, and then turned again and left. Despite his errand, even Rosencrantz was smiling, but Hamlet was not when he turned to him and Guildenstern and said, "Leave us...friends."

Rosencrantz's smile faded immediately. He and Guildenstern bowed very low, turned, and followed Polonius.

I wish I might say that nothing more significant happened that night. But of course I would be so wrong.

It suddenly became dark. With a last sputter, the candle dimmed and then guttered out. Horatio put down his quill and rubbed his eyes absently. Then he started at a movement in the room, a sound. He whirled around, standing as he did so. Then he stumbled and fell onto his side on the floor. But before he landed he was already laughing. Cleopatra had returned. He had tripped over her.

As his eyes adjusted to the starlight from the lone window he heard the cat begin to purr and felt the tug of its claws in his jerkin.

You silly beast, he mused to himself, and reached to stroke the animal's back. For a moment he thought how easy it would be simply to kill a cat, to grasp its head and snap its neck, and he felt mildly ashamed that he would even think such a thing. But contemplating their unequal power reminded him of Claudius and Hamlet. *How easily death may be delivered*, he thought more seriously.

He thrust the cat aside and got a bit unsteadily to his feet in the darkness. By touch he gathered his papers together. He could still smell burnt wax. He turned, felt his way to the door, and carrying a few papers he wished to review once more under his arm, left the chamber.

Chapter 32

The Possibilities of Forgiveness

Claudius sat on the front pew in the main chapel. He gazed pensively at the *Last Judgment* painting above the altar once again, but despite the expertise of its rendition, it held no power for him. He tried to imagine himself tumbling into Hell with the sinners on Christ's left. He could not. For all the terror and shame in their expressions he simply could not see himself, a king, among them. He looked at the Christ's chosen, stepping up the stairway into Heaven. Neither could he see himself there, the figures self-righteous and smug in their superior confidence. *A man without doubts is not a man*, he thought to himself, though he smiled grimly at his own royal pretensions, the public confidence he felt continually obliged to display.

Then he thought of Hamlet—and of the play. *What might he know? Or suspect? Or was the whole episode some bizarre accident or coincidence? That seems unlikely, and yet how could Hamlet have any notion of his father's murder? No one else knows. The servant who signaled me into the garden has long ago been silenced—an 'accidental' fall off the pier late at night with a cut throat. Such minor tragedies are common enough in a seaport town, especially down by the docks. And certainly the players are innocent. They seemed utterly stupefied by the turn of events in the theater.*

Hamlet must be sent away as I planned, he thought. *Even Polonius was agreed, although he is consistently all too ready to agree to any kingly opinion.*

Claudius straightened up. Hamlet was to visit his mother tonight, some time after the play. *It is time to find out what Polonius knows. Why has he not come to report*? Claudius passed a hand across his brow. He had a minor headache. He decided to go to Gertrude, get her version of events. But first he would try to pray. What could the gesture hurt?

On a silk cushion he knelt facing the altar, above and to one side of which hung a nearly life-sized sculpture of Jesus hanging on the cross, a postural agony, head lowered under a crown of thorns. Claudius crossed himself. He tried to pray but had difficulty deciding how to begin. None of the formulaic prayers he had absorbed since childhood seemed either adequate or appropriate.

He thought for a time about the purpose of prayer itself. It was meant, he knew, to secure forgiveness, or even better, to derive through God's intervention the moral resolve not to sin in the first place. Yet here he was, and as if sharing God's perfect insight, he recognized a part of himself that was foul, a vicious killer and thief, a semi-incestuous, lustful creature who had likely wallowed in every deadly sin.

What was there he might say that almighty God in all His incomparable majesty and justice might hear with an approving ear? 'Forgive me my foul murder?' Surely that could never be, because without even a quiver of doubt Claudius knew that he would never give up the rewards of his act: his crown and his queen.

He thought of the repetitive, mumbled phrases that constituted most prayer as he had experienced it. *Thoughtless*, he concluded. *Most prayer is thoughtless.* He almost snickered at the absurd image of hundreds of people, urged on by dogmatic priests, crowding the great churches, muttering memorized appeals and responses to an indifferent sky.

Yet a part of him remained afraid--afraid of the eternity after death and what it might be, what it might mean for him. He knew that here on Earth many crimes might pay, in fact, that stolen coins used as bribes were part of what enabled his magistrates to live so well. If a felon could afford it, he could buy out the law. And indeed, had he himself not been richly rewarded for his own crimes? However, God in His purity could not be so easily bought off, and might through His immutable power force anyone, even a king, to confess his sins.

Claudius remained piously bent, palms together before his chest in supplication to Christ.

It was at this moment that Hamlet chose to walk past the chapel entrance on a circuitous route to his mother's chambers. He needed time to think, at least partly to prepare his words. His mother might be venal and weak, but she deserved the truth; and if such truth were to prove painful, so be it.

He moved softly in his palace slippers, and no one was about. But when he glanced through the chapel's entryway he saw a figure at prayer. He was about to move on without another thought when he recognized the figure's familiar outline, especially the heavy hair above the rich robe. It was the king! And he was alone!

Hamlet's hand moved reflexively to his sword hilt. There he was, as simple a target and potential victim as had ever been offered any assassin. The image of his own father, horrified and tormented passed through Hamlet's mind. He very quietly began to draw the familiar weight of his sword. *Uncle Claudius alone...now I can kill him*, he thought with a sudden thrill. And then he paused. The king was praying.

There he is, thought Hamlet, *making everything up with God, fully prepared for his passage to Heaven.* The very thought revolted Hamlet. *He took my father's life when no priest or prayer had absolved him and now my father suffers in Purgatory! I cannot kill Claudius now, when his prayers have purified his soul! That's not revenge; it's a blessing!*

He slipped his sword, whisper softly, back into its wool-lined sheath. *No*, Hamlet concluded, *I must be patient a little longer, find the king when he's been in the pleasure of his incestuous bed, or drunk, or in the midst of some act whose sinful character and evil nature will send him kicking to Hell where he belongs.* He grimaced at Claudius, who had not changed his posture but remained at prayer.

Hamlet paced softly away, back the way he had come. His mind whirled with images of all that had happened. His murdered father, the perfidy of Rosencrantz and Guildenstern, his self-satisfied mother...his mother. He found he had gone all the way back to his own quarters before he remembered that his mother expected him. Seeing the king as a potential victim had nearly completely erased the thought of his initial errand. He turned once more on his way to see the queen.

In the chapel, Claudius straightened. Christ had not moved. There was no indication that God had overheard his silent thoughts, perused them for blasphemy, or judged of his guilt or innocence. He felt the momentary despair of his conclusion that no matter the forms in which they are delivered, insincere prayers can never move Heaven.

Finally he again got to his feet. He would have some wine in his own quarters, he decided, and then go to see Gertrude.

Chapter 33

Dead, for a Ducat

Gertrude sat in front of her glass, quietly unbraiding her hair. She examined the woman in the mirror—her sure hands, her implacable face. Was this the face she presented to the world? Truly it must be.

She looked down at her hairbrushes, and then once again at her mirrored countenance, which stared back at her with the same inscrutability. She finished loosening her hair and shook it out behind her. Hamlet was her son, after all. It would not be inappropriate for him to see it thus.

Her thoughts of Hamlet were a mixture of outrage and maternal solicitude. How could he present such an offensive play before his royal father! How could he? She was offended herself. She felt stained by the pseudo-righteousness of the duchess, with all her idealistic talk of marrying only once. And Hamlet's sarcastic commentary was offensive, as well. And albeit indirectly, to accuse the king of murder! It was almost unthinkable. She blushed with anger, and shame that her son might do such a thing.

Just then someone knocked. Where were servants when you needed them! The knock repeated. She threw an embroidered robe over her, its folds tumbling to her slippered feet, and knotted its golden cord at the waist. Then she crossed the room and opened the door. Polonius looked at her as if about to ask a question.

"My lady queen," he said, and he bowed. Glancing at him she could only think of how old he seemed to have become—graying hair and beard, a wrinkled neck. She did not smile.

"Polonius. What would you at this hour?"

"Lord Hamlet is coming to your chamber, to speak with you as you requested. The king would have me—hear the conversation."

"Surely a queen must have her privacy," she said curtly.

Polonius made a gesture, a half shrug that seemed to say, you know the way of kings.

"Oh, all right," she said. "But Hamlet mustn't know you're here. Get behind that tapestry over there, and don't move or make any unnecessary sound."

"Mother!" a voice cried out from down the corridor. "Mother!"

"He's coming," said Gertrude. "Hurry."

"You be plain with him," said Polonius quietly, as he moved toward the wall. "His pranks have gone too far. His majesty is very displeased."

Polonius stepped quickly to the large tapestry depicting an angel announcing to Mary her coming Holy motherhood. He slipped behind it and stood soundlessly. The heavy cloth wavered for a moment or two and then was still.

Moments later Hamlet knocked on the still open door and entered. He appeared distracted, somewhat disoriented, and his hand kept straying to the handle of his sword. He looked expectantly at Gertrude, who clasped her hands together, then separated them, and stepped up to Hamlet to look him in the eye.

"Now, Mother, what do you need from me so urgently at this late hour?"

"Hamlet, you have grievously offended your father!"

Hamlet's rolled his eyes upward as if reacting to some mockery or absurdity. "Mother, *you* have grievously offended my father!"

"Oh, Hamlet!" she cried out in exasperation. She moved to her sofa and sat.

Hamlet sat on the arm of her sofa. "What's the matter now?" he asked.

"Hamlet, have you forgotten me? You act as if I'm some servant who can be carelessly chastised without consequence. Consider to whom you speak!" She was becoming angry now.

"Marry, you're your husband's brother's wife. And though I might wish it were not so, you *are* my mother." He looked at his feet, an expression of utter gloom and disgust on his face.

Gertrude finally exploded with anger. She stood and shook her fist at him. "You ungrateful child!" she hissed. "By Christ, if you will not speak properly to me, I'll set those onto you who will make you!" With this threat she moved toward the bell-pull to call a servant. Hamlet leaped to his feet, and drawing his sword, interposed himself between his mother and the pull.

"Oh, no you don't!" he said, equally angrily. He waved his blade at her. It was a feeble flourish, but she stepped abruptly backward, her hands out as if to protect herself.

For a moment she felt an unreasoning terror, and her voice rose even further. "My God, Hamlet," she cried out. "Don't murder me!" Then, turning from him she fled to the other side of her large bed, crying out, "Help! Help!"

There was a bustle of clumsy movement behind the tapestry, and a male voice cried out to supplement hers. "Help, guards, help!"

Hamlet spun to face the sound. "What? A rat?"

Behind the tapestry Polonius seemed to have become briefly entangled. For a moment his hidden body bulged against the fabric.

In two steps Hamlet was there. He drew back his sword and plunged the shining blade through the tapestry, once, twice—a third time for measure. For a moment he couldn't draw the sword free. Then, pushing on the collapsing bulk behind the cloth, he drew the blade out. Fresh blood and what looked a little like some gut clung to it and dripped onto the polished flagstones. Still behind it, Polonius was grasping the heavy tapestry, trying to stay upright. The angel wavered wildly above the awestruck Mary. Polonius emitted a hoarse, gasping sound. Then his grip slackened, and his body tumbled to the floor, still hidden from view.

"Dead, for a ducat," Hamlet muttered.

Gertrude rushed forward once more. "Oh, God, Hamlet, what have you done?"

"I know not," Hamlet answered her. He wiped his blade on the tapestry and slid it back into its sheath with a whisper. He turned to her and asked, "Is it the king?" He trembled in a near delirium of excitement, a rolling of his shoulders that he could scarcely get under control. After a few seconds he calmed himself.

Gertrude shuddered and groaned softly, a kind of "No, no, no…"

Hamlet lifted the bottom of the tapestry upward. Polonius' sightless eyes looked up at him; his face held an expression of curious surprise, as if a bee had stung him, or he had stubbed his toe. Hamlet drew back momentarily.

Then he knelt beside Polonius. "You intruding fool!" he said. Blood seeped through a rent in Polonius' robe, but as the heart had stopped, the heavy bleeding had more or less ceased, too. Hamlet touched the old face, marveling at its wrinkled detail, its stillness. "Fool," he said again, as if for emphasis. "I took you for your better."

He turned to Gertrude, who was wringing her hands in an agony of tension. "Oh, Hamlet," she began, but when he glared at her she stopped.

"Be quiet," he said to her emphatically. "And stop wringing your hands."

She sat back on the edge of her big bed and tugged her robe about her. She looked at Hamlet, aghast.

"It's time I squeezed your heart a little, if anything can penetrate the shield of your ambition and indifference." Hamlet stared at her, then moved toward her, hands out showing that he no longer held a weapon.

Gertrude crossed her arms in front of her bosom, squeezing her shoulders together as if chilled. "What have *I* done, that makes you so hate your own mother? Well?"

"If you hold yourself your husband's other half—what about kill a king, and marry with his brother?"

"Kill a king?" she gasped.

"Those were my words," he said.

Hamlet clasped her hands in his and sat beside her, gazing into her face all the while. She could not meet his eye.

"Look at me," he said hoarsely, but she stared at the floor. "Look at me."

With great effort, she turned her head to him. He reached under her chin and tugged by its silver chain, up from her cleavage, the cameo of Claudius she had worn since their recent marriage. It was a common image, one owned by many wealthier Danes as a symbol of their station and loyalty, although hers was pure ivory. He grasped too, his own cameo. But his was different. He pulled her close so that the two cameos could be seen side by side.

"Use your eyes! Explore these two counterfeits," he said sternly. "Two brothers." He pointed to his own, a representation of Old Hamlet. "Look you here. Look at the nobility on his brow, the representation of grace and wisdom created to say to all the world, '*This* is a man!' This *was* your husband."

He jerked her cameo, and her head snapped forward. He lifted it for her inspection. "Look at what follows: like mildewed maize, infecting his wholesome brother. Have you eyes? Look! How could you be queen to this…gargoyle…after being married to a human angel? Have you eyes? I know it's common for young women to fall into the thrall of fantasy…" For a moment he paused, eyes on some inward vision, then said, "But a woman of your age? At your age the heyday in the blood is tame, it waits upon the judgment! And what judgment would stoop from *this…*" at this moment he thrust Old Hamlet's cameo before her unwilling eyes… "to *this?*" and here he pushed Claudius' image before her.

All Gertrude's power and confidence seemed to be melting within her. Her shoulders sank, and she lowered her head. "Oh, Hamlet," she said, but did not finish her thought.

"Your new master is nothing but a charlatan, a cutpurse of the empire, not half the twentieth part of your precedent lord!" Hamlet spat to one side. "My uncle is a king of shreds and patches, a murdering felon who took the crown into his crooked hands and put it in his pocket!"

Gertrude was weeping openly now, shuddering with her grief and anxiety. "No more Hamlet, no more!"

"Hah! I can scarcely bear to imagine it, you and that grotesque swine making love in the malodorous sty of his bed, sweating and grunting like pigs!"

"No more, sweet Hamlet, no more!"

Hamlet suddenly started, as if an icy hand had slid inside his shirt and down his back. He let go his mother and slid to the floor, gazing at the doorway, which still stood open. He groaned and recoiled, and stared at the door as if the angel of death stood there. "What would your gracious figure?" he asked the open space. He shivered.

Gertrude stared at him in amazement. She could hardly believe his transformation.

Hamlet nearly whispered. "Have you come to chide your tardy son?" he croaked. "Oh, do not look upon me, lest you further compromise my stern intents." He cocked his head, as if to listen.

"Hamlet?" his mother asked in a low voice. He ignored her, or appeared not to hear her. After some moments he turned to her.

"How is it with you lady?" he asked.

Gertrude stared at him in amazement. "How is it with *you*, that you speak to an empty space?" she finally asked.

"Do you see nothing there?" Hamlet asked, eyes wide.

"Nothing at all, yet all there is, I see," she replied.

"And hear nothing?"

"What, Hamlet?"

"My father! There! At the portal! Look there, where he steals away!" He pointed at the empty doorway. "Father?" he called plaintively.

Gertrude's heart skipped erratically. She took a deep breath to steady herself, then she grasped Hamlet by the shoulders and twisted him to look at her and said, "This is but the coinage of your brain. Such visions are common…in various forms of…madness…"

She had nearly swallowed the last word, but it had an electric effect on Hamlet, who straightened and shook off her hands. He stood and gazed over his shoulder at the empty doorway, then looked back at Gertrude and smiled—a bitter smile, almost a hateful smile.

"Madness?" The word was articulate, slick, like a blade slicing a peach or a block of butter.

"Madness?" he said again, almost disbelieving what he had heard. "Mother, for love of grace, never flatter yourself that rather than your sin my madness is the author of all this! Mother?"

She looked at him, and expression of dismay and puzzlement on her face.

"Put me to the test," he said at once. "Tell me a story, any story. I'll repeat it, if not word for word, at least the same in meaning. Madness would stray from such an accomplishment in minutes, if not moments!" He paused. "Do you think I'm sailing to the wind of my emotions? Check my pulse. It beats regularly, evenly, as it usually does."

Gertrude now looked down. Finally she said, "Hamlet, you've turned my gaze into my blackened soul; you've broken my heart in two."

"Then throw away the poisoned half," he answered, "and live the purer with what remains."

He moved from the bed and back to Polonius, whose corpse emitted a soft fart. Hamlet backed away momentarily, then closed Polonius' eyes and crossed his arms.

"This councilor is now most grave," Hamlet said ironically. "Who was, in life, a foolish, prating knave," he finally rhymed, and smiled a moment at his wit. Then, once more, he straightened up and moved to rejoin his mother.

"Mother," he said, and he lifted her chin so that she would look him in the eye. "Don't go to my uncle's bed tonight." She raised her eyes in weak protest, but remained silent. "This abstinence will make the next abstinence only easier, the one after that easier still." She twisted her face down again.

Hamlet went on. "God must have chosen me to be his minister." He pointed at Polonius' corpse, now straightened but silent on the flagstone floor. "He hath plagued it with me, and me with it, and I, too, shall suffer for these acts," he prophesied.

Hamlet clasped Gertrude's hands between his own, and she looked at him once again. "Mother. Suppose you do return to my uncle's bed. Perhaps he strokes your neck," and at this Hamlet demonstrated by stroking his mother's neck, although she backed away somewhat. "Or maybe he gives you a couple of wet, sucking kisses." He sneered, and then after a moment added in a soft, meaningful voice, "If you truly love this goat as your rightful lord, it were good you let him know—I am not truly mad, but mad in craft."

Gertrude gave him a long, examining look. Finally she sighed, and said, "I cannot tell him this. You are my son." She crossed herself. "If life be made of breath, I have no breath to reveal this to him."

Hamlet straightened, then said, "I have discovered that the king has plans concerning me. If I am any predictor of events, I suspect I am to be sent to England."

Gertrude stiffened.

"You knew that?" Hamlet said.

"Alas, I had forgot," she answered.

"Then I'll likely be escorted by my old schoolfellows, Rosencrantz and Guildenstern, two completely untrustworthy companions. They'll bear a mandate from the king."

Gertrude grimaced and placed a hand on Hamlet's arm.

"Worry not, Mother," Hamlet said. "In any game of wits it is foolish to play unarmed (as Guildenstern is), and although Rosencrantz might style himself a worthy opponent, I am not intimidated by any schemes he might offer up. I shall dig well beneath their mines and blow *them* at the moon! I embrace the challenge—wit against wit, craft against craft."

Again Gertrude looked down. She shuddered briefly and once more clasped her hands together.

Hamlet stood and turned once again to the body. He grasped it by the legs and began pulling it toward the exit. "Come, sir," he said. "Let's toward an end with you. Good night, Mother." He dragged the body along the floor and out the open doorway.

Gertrude stared after him at the open portal, the image of his exit even now a ghost in her own memory. Even when she looked down she could see his departure—again, and again, and again.

Chapter 34

Claudius Takes Charge

At Gertrude's door Claudius paused. He put his ear to the door, but no sound came from within. He straightened and knocked, soundly. After a moment he heard her familiar step moving his way. The latch clicked, the door opened, and Gertrude stood looking at him, a candle in her hand. She bowed her head briefly and opened the door wider to let him in.

"Well, Gertrude? Did you speak to Hamlet?" Claudius' voice was slightly impatient, a bit querulous.

She led him into her main living area and sat on one of her sofas. She finally nodded. "Yes. I spoke to him."

"Well? What did he say? How is he?"

Gertrude took a long moment before replying. "Polonius was right. He's mad. I've never seen him so."

"What happened?"

Gertrude began to cry softly. Her tears slid remorselessly down her cheeks, and she dabbed at them fruitlessly with her handkerchief. Claudius moved to comfort her, but she avoided his arm. He gave her a wary glance at her rejection. Finally she spoke again.

"I was trying to explain to him that this 'prank' play was simply too much, too offensive for you, for me, for us at court. But he would have none of it. He was waving his sword around looking for all the world as if he were seeking some Turk to kill. Then he heard something stir behind the arras where Polonius was hiding. Crying 'A rat! A rat!' he plunged his sword through the tapestry there and killed the unseen, good old man."

Claudius got up swiftly and moved to the wall where the tapestry hung. The angel still gazed lovingly at Mary, but there was a bloody rent through Mary's thigh where she was seated on a stool. The blood was darkening now, but still fresh. Claudius touched it speculatively, then jerked his hand away and examined the red stain on his fingers. He rubbed it off on another portion of the cloth.

"It would have been so with me if I'd been there!" he exclaimed softly. He turned to Gertrude, who still wept softly on the bench.

"He weeps for what he has done," Gertrude said lamely. "But he *is* mad. He's *mad*."

"Still," Claudius emphasized, "how can I answer for this bloody deed, committed here in the confines of a royal apartment? You know how people talk! Servants, courtiers, everyone! They will say it's my fault! I should have kept this mad young man under closer supervision, perhaps even locked away. But for love of you, and for *him,* my nephew and my son, I did not do what was right—only what was expedient." He calmed himself a moment, then asked, "Gertrude, where is the body?"

"Hamlet took it. He threatened me briefly, then took the body away." She sighed. She was no longer crying. She made an erratic gesture with her hand. "I had dismissed my servants for the night. After all, Polonius was there. Hamlet is my son. What had I to fear?"

Claudius moved to the doorway at the main hallway entrance. Opening it forcefully, he called loudly, "Guard!" Moments later he returned with two beefy Swiss guards beside him. To the first, he said, "Hamlet, in his madness, has slain Polonius. Get Rosencrantz and Guildenstern. Find Hamlet. Get him to reveal where he has put Polonius' body. Be diplomatic. Don't force any issues. He's unpredictable."

The first guard bowed and left.

To the second, Claudius was extremely pointed. "You will stay here, just outside the queen's entrance. Do not allow anyone in here but me, do you understand? The queen's life may be in your hands. I will send you another to accompany you."

The guard bowed. He turned, and holding his pike firmly erect, he stepped outside the room.

"Gertrude," Claudius finally said. "I must sort these affairs immediately, or as soon as possible. I will not disturb you further tonight. Is there a waiting lady you wish as company?"

Gertrude looked at him listlessly. "No, my lord," she said.

"I will leave you then." Claudius looked at her, a measured expression as if it held unspoken questions. Then he turned and left.

Gertrude watched him go. For a moment it seemed as if two men were alternating their way out through the doorway—Claudius, and Old Hamlet, one bowing to the other to take the lead, only to have the other demur and insist that the first take precedence. Then to her imagination came the image of young Hamlet, bent over, dragging Polonius' body through the portal. She closed her eyes and turned away. Her heart was still beating very fast. Try as she might, she could not will it to be still.

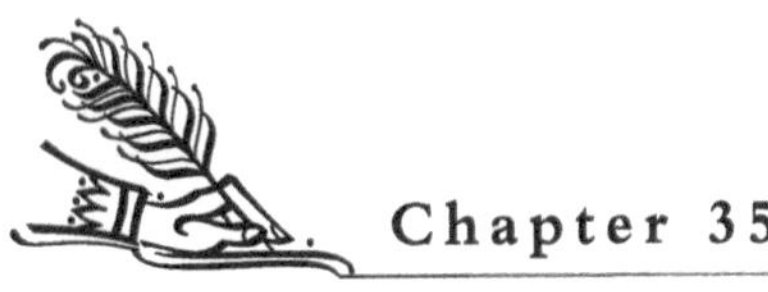

Chapter 35

Crime and Punishment

Horatio sat staring into space, unmoving at his writing table, quill poised above the paper but still. A drop of ink gathered at the nib and after a seemingly interminable moment fell with a soft "plop" onto the page. Horatio started, then blotted the drop with a napkin. The cat looked at him curiously from its cushion. Horatio dipped the quill into the ink once more and began to write.

Have you ever had a premonition? I have.

After the play and our encounter with Rosencrantz and Guildenstern, Hamlet sent me away. Perhaps he meant to save me from whatever dangers he anticipated might await him. I walked to my rooms, barely aware of my surroundings. The evening's events—images, comments, facial expressions—all kept crowding into my attention, each seeming to cry out, "Me, me, me, pay attention to me!" I didn't remember having entered my room, so distracted was I.

But I had cast off my cloak and now sat woodenly at my table. A half-finished loaf still lay on my board there surrounded by crumbs. I picked up my knife and toyed with it, tapping its blade on the table as I thought.

What would happen now? How angry was the king? What was he likely to do? Was Hamlet reconciled with Ophelia? Where would the players go now? What did the queen think? These and other questions roiled in my mind like some swirling whirlpool, sucking everything into its depths.

At length, I must have laid my head on my arms and begun to doze, for I woke with a shiver and a start. For some unaccountable reason, I knew something was wrong. This was the premonition, yelling at me its inaudible command: *Go find Hamlet*!

I clambered to my feet once more, collected my cloak from the bench on which it was crumpled, and left my chambers.

It was dark in the corridor, although a few yards away I could see torchlight from a connecting hallway. I moved in that direction, and instinct and apprehension drove me to head toward the royal apartments.

Normally I would be reluctant to enter that section of the palace, which was usually carefully patrolled by the king's Swiss mercenaries. But I encountered no one until I was in the hallway outside the queen's apartments. It was there I met Hamlet. My heart bounded with joy that he was alive.

Hamlet had his back to me and was dragging some heavy, irregular object toward me along the hallway floor.

"Hamlet," I called softly.

He turned to me in what seemed like a bit of a fright; then he smiled when he saw that it was I. "Help me," he said.

I hurried to his side. On the floor lay Polonius. His eyes were closed, but it was apparent from the near-grayness of his skin that he was dead. A small dribble of blood had leaked out of the corner of his mouth and dried to a semi-crust in his beard. My stomach nearly turned over. I crossed myself, more than once, I think.

"I need to move him," Hamlet said, heedless of my reaction.

I stifled my nausea and bent to take the old man under the armpits. Hamlet hefted his legs, and we straightened up together.

One of Polonius' arms slipped off his chest and his hand with the signet ring slapped onto the floor. I shoved my knee under his back and moved my hand down to pull the arm up again and position it across the chest.

"This way," Hamlet said, and jerked his head to indicate a narrow hallway leading vaguely toward the area of the chapel. He backed into the passage, and I necessarily followed, the body swaying irregularly between us.

The hallway was longer than I anticipated, at least 30 paces. At its end Hamlet turned into a small anteroom that led into the apse of the chapel. Against the anteroom wall stood a long oak table covered with heavy damask, which hung nearly to the floor. Using Hamlet's nods as gestures, I helped him lay Polonius on the floor next to the table. Then the two of us shoved the body under the table, allowing the damask cloth to fall down to cover it. Until it began to smell, at least, it would be hard to find.

Hamlet gestured to me again to follow him. "Come," he said tersely. We retraced our steps quietly. At one point, Hamlet placed his fingers on his lips and we paused as a pair of guards passed by the entrance to our hallway. When the way was clear, I followed him to his quarters.

Although I had not spent much time here, it was familiar enough, and at his further nod I sat on a small sofa near the hearth. As Hamlet was pouring some wine, I could hear snoring from an adjacent room, and raised my eyes in inquiry.

"Yedric," he said softly. He handed me a glass of wine for which I thanked him, and he sat opposite.

"You must be bursting with curiosity," he said after we had drunk.

"Of course." I leaned forward.

"I was—conversing—with my mother," he said after a moment's hesitation. His hesitation before using the word 'conversing' suggested that it was no ordinary conversation.

"Polonius was hiding behind the arras. When he shouted, I reacted quickly, perhaps with insufficient thought, on reflection. I stabbed the figure." He drank again and wiped his mouth with a silk handkerchief. "I think I hoped it was the king."

My expression must have revealed my shock.

"I know, I know," he continued. "It was, perhaps, careless."

"What now, do you imagine?" I asked him.

"The king has plans in place to send me to our territory in England—tax collector has apparently become one of the prince's roles in today's Denmark. If my mother can prevail upon him not to have me executed for this killing, I expect he will follow through with his plan and send me there."

He drank again. I hoped he would not become drunk. He would need all his wits in the hours to come. "Rosencrantz and Guildenstern, our 'friends,' will likely escort me."

"Surely *they* can be trusted," I ventured.

"In a world of ambition, no one can be trusted. That is why I trust *you*."

I lowered my eyes at this mixed compliment, but at that moment there came a knocking at his door.

"Oh, here they come," Hamlet said. "Yedric!" he called. Moments later Yedric entered from his sleeping chamber, rubbing his eyes, as the knocking resumed even more loudly. He looked at Hamlet, who nodded toward the disturbance.

We heard the bolts slide free and the latch click.

"What is the meaning of this loud intrusion, sir?" Yedric asked with uncharacteristic indignation.

"We seek the lord Hamlet." It was Rosencrantz's voice.

"I shall see if he is available," Yedric responded, and we could hear the door close once more. In my mind's eye I could see the impatient Rosencrantz, who had never thought much of Yedric, tapping his restless foot outside. Yedric came into the room where we were sitting, but before he could speak Hamlet said, "Let them in."

A few seconds later, Yedric led Rosencrantz and Guildenstern into the room. Each of them bowed low to Hamlet, and he nodded in recognition.

Uncharacteristically, Guildenstern spoke first. "My lord, the king has instructed us to seek you out, and to deliver both you and the body of Polonius to him. Where is Polonius, my lord?"

"Do not believe it," said Hamlet, but he directed his remark at Rosencrantz. Guildenstern looked at his friend.

"Believe what, my lord?" Rosencrantz responded.

"That I can keep *your* counsel, and not my own. Besides, what kind of answer is suitable to be given to a sponge?"

Rosencrantz straightened, a slight increase in tension in his stance. "Do you take me for a sponge, my lord?"

"Oh, a perfect sponge, a wonderful sponge, one that soaks up the king's instructions and largesse with smiles and bows 'til he positively drips! But such officers do a king like my uncle yeoman's service, perfect service, for he knows he can keep you like a morsel in the corner of his jaw, ready to swallow at any time. When he needs what you know he need only squeeze you, and you shall be dry again."

Hamlet chuckled malevolently, and I hid a smile behind my fist. Rosencrantz's expression darkened. "I don't understand you, my lord."

"All the better," Hamlet snorted. "A knavish speech sleeps in a fool's ear."

"My lord, where is the body?" interjected Guildenstern once more.

"The body is with the king, but the king is not with the body. The king is a thing..." Hamlet's voice trailed off.

"A *thing*, my lord!"

"Of nothing. Nothing." Then his face brightened. "By all means, take me to him. Horatio, accompany us."

Rosencrantz frowned, but the two of them bowed once more. Yedric brought Hamlet his cloak, and we went out into the hallway. Hamlet winked at me broadly. Then, at the entrance to a side corridor, he shouted, "Hide fox, and all after!" and he was gone, running down the narrow hall.

"Where's he *going*?" Rosencrantz snarled at me, but I merely shrugged. Guildenstern started after Hamlet, and Rosencrantz signaled to two guards who had just entered the corridor from another direction.

"Hamlet has slain Polonius," he said to them. "Go help Guildenstern find him and bring him to the west parlor where the king will be waiting." The men turned, but Rosencrantz added loudly, "Don't upset him!"

The two men hustled away calling, "Hamlet! Prince Hamlet!" One of them scooped a torch from a wall sconce.

Rosencrantz looked at me and said, "You might as well come with me. They'll find him eventually."

I smiled inwardly, but showed only calm agreement in my outward expression. "Of course," I answered. "Whatever the king demands."

Horatio paused in his writing. He knew he was far from finished here, but his back ached. He put down the quill and stood to stretch. Cleopatra watched him from her cushion, then got to her feet and stretched herself, as well.

Horatio smiled at it. "I should call you Gertrude," he said to her. "Closer to home." He smiled at his own somewhat silly imaginings. "What would your ladyship?" he said to the cat, but it merely looked at him, then sat and began to clean its face by licking its paw and rubbing behind its whiskers.

Chapter 36

Attack Readiness

It was sunnier than expected. All last night, rain had been pounding on the shingled roof, and the stream leading down to the fjord was in spate, boulders thumping and grinding down the river bed, and torn vegetation riding the wild riffles down the slope. Fortinbras grinned. Sun was always pleasing, and this morning's sunlight was spangling off the choppy waters of the fjord and pushing back the shadows at the edge of the forest.

"Well, do you think they're ready?" Fortinbras directed his question to Lars, his second-in-command. They were watching a troop of men in training, 24 pairs of them squared off against one another in single combat. The sound of swords rang through the valley.

"They're good men, and they're hungry for glory. Such hunger counts for a lot of skill. Yes, I think they're ready.

Fortinbras turned to Lars, who was chewing on some dried fish while he watched the men exercise. Fortinbras made a sour expression. He didn't like fish, nearly a sin for a Norwegian, but what could he do? He didn't like fish.

"With King Olav's permission, we'll begin our expedition with the next tide."

Fortinbras felt vindicated, energetic and alive, all in one.

Lars looked at him inquiringly and asked, "Will the men receive any advance on their pay?"

Fortinbras scowled at him.

"I only ask because aside from the event of King Olav's 'visit,' when he most generously granted each man three silver coins, it has been over four months since any of the men has been paid even one copper piece. They are men with obligations, in many ways much like us, my lord."

"Have they not been well fed?" asked Fortinbras.

"Yes, my lord."

"Were there no women available?"

"There were, my lord."

"Did they all sleep in the rain?"

"No, my lord, they have been well cared for."

"Then they have no cause for complaint. Warriors who wish wealth need to earn it. There will be plenty of opportunity for plunder once we get to Poland."

Fortinbras looked out to the strand, where a couple of dozen long ships were beached against the gravel. More were anchored offshore. He could hear some rope from a stay slapping against a mast somewhere. The planking on at least half the ships was still nearly white—new wood. But they had been sailed up and down the fjord twice in variable weather. They were good, seaworthy boats. They would serve.

"I expect the messenger from King Olav tomorrow, or the next day (Wodin's day) at the latest. Of course he will approve our expedition, especially as it is his plan. There will be real action soon. It is important, however, that we stop at Elsinore to reaffirm our agreement with the Danish king to allow us unobstructed passage through Danish waters. The sail is a short one," he said. He paused as if thinking.

Lars smiled. "Then, with your permission, I will allow some 'entertainments' tonight, women from the village, as well as a pair of magicians from Borgstein up the coast. There is ample ale, and good beef remaining from the cattle we slaughtered for jerky."

"Granted," said Fortinbras. Since his recent interview with king Olav, and his acceptance of Olav's plan to attack a settlement in Poland instead of Denmark, he had felt strengthened and elated. True, his king had chastised him. But in recognition of Fortinbras' agreement to the new plan, Olav had funded him with seventy-five thousand kroner in gold, plenty to manage the expedition, with some left over besides. It would not hurt to be at least a little generous. He whiffed the air and scented some kind of stew, probably cooked in ale.

"Call the men in," he said to Lars. "Let's get them well fed and happy, ready to go. Some of them, ultimately, will not come back. We leave in two days."

Lars nodded and signaled the training officers. Fortinbras returned his attention to the sky above the fjord. A pair of distant birds sailed, almost immovably, on thermals high above the cliffs overlooking the water. Fortinbras wasn't sure he believed in omens, but he watched their gliding appreciatively, their graceful dark outlines against the bright sky. *At least it is sunny today*, he thought to himself. *One has to take goodness when one can get it.*

He turned and headed toward his quarters. There was still much to prepare.

Chapter 37

Where's Polonius?

Claudius hastened from Gertrude's apartments to the office attached to his own quarters. He wakened the office custodian, an older man dozing in the anteroom, who hastily and nervously lit a couple of torches and the double candelabra that lit Claudius' desk.

"Leave us," Claudius said, as he took his seat.

The servant bowed hastily and left the room. Claudius sat with his elbows on the desk, his hands forming a double fan of fingers. He couldn't stop thinking, even if he wanted to. Everything was becoming much too complicated, too quickly. Finally he drew paper and a quill toward him, dipped the quill in the silver inkpot, and began to write.

He wrote for a full ten minutes. When finished, he picked up the page and reread it slowly. Then, apparently satisfied with its contents, he folded it carefully and used one of the candles from the candelabra to seal it. The hot wax sputtered, and Claudius briefly sucked his finger where he had accidentally splashed it. He bent his wrist to press the image from his royal signet ring into the wax to indicate its importance: this was a letter from the king!

A moment or two later a knock sounded at the door.

"Come," said Claudius.

Rosencrantz entered, along with one of the Swiss guards carrying a torch.

"Well, where is Hamlet?" Claudius demanded.

"Outside, to know your pleasure. Horatio is with him. Hamlet won't tell us where Polonius is, and whether or not Horatio knows..." He shrugged.

"No matter. Bring them in."

Rosencrantz went back to the entrance and called, "Guildenstern, bring in the prince."

Hamlet entered, squinting at first at the brightness. He looked around quickly, sizing up the situation. Guildenstern stood behind him. A moment later, Horatio also entered, brushing off the hand of one of the guards. He moved to one side and stood silently, watching.

Claudius looked at Hamlet closely. "Hamlet," he said in a stern tone, "where's Polonius?"

Hamlet stared at the king a moment, then replied, "At supper."

"At supper?"

"Supper of a sort, I suppose. Not one where he eats, but where he is eaten. A gathering of expedient worms has already begun to make short work of him."

He gazed thoughtfully off into the ceiling's corner, as if plumbing some universal question. Then he smiled grimly.

"You know," he said, "a worm is our only emperor for diet...we fatten all other creatures to fatten ourselves, and we fatten ourselves for worms. Variable service but to one table." He sighed, then added in a subdued voice, almost reverent, "That's the end. Amen." He regarded the king blankly.

"Hamlet," Claudius began reasonably, "What do you mean by this...this explanation?"

Hamlet looked up again. He had been tugging on a hangnail. He dropped his hands to his sides and shrugged.

"Nothing important. Merely to show you how a king can march a procession through the guts of a beggar." He grinned at Claudius' evident discomfiture. "Marry, how? A worm eats of a dead king's body; a fisherman uses that worm to catch a fish; a beggar eats the fish. Q.E.D."

"Oh, Hamlet," Claudius finally said. "Stop this foolish riddling. Please. Tell us where Polonius is."

"In Heaven," Hamlet said cheerfully. "Send for him there." Then, more seriously, he said, "Or, if your messenger find him not there, seek him 'below' yourself."

Rosencrantz gasped audibly.

Hamlet turned toward Horatio and gave a pained smile, but then turned back to Claudius and said, "But, if you don't find him within a month, I'm sure someone will nose him one Sunday or the next at chapel…assuming, of course, that God's observances remain important these days."

"Go search the chapel!" Claudius said to one of the guards, several of which were now in attendance.

"He will stay 'til you come," Hamlet called out as two of the guards hastened from the room.

"Hamlet, I have made a decision regarding your safety, which, as you know, I tender as dearly as I do my own." He looked at Hamlet to see his reaction.

Hamlet looked skeptically at the king, but said nothing.

"I have need of an ambassador to attend to our pressing interests in England. I have decided to send you, along with Rosencrantz and Guildenstern. Taxes from our territories are in arrears. Your presence, a *prince* as ambassador, will lend authority." Claudius coughed into his hand. "As well, given recent events, it is important that the court, and the kingdom in general, be given the chance to recover from their shock. Polonius, as you know, was a popular figure about the court, and a man upon whom we relied."

"England? Good, good," murmured Hamlet.

"The more so now that you understand our purposes."

"I may not know them perfectly," said Hamlet, "but I'm sure that God sees them. What more confidence need any man have than the assurance of *His* holy direction?"

Claudius lowered his eyes briefly, then looked up again, as Hamlet had already turned to Rosencrantz to speak once more. "Come then! For England!" But he once more turned to Claudius and said brightly, "Good-bye, Mother!"

In puzzlement once more, Claudius corrected him. "Thy loving *father*, Hamlet."

"Are not husband and wife one flesh, as it tells us in scripture? Therefore, 'my mother.'" He turned to leave. Horatio came to him and whispered in his ear, but Hamlet merely shook his head.

"Guildenstern! Stay," said Claudius. Guildenstern looked at Rosencrantz, who simply nodded at him, then turned and escorted Hamlet from the room. Guildenstern approached Claudius.

Claudius took the document he had been writing from his desk. He bound it in a scarlet ribbon and handed it to Guildenstern.

"Take this," Claudius said. "It contains important instructions to my governor in England. Under no circumstances open this paper, but ensure that he receive it, seals intact."

He looked sternly at Guildenstern, who tucked the paper into an interior pocket in his doublet. He bowed to the king, but said nothing for a moment.

"Well?" Claudius said to him.

"Of course, your majesty. And may I add, I hope you are certain in your confidence that we—Rosencrantz and myself—are your perfect and loyal servants in this matter. A ship leaves for England on tomorrow's afternoon tide. We, and the prince, will be on it."

Claudius nodded and waved him away. Guildenstern bowed, turned, and left. Claudius sat once more—for some reason he had risen to his feet at some point during the conversations. He bowed his head.

Let England take care of Hamlet, he thought. He smiled at his own cleverness. *This is power*, he thought. *My power.*

Chapter 38

Departure for England

A pale sun showed through the high windows of the hallway outside Hamlet's quarters. Rosencrantz approached the two guards who had been posted outside Hamlet's door. He nodded, and the larger of the two nodded in return. Rosencrantz raised his gloved fist and knocked. It was a dignified knock—not forceful or peremptory—merely notification of arrival—and of Hamlet's departure, he knew.

Yedric opened the door, and Rosencrantz could see Hamlet wrapping a cloak about himself in the background.

"The lord Hamlet will be ready in a few minutes," Yedric said curtly and closed the door once more. Rosencrantz rolled his eyes in impatience, and out of his vision one of the guards smiled. Rosencrantz turned to the large one.

"Accompany us to the dock," he said. "Just in the unlikely event that the prince should decide to do something—erratic."

The guard nodded. He knew his job. And he knew that Rosencrantz had the authority of the king.

Guildenstern approached along the hallway. "The coach is waiting at the west entrance," he said. Rosencrantz nodded.

The door opened once more. Hamlet stood there, surprisingly imperious, a purple cloak wrapped about him. Rosencrantz and Guildenstern bowed to him, and he nodded in recognition. "We are at your, and the king's, service," said Rosencrantz with a kind of officious formality.

"So much service," responded Hamlet. "I suppose you will carry me to the boat, if need be."

"And what eventuality should ever cause such a need to arise?" asked Guildenstern.

"Well, I might be smitten with plague, for example, or remorse, or even a plague of remorse, an ailment sufficient to render my very limbs incapable," Hamlet replied.

"My lord, you above all save the king must understand the seriousness of our mandate—the kingdom's taxes must be collected. And we all know the English as the irresponsible vagabonds they are. Surely such considerations will lend you strength." Guildenstern smiled.

"I think I *do* understand the seriousness of *our* mandate." Hamlet glanced about him, allowing his eye to rest a moment on the two beefy guards who were preparing to accompany them. "Do you really believe these are necessary?" he asked Rosencrantz, who colored visibly, then shook his head.

"Only for your safety, my lord."

"Of course, of course. For my safety." Hamlet took a deep breath. "All right. Lead on." But it was he who walked ahead before they could move, and they hastened to accompany him.

When the coach clattered over the last of the cobbles onto the pier, the afternoon sun was already well advanced. A soft breeze riffled the water and set the king's banners on the customs house flapping. A few gulls squawked, and the shouts of dockworkers could be heard along the quay. The royal party descended from the coach, their boots loud on the rough planking. In front of them waited a captain and two ship's officers at the foot of a gangplank leading onto a sturdy merchant ship.

Although a vessel of only two comparatively short masts, it appeared fairly elegant in appointment. The paintwork was new, as was the rigging, and the uniforms of the officers were bright and in good repair. The ship even featured two small cannon in the bow, brass guns that had been polished until they gleamed, although they would be hopelessly inadequate in any truly threatening encounter.

The officers bowed deeply, but Hamlet took little notice. His gaze was focused on the next pier over, where half a dozen uniformed men were disembarking under the direction of an officer in a foreign uniform. Beyond their ship, a new longboat in the Norwegian style, several other longboats were sitting at anchor, and more sails were to be seen at the harbor's mouth. Waiting at the head of their pier was an armed contingent of Danish troops including a squadron of cavalry.

"Whose troops are those?" Hamlet had turned to the ship's captain and directed his question to him.

"They are Norwegians, my lord," he answered gravely.

Hamlet looked again at the Danish troops who appeared alert but not alarmed.

"How are they purposed? Who leads them?"

The captain looked up and said, "Fortinbras, the prince of Norway, has been promised by your father," and at this Hamlet winced, "conveyance through Denmark's waters to attack Poland."

Hamlet cocked his head. "The main part of Poland, sir, or some frontier?"

The older of the two junior officers stepped forward and offered, "With your permission, sir," (and it was unclear whether 'sir' referred to Hamlet or to his commanding officer). He came closer to Hamlet. "They go to attack a tiny enclave hardly worth living in, a village and a few farmsteads." He cleared his throat. "You couldn't pay me enough to farm it."

Hamlet snorted his derision. "Well then, surely the Poles will not bother to defend it."

"Oh, yes," the captain added once more. "They're aware of the threat, at least according to some traders who arrived from Poland a day or two ago. It is already garrisoned."

This is madness, Hamlet thought. *Madness. Hundreds, perhaps thousands of men will die fighting over a straw.* He sighed. *And yet, it's a fine madness,* he concluded.

He gazed across at the young Norwegian officer, who was parlaying with the commandant of the Danish troops. Flinging back his scarlet cloak, Fortinbras gestured with his left hand at his ships entering the harbor, and the Danish officer followed his gaze.

Look at him, Hamlet thought again. *Ready to brave any form of death and destruction with total equanimity, all for 'honor', for a word, a puff of air. But if he lives it will change his life. Yet I, son of a murdered father, with time and opportunity for my revenge repeatedly at my disposal, have not acted. I am shamed in my own eyes.*

Beneath his cloak his hand closed over the ribbed handle of the dagger he always wore.

"My lord," the captain resumed. "You will, of course, occupy the captain's cabin, there on the rear of the main deck." Hamlet glanced at it. "May we welcome you aboard?"

"Yes, of course," Hamlet replied. "Rosencrantz, ensure that my trunks are brought aboard and stowed properly." Hamlet didn't even look at him, though Rosencrantz bowed in acquiescence. Hamlet strode up the gangplank onto the deck.

From the elevation of the ship's deck he stared intently at Fortinbras once more. Fortinbras appeared to be giving some orders to a junior officer, who was nodding in agreement. Then, as if someone had called him, he looked across to where Hamlet stood. The two men exchanged a long glance. Then Hamlet turned and entered the ship's main cabin, closing its doorway behind him.

Chapter 39

Madness Compounded

Horatio toyed with his quill, allowing the tip of its feather to scratch his forehead as he thought. Although the next part of the story largely concerned relatively minor figures, he realized how it important was that they be treated in detail. After all, in some ways they and their fates reflected the characters and fates of members of the royal family.

Horatio knew little of women, and although he understood their intellectual attractions (and was not immune to their sexual allure), he was reserved and cautious by nature. In addition, he was observant and intelligent, diligent and loyal. For such a man, devotion to ideals and to a world of ideas is safe, the second more so than the first. To Horatio, honor had less to do with ambition and more to do with understanding, and achievement was less a physical or legal status within a social hierarchy and more an improved knowledge derived from a process of inquiry and cogitation.

When he finally began to write, Cleopatra yawning at his elbow, it was this latter achievement that was his object. He had to think this through.

I was thunderstruck by the events surrounding the death of Polonius and the departure of Hamlet for England. The murder itself was shocking, and Hamlet's confrontation with the king was bizarre, filled with insult and venom (barely hidden), and hypocritically sugared with Claudius' semblance of familial solicitude and care.

Only Hamlet, of course, could originate such exact phrases as, "Farewell, Mother," to Claudius and logically rationalize them. And Claudius' protests that his actions were for Hamlet's wellbeing were simply lies. But I'm rushing.

I was able to retrieve some documents from Polonius' apartments. (What a suite! The king obviously believed in rewarding his chief councilor. It was luxurious beyond belief! At least compared to mine...)

Among the documents were many letters, diary entries, even poems composed by Ophelia. I admit that I tended to underestimate her. I should have known that Hamlet could not give his heart, or his body, to one unequal to him. The following poem, though perhaps a bit trite, gives some insight into Ophelia's heart:

I felt his hand upon my breast, and laughed with joy;
I urged on his passion, lest he'd think me coy.
And when he left his sweet release with me,
I throbbed in concord like the heaving sea.
And having all his love within, I trust
I'll have his faith until we two are dust.

Of course, few if any of us thought then that she might carry Hamlet's child. Who knows, indeed, whether or not she did? But as events unfolded, such likelihood is certainly possible.

Hamlet was gone—to England, we were to believe, or God knows where.

Polonius was dead and in the ground. The king had arranged his burial, a quiet ceremony in a minor chapel, followed by interment in a poor country churchyard. Even the priest had threadbare vestments!

Ophelia's only living family, Laertes, had been informed by messenger, but he was still likely on the way from France. It is small wonder that she felt lost and abandoned. I only happened to see her in one of the palace corridors, a haunted ghost of a thing, not even properly dressed, eyes flicking this way and that as if watching for something horrible. I asked her whether or not I could be of service, but she merely glared at me and said, "My brother shall know of it!" and paced away as if some purpose demanded her presence.

I too felt alone. My presence in Elsinore was essentially at the bidding of my prince. With his departure I felt certain that my own eviction would be forthcoming, but for some reason it wasn't. Perhaps the royal couple was preoccupied with more important things. But I missed Hamlet. We used to spend much time together.

Memorable among these now lost hours were his practice periods at fencing. I would call on him (at his previous request, of course), and he would set down his reading, gather his foils, and direct us to the gymnasium above the jails. Here I would sit, often reading patiently, while the prince was put through his paces by his fencing instructor, Dean Mastresen, a man who once defeated the renowned Sir Alfred Ericson, known to those in his field as one of the finest swordsmen in Europe. The foils would clash in their erratic rhythms, while I pondered the finer points of Pythagorus and Aristotle. Every now and then I would hear a curse or a change in tempo, and I would look up, only to see one or the other with his sword's point at the other's neck. (Hamlet's instructor must have been incredibly brave, for to put a sword to the neck of any royal is to invite death. But Hamlet would merely sweep off his mask and laughingly offer the man his hand, contemptuous of what might have been his fate.)

Ah, yes, fate. On other occasions Hamlet and I conversed *about* fate.

What *is* fate, except the ordination of what must be? And yet, Hamlet always questioned how it might come about. His perception would leap ahead of my semi-tutored mind, willing to question the standard explanation of God's will. But his questioning almost made me apprehensive with its audacity, his willingness to suggest that something more than God's supreme will *might* be at work.

Philosophers look at effects and causes. The chicken causes the egg. The fire causes the water to boil, and so on. We assume that all these created phenomena are the work of God. But Hamlet would challenge such mundanities further.

"Suppose," he would say, "that God did not want the water to boil, no matter how much fire we applied to its pot. Would it boil, or not?" And, "Suppose a partridge wanted to lay a puppy—could it do so? Or, could it do so if God gave permission?"

But most of all he was interested in his own fate. We all know the mythic tale of the three sisters—one who spins the thread of life, one who measures it, and a third who cuts it off—but surely these tales are simply metaphors. How are the grand creations done—the spinning, the measuring, the cutting—and who or what, really, is responsible for their outcomes? Might innocence or guilt come into destiny's remorseless processes? Is it possible to find oneself in a dilemma from which, through no fault of one's own, it is impossible to extricate oneself?

Hamlet certainly understood that he was in such a predicament. After all, the murder of a family member *demands* revenge. But to kill a king, God's anointed earthly minister, is the worst crime of all. I'm confident that he wished that God would release him in the same way that Christ prayed on Golgotha. "Oh my Father, let this cup pass from me..." something like that. I remember Hamlet's haunted voice on the night of the ghost: "My fate cries out!" He must have believed at that moment that he had no choice, no freedom of will--only the acceptance of what must be.

But Hamlet is gone. I wish to speak more of Ophelia.

She must have managed all alone for a few days. I am sure that Polonius' servants did their best for her, but they were always trained by the old man to remain aloof, and I suspect that what she needed was simply a loving breast to cry upon. None such was to be had.

It was a few days later when I happened upon her in the corridor once more. I had been trying to commit a part of *Nichomachean Ethics* to memory, and I have found that memorization always comes more easily while walking or pacing up and down. Corridors are good for that.

I had successfully managed three important principles, along with their supporting arguments, when she came lurching down the hallway, almost as if drunk, headed for the queen's apartments. It was hardly possible to believe that it was really she. Her hair was wild and unwashed, and she was only half dressed. She approached me warily and asked, perhaps somewhat skeptically, "Where is the royal majesty of Denmark?"

I assumed she meant the queen, only because of her location (the king's apartments are in the next wing, only accessible from the queen's through the chapel).

"Lady Ophelia?" I said.

She merely backed up against the wall and slumping to the floor, said, "I need to see the queen. I need to see the queen. I need to see the queen." She repeated this again and again until I squatted beside her and asked, "And why do you need to see the queen?"

She smirked at me, then bowed her head in prayer, saying, "Our father, our father, our father...art thou in Heaven?"

I helped her up from the floor and she looked at me vacantly, an expression far from the vivacity and readiness to tease that those of us who knew her were once accustomed to. I led her to an upholstered bench under a window. Light streamed through, illuminating her hair like that of a fallen angel.

"Lady Ophelia, I will try to convince the queen to see you."

She stared at me with the vague hint of a smile, then swept her feet up onto the bench and faced out the window, arms around her knees, gazing at Lord knows what. I stepped away from her, looked at her once more, then walked the twenty or so paces to the entry to the queen's apartments where a sleepy guard stood holding his pike.

"With your permission?" I queried, and indicated that I should like to knock. He nodded and moved aside a little. I rapped tentatively on the door, then once more with a little more force.

Moments later a female servant opened and asked my errand. I explained that I needed to see Queen Gertrude on urgent business—concerning Polonius, I told her. The maid looked at me questioningly. Then instructing me to wait, she disappeared within. She returned shortly and said somewhat breathlessly, "The queen will see you. She has been speaking to Reynaldo, who will remain present."

It was my turn for to be surprised. Reynaldo had been one of Polonius' most faithful servants, but he had been sent to France, or so I thought, to inform Laertes of his father's murder. Another messenger must have been sent.

"Come with me," the girl said.

She led me into one of the queen's parlors. I could not help but notice what appeared to be a new tapestry along one of the walls. It did not quite match the others.

The queen, in an ivory gown, sat on a low bench, and Reynaldo, dressed in black velvet and wearing a rapier at his hip, stood beside her. I wondered whether he might be positioning himself to replace his former master. They eyed me suspiciously.

I bowed low. "Lady queen," I began, and straightened. "Reynaldo," I acknowledged, and dipped my head in his direction. He returned the gesture.

"What is it you require, Horatio," the queen asked directly, "particularly concerning Polonius?" She appraised me coolly, eyes direct, her person clearly not frightened or abashed in any way.

"My lady, Polonius' daughter Ophelia is without, evidently in some distress. She is begging to speak with you. And to you, I say, 'Well met,' Reynaldo. You among all of us might have some clearer understanding of Ophelia, given your experience with the family."

"With your permission, your majesty," he began, "I have not seen the young lady for days, as I have been with my own family. I am only just now returned, and was directed to see your majesty by the royal chamberlain, whom I encountered by chance at the palace entry." He lowered his head a moment. "Perhaps I should have been more attentive to young Ophelia under these circumstances."

Gertrude cleared her throat. "I cannot imagine what young Ophelia might desire of *me*. Especially without going through the proper procedures to obtain audience. Let her return in three days time when I have my regular appointments to examine the minor suits within my purview."

"My lady," I went on, "It may be good she were spoken with now. Her appearance is not that of the young lady we once knew and admired. Palace servants have informed me that her speech is wild, often irrational, although composed of language that might suggest that there *is* meaning. Listeners find themselves compelled to try to interpret her conversation in ways that might make sense to them, and yet she may mean other things altogether. She speaks often of her father and her brother" (at this Reynaldo lifted his head expectantly) "and complains that conspirators may have eliminated her father for unknown reasons. Of course, it is well known that our Hamlet was the instrument of Polonius' demise, but such considerations seem beyond Ophelia's understanding, or at least her willingness to comprehend."

I paused to assess the impact of my words. Reynaldo leaned down and whispered something in the queen's ear. She turned to him and mouthed something back that I couldn't decipher. He nodded, as if in agreement.

"Very well," she said. "Let her come in."

"I will get her," I said. I bowed and went back out into the corridor. Ophelia was still in the window down the hall, singing some incomprehensible tune and drawing with her finger on the windowpane.

"Lady Ophelia," I said as I approached. She looked at me and gave me a smile and a wink. "If you will permit me to escort you, queen Gertrude will see you now."

"Oh, brave knight!" she exclaimed, and bounded to her feet, which I only now noticed were bare, and not very clean. Her own gaze followed my eyes, and she lifted one foot and wiggled its toes.

"Christ had nails in his feet," she said, frowning. "Ah, what smith could be so bold as to shoe our Lord? Desert dust and cobwebs, and especially snakes make wary walking. But I don't walk so much as dance!" She smiled at me winningly and whirled two quick pirouettes past me down the hall toward the queen's entry.

She moved up to the guard, and to his obvious discomfiture kissed his cheek. "Come, my cavalier!" she beckoned me. I caught up with her, allowed her to take my arm, and with my free hand knocked on the door once more. The guard resumed his station.

When we entered the queen's parlor, Gertrude's consternation became immediately evident. Reynaldo looked white, whether with fury or disbelief, I couldn't say. Gertrude stood and approached Ophelia, who stood motionless with her hands clasped, as if in prayer, her eyes lowered.

"Lady Ophelia," the queen began, but Ophelia put her hand up, palm outward, and said, "Shush! There's a song!" She cocked her head as if listening to some otherworldly voice, then began to sing herself, with tears coursing down her cheeks.

They bore my father soft away,
No, ah no, his death was wrong!
And in a grave his body laid,
No, ah no; no life lasts long.
And so his body lies there still,
No, ah no, his death was wrong!
Within the churchyard, on the hill,
No, ah no; no life lasts long.
His face was pale; his hair was white,
No, ah no, his death was wrong!
His body buried in the night,
No, ah no; no life lasts long.
And when such cold comes call for you,
No, ah no, such death is wrong!
Remember: it is all men's due,
No—ah no—no life lasts long.

The last syllable died away on a long, mournful note, and truth be told, I was enchanted by the beauty of her voice and by the pathos of her message.

The queen went to Ophelia, who had now slumped to sit on the floor again, her face hidden in her hands and wild hair.

Gertrude bent to comfort Ophelia, but Ophelia shrugged off her hand.

Gertrude straightened again and shrugged at the two of us as if to ask, what should I do? At that moment King Claudius entered the chamber. Reynaldo and I instinctively bowed and he nodded at us. He looked at Ophelia and Gertrude, who gestured at the now silent girl. The king moved to look down at her.

"How do you, pretty lady?" the king asked gently. (I had not known him capable of such solicitude!)

Ophelia peeked up at him through spread fingers. She examined him for a moment, then sighed heavily and got to her feet. For several seconds she looked around at all of us present—Reynaldo staring at her from his position across the room, me staring much as he, I should imagine, and the king and queen in front of and beside her. Then she giggled.

"As a bird or a beast dressed for table, I think," she finally said. "Defeathered or defurred, but not yet flayed."

She moved very close to the king now, and began to stroke his chest. He stepped back, startled, but she followed and put her ear to his chest, her arm around his waist to hold herself close.

"Have you a heart?" she asked him, and she smiled up into his bewildered face. "Does it sing?" She laughed again. "Mine does," she said, and breaking away from him moved to the window. Her expression twisted from her smile and she began to cry once more. Her nose was running, and she wiped it away with one hand and onto her skirt. She began to sing once more, each couple of lines separated by audible hiccups of grief.

His soul now rests on God's great scale,
No, ah no, such death is wrong!
The echoes of condemned souls wail,
No, ah no; no life lasts long.
We wait, God waits, for our great test,

No, ah no, can death be wrong?
That presages eternal rest,
No, ah no; no life lasts long.

Then suddenly she snarled at Claudius, venom in her voice: "My brother shall know of it." And once more, more softly but emphatically, "My brother shall know of it."

Turning to me, she held out her hand and said, "Come, my cavalier, come." Hardly knowing what to do, I took her hand, and she led me (rather than the other way around) toward the door.

"Oh, take her home, Horatio; keep her safe," the king said, and I nodded. As Ophelia and I were moving to the exit, I heard him say, "Reynaldo?"

Reynaldo replied, "At your service, my liege," and he bowed, and moved toward Claudius.

I took Ophelia's hand and tucked it under my arm. She seemed utterly distracted now, and once outside the queen's apartments it was no difficulty to walk her down the several echoing corridors to Polonius' apartments. Ophelia looked around us warily, as if she expected us to be accosted by danger at every turn.

On the way I stopped one of the maidservants, who was carrying a basket of linens along one of the hallways.

"When you have done with your delivery, come to Polonius' apartments at once. The king has an important task for you," I told her. She took a deep breath, and with a 'Yes, my lord,' curtsied agreement. I felt suddenly flush with power, a strange rush of feeling. 'My lord!'

The maid must have hurried, because by the time we had reached Polonius' apartments she was already catching up to us. Between us, we took Ophelia inside.

Ophelia seemed to know where to go, by habit I suppose. She tugged free of my arm and walked directly to her bedchamber.

"Stay with her," I instructed the maid. "I am sure Reynaldo will be here soon, and I will send you further help. The lady is distraught. She needs rest."

"I will, my lord," the maid replied.

I turned and left the quarters, and I could see Reynaldo just rounding a corner towards me. But I pretended not to notice, and turning the other way, went to my own quarters. I needed time to think.

At this point Horatio put down his quill and rubbed his writing hand with the other. It ached. He felt somehow anxious, irritated. Only the cat appeared at peace, asleep on its cushion. And it was cold in the room. Brother Henrik would have to start supplying coal along with the supplies of paper, quills and ink.

Horatio gathered his papers carefully, slipped them into a large interior pocket in his robe, and blew out the candle. Candle smoke lingered in the air, a scent like sour honey. He closed his eyes a moment, remembering the image of Ophelia singing through her tears before the king and queen. He opened them again, and still feeling Ophelia's presence in the dimness of the window's moonlight, turned and left the room.

Chapter 40

Laertes Returns

His cheeks burned with anger, with anxiety, with shock.

"Dead?"

"I am sorry, lord Laertes, there is no doubt. Your father's servant Reynaldo, who had been planning to come to Paris himself when these events unfolded, sent me with the grievous news. Your father was murdered." Jan lowered his head, waiting what he knew must come next.

"Murdered!"

"Yes, lord. While carrying out an important mission for the king, he was killed by Prince Hamlet."

"Hamlet!"

"Yes, lord." Jan stood silently, awaiting further interrogation. Laertes' cheeks continued to burn, as if blushes could ignite a forest, a continent! He stood leaning against his desk, fingers clutching the edge of the writing surface. He gazed out the window of his third-floor rooms at the Paris blue sky. A pigeon sailed in and settled on the sill, looked briefly into the room, and flew away again. Finally Laertes spoke once more.

"You are the bearer of evil news. I am..." At this, he gesticulated wildly with his right arm. "I am aghast, aghast."

He settled into his chair, gazing wildly about himself while his discomfited family servant waited. Then he stared pointedly at Jan.

"My sister!" Laertes said. "What of her?"

"The minor house servants, Peder, Emily, and Betta, have their instructions to care for her." He paused, then said, "Peder, as you know, is infirm, and Betta can be difficult to instruct, but Reynaldo is still there.

"Yes," Laertes answered. "Yes, he's a reliable man." He thought for a moment. "I will return on the next available boat." He looked at Jan pointedly. "See to it. Arrange passage. I will wrap up my affairs here, as necessary; be prepared to leave immediately. See to it," he said once more. Jan bowed and left the chamber.

There were many Danish merchants and their retinues on the boat returning from France. The seas were largely calm, (*God be thanked*, Laertes thought), and the merchant ship made good headway. On the way he spoke with several of the passengers, telling them of the death of his father at the hands of the prince. (Perhaps he embellished the tale with imagined details, but what of it?)

With very few exceptions they, too, were shocked and upset. Some made strong efforts to appear even-handed in their judgment of events, for they were getting news third-hand. Further, many had no wish to be involved in court politics or intrigue. Still, the very idea of a prince murdering a chief councilor was unsettling. Who knew what implications this might have for trade?

The day the boat reached Elsinore harbor was sunny and cool. A cutting breeze whipped off the sound, turning the harbor to chop. But despite the somber motive for his journey, Laertes found himself nearly elated to be back in Denmark. He gazed at the familiar church towers, and further up the slope to the imposing defensive works around the palace.

He had spent many days talking with his fellow passengers, asking them questions, posing them dilemmas.

What kind of king promotes a murderer to the role of ambassador?

What kind of king fails to protect his closest advisor and supporter?

Is it just for a king to allow a loyal courtier to die unnecessarily (he added this last word on purpose) in the service of royal interests?

Laertes was no fool. He knew that the king was now vulnerable, and while public opinion was more or less worthless, the support of the merchant class was essential to a stable state. Laertes' father was a victim, perhaps a needless victim. Might Laertes himself not profit from this sacrifice? (This last was a question he asked only himself. He felt a bit tarnished, a bit vile for considering it. But he could not help but entertain the idea.)

He stood near the bow watching as the ship approached the pier. When it scraped against the pier's timbers and the gangplank had clattered onto the landing, he instructed Jan once more.

"Jan," he said, in as reasonable a tone as he could muster, "I wish to see my sister. Reynaldo must not know. Make sure you bring her to me, here, at the Falcon's Rest (he indicated one of the waterside inns nearby) by the ninth hour tonight."

Jan bowed his obedience, and once ashore, moved off through the crowd of hawkers and fishermen that made up much of the harbor crowd. Laertes watched him, the quiet, graceful movements of a practiced servant—unobtrusive, purposeful without being frantic. He could further use this man, he thought.

Later that evening Laertes sat, wrapped in his cloak in front of the fire in his room. When the owner of the Falcon's Rest had seen a sample of this fine traveler's gold, he had been more than eager to ensure comfort and privacy for his guest. He had assigned two of his servants to be available at any hour to serve the illustrious newcomer. The dinner had been filling, if not quite delicious, and Laertes reclined on his bench with a cup of wine, staring into the flames, thinking.

He needed to speak to the Council of Eleven, the chief lords of the realm without whose commitment and assent any claim to royal leadership would naturally fail. They were not fools. They would know by now the precarious nature of Claudius' current position. If anyone could see Laertes' worth as pretender to the throne, it would be these men. He smiled to himself, and sipped once more. The eighth hour had rung on the church's great bell several minutes ago. Then someone knocked on the door. Laertes started.

"Enter," he called.

Someone pushed open the door. Then Jan stood in the flickering light, looking abashed and contrite, as if expecting to be punished.

"Well?" Laertes inquired.

"My lord, the lady Ophelia is not able to attend you. She is in the family apartments in the palace. Reynaldo and, oddly enough, Horatio (Hamlet's friend, the scholar) are with her." He paused, then said, "She is ill, my lord."

"Ill? What kind of illness?" he asked sharply. Laertes had seen plague and its victims once when quite young. He knew how terrifying it could be. Still, there had been no rumors of contagion on the waterfront.

"It is important that you see her and judge her condition for yourself, my lord. According to Reynaldo, she cannot be left alone, and I was unable to see her in person. I deemed it right that you should know this from my own mouth."

Laertes scowled. "I am unable to approach the palace yet," he said roughly. Then, more softly, he added, "I am anxious for my sister, as I'm sure you understand. However, I am uncertain as to my welcome. As you are able, make contact with Reynaldo and even with my sister, if she is able. Report to me all that you can, each evening roughly at this hour. Say nothing of me, or, if pressed, that to your knowledge I am still on my way from Paris."

He waved away the uneasiness in Jan's expression. "Oh, do not worry. No one expects me here in such exceptional haste. Follow my instructions, and all will be well—perhaps marvelously so."

Jan bowed and retreated out the door.

Laertes returned his attention to the fire, the curl of flames licking at the charred wood, the glow of coals, the flickering of light and shadow. *How like fortune is fire,* he thought to himself. *Unpredictable in its particulars, but leading to a predictable end…* Then he wondered to himself just how predictable his own end would be.

The flames flickered their reflections in the pewter wine cup he had set on the small table beside him. He continued to stare into the fire.

Chapter 41

King or Usurper?

Horatio yawned. It would not do, he knew, to be sleepy at this time, for his memory had to be sharp for the events he must now record. He had to speak of Ophelia again.

He rubbed his right eye with the knuckle of his right fist and yawned deeply once more. He wished he had some tea. Finally he got up from his writing table and went over to the window, where it was still nearly dark outside. Only the glimmerings of near dawn were silvering the harbor water far off and below, and the quarter moon still glowed off to his left.

He took a deep breath and stretched his back, then returned to the table. He lifted his right arm and rotated his shoulder. Cleopatra watched from her cushion in fascinated silence. Finally Horatio reached for his quill, dipped it into the ink, and began to write.

> "The king! The king! The queen! The queen! My brother!" These words Ophelia had been repeating for days now, as if there were no other words in her head. Except, of course, for, "Oh, Hamlet," which she would utter every now and then at irregular intervals, in a voice drawn out by some emotional state that perhaps only the condemned or dying might understand.

I had been sleeping in Polonius' quarters on a thick rug near his parlor fire for days, 'keeping good watch' as commanded by the king. Reynaldo was present, of course, as were two or three other servants. But none of them seemed to wish to have me gone.

Reynaldo moped around the quarters like an old hound, obviously somewhat demoralized by the death of his master, but only when he wasn't going through Polonius' papers. He would sit at Polonius' desk, reading some note or bygone regal order. He would grunt and sniff, as their effects hit his understanding. Once or twice he consigned a file to the flames in the small fire that burned in the grate to the left of Polonius' desk. Then he would turn to me, if I were in the room, and scowl as if to say, 'I know you've seen me destroy these documents. Utter a word of this at your own peril,' and I got the message. In any case, I was more concerned at the moment with Ophelia.

Ophelia seemed to have completely lost her wits. At one point or another she could gather her faculties together to the point at which she could ask for a bath (Emily or Betta would help her), though truth to say, she remained sweaty and unkempt most of the time, her hair as wild as her eyes.

I arranged that food would be brought, and when I thought she might be calm enough, I would try to converse with Ophelia.

Have you ever seen a jungle bird called a parrot? It's a brilliantly colored bird with a hooked bill brought from Africa by sailors. Such a bird can often reproduce human speech, and it will repeat a word or phrase again and again in such a way as to make any listener suspect that it has no knowledge of *what* it says, only of how to say it. Ophelia was just such a bird, repeating in a mournful tone, "The king! The king! The queen! The queen!...Oh, Hamlet!" On it went.

On the fourth afternoon, just after Betta and Emily had managed to wash and dress Ophelia, Reynaldo appeared in the doorway once more. (For some reason he had been gone for several hours. He always came and went unannounced.) He had a troubled expression, and for a few moments he did not know precisely how to address us.

"We must...the king...it is necessary that we go see the king and queen," he finally managed. This uncertainty of speech was quite unlike Reynaldo.

I nodded to Betta to bring Ophelia, but when Betta tried to take her arm, Ophelia said emphatically, "No! No! My cavalier must escort me!" I knew she meant me.

I approached her and bowed, and in my most sophisticated tones said, "My lady," and extended my hand. She took it regally, and we moved together toward the doorway. Reynaldo opened it, and once we were through, closed it behind us and led us down the hallway toward the king's quarters.

There was an unusual amount of activity in the hallways. Armed men moved here and there, some wearing the livery of the king's guard, others in more ordinary clothing. Faces were grim, and although weapons were not drawn, they were in no way hidden, and I was impressed by an apparent chaotic urgency, suspicion, and nervous tension present in the men.

Four guards were at the king's entrance. Two were the familiar Swiss mercenaries who traditionally guarded the king and his family. Two were rather roughly appointed, dressed in near homespun, yet well armed and sober in appearance for all that.

I was at first unsure what these changes meant. Ophelia clung somewhat inelegantly to my left arm, occasionally mumbling, 'king,' or something similar. The guards looked at her uncertainly, but as we were obviously expected within, they half bowed, and one of them opened the doorway and ushered us inside.

The first person I saw was the queen, Gertrude, sitting on a sofa opposite, pale and in obvious displeasure. I glanced to my left to where she was looking. There, the king and Laertes (Laertes!) sat opposite one another at a small table. To my amazement,

Laertes held a rapier in his right hand, although its blade lay on the table.

The king had been speaking when we entered, but he broke off at our appearance, then said, "You will see." Laertes merely scowled, then turned to us. In an instant he was up and moving to us, sliding the sword into its sheath and out of the way.

"Ophelia!" he said. "Sweet sister!" Ophelia simply gripped my arm harder, cringing away from him at first. But only a moment later she had released me and had her arms around her brother's neck, planting a profusion of kisses on his cheeks.

"Oh, brother, brother!" she panted. "So they have not killed you? Not dead yet?" She backed momentarily away and stared at him. Then she said more softly, "Do not doubt that it will come."

He looked at her, uncomprehending, but she slipped away and crossed the room past the queen, who eyed her nervously.

"Horatio?" Laertes said, as if to inquire whether or not it was really I. I nodded. He turned again to watch Ophelia, who had scooped a huge handful of flowers from the great vase standing on a sideboard beneath a mirror. She rubbed them lightly across the skin of her cheeks, inhaling deeply. Then she gazed at herself for a moment in the mirror and began to cry.

"Oh, Ophelia," the queen said, in as tender a voice as I'd ever heard her use. But she didn't get up. Then Ophelia began to sing an old, well-known lament, her voice tremulous and arrhythmic through her sobs.

Tomorrow is St. Valentine's Day,
All in the morning betime...
And I a maid at your window,
To be your valentine.

It seemed as if she were singing to someone else, someone behind the mirror. She gripped one of the flowers, singled from the bunch, and kissed it, closing her eyes as she did so. Tears continued to trickle down her cheeks. She sang again.

Then up he rose and donned his clothes,
And oped the chamber door...
Let in a maid, that out a maid,
Never departed more.

At this she lowered her head, almost as if in shame, then gazed into the mirror once more and sang.

By Jis, and by Saint Charity,
Alack, and fie for shame...
Young men will do it, if they come to it,
By cock, they are to blame.
You said, before you tumbled me,
You promised me to wed...

At this she turned to us all and smiled, a wan, hopeless smile. "Then he answers," she said.

"So would I ha' done, by yonder sun,
Hadst thou not come to my bed."

But she didn't pause there. Instead, she walked to the king while the rest of us regarded her in shock and stupefaction. She held out a few blossoms to Claudius, who took them. He looked at them briefly, then back at Ophelia, who stood smiling salaciously at him.

"There's fennel and columbines for you," she said matter-of-factly. "Oh, and also rue. For have we not all cause for sadness?"

She turned back to her brother, who had been softly approaching. "And you deserve some, too, no? Well, I'd give you some violets, but they all withered when my father died." Then, as if in afterthought, she said, "But here's a daisy," and she thrust one into his outstretched palm.

Then she turned to me and said, "Cavalier? Is my coach ready? Come," she said to me imperiously, "my coach!" and she snapped her fingers. She grasped my arm, and turning to the others said, "Good night, ladies, good night! Sweet ladies. Good night." And she led me to the exit.

I turned and looked at the others. Laertes appeared stricken, the queen mournful. She glanced once at Claudius and Laertes, then got to her feet and left by the side entrance to her own quarters. Claudius looked after her, then back at us. He appeared thoughtful, calculating. He called after us, "Look after her, Horatio. Keep her safe."

At that point we left the room, but as the door was closing I heard something like a roar or scream of impotent fury—Laertes' voice. It chilled me.

At this point Horatio ceased writing. He felt drained, unhappy. The importance of his personal participation was eclipsed by the ugliness of the memories. He needed sleep. In fact, he found he needed more sleep than ever before, as if each extended period of composition drained him like some athletic event. He yawned, a great stretching yawn that seemed to suck the whole atmosphere into his chest, only to release it in a long, slow exhalation. He would take an hour or so off, he decided, and then begin again. The cat was looking at him, as if in skepticism, but he had already lowered his head and begun to sleep.

Chapter 42

Victory in Poland

"Why didn't they surrender?" Fortinbras asked.

One of his lieutenants looked up. "Pride, I imagine. Pride."

Using his dagger, he was sawing at the ring finger of a dead Polish officer. There came a muffled 'pop,' and the finger came free. "There," the lieutenant said to himself. He tugged the ring from the bloody stump. Fortinbras looked away.

It had been a spectacular, coordinated attack. The Poles had been massed in fortifications along the shore, focused on Fortinbras' arriving ships. They had not anticipated the landward attack by the force of Norwegians that he had set ashore two days' march down the coast. The land force had swept into the town and launched a murderous attack into the Polish rear, even as those attacking from the sea were storming into the low surf to engage the Polish lines. Although the surprised Poles had generated a fierce resistance given the surprise attack from the rear, the outcome had essentially been a massacre.

Now Norwegian troops were active everywhere. Two were arguing over a large grey horse, once the property of a now dead Pole. A specially designated group was patrolling through the chaos of dead littering the sloped field on which the battle had been fought, sticking here and there with their pikes, finishing off the groaning Polish wounded.

One elated soldier came trotting past his commander carrying a large shield inlaid with a golden eagle. He glanced uncertainly at Fortinbras, but continued toward the rear, where cooks were already preparing food over several dozen campfires. There would be ale tonight, he knew.

Fortinbras slapped his own cheek where a mosquito had been sucking. A fresh blood spot appeared amid the splotches of enemy blood that were drying there. He felt a frisson of pride overriding his disgust. He had prevailed.

Beyond the field several houses in the village were ablaze. Smoke swirled into the air on the chilly sea breeze. That breeze would be welcome when the dead began to rot. The fires' infernal crackling could be heard over the shouts of the looting and the mournful cries of Polish women. Dogs barked and howled, and oddly, a rooster began to crow.

Lars approached Fortinbras and nodded what passed for a bow. "My lord," he said, out of breath, "the village is ours. Not a Polack man is left alive."

Fortinbras nodded his approval. "We will feast tonight. There must be food in storage here, and there are cattle in the pasture beyond. Ensure that our wounded are treated with all skill and speed. By tomorrow there must be an account of our dead."

He paused and then said, "Apart from legitimate acquisition of personal spoils from troops in the field, ensure that our men do not take private goods from the village, or from the church." He nodded toward the spire at the far end of the village. "The church is off limits. Other valuables in the village are ours, not for our soldiers except as pay or reward to be determined by me."

Lars bowed his head once more and moved off into the field, shouting for his officers. A swirl of wood smoke enveloped Fortinbras for a moment, and he fanned before himself a moment until the breeze pushed it off again. Finally he turned and trudged back toward the tents that had been put up for him on a small rise to the rear of what had been the landward battle lines.

He looked at the muck on his boots. He would need to clean his sword, he thought. He remembered the grimace of surprise on the Polish prince's face just as his sword jammed into the man's chest—a look of shock, of disappointment, then of emptiness.

At that moment one of his naval officers appeared before him, somewhat out of breath.

"Lord Fortinbras," he said quickly. Fortinbras nodded. "Two of our scouting ships have informed us that a Polish fleet is slowly approaching from the northeast. A naval encounter could set us back."

Fortinbras thought a few moments. It would take at least a day to gather their plunder. "How far away are they, in time, I mean?" he asked.

"At their present pace, a day and a half to two days, sir," the man responded.

"Have our ships ready to leave within two hours. We don't want a naval engagement with a force of unknown strength. Sail westward along the coast to the rocky bay we anchored in before splitting our forces for the attack. Our fighters will march west with our booty to meet you there in two days. Wait just offshore for our arrival." He paused. "We've achieved what we came to do." He thought a moment of how tired he and the men were, but they would have to pack swiftly and be off by morning.

The officer gave a half bow and stepped briskly back off toward the shore where the ships of the seaward attack bobbed in the light chop. Farther out he could see another dozen or so at anchor. *We will have to hurry*, he thought, breaking into a clumsy trot.

Fortinbras watched him go. He kicked a stone out of his way, then kicked it again when it hadn't rolled far enough. What had he expected? He didn't know. He had picked a fight. He had won. And? Two words echoed in his brain, over and over again. *Now what?*

Finally, barring other considerations from his mind, he turned to find Lars to get their retreat march organized. *What has been won can as easily be lost,* he thought to himself. *Tired or not, we will have to get moving.*

Chapter 43

Escape Into the Trap

The night was chaos. Hamlet's ship, a basic trading vessel, floated grappled to a long, sleek warship, a pirate raider. Torchlight glittered on the water, and sounds of shouted orders in a Frisian dialect rang out.

Several Danish sailors were already dead, and another lay groaning, bleeding heavily from his side onto the oak planking. The captain of the Danish ship knelt, offering his sword to the intruder leader, who snatched it by the handle, then planted a kick on the captain's chin, knocking him backward. One of the raiders was about to open the door to the companionway below deck when it seemed to open of itself, drawing everyone's attention.

Hamlet stepped out, wrapped in a purple cloak that he hugged about himself. He closed the door again behind him. He spoke to the intruders in their own dialect. They stopped and gazed at him, startled, nearly stupefied.

"I believe it is I whom you seek so rapaciously," Hamlet said calmly. He looked at the pirate leader. "You are a bold fellow, aren't you?" Hamlet observed.

The man scowled and approached gingerly. Hamlet put up his hand, and unaccountably, the man halted.

"I will accompany you willingly," Hamlet said to the puzzled leader. "As you can see, I can make it worth your while to accommodate me."

Although one of the pirates made to threaten Hamlet with his sabre, the leader motioned him away. He waited for Hamlet to continue.

"Come here, fellow," Hamlet said in a tone of one accustomed to command. His manner was so obviously royal the man nearly automatically obeyed. He came closer. Hamlet extended his fist to show off his signet ring. "I am the Danish crown prince. You must return me to Denmark."

The leader frowned skeptically. He spat on the deck and pointed his sword at Hamlet. He sneered.

"Oh, don't worry, I'll ensure that you're paid for your pains. Shall we say ten thousand crowns?"

The man gasped. One could build four ships for ten thousand crowns.

Hamlet went on. "You must leave this ship and take me with you. This ship has its own destiny that has nothing more to do with gentlemen such as you. Return me to the Danish shore, deliver some letters from me to the castle in Elsinore, and I will ensure you get your ransom money."

The pirate group, who numbered no more than twenty or so well armed men, was now gathered around. Some stared at Hamlet with open hostility. Several looked to their leader, who gazed at Hamlet for several moments. Hamlet returned his stare.

Finally the man stabbed his sword into the deck, where it stood quivering. He gestured to his men, and pointed toward his ship. Reluctantly they began to move to the gunwale where the pirate vessel bumped alongside. He waved his hand again and they clambered over the rail and dropped onto the deck of the raiding vessel, one by one. Then the leader gave a half bow and gestured for Hamlet to precede him.

Hamlet nodded. The leader wrenched his sword free and the two men paced to the gunwale. Hamlet vaulted over it with ease, landing on his boots amid the pirate crew with a thud. The pirate leader followed.

Behind the companionway door, Guildenstern stooped, squinting through a crack beside the jamb. He and Rosencrantz had been hiding in a large cupboard in their cabin. "I can't believe it," he said.

"Move and let me look," Rosencrantz said from behind him. Guildenstern felt himself being pushed aside, and Rosencrantz applied his eye to the crack.

"What's he done?" he asked in puzzlement. "Where is he?" Hamlet was no longer visible.

"He's in their boat!" Guildenstern croaked.

A moment later the grappling hooks were removed. Rosencrantz could see sails being raised and could hear the familiar noise of a ship's crew at work. A few more moments and the pirate ship began to pull away.

Both felt a mixture of vast relief and a new apprehension.

"My God, he's gone!" Rosencrantz said.

"Gone?"

"He's with the pirates. Hamlet! You said so yourself. They're leaving!"

Guildenstern crossed himself. "Thank God," he said.

"Hamlet is *our* responsibility!" Rosencrantz protested.

Guildenstern remained silent for a moment. He allowed Rosencrantz to elbow him further out of the way and open the door, and the two of them climbed up onto the deck. Torchlight on the deck of the pirate ship could still be seen, but it was already a hundred yards away or more and receding into the blackness. A man nearby groaned pitiably, and Guildenstern moved to help him. Rosencrantz stepped over to the rail and fixed his eyes on the departing pirate vessel, which continued to shrink into the distance. Although several torches burned on their own deck, it had never seemed so dark.

The Danish captain groped his way unsteadily to his feet. He looked around him. A whiff of breeze snapped a sail, which slapped briefly and bellied out. The ship responded gently, moving slowly with the wind. The captain approached Rosencrantz and said, "Now what?"

Rosencrantz seemed uncertain for a moment, then decided. "We continue for England. We still have enough men?"

The captain looked around at the dead and wounded. Here and there a sailor emerged from another area of the deck. Two Danish sailors clumsily muscled a dead pirate up and over the starboard rail. Rosencrantz heard a muted splash.

After a brief mental count, the captain said, "We'll have to make do, whichever way we sail." He turned to his two remaining noble passengers. "You'll pull a rope if you have to." It was a statement, not a question.

Rosencrantz frowned, then moved to help Guildenstern. Only a distant flickering light showed where the pirate vessel was moving back toward Denmark.

Chapter 44

The King Counsels Poison

The door closed behind Horatio and Ophelia with a solid 'thunk,' leaving the other two men alone. But even as it was closing, Laertes let out a howl. His face was blotched red and white, and tears wet his cheeks.

"Oh, God!" he shouted. Then, to Claudius he cried, "Did you see that? Did you?" He pounded his fist on the table between them, and Claudius looked down, reflexively mouthing a small prayer.

When he looked up, Laertes had stood quietly, the rapier in his hand. Although the blade pointed at the floor, indecision seemed to flit across Laertes' features.

"Laertes," he said firmly, almost like a father. "Laertes. Your grief is mine and mine is yours."

The tip of the blade wavered side to side slowly before him like a snake seeking prey. It was obvious: Laertes was an expert swordsman.

"Do not wave that blade toward us!" Claudius' voice was sharper now, fueled by anxiety, but also an expression of his assumed authority. "As your father's son, you above all must understand that I am God's anointed ruler. Treason and regicide would not become you."

The hardness in his voice softened. "Laertes," he said, again. "Tell me your grievances, and I swear that I will do all in my power to salve them. I swear." He paused. "I put it to you, select those of your friends whom you will and let them judge my actions. If they find me in any way responsible for your father's death, I will give you my life and crown in satisfaction."

Laertes regarded him thoughtfully, still angry, but considering. Finally he answered, bitterness in his voice, "You must realize, the obscure funeral rites, the private burial, the unconscionable lack of recognition for my father's loyalty and service. Now my beautiful sister marred by madness as a result. Surely I must call it into question."

He looked down at his sword, and then slowly slid it back into its scabbard. He walked to the window, a vantage from where he could see the sun setting over the harbor; then he returned and sat again opposite the king.

"Laertes you must understand. It was Hamlet, who suffering from madness, murdered your father. He has been sent…away. To England, where he will doubtless suffer a just punishment for his crime."

"You know this?" Laertes asked. "Why did you not simply try him in your own court and assess the natural punishment yourself?"

Claudius looked away and sighed. "For two reasons—special reasons. They may not seem adequate to you, and I can understand why they might not. For me they served."

"First, the general population, not only in the palace area but in the city and in the countryside as well…they *love* him. I know, I know, they exhibit that typical stupidity that people often show—they don't judge the crime but instead sympathize with the travails of the criminal. They judge with their hearts, not their minds." His tone was frustrated yet resigned. He sighed.

"My position as king may be granted by God, but God himself knows that it is the people who buttress our security, and to go dramatically against their inclinations would be a foolish act." Claudius wondered a moment how the people in question would react to Laertes' ambitions, but he let it go.

Laertes turned away. *Surely the king is a calculating coward*, he thought. But even as he considered this, he couldn't help but admit to himself how his own anger had already leaked away. He wasn't completely sure what drove him most any more—his sister's distress, innate rage at the death of his father, his clinging to principles of courtly behavior, or his image of his powerful father, high in the noble Danish court. He was sure that it wasn't possible that the king would hand over his power, whatever the facts of the case were. But Laertes' own ambition had already shrunk when tested. He felt momentarily diminished.

"The second reason," Claudius went on, "is the fact that the queen, his mother, is so conjunctive to my life and soul that I could not bear to execute her son—here." He stressed the last word, and Laertes gave him an appraising glance.

Straightening up, Laertes said, "There must be justice, wherever and however it is to be administered."

"Of course, of course," Claudius answered. "Do not imagine I am willing to let myself and my queen be threatened, my officers murdered, and the kingdom stirred into weakness and unease without using my powers to remedy affairs. Where the guilt lies, there let the great axe fall." The last sentence dropped between them, a great linguistic axe, potent with bloody meaning.

At that moment a servant knocked.

"Come," Claudius called.

One of the lesser servants approached softly. He bowed twice.

"Yes, yes, what is it?" Claudius asked impatiently.

"I have letters, your majesty." He extended a packet. "One is there for the queen, and one for you. One also for Ophelia." Laertes looked up at the sound of her name.

"From whom?" Claudius demanded.

"From the lord Hamlet, my liege."

Claudius took them, scanning their exteriors briefly. Laertes was even more alert now.

"Who brought them?" Claudius demanded.

"Some sailors, I think. I didn't meet them. Rolf received the letters and gave them to me to deliver." The servant stood carefully erect, watching as the king opened one of the letters.

"Leave us," the king commanded. The servant bowed and left the room.

"You shall hear them," Claudius said to Laertes. He began to read aloud.

Your Royal Highness,

I have recently, and very strangely I might add, come back to Denmark, and I beg leave to meet with you at which time I will recount to you the occasion of my strange return.

It would be best if we might meet alone, for surely the business that might occur between king and prince requires the protection of privacy.

Hamlet

"Can you make anything of that?" Claudius asked Laertes.

"Is it Hamlet's writing?"

"It is. How could he have returned? The ship was bound for England."

"Perhaps," Laertes said, "more to the point would be to discover what he wants. In any case, let him come. If he is, indeed, my father's killer, does it not fall right that he be here where I can take my requisite revenge?"

"You are right," Claudius replied. He got up and went to a sideboard. He poured two glasses of wine from a decanter and brought one back to Laertes, who took it and looked at it suspiciously. Claudius smiled knowingly and drank. Seeing this, Laertes sipped his own, tentatively.

"Laertes, tell me," Claudius said, more genially now. "Did you truly love your father?"

Laertes colored and answered sharply, "Why do you ask this?"

"It's not that I think you did not love your father," Claudius continued. "But like most feelings, time can qualify a feeling's fire in the same way a candle burning lower has smaller flame, one that ultimately goes out by itself, quenched by its own molten wax."

He smiled at the aptness of his own comparison. Then he said, "If you truly want revenge for your father's death, you need to burn at full flame. What kind of risks would you willingly take to achieve your revenge?"

"I'd cut his throat in the church," Laertes answered indifferently.

Claudius gave a light guffaw of approval. "It *is* true; revenge should know no boundaries. Listen. If I can arrange the opportunity for your revenge, will you be ruled by me?"

"So long as you do not rule me to sue for some sort of peace."

"Only to your own peace." Claudius took another swallow of wine, then gestured with his cup toward Laertes.

"I have heard tell, from various sources, of your skill at fencing. In fact, the most recent court visitor from France claimed that he doubted whether *any*one could match you."

Laertes colored slightly, then inclined his head slightly, a gesture of false humility perhaps.

The king went on. "Suppose we were to arrange a practice bout between you and Hamlet, assuming in fact he is returned. Although a shrewd young man, he harbors little suspicion. He may be annoying in the instability of his mental states, but he does not think ill of the world. With a little shuffling of the foils, we could arrange for you to use an unblunted sword. With a bit of casual swordplay you could requite him for your father." Claudius beamed. The idea seemed perfect.

Laertes weighed his options for a few moments. Then he said decisively, "Yes. I will do it. It warms my heart that I might avenge my father using the same means by which Hamlet killed him."

He paused a moment, then said, "To be utterly certain of our desired outcome, I'll poison the blade's tip. I have access to a poisonous paste concocted from a variety of noxious herbs—I bought it from a mountebank in the Latin Quarter in Paris. (One never knows when one might need such a compound.) If I but scratch him in any significant way, it will kill."

He felt a sense of satisfaction, almost elation, now that some kind of physical action was in the offing. *Thought and planning are never so gratifying as doing,* he thought. Even now he was imagining the swift flashing of his rapier, disarming the enemy prince, slipping his riposte into Hamlet's abdomen.

"Excellent!" Claudius said. He knew he had Laertes on side now. The control that had been so dizzily slipping away only a short time before was back.

He drank again, then said, "However, even the finest plan should have a back-up, a second option in the unlikely event our first plan should fail. Let me think."

He tapped his forefinger on the table in front of him. Laertes frowned as if irritated, but then Claudius added, "Ah, I have it. Fencing is very strenuous, is it not?"

It was unclear whether or not this was a rhetorical question, but Laertes nodded.

"And surely the stress of manly combat can make a man hot and thirsty?"

Laertes nodded again.

Claudius smiled grimly and explained, "Well, our back-up plan will include a method that even the queen would call accidental. I will prepare a cup of wine for the occasion, a cup of poisoned wine. Make your bout with Hamlet vigorous and tiring. If you fail to gain the needed hit, unlikely as such a consequence may be, for his thirst I will offer him the wine. If or when he drinks, he still will fall."

Laertes looked at Claudius with a new expression, one not quite of respect, but of grudging admiration, much as a dog that has wrestled a bone away from another looks with envy at one that has taken some meat. He gazed openly at the king with a mix of apprehension and appraisal. Finally he nodded decisively.

He relaxed in his seat and drank again. It was a sweet wine with a floral nose, soft on the tongue. He lowered his glass and looked again at the window, where only the last rays of the sun could be discerned. He turned again to the king.

Claudius was smiling. Laertes smiled back. The two men raised their glasses to one another.

Chapter 45

In the Service of the King

Guildenstern retched over the port rail as the bow of their ship rose once more, only to plunge again into the trough of the North Sea swell. From his seat on a coil of rope, Rosencrantz watched critically, a look of despair on his face. Guildenstern turned and gave him a piteous expression, then brought up some more smelly fluid that splashed on the deck and on his boots. Finally he wiped his mouth with his sleeve (his handkerchief was far too soiled—he had thrown it overboard), and he turned to Rosencrantz again. He staggered over to the coil of rope where Rosencrantz sat, somewhat green with nausea himself.

"Are you finished?" Rosencrantz asked.

Guildenstern grimaced, but nodded. "I think so," he muttered weakly.

"Help me up," Rosencrantz said, extending his hand. Guildenstern rubbed his own hand briefly on his breeches and helped Rosencrantz to his feet. The wind stung with salt. It tugged at their hair and their sleeves, a chilly insistence.

"Let's go below." It was rather more a demand than a suggestion. Rosencrantz led the way to the hatch, and the two descended to the companionway that led to their quarters, directly beneath the cabin where Hamlet had been.

It was dark below, and reeked of oil and sweat. One of the regular seamen glanced at them suspiciously as he squeezed past on the way up to the deck. His arm was bandaged with someone's shirtsleeve, and he had a black eye. But he scuttled up the short stair with practiced ease.

Rosencrantz ducked through the low entrance into their cabin, and Guildenstern followed. The cabin floor still heaved up and down with the swells, and neither of them felt safe.

Rosencrantz sat on the edge of his bunk, a narrow wooden shelf with a heavy straw pallet, covered comfortably enough with several woolen fleeces. Guildenstern sat opposite. Two narrow glass portholes near the ceiling emitted an intermittent, dim light.

"Are you sure we've done the right thing?" Guildenstern said.

"As you informed *me*, king Claudius demanded we provide the English with his letter," Rosencrantz said. "That is what we shall do."

"I know, I know. But you know my reservations. Now that the prince has been taken everything might be different." Guildenstern coughed softly into a fresh handkerchief he had retrieved from his trunk.

"I daresay it is," Rosencrantz countered. "But who are we to disobey the king? Besides, Hamlet is likely to be dead now in any event." Rosencrantz crossed himself reflexively, and Guildenstern did likewise. "I'm surprised we survived the skirmish ourselves. It's only the fog and the currents that saved us." This last statement was a comforting lie, but Guildenstern did not correct him.

"Is there any wine left?" Guildenstern asked.

Rosencrantz pointed to a built-in cupboard above a small table attached to the hull. Guildenstern rose, pulled it open, and removed a bottle containing some dark liquid. He poured measures into two mugs on the table, recorked the bottle, and put it back in the cupboard. He handed one of the mugs to Rosencrantz.

Rosencrantz winced as he gripped it with his blistered palm. He hadn't complained much, but 'pulling a rope,' as the captain had put it, was hard, unaccustomed work.

He sipped and then said, "We will deliver the letter as instructed. We cannot be blamed for carrying out a royal command." It was a rationalization, but it was the best and safest course of action he could think of.

After a few quiet moments Guildenstern finally asked, "You never really liked him in Wittenberg, did you?" Rosencrantz looked up.

"The prince? Of course I liked him." His mouth twisted into half a sneer. "It is every subject's duty to *love* the prince."

Then, more quietly, he said, "No, I didn't like him. Each day in Wittenberg I'd watch the professors, with their sheep-like acquiescence to his questions and proposals, and the other students deferring to his status, as if he were some purebred greyhound amid a pack of mutts. He was condescending and superior." He began to warm to his critical theme.

"And Horatio! God, there was another! A self-styled 'philosopher,' absorbing classical platitudes and aphorisms as if all that half-baked nonsense can change the direction of the world." He snorted. "I didn't like him, either." He paused, but then said, "I gather you did." He was disappointed in Guildenstern, whom he judged as deferential and acquiescent as the professors in Wittenberg. But he had to admit to himself that he had always enjoyed his social authority over the man.

Guildenstern answered surprisingly readily. "I admired him—Hamlet, I mean. He accepted his power and lived with it, much as a man lives within his skin. God gives us our roles to play. I thought he played his well. Until he went mad, anyway."

He mused for a moment, and then said, "I would never have imagined such a man could lose his wits the way he did. The contrast to his public person between Wittenberg and Elsinore was so strange. Once back in Elsinore each time we saw him I felt we were looking at someone through an imperfect window, revealing a wavy image with blots and imperfections, the picture of a person who somehow lacks dimension, but whose outline creates something a bit fearful. I actually became afraid of him. My fear of the king is rational. My fear of Hamlet was not so."

Guildenstern drank again and looked at the unsteady floor. The drink seemed to have steadied him somewhat.

A knock resounded on the cabin door. "Masters?" a voice called. "We are approaching the English coast. If weather permits, we will reach the town they call Scarborough within two or three hours. You will disembark there." Steps could be heard pacing away from their door.

"Cheer up," Rosencrantz said. "It is only two days ride from Scarborough to York, or so I am told. We will deliver the king's missive and, God willing, return speedily to Elsinore."

Guildenstern looked at Rosencrantz. "Well. Let us hope so," he said.

Chapter 46

Earth, Air, Fire and Water

Horatio took a fresh quill, and with a small blade he kept in one of the table's drawers, he sharpened its tip. He had much to think about, much to write, much to admit. He selected a new sheet from the several remaining beside the inkpot, positioned it carefully before him, bent forward, and began to write.

I sometimes blame myself. Indeed, if I were not so inured to feeling the guilt those pestilent priests continually foist on us I would be wracked with regret. And truly, I do feel regret for the events I am about to recount—or for some of them, at least--but not guilt.

When we left Laertes and the king, Ophelia clung to my arm as if she were drowning and I were some nearby log, a floating sanctuary to which she could adhere for safety. Truly, I felt both impotent and empowered, for I knew that I had been entrusted with a jewel of great value, and yet I knew not how I might help other than try to keep her safe.

We walked along the corridors toward her family's quarters. The usual guards, stationed at intervals throughout the palace, nodded their deference as we passed. Ophelia would gesture regally to them (as if her gestures in any way mattered), and they would bow their heads lower. None of them smiled, yet they looked on in near wonder.

At her doorway I fumbled for the latch and let us in. The rooms were dark, and somewhat musty-smelling, as if some earthy garden below the window were rotting composted material on its surface.

The air was cold, and I noticed the outer window had been left unlatched. I let Ophelia go for a moment and strode to it. Outside the evening had given way to night. A cold breeze whipped off the harbor, and I tugged the casement closed. Then I felt for a flint, and finding one, struck sufficient flame to light two candles I had discerned on the table.

There is something about fire that encourages us, and that makes us feel safe, and so I took one of the candles to the hearth on the outer wall. A fire had been laid there, in preparation for lady Ophelia's return, but it was unlit. The servants seemed to have gone, Reynaldo and the women, though I could not for the life of me understand where or why. The place was silent as the grave, but I felt reassured when the kindling caught ablaze and the larger wood chunks began to smoke.

I felt Ophelia's hand on my arm once more. I turned to her and asked, "Do you know where Reynaldo and the others might have gone?"

She shook her head. She pulled herself closer and murmured into my ear, "My cavalier, my cavalier," and she laid her head upon my shoulder. I caught the scent of her hair. I stiffened with fear and desire. I turned, and she raised her face to mine, an expression unguarded, pitiful, and utterly ravishing. I stared at her, the blood coursing through me, then looked away.

"Do not fear my brother," she said, as if she thought his possible influence was choking off my most natural response. My desire for her nearly overwhelmed me, but also nearly appalled me. Whatever her beauty and lusty openness, she was the lady of my prince—Hamlet's lady. Whatever her or my need, she would always be, to me, Hamlet's lady.

She stood on tiptoe to kiss me, and God help me, I allowed her to, this mad, beautiful maid. We kissed for perhaps five seconds, five seconds of sensual joy. I broke from her, gently, very gently pushing her away by her shoulders, though she held onto my hands, which were shaking a little. Apparently unoffended by my anxiety, she gave me a small, secret smile.

"Thank you, my prince," she said. Then, abruptly she let *me* go and walked through the door that led to her bedchamber. She closed it behind her and I heard the bolt slam shut.

My face burned with shame and fear. My body trembled, a kind of shudder that forced me to lean against the hearth, where the fire crackled cheerfully. I gathered my breath and my wits.

Only moments later the hallway door opened once more. Reynaldo stepped in and looked at me inquisitively. I must have appeared shaken, for he moved quickly to me, saying, "Horatio?"

I nodded and babbled something about some servants' irresponsibility, mentioning, I am sure, Ophelia's female helpers. At first he frowned, thinking I had lumped him in with some of the human dross we had as servants in the palace precincts.

"Not you, of course," I reassured him. I moved to a sofa and carefully sat down. "Twenty minutes or so ago I brought Ophelia from seeing her brother and the king," I said.

Reynaldo raised his eyes. "No wonder you look upset," he said. "I've just come from the king. Laertes was positively smoking with frustration. He and the king appeared reconciled well enough, though. King Claudius merely reaffirmed that we—that you and I—continue to look after Ophelia."

"You must pardon me tomorrow," I said. "The ladies will return, will they not?"

Reynaldo shrugged, and then said, "I expect so. I told them so."

"My father's brother, a merchant, has been at sea for several months and is only recently returned. I have committed to assisting him to find new accommodations on the morrow. You and the ladies can manage, can you not?"

I was lying about my uncle, of course. I thought momentarily of my conversations with Hamlet about honesty. But I felt strongly that I needed a ruse, for I had other obligations. I brushed off my compunctions like dust off my tunic.

At this moment one of the ladies knocked politely and then let herself in. She glanced warily at Reynaldo and me, and asked, "The lady Ophelia? She is well?" Reynaldo looked at me as if the answer to this question interested him, too.

"There is little change in her demeanor," I said. "I brought her from the king and her brother, and she seems to have gone to bed." I nodded toward her door.

Reynaldo went to a sideboard and poured himself some wine. I finally got to my feet to leave.

When Reynaldo looked up from his cup I said to him, "I will contact you within the space of two days at the latest. If you need me, send messages to my quarters and to The Hawk and Hounds tavern, where I am expecting to meet my uncle."

Reynaldo nodded absently.

Without waiting for any more questions I let myself into the corridor and closed the door behind me. For moments back in Polonius' apartments I had felt as if I were drowning (or how I imagine drowning feels). I ached with a great feeling of emptiness, as if a capacity I had not known existed within myself had suddenly become apparent, but once more existed only as empty potential. I felt extraordinarily alone.

I fished in my pocket once more, and pulled out the brief note one of the servants had passed me only hours before. "If you value your friend's life, you will come to the Hawk and Hounds tomorrow. We will contact you."

Chapter 47

Heads You Lose

Governor Berndt eyed the newcomers from Denmark distastefully. They stood before him, rather arrogantly he thought. The one called Rosencrantz had proffered a letter with the king's seal, as if no other politeness or ceremony were necessary.

Berndt lowered his eyes once more to the document. *Let them stew*, he thought.

He cracked the seal and unfolded the single sheet of instruction from the king. "To the Governor," it said, simply and plainly.

To the Governor:

Insofar as our peoples both prosper and profit from our mutual cooperation; And since this new decade continues our many years of amity; And whereas the York province of England is the faithful tributary of Denmark's royal house; Therefore I, Claudius, king of Demark would that you carry out our royal will through the following act, namely that the two bearers of this letter (known by their surnames Rosencrantz and Guildenstern) be put to immediate death through beheading. It is also our will that neither be shriven prior to your delivery of our justice, as neither has proven to be a trustworthy liegeman in our service. When evidence of their execution has been delivered to Elsinore, your person will be amply rewarded, more specifically with the title 'Earl of Northumberland,' such title to include all revenues from the estates and rents to be listed by Denmark's chamberlain within thirty (30) days of the receipt of such evidence. We are gratified by your humble and reliable service to the crown and to the state of Denmark.

The letter was signed with a semi-legible flourish. Berndt looked up.

The one called Guildenstern was gazing about himself—at the guards, at the ceiling (Lord knew what he saw there), at the windows. He turned and whispered something to Rosencrantz, who half turned to him and whispered something back, something apparently salving, for Guildenstern took a deep breath and bent once more toward the governor.

Berndt refolded the letter and placed it in the inner pocket of his robe. He beckoned the head of his personal guard, a beefy man armed with a large pike.

The guard approached and leaned toward the governor, who whispered in his ear, softly and earnestly for a moment. The guard looked at the two ambassadors appraisingly and then straightened up, nodding to the governor.

He snapped his fingers at the four guards who stood alertly along the walls. Four would do it; he could leave the guards at the doorway. He indicated the two men before him.

Guildenstern glanced up, as if momentarily puzzled. Rosencrantz looked back over his shoulder, just in time to feel the steely grip of two men grasping his arms.

"Wait! What is this?" he demanded, but the guards had already forced him and Guildenstern to turn back toward the entrance. "Governor?" he shouted over his shoulder.

"Don't make this any harder," said one of the guards in a soft voice, and the six men moved quickly, if erratically, out of the room.

"There must be some mistake, some misunderstanding!" Rosencrantz was shouting, and then they were through the door.

Berndt watched them go with curious, mixed feelings of pity and contempt. *No one should cross a king*, he thought to himself. His mind turned to the title 'Earl of Northumberland.' *Ah, yes*, he thought to himself. *It has a nice ring to it.*

It wasn't yet raining, at least not in the prison courtyard. The two men being hustled along by the husky guards strained to look about them but couldn't seem to get any bearings. It was cold. *Do these men speak Danish*?, thought Rosencrantz.

The courtyard was drab and empty, save for the execution block near the middle of its back wall.

"Now see here..." Rosencrantz remonstrated, but one of his captors unceremoniously slapped him with a heavy hand across the side of his head. For a moment, Rosencrantz's eyes filled with tears. He felt a ringing in his ear.

Guildenstern looked fearfully at his companion. He felt a sharp pain in the twist of his elbow as his guard forced him to his knees before a large, oak block, anchored in the sand of the courtyard.

"Head down!" the guard barked. Guildenstern turned again to question such an impertinent order, but an armored fist smacked his head sideways, then shoved it down onto the block.

"Rosencrantz!" Guildenstern shouted, but again, his head and chin were jammed roughly onto the block. Guildenstern had bitten his tongue, felt the salt blood on his lip, and the sensation of vertigo.

The swish of the axe was the last thing he heard.

Rosencrantz looked up to see blood everywhere—a scarlet runnel sliding down the block, a smear being wiped off a large axe-head by a muscular masked executioner, a few dribbles leaking out of the neck of his friend's head, which lay lopsided on the sand, staring emptily at him as if to say, "Is this what you had in mind?"

"You're next," growled his captor. Two more armored men dragged Guildenstern's body from the block. Rosencrantz felt his bowls releasing as he was dragged into its place.

"This is all wrong!" he said urgently, as he was forced to his knees.

Chapter 48

A Letter for Horatio

Horatio was tired. Bent as he was, he straightened from the table where he had been trying to write, and he shrugged his shoulders several times to try to loosen the knots in the muscles of his back.

Cleopatra looked at him curiously from her cushion, that impenetrably feline stare so alien that the Egyptians had seen within it forces of their gods at work. Horatio reached over and scratched behind the cat's head. It rolled backward and swatted at Horatio's hand. One of its claws drew a nip of blood.

Horatio withdrew his hand and glared at the cat. It glared back at him. *A standoff*, Horatio thought. Then he thought, *perhaps a standoff would have been better for Hamlet, nay, for us all.*

He turned once again to his papers, thinking, *the story is almost over. I must get it right. I must be very careful.* He picked up his quill, drew a fresh sheet of paper toward him, and began once again to write.

It was late afternoon when I received Hamlet's letter. I was sitting in the pub known as *The Hawk and Hounds*, a somewhat less than salutary place near the docks. (I was not prone to wasting my time or my very modest income in pubs, but the note had been insistent.) The book I had brought with me, *The Decameron*, was far too lighthearted for my mood, and it lay unopened on the table.

The pub smelled of fish and ale, only to be expected. To my left, three sailors were quarrelling amiably over a game of dice. The middle-aged woman who had brought me my ale now stood across the room, stirring some kind of soup, herring perhaps, in a great pot hanging over the fire in the hearth. I supposed I would have some later. She looked up at me and smiled suggestively (one of her front teeth was missing), but I shook my head and looked away. After what I had so recently experienced? Never.

I drew my book toward me and was about to pull back the cover when the pub door swung open. I watched as two foreign-dressed seamen slipped inside, closing the door behind them. One of them, a heavy, bearded man with a slight limp, went to the woman and showed her the writing on a sealed message he carried. She shook her head and shrugged to indicate that she didn't read, and he drew it back, frowning. Then glancing over, he noticed me with my book.

He moved over to me, surprisingly quickly given his game leg, and he thrust the letter toward me, pointing at the writing on its surface. I was shocked to see my own name and occupation: Horatio Landor, Tutor. It was Hamlet's handwriting.

"I am he," I said to the man, and then, realizing that his capacity to speak the Danish tongue might be rather limited, I pointed at my chest and then to the addressee on the letter, saying once more, "Me. I am he."

He grasped me by the wrist and held it hard for a moment, looking at me in what might have been interpreted as a threatening manner. I pointed at the name on the letter once more, and then at myself, and waited.

He sized me up for another moment or two, but apparently unable to think of any better plan, passed the letter to me. His companion, a beefy looking fellow smelling of salt and sweat, moved from the door to sit beside me. Putting my hands up, palms toward him, I indicated that I would not make trouble.

Across the fold of the letter was stuck a crimson royal seal, a feature that surprised me. But the message was clearly addressed to me, and I cracked the wax and opened the page.

Horatio,

Please give one of these men access to the king's chamberlain and household manager, a man who, I know, has command of the Frisian dialect that they speak. These men have done me a good turn, and in return should be promptly rewarded. The chamberlain will do as I ask without involving the king. Although the payment of ten thousand may seem extraordinary, the chamberlain is a man who can manage to provide it without its being unduly missed. And he trusts me implicitly, a not insignificant factor in this affair.

When you have paid these men (who have treated me with dignity), contrive to walk each morning to the sexton's cottage at the graveyard beside the Church of Saint Sebastian near the west edge of the royal park. It may be a day or two, but I will meet you there. I have much news for you, news that will both surprise you and, if I know you as I think, offend your sense of right. Its weighty nature should have been my burden alone, but in light of recent developments, I am in need of your counsel and support.

He that thou knowest thine,
Hamlet

I turned to the bearded man and nodded. Gathering up my book, and leaving the remainder of my ale untouched, I indicated that they should accompany me. The chamberlain was not a difficult man to find, and as it was still early enough, I knew we would locate him in the lower precincts of the castle complex in the small office where he kept his accounts, as well as a sizeable amount of ready cash in a guarded strong room.

At the pub door I looked briefly back into the room, then out into the fresh sunlight. I realized vividly that I was more than happy to be leaving. Hamlet's letter had given me new hope. I closed the door behind us with a thump, pleased as well by the fact that I would not be troubled by further commerce, of whatever nature, with the innkeeper's vulgar servant woman.

The air was cool and the breeze was invigorating, causing me to shiver for a moment. We made our way up the street toward the castle's bulky precincts, and I was both wary and amused by the watchful way these rustic companions kept pace with me. One of them kept touching my elbow, occasionally pinching the muscle on the back of my arm, a reminder, I suppose, not to double-cross them in any way. That gesture, and the way the other held his hand to the hilt of a long knife he kept in his belt, continually fed my alertness.

When we reached the castle walls and the north gate, I paused. Neither of these men seemed the type to have business in the castle, but I was also sure that neither would let me out of his sight for even a moment. Then I remembered the letter. I took it from the pocket where I had stowed it and refolded it so that the wax seal fit together once more. Yes, it was broken, but the crack was barely visible. I held it carefully between my thumb and middle finger and beckoned the men on with my other hand.

At the gate, the guard looked at my companions suspiciously.

"Who're these, then?" he asked, somewhat insolently, I thought. He knew me (and probably took me for another 'useless' scholar, for such is the common attitude of many men and women in service toward the educated. Will it always be thus?). He did not, however, know the two unsavory characters that accompanied me. I held up the letter in such a fashion as to reveal the seal, hoping the crack would remain unnoticed.

"No need to trouble yourself," I muttered cheerfully, if unhelpfully.

The seal did its work admirably, and the man backed away and waved us through. He still glared at us, and the armed Frisian grimaced back at him, but at my beckoning they followed me through the gate.

Once inside it was only a four-minute walk to the chamberlain's office, located in an adjunct room in the castle's fortified cellars. We walked sixty paces or so from the entry walls, then down an exterior staircase and through a door guarded by three husky soldiers. Accompanied by one of these, we stepped hastily down a long subterranean passage and around two dark corners until we reached the corridor's end. There I knocked tentatively on a thick oak door that was fortified by large iron bands connected to its massive hinges. At my nod the guard turned and made his way back to his post.

My companions looked around uneasily. For a moment there was silence, then a shuffling sound could be heard from inside and the door swung open.

"Horatio?"

"Ah, then you recognize me," I said.

He dubiously eyed the two men at my side, but they resolutely met his examination with doubtful looks of their own. I held out the letter, as well as the instructions written especially for him enfolded within. I momentarily imagined some code, but smiled at my own suspicion.

He took the letter and glanced through the contents carefully, all the while blocking entrance, an unnecessary gesture given that he had an armed guard within at all times.

When he had measured its import, he beckoned swiftly that we should enter, and we did so, crowding into the small office. Seated against the far wall, sharpening a sword was one of the king's guards.

He regarded us coolly, and truth be told, I knew he was capable of having all three of us skewered and dismembered within the space of a few seconds, so I was not surprised at his casual posture. The Frisian with the knife looked at him uneasily. The soldier only smiled back, tested the edge of his blade with his thumb, and continued his sharpening.

"And how fares the prince?" Jacob asked, as he moved toward a chest against another wall. He lifted a woven rug from its lid, and removing a large key from his pocket, fitted it into the lock set into the chest's front. He paused before turning it, and he turned to look at me.

"All I know is what I have shared with you," I answered.

He held my eye for a moment. Then he turned the key and raised the lid. He removed four sizable bags containing coins from its interior and placed them heavily on his desk.

He turned to me and said, "Eight thousand is all I can manage, at least at present. For the lord Hamlet I would give my life and soul, but I think these 'gentlemen' will accept the amount. I fervently hope so, for that is all I have at my disposal for another three days."

He opened one of the bags by loosening its drawstring, and he poured some of its golden contents out onto his desk, a polished surface surprisingly elegant for so ordinary an office. The coins clattered and spun, falling finally into a shiny heap. I held my breath.

The Frisian with the knife gasped. His companion stepped to the table and picked one of the larger coins at random. He bit it carefully, and thus satisfied, nodded to the other.

"How will they carry it?" Jacob asked.

I shrugged. I hadn't thought of this eventuality. We couldn't be seen to be removing bags of money from the castle.

"Never mind," Jacob said. "Eric can help."

The soldier looked up upon hearing his name and frowned. Hans rummaged in a cupboard and removed two leather sacks. He swept the coins back into their bag. Then he placed two bags in each sack, stuffing each also with some raw wool from a bale beside the door. There would be no jingle of coins to reveal this cargo. I hefted one. It was heavy, perhaps forty pounds.

I turned to the Frisian with the knife. "Where is the prince?" I asked. He shrugged in incomprehension, but his companion turned and said in clear Danish, "We will release him when the gold is delivered to our leader. Your soldier friend may accompany us—no one else."

He paused, considering. "Though we may appear foreign dullards, you above all, a 'scholar,' should realize that rarely are things as they seem."

Then, almost as an afterthought, he said, "You'd best hope that eight thousand is acceptable, hadn't you?" I looked at Jacob with apprehension, although he remained surprisingly calm.

"Eric," he said. "Accompany these men, please, and lend a hand with their luggage. Also send me another guard to stay with me until you return."

Eric stood and sheathed his sword slowly. He approached the table and lifted one of the two sacks. His very bearing breathed the threat of unpredictable violence, but nearly effortlessly he hoisted one of the two sacks over his left shoulder (leaving his right hand free to act) and indicated that one of the Frisians should take the other.

I moved to accompany them as they approached the doorway. The Danish speaker opened the door and gestured the others to precede him. Once we were out, Jacob looked at me, eyebrows raised, but he said nothing. He closed the door behind us. The locking bar dropped into place with a heavy thump.

Chapter 49

Ambition and Loyalty

Poland is surprisingly pretty coming up to harvest season, Fortinbras thought. The air was mild, smelling of cut hay. Although the horizon appeared unbearably far away, the landscape itself was green and golden with ripening crops. In another few miles they would camp before rejoining his fleet the next day.

He felt his horse's muscles ripple beneath his thighs in its regular walking pace. He pulled in off the track and gazed back down the line of his men that stretched to the east for half a mile or more. Some were bandaged on various limbs, and a few were borne on makeshift litters by their comrades. He was proud of them. They might be a crew of cutthroats and ruffians, but they were *his* cutthroats and ruffians.

He waved to Lars, who was riding fifty or so paces behind him, signaling him over. Lars cantered toward him and pulled up casually, the horse breathing easily as if a short run was just what it had been missing.

"How are the men holding up?" Fortinbras asked him.

Lars grinned. Fortinbras had asked this question at least a dozen times over the past two days as they had made away from the coastal village (now a smoking ruin somewhere back over the horizon), and toward the rendezvous with the ships. "Well enough, I think, your lordship," Lars replied. "These men despise marching, but once back aboard our fleet tomorrow they will feel more at home. We've been moving fast, and they are tired."

"No grumbling, though? No complaints?"

"Only the usual—sore feet, insufficient women."

Fortinbras grimaced at the last item. It wasn't uncommon for invading soldiers to rape, he knew. Yet surely God could not smile on violence done to the weaker sex. He knew that his command that the Polish women en route be left alone was not popular. Still, it was unseemly for a prince to condone such acts.

A few dozen of the men had already passed them, heading along the faded track, always southwestward.

"Come," said Fortinbras to Lars, and he trotted up the file to its head once more. Lars followed, and once caught up, fell in at his side. Fortinbras' horse blew noisily and turned to nip at Lars's brown stallion. Fortinbras pulled the horse's head sharply away, then patted its neck reassuringly. It was a spirited beast, like himself, he thought.

"Once aboard ship we will soon be back into Danish territory," he said to Lars. "For the approach to the main island and Elsinore count another few days, depending on the weather."

Lars nodded noncommittally.

"Once there, at Elsinore I mean, we shall have to assess things carefully. We held to our agreement with the Danes carefully on the way through their area of control to our Polish raid; things may be different on our way home."

Lars glanced at Fortinbras and nodded. He had been waiting for this conversation. The men were blooded and still feeling the lift of their recent victory. Any move against Denmark would be more easily taken with the troops in such a spirit than to have to wait one or two seasons and prepare them once more for war. He felt a surge of affection and admiration for his prince. Now might indeed be the time for such a bold move.

Fortinbras continued. "Before leaving Norway I had a long meeting with King Olav—you remember."

Lars nodded.

"Although our king was displeased with our secret preparations to invade Danish territory, he and I compromised."

Lars knew this actually meant that Prince Fortinbras had fallen into line. But he held his tongue.

"Olav suggested that without being too obvious we examine Elsinore's defensive capability when we were to pass through on our outward journey. If, in my best judgment, the Danes showed some weakness, he gave his general approval to our moving against them later, depending on our success in Poland. After all, our initial objective was simply two islands; but why not go after Elsinore itself?"

He paused a moment, as if reconsidering the confidence he had begun to share. But Lars had always proven himself trustworthy. He continued, and Lars listened carefully.

"When we were moving through Elsinore I spent an hour's conversation with one of our spies there. Despite the strength with which their king Claudius answered our initial challenge, there was much uncertainty in the Danish court. The young prince Hamlet was leaving for England, ostensibly on a tax-collecting voyage. But many in the court were aware that he suffers mental instability. He murdered Claudius' chief councilor in the queen's bedroom, of all places!"

"Truly!" Lars exclaimed. The idea was bizarre, almost unbelievable.

"Although Claudius may yet be in control, surely there exist murmurings of discontent and unease. Perhaps the country is not nearly as prepared for war as it was previously. We, on the other hand, are sailing on a high tide, as it were. Timing, as always, is half of any battle's advantage, is it not?"

"Almost certainly."

The two men rode without speaking for a few moments, listening to birdsong and the long, low rumble of irregularly tramping feet. Then Lars spoke.

"My liege, might I ask what may be a sensitive question?"

Fortinbras looked at him sharply, but Lars pressed on.

"We have been acquainted since our youth, have we not? And have I not proven my loyalty to you in all things?"

"If it is a matter of money, have you not been amply rewarded in this latest venture?"

"Oh, yes, amply," Lars replied. "I am not the least dissatisfied." He lowered his eyes a moment, then turned to Fortinbras. "No, it's a more personal matter."

"Go on, then," Fortinbras said.

"I am curious. How is it that your uncle is the king of Norway? I know that you were very young when your father suffered his defeat to the Danes. But is there no provision in Norwegian law or precedence that a son and prince should claim kingship upon reaching a suitable age? And surely you are of suitable age?"

"Ah," said Fortinbras. He gave Lars a long glance, one of appraisal, such that Lars himself turned away blushing, as if for some shame he were not quite prepared to admit but that some unaccountable part of himself nonetheless reacted to.

Fortinbras finally responded. "You are right, I was very young, when Denmark's King Hamlet killed my father. There was little option but for my Uncle Olav to take control."

He blew out his breath in what, in other circumstances, might have been a sigh.

"Olav is a strong king. He might have had me killed. It is not uncommon for ambitious men to murder their potential rivals." He paused and thought, listening to the breathing of the horses.

"Because I am alive, I am grateful. As for rights or the provisions of tradition," (he spat to the side in derision), "rights are what you claim if you are able and willing. No one will seek you out and give them to you. You must take them—when you are sure you are able, and when you are convinced you are in the right, and that God approves." He wiped some spit from his stubble onto the back of his gauntlet.

"That last insurance is, of course, somewhat tricky, and may fall to our conscience." He turned to Lars and smiled.

Lars gave Fortinbras a tentative look, then answered, "If that is true, then I can see your difficulty." He paused, but then continued more assertively than before. "You know, of course, that in all things I am *your* man—even with respect to Olav." It was a brave admission, perhaps even foolhardy, a risk.

But Fortinbras replied candidly, "If I judged otherwise, you would not be here, would you?"

Lars glanced at him again, then chuckled. "No, probably not." Then, after a pause, he said, "I think it best that things be clear, though, don't you?"

"Yes," Fortinbras said. "I do."

Ahead of them the sun was lowering beyond some rolling hills. The broad, low valley through which they progressed was dappled with late sunlight and smelled of hay and wildflowers. A light breeze stirred the barley in the fields along the road.

"We'll camp in the lee of those hills yonder, I think," Fortinbras added finally. "See to the dispositions. Tomorrow we meet the ships."

Lars straightened in the saddle, then turned his horse back to the column. He was already picking out the cohort commanders to relay the orders. He trotted confidently away to meet the troops.

Chapter 50

Willow and Water

It was very early, just hinting of first light. Jonas, the guard in charge at the south gate to the palace grounds, was barely awake. He forced himself to his feet and to get his blood moving, stamped a small circle around in front of the massive oak barrier, which he himself had closed the previous night when the church bells tolled the eleventh hour. *Thank God,* he thought to himself, *I can go to my barracks and get some sleep in another half hour.*

He turned to gaze up the thoroughfare toward the palace. He shook his head, as if to clear it, and looked again. There she was.

Ophelia stepped carefully down the dimly lit cobbles. She remembered having tripped on a cobble once, as a little girl, and her knee still showed a small scar where the skin had separated and the blood had flowed. She smiled, remembering.

Childhood had been such fun. She remembered her mother, helping her with her clothing, and remembered 'helping' her mother supervise the creation of dinner for her important father. She could still smell the aromas of bread and beef, of pudding and wine!

She paused for a moment, looking about her, as if she had forgotten her errand. Yes! That was it. She must go for fish, the best second course! And where do you go for fish? To the water, of course. She resumed her way, gazing toward the gate, where a young soldier stood staring back at her.

Jonas looked again. Yes, it was Ophelia, the dead chief councilor's daughter. What was she doing here at this hour?

The young man was very handsome, but most young men were. And if he were like most young men, Ophelia knew he would do as she asked. After all, love was in her heart, love was in her belly, like a little fish, tickling deep inside her. Who could now deny her? As she approached him, Ophelia smiled sweetly, as if struck by some positive impression. She wrapped her cloak closely about her, as it would not do for him to see her in her night things.

"My lady?" he asked as she approached.

Ophelia came up to him and touched his arm, firmly yet gently. "Oh good sir," she said, "I must go beyond the walls. I have been summoned," she said.

Jonas looked at her, puzzled for a moment. "May I inquire who it is who has summoned you?"

"Now that would be telling, wouldn't it?" she said with a sort of giggle. Then she became more serious. "You knew of my father, did you not?"

"Of course, my lady. Everyone in service knew of the lord Polonius."

"Think then, perhaps, that such power as he possessed is what has summoned me. Can you not do that?" She squeezed his forearm slightly and smiled at him innocently. "For me?"

"My lady, you are unaccompanied. I should be remiss in my duties were I to allow you to fall into any danger."

"Falling is such a weighted word, is it not?" she asked. "For it suggests loss of control, an absence of balance, perhaps even foolishness. Surely you do not think me a fool? Or a fallen woman?" She smiled at him coquettishly.

Jonas blushed. Within him pulsed feelings of foolishness, of solicitude, and yes, even erotic attraction.

"I would never consider your desires foolish, madam," he said, and he lowered his eyes in deference.

"Please, then," she said, "allow me to exit the gate." She paused, and then added, "You will not be in any trouble, I swear."

He looked up at her angelic face, at the dark eyes that gazed back at him frankly.

"My lady, it is not my troubles that I am sworn to defend and protect. But as it is nearly dawn, and since it is you asking, and not some surly servant, I will open just this once for you."

He slipped his arm from her grasp and moved to the small portal found within the larger gate. He unlatched the bolt and slid it free, then opened the doorway. Ophelia approached the threshold.

"You are kind, good sir," she said, and smiled sweetly.

His heart thumped, and he flushed slightly. Finally he said, "I am at your service always, my lady."

Ophelia stepped through the portal, looked back at him with a grateful smile, then turned and proceeded down the cobbled roadway.

Jonas watched her go. Then, as if awakening to his true duties, he closed the door once more. He would open the whole gate in another twenty minutes or so. What difference could twenty minutes make?

Ophelia fairly danced down the cobbles. She knew where she was going. It would be beautiful in the dawn light, she thought.

An old woman sweeping the steps in front of the Black Cock Inn watched her pass. It was strange to see a young woman alone at this early time of the morning. It was a rich cloak the young woman wore, that was for certain.

Ophelia smiled conspiratorially at the old woman, who bowed slightly (though she frowned thoughtfully) before resuming her sweeping. At the next opportunity Ophelia turned right, into a lane between a hostler's and a bakery, from whose premises the infatuating aroma of fresh bread impregnated the morning air. A spangle of light danced on the chapel's peaked roof not far before her. She took an excited breath and moved on. Morning was here!

She bent to the grass beside her path. Here she picked a handful of wildflowers that grew there in profusion. She lavishly adorned her hair and clothing with posies and blossoms, nearly ecstatic with their beauty.

Beyond the chapel, from which she could hear monks' muffled chanting, she hastened past a few simple cottages. A dog looked up from where it had been sleeping on a doorstep, eyed her dubiously, nearly barked, but lowered its head once more as she passed on. Some sparrows began to chirp in the hedge to her left. They lifted her spirits.

Hamlet would love such a morning, she imagined happily. Hamlet…my cavalier…my cavalier Hamlet… Her thoughts grew a bit muddy, and she faltered in her walk a moment, thinking. Then she heard the great cathedral bell begin to toll the arrival of morning. She smiled and moved more quickly.

At the end of the lane she passed a youngster leading two lean cows toward pasture. He nodded to her and tugged his forelock, a gesture of respect. She smiled and nodded, and hurried along.

Past the lane a path branched off to the left, leading to one of the old mills. There was the pond! There was the millrace! The sun on the water drew her along. There was the willow! She longed for its embrace. *Everyone knows that the willow has holy healing properties,* she remembered. *The willow loves water. I am like the willow,* she thought, and smiled once more.

The boy with the cows watched her hurry down the path toward the mill. *Not every morning you see a noblewoman out this early*, he thought. Then he turned uphill to one of the common pastures that surrounded Elsinore on the landward side. He tapped each cow on the flank with his willow switch, and they obligingly stepped ahead more quickly. They knew from experience that there was fresh grass waiting. The repetitive drumming of a woodpecker echoed from the copse across the pasture. Sunlight was slanting up over the trees now, lending a golden radiance to the lightening sky.

Ophelia stood beside the millstream and watched the water pushing into the stony channel leading to the millwheel, which creaked slightly as it turned. The rush of the water was mesmerizing. There was something inevitable about it, something reassuring. Its gurgle, and the splash off the wheel as it turned over, were voices she knew and trusted. There was almost a sleepiness to it, the sound of a caress, of liquid inevitability.

There was the willow, on the opposite bank, leaning out over the pond. It was a huge old tree whose roots were dug deeply into the moist ground. Ophelia proceeded across the narrow footbridge that fronted the mill. The miller would still be sleeping, she thought. Her footsteps were soft, but audible, and the boards of the bridge creaked as they gave slightly.

She stepped off the bridge and moved to her left to the base of the tree. *Fish and willows must be kin*, she thought; *they both love water so!*

She leaned her body against the tree, hugging it to her, her to it. She felt the rough bark with her cheek, moist with dew, yet charged with life. It lifted her spirits, which a moment ago, had felt almost sad...almost sad. She kissed the bark. Then, looking up the trunk, she noted with satisfaction the great branch that spread horizontally over the pond. It seemed to beckon, and she bent to remove her shoes. In her bare feet, she clambered up the sloping trunk and maneuvered herself around it onto the branch. She took a deep breath, holding the trunk with one hand, and stepping gingerly onto the branch, which dipped only very slightly under her weight. She paused only a moment, as she scented a whiff of smoke. *Someone is awake*, she thought. She smiled again.

In the mill house, the miller's wife, wakened by some sound outside (it had sounded like footsteps on the bridge) fussed at her stove. After several strikes of her flint, the kindling finally lit, and she smiled cheerfully as the small sticks began to crackle. She could smell the smoke as it spread into the chimney where, she knew, it drifted upward. She added a couple of larger sticks, laid gently so as not to disturb the new flame. They were dry, and they caught quickly. She pushed the door partway shut as the chimney began to draw. Then she moved over to the window to watch the sun rising over the copse a few dozen yards away to the east. To her left, she could see the willow leaning over the millpond. She started, rubbed her eyes a moment and looked again.

Ophelia stepped further out onto the branch. For security, she held onto some thinner, 'weeping' branches that descended from a major branch above. The bark beneath her bare feet was damp, a bit slick with dew, cold. She laughed, though, a silent laugh. No damp tree was going to spoil her morning. Just to show him, she raised her foot to stamp on him! Her other foot slid, caught a moment on a bark crevice, then slipped completely. She cried out.

The miller's wife hastily slipped out the door and onto the bridge. There she gasped in surprise. On the willow branch stood a barefoot young lady, her cloak open to reveal what appeared to be a nightdress. Blooms of various wildflowers decorated the girl's hair. She clutched some branches from above in her right hand, and she raised her foot as if to stamp on the branch that was her only footing. The miller's wife stared in disbelief and watched, as the young woman slipped from the branch, held for a moment by her right hand, and then fell five or six feet downward into the mill pond in a great splash.

The shock of the cold water made Ophelia's heart race, and she kicked her way to the bright surface. She took a great breath and laughed for joy. The water was cold but so alive! The sun spangles on its surface laughed with her, a tinkling rustling sound like elves in the grass sharing secrets. She twisted onto her back and began to sing.

O God from whom all blessings flow,
Unto all creatures here below...

How did it go from there? "All creatures here…heavenly host…?" She shivered involuntarily. Her nightdress was so wet and cold. It was heavy.

The princess had a suitor, o,
A man all strong and fair,
He clasped the princess to him, o,
A prize both rich and rare;
All lusty was his manner, o,
He carried her away,
He promised her his love, o,
Forever and a day…

She tried to lift her head from the water, which had somehow slid over her cheek and into her mouth. She coughed, and flailed with her right arm, even while trying to push the water from her face.

The miller's wife was now on the bridge. The girl was obviously in trouble. The millpond was deep, fifteen or more feet in some places. "Miller!!" she cried aloud. "Miller!"

Ophelia felt a kind of heaviness pulling at her legs now. Her nightdress was tangled around her knees, and she couldn't quite kick. Someone was shouting. She felt alarm, gave a swift, fleeting glance at the sunlight on the willow leaves overhead, and then slid under the surface. Her mouth opened in surprise. She tried to breathe.

The miller burst out of his doorway, a small axe in his hand, ready to ward off invaders. He could see his wife on the bridge, gazing at the millpond.

"Oh, Miller," she cried, and pointed at some bubbles filtering to the pond's surface from below. A few bedraggled blossoms floated on the glistening surface. "Amidst those weeds! A woman," she said, pointing again. "There."

Chapter 51

An Earthy Perspective

Andred, the sexton, leaned on his shovel and grinned at his companion, a scrawny fellow named Tim who sometimes assisted around the churchyard. Only now noticing that his overseer had ceased digging some moments ago, Tim, too, thrust his spade into the ground and grinned back. He had learned that more often than not it was useful to emulate one's superiors. And there was little doubt that the sexton he worked with was his superior—after all, the sexton had hired him, and for two pennies a day, at that!

"So, what do you think of this affair then, eh?" the sexton demanded.

Tim paused to think.

"Ah, come on, this young lady's death," the sexton added.

"A sad thing, that," Tim said, noncommittally. He looked back at the sexton, searching for another clue.

"I tell you," the sexton finally said, "if she hadn't been part of the royal court, she would never be given Christian burial."

He was indignant, and just a little angry. He knew injustice. He frowned at his helper sharply, as if to emphasize the gravity of his judgment.

It was a shocking statement, and Tim felt obliged to defend the poor girl.

"Ah, go on, then," he said. "God will take all to Himself one day." He had heard a priest say that once.

Andred scowled.

"And yet, there is some doubt," Tim added.

Andred's expression softened.

"Listen," Andred said. "If water were to come to a man and drown him, clearly the man would be innocent, right?"

Tim thought for a moment, scratched under his chin, and nodded. "Aye."

"But," Andred went on, "if that same man were to go find water (of sufficient depth and magnitude, mind you), and drown himself, that man would have killed himself, would he not?"

"Does the law find so?" asked Tim. He had heard about the court inquest, the one looking into the death of old Polonius' daughter. One night in the Hawk and Hounds the miller had described in eloquent detail his ordeal being questioned by the king's coroner, but Tim had not heard of the coroner's decision. Was it suicide, or not?

"It does, indeed," claimed Andred, and he slapped the front of his thigh for emphasis. A small cloud of dust emanated from his leather breeches, and he waved it away. "The coroner has found so; I heard it this morning." He grinned, as if possession of the latest gossip were some virtue to be rewarded.

Tim looked down, then glanced behind Andred. A small rodent of some kind scurried to the far corner of the grave they were digging. Andred turned slowly. He lifted his heavy spade and whacked it, once, twice to make sure. He lifted its senseless form with the spade and tossed it out of the hole where they were working.

Andred stuffed the blade of the spade back into the earth and leaned once more on the handle. He smiled slyly. "I have a riddle for you," he said to Tim.

Tim grimaced toward the ground, then raised his head and smiled at Andred. "All right," he said.

"What builds stronger than the carpenter, the shipwright, or the mason?" Andred leered at Tim triumphantly.

"Aha," said Tim, after thinking a moment. He pointed at Andred triumphantly. "A gallows-maker, for his frame outlives a thousand tenants!"

Andred chuckled heartily, startled at this turn of thought. His young companion was not entirely witless, then! He raised his eyebrows in appreciation, but frowning, said, "I like your wit well, but it *is* a dangerous suggestion. After all, your answer does well to those that do ill! And you do ill to suggest that the gallows is built stronger than the church. For such a suggestion the gallows might do ill to thee!"

Tim felt his chest tighten in apprehension, and he crossed himself.

"Try again," Andred said, and he waited expectantly. Tim had surprised him once, but surely could not do so again.

"I can tell you," Tim said. "A moment, though," he added. He screwed up his face, puzzling mightily. After a few long seconds, though, he conceded. "By the mass, I cannot tell," he admitted lamely.

Andred smiled condescendingly and said, "Trouble yourself no more about it. After all, a dull ass will not mend its pace with beating." He sniffed ostentatiously, then said, "If someone ever asks you this again, say, 'A grave-maker, for the houses he makes last until doomsday!"

Tim groaned inwardly, then turned and tried once again to dig.

Smug with self-satisfaction, Andred clapped a calloused hand on Tim's shoulder and said to him, "No, no, that's enough. I'll finish, but only if you go down to the Captain's Cabin and fetch me some sack, say a bottle or two. Would that be fair?"

Tim nodded energetically. He really hated digging, though he needed the work. He held his palm out, where Andred deposited two greasy coins. Then he hoisted himself out of the hole and leaving his shovel leaning on the trunk of a mature oak, made his way between the gravestones and through the gate to the roadway that led back toward the more inhabited parts of Elsinore.

In his haste he failed to notice the richly-dressed young man leaning on another oak tree near the cemetery wall, and just managed to express a 'Good day t'ya, sirs' to the youngish, scholarly gentleman (accompanied by two foreigners) coming toward the cemetery gate from town. One of the foreigners scowled, but the Dane (obvious by the cut of his hair and the color of his waistcoat) nodded. Tim turned to watch them pass, then headed up the road toward the Captain's Cabin.

Chapter 52

Burial and Resurrection

It is unusual. Last night I gathered twenty sheets of the paper brother Henrik left for me in the small pile beside the inkwell, and along with three quills and a bottle of ink, I removed them to my own quarters. (Cleopatra will have to fend for herself.) Thus I find myself at my own table, cramped between my bed and the small hearth, continuing my tale.

Perhaps in the last section of my report I recorded more detail than was necessary. The Frisians took their money. Before they departed they accompanied me to the churchyard gate. There I saw Hamlet, standing shivering within his cloak, beside the entrance to his family's crypt, Old Hamlet's final resting place. I never saw a lonelier figure. Still, on seeing me he raised his hand in a kind of welcoming gesture, and I made my way to him between the mounds and headstones.

Forty or so paces to my left, a gravedigger was thrusting a spade into a pit he was enlarging. Indeed, I could see only his shoulders, head, and the bright cap he was wearing. As if to a drummer's beat, the spade lifted and tossed moist clods onto the earth beside the grave. The repetitive 'chuff' of the spade and the muffled 'clump' of the tossed earth carried in the cold air.

Hamlet threw his arms round my shoulders and hugged me hard, perhaps the nearest I have ever come to royalty.

"Friend," he said gravely. I lowered my head, for I feared he might see the tears of happiness and gratitude that were on my cheeks. Evidence of his generosity of spirit showed in his letting me go and turning to gaze at the gravedigger, who was whistling gustily, and Hamlet said, "Well, that gentleman enjoys cheerful employment, does he not?"

I chuckled in spite of my relieved sentiment, and replied, "Better dirty employment than none, wouldn't you say?"

Hamlet looked over and smiled.

I expected some immediate clarification of the reasons for his unexpected return, but the gravedigger had caught his attention, the more so because in rhythm to the sound of the spade, the man had begun to sing.

In youth when I did love, did love,
Methought it was very sweet,
To contract the time for my behove,
O, methought there was nothing meet...

"Has this man no sense of the 'gravity' of his business, that he sings while grave-making?" Hamlet pondered.

He looked at me as if for an answer, and I stammered, "Eventually we tend to come to terms with familiar tasks, however gruesome. Even a king's executioner must accustom himself to the blood of his victims, clean his great axe (with whatever distaste), yet smile in the eve as he sups with his family."

"Indeed," Hamlet replied, and he seemed to think a moment. Then he walked over to the gravesite. I hastily moved to accompany him.

"Whose grave's this, sir?" he asked with his customary confidence. I was sure that the man digging would not know my prince, and I was curious as to the outcome of this conversation.

The grave digger looked up, pausing only for a moment, and said, "Mine, sir." Then, before Hamlet could pursue the matter, he gave a great grunt and tossed a skull up with his shovel, one that must have been buried many years ago. He sang on.

But age with his stealing steps,
Hath clawed me in his clutch,
And hath shipped me into the ground,
As if I had never been such.

The skull's empty eye sockets gazed up at us mockingly, and Hamlet smiled, as if sharing a great joke.

"That skull had a tongue in it and could sing once," he said to me. "Now this rascal bounces it onto the ground like any other piece of waste matter. Yet once it could have been the living head of a diplomat or negotiator, one who might out-bargain God himself, could it not?" He chuckled cheerfully.

I smiled in spite of his irreverence. "It might," I conceded.

"Or he might have been a courtier, like Laertes or his busy father, a man who knew how to flatter, cajole or beg, to say 'dear lord' or 'sweet lord' when the occasion demanded it?"

"Yes," I admitted.

A pickaxe and a spade, a spade,
For and a shrouding-sheet,
A pit of clay for to be made,
For such a guest is meet.

Hamlet's expression softened at these words, these ghosts of meaning flung into the morning air by the gravedigger's song.

He pushed the skull with the toe of his boot, turned it sideways in the soft earth.

"Methinks this boney countenance has the smile of a lawyer, one who knew all the tricks of his profession—the sophistry and the Latin phrases that confound the uninitiated—and yet one utterly unable to charge this digging fellow with battery. Ironic, is it not? The conveyances of a lawyer's career might thickly pack a little box. Yet what are these documents to him now?" Hamlet looked at the ground.

Not just this one. Hamlet's ironies seemed uncountable. Everywhere he appeared to see the foolishness of human ambition and the senselessness of hope. But he pressed on by addressing the gravedigger again.

"It must, indeed, be your grave, sir," he said to the man loudly, "for you lie in it."

The man ceased his shoveling a moment and regarded Hamlet slyly. "I do *not* lie in it, yet it *is* mine."

"To be in it alive and say 'tis thine is a lie, for a grave is for the dead, not for the quick or living. Therefore you have lied."

The man smirked at Hamlet. "'T'is a quick lie that can travel from me to you."

Hamlet smiled shrewdly back at him, and squatted beside the pit. "What man do you dig this for?" he asked.

"For no man, sir."

"What woman, then?"

"For none neither."

Hamlet looked at me and grinned. More emphatically, he said, "Who is to be buried in it?" He looked back at the grave-digger.

"One that *was* a woman, sir, but rest her soul, she's dead."

Hamlet turned to me. "Well, that clears things up, doesn't it?" he exclaimed jovially. Once more he turned to the gravedigger, who paused in his work, was smiling smugly at his own wit.

"How long have you been a gravedigger?"

The man rubbed under his nose a moment, pondering briefly, then answered, "I came to this job the day the young prince Hamlet was born, the prince that is mad and sent to England."

"Aha!" Hamlet exclaimed. "And tell me, if you can, why was he sent to England?"

"Because he was mad! He shall recover his wits there. Or if not, it will not matter there."

"Why not?" Hamlet asked him, genuinely puzzled.

"It won't be seen in him there. *There* all men are as mad as he."

Hamlet snickered, and I laughed too. The gravedigger merely smiled; a man must not laugh too hard at his own joke.

Hamlet stood once more and once again touched the skull near the grave with the toe of his boot. "Tell me," he said to the gravedigger. "How long will a man lie buried in the earth until his flesh completely rots away?"

The gravedigger looked at Hamlet, perhaps more closely than he had before. He considered a moment.

"Well," he said, "He'll last eight or nine years if he's not rotten before he dies—the recurrent plague (God save us!) gives quite a start to the process, you know; some will hardly last the burial ceremony. He thought a moment. "A tanner will last nine years."

He grinned, then laughed out loud. When he ceased laughing, he said, "His skin is so tanned with his trade that it keeps out water, and water truly hastens the decay of any whoreson dead body."

He reached down into his pit, wrestled with something unseen for a moment, and then tossed another skull up onto the loose soil from the hole. "Here's a skull that's been in the earth for about twenty-three years."

"You know it?" Hamlet asked. "Whose was it?"

"Ah, he was a mad rogue, that one. He poured a flagon of wine on my head once. A joke, of course, but he was full of pranks. This skull, sir, is Yorick's skull, the old king Hamlet's jester."

"This?!" Hamlet took the skull up and peered with fascination into what once must have been its face. The skull seemed to leer back at him, as if holding back some naughty witticism. But Hamlet was not amused. Rather dismay clouded his features.

"Alas, poor Yorick." Hamlet said. I crossed myself. Hamlet turned to me and said, "I knew him, Horatio. He used to carry me on his back up and down the halls of the palace. I used to kiss his cheek and he mine!"

He looked again into the lost face. "Where be your jokes now, those flashes of merriment that set the table roaring with laughter? You're not even capable now of mocking your own grin."

He sighed, paused, and then said in a bitter tone to its vacant eyes and grinning jaws, "Why don't you go to my lady's chamber and tell *her*, that though she paint her face an inch thick, to this end she must come. Make *her* laugh at that."

I shivered when I heard these bitter words, but quickly answered when he asked, "Do you imagine the great Alexander or Julius Caesar looked this way after death?"

"Yes," I said, although I had never thought of such men as dead bodies before, except of course with respect to the infamous murder of Caesar in the Roman capitol.

Hamlet sniffed the skull and grimaced. "And smelt so?" he asked. He held his nose.

"Just so," I answered truthfully, a kind of depressed resolve.

"'From dust to dust...' To what base uses we return, Horatio."

I couldn't answer him. Instead, my mind kept repeating the phrase from the church's liturgy: the resurrection of the body, and life everlasting...the resurrection of the body and life everlasting. But only a moment later everything changed once more.

Chapter 53

To Honor the Dead

Two priests were chanting, a dirge, by the sound of its minor key, and their mournful voices. The Latin remained yet indistinct. I looked at Hamlet, who was gazing down the roadway toward the palace district. A procession was moving slowly in our direction. Two priests led the way, and some rather elaborately dressed individuals, behind what appeared to be a corpse on a bier, were following them.

"Those are members of the court!" Hamlet said to me softly. "Look. Is that not the king?"

I placed my hand to shade out the early sun's glare and followed his gaze. It did, indeed, appear to be the king, as well as the queen and some other noble figures.

Hamlet turned to me. "Let us slip behind that great oak, and see who is to be buried." He indicated a large old oak some fifteen paces behind the new grave.

I followed him quickly. The gravedigger watched us skeptically, then hoisted himself out of his pit, and placing his shovel over his shoulder, strolled off toward the sexton's cottage near the church.

Hamlet stood behind the oak, fully concealed from the funeral party, I have no doubt, except perhaps for his eye and the edge of his head, which would have appeared as no more than a bump of bark at their distance. I lay prone, with my head raised over a root just sufficiently to see the events as they unfolded. The funeral music drew closer.

When the procession reached the newly dug grave, all went silent for a moment. Then a male voice rang out clearly.

"Is there no more to be done?"

I barely heard the muffled reply, as a priest beside a young man, Laertes by his profile, answered, "No more. We should profane the service of the dead to offer the same prayers to this woman as to peace parted souls."

There was a pause. Then the priest added, "You know her death was doubtful, that she may have profaned God's will by taking her own life. We have granted her bell and burial, her maiden raiment to indicate the purity of her virgin status. We can no more."

I recognized the king's voice. "Laertes, let it go. Let her go. We cannot argue with God's will."

"Laertes!" Hamlet whispered to me.

I peered more closely. It was, indeed, he. Laertes turned to the priest and said caustically, "I tell thee, priest, my sister will be a ministering angel at God's right hand when you are howling in hell!"

"The lady Ophelia!" Hamlet said to me, softly but with a tone that seemed so full of agony I thought his grip on the oak trunk might tear it from the earth.

I looked back to the graveside. The queen was dropping flower petals into the grave, as two servants lowered the linen-wrapped body into its elemental space.

"Sweets to the sweet," she said, and then, as if an afterthought, "I had hoped you might be my Hamlet's wife..."

Laertes looked at her darkly. The king took his arm, roughly it seemed to me, and Laertes shook it off.

I turned again to see Hamlet's reaction, but it was already too late. He was pacing impatiently toward the grave.

Laertes didn't see him at first, but instead, began, "My sister was a paragon of beauty and virtue, the image of my mother and the joy of my father's eye. Only violets and other flowers of beauty will grow from this ground. I can scarcely bear her loss, as I loved my sister like no other."

At this point Hamlet reached the party, and Laertes looked up in shock.

"Ah, yes, and I suppose you'll be buried with her, too, will you? Join with her in everlasting bonds of familial love? Lock hands with your father around her virgin perfection? Sing with flute and harp the family hymns of blood and wine?" Hamlet spat to one side. "You don't know what love is! It is I who loved Ophelia! A thousand brothers with all their love could not make up my sum."

I had sprung to my feet and made to follow, although I tripped on the root and went sprawling. Getting to my feet, I heard Laertes cry, "The devil take thee!" and he threw himself at Hamlet.

Gertrude backed away, clutching the arm of the priest reflexively, aghast at such violence in the churchyard.

"Part them!" shouted the king to two men-at-arms who had accompanied the funeral party.

Laertes had his hands on Hamlet's throat, and Hamlet swung his fist at Laertes' cheek, a blow that appeared to stun him momentarily, at which moment the men-at-arms parted them. The pallbearers stared open-mouthed.

"Horatio," the king ordered, "Wait upon him," indicating Hamlet, but Hamlet was not through. He freed himself from the soldier, who doubtless felt embarrassed and ashamed at putting his hands on the prince.

"Why do you abuse me thus?" Hamlet demanded of Laertes, who could only spit defiance in answer. He could not free himself from the grip of the burly soldier who held his arms from behind.

"It is no matter," Hamlet went on. "Let Hercules himself do what he may, cat will mew and dog will have his day." He lowered his head, as if only now realizing the sorrow that faced him.

"I said 'Wait upon him,'" the king reiterated to me. I took Hamlet's arm and squeezed it, if only to reassure him that I was there. He looked at me vacantly, and then, as if obeying some preordained command, moved away from the party toward the palace.

We walked together, my hand locked onto his arm. Glancing back, I could see the king remonstrating with Laertes, who glared sullenly at him, still restrained securely by the soldier.

The queen stood with her head bowed, and the priest had moved behind a tall gravestone, where he appeared to be praying, though not on his knees. The servants simply stood agog.

I kept my attention on Hamlet as we paced away, he gazing at the ground, walking as if at any moment the very earth beneath us might open our way into Hell.

Despite the emotion of the event, he never looked back, although he once glared at me as if to say, 'Who are you to manhandle a prince thus?' I pretended not to notice and hurried him toward his quarters in the palace.

When I once had the door of his quarters secured behind us, I let go of his arm. He looked at me with a long glance filled with some horrifying mixture of longing and despair. There were tears at the corners of his eyes. Then he stepped to a sideboard and filled a glass with whatever wine was in the decanter. He drank it down and poured another, then turned to me. He put his hand before his mouth and belched softly.

I could not fully read his countenance, yet stared at him, feeling his despair in my own heart. After a long moment, he took the remainder of his wine to a table beside one of the palace windows overlooking the town. He sat, gazing out the window a long moment. The tears reappeared at the edge of his eyes. He brushed them away. Finally he took another long drink, and then turned to me. He blinked several times and clearing his throat, finally spoke.

"I know not," he said soberly, "the debts I owe you—as both servant and friend."

"My lord," I said, more or less speechless.

He indicated that I might sit, and I crossed the room from the entrance to sit opposite him.

"I must explain to you," Hamlet said, but I shook my head in demurral—after all, what explanation does any prince owe a commoner?

He continued, "No, truly, I must. It is only now that I understand Laertes' rage, for I see in it the mirror image of my own."

He lifted his cup and drank a swallow or two. "I know not how the lady Ophelia has passed." I watched another tear slide down his cheek. "Yet still, must we not seek the solace of justice, even in the midst of despair, to remedy perfidy and evil?"

I simply stared at him. He drank again and wiped his cheek with the back of his hand. Then he looked at me more directly, more compassion in his expression than anything else.

"I must tell you of my return," he said. "Surely you must wonder how it is, despite the king's best connivance, that I happen to be here?"

I nodded. Indeed, although I understood the role of the ransom, what preceded it was a mystery that had eluded me.

"Well, then," he said. "It was apparent to me that my mission to England was a complete travesty. The king himself had shared with me knowledge of Denmark's finances not that long ago, though he must have forgotten. England was not in arrears. Thus he could only be sending me thence to get me out of the way. And what is more 'out of the way' than in a grave?"

He must have seen the upset in my face, for he added, "Oh, don't look so shocked. Let me tell you." He took another swallow of wine, and licked an errant scarlet drop from his lower lip.

"My two keepers, though earnest in their endeavors, lacked subtlety. While they slept, I managed to open their packet, the one containing my uncle's message to his governor in England. Upon opening it I found his intentions, written in clear, precise instructions. Though larded with many eloquent phrases extolling England's loyalty, Denmark's regal responsibility and care, and so on, the letter went on to demand my immediate execution—that my head should be struck off."

"The king wrote this?" I demanded, the alarm coursing through me like rough brandy.

"Oh, indeed," Hamlet replied. "And are you not curious how I then proceeded?"

"By all means!" I said.

Hamlet sighed. "I once judged diplomatic language to be worth little more than a bucket of sugared swill," he said. "In fact, I did my best to be more direct in my own communication. But now, my exposure to such trite treacle did me great service. I replaced the king's instructions with a letter of my own, one demanding the execution of its carriers—no shriving time allowed."

Hamlet looked at me expectantly. I shivered. "So Rosencrantz and Guildenstern...go to it?" I asked lamely.

Hamlet's expression darkened for a moment. He shrugged. "They are not near my conscience," he finally said. "They made love to their employment. Rosencrantz was always ambitious, and Guildenstern foolish enough to emulate him. I need not point out that I should surely not be here to tell you of this had they succeeded." He lowered his gaze a moment.

"How was your letter sealed?" I asked, for all royal commands are sealed with the king's signet.

"Ah, God Himself must have been at my shoulder, for even in this was Heaven ordinant. I had my father's old seal in my purse. A king's seal is a king's seal, at least to some provincial official."

He paused a moment, then said, "Great Caesar was lucky, he thought, at least until he was killed. Perhaps Fortuna is at my side, too."

I lowered my head, looked blankly at my hands, with which I had been unconsciously gripping my chair arms. I relaxed them willfully.

"How can such a man be king?" I finally squeezed out in an exasperated tone.

Hamlet grunted his agreement, and added, "Does he not, in this ripening moment, deserve to die—the man who killed my father, whored my mother, and raised his powers against my very life? How can I in all conscience allow this rotten canker to continue to fester, to commit further evils, when I might remove him with this arm?" He stretched his hand out before him, holding the dagger he always wore at his belt, then looked down again to sheathe it carefully.

"You haven't much time," I offered. "Surely the news from England will be here soon. The time is short."

He glanced up. "It *will* be short," he agreed. Then an expression of realization crossed his face. "I regret, you know, losing my temper to Laertes as I did. After all, we face the same conundrum—a father's murder, recent loss of a loved one, and the presumed guilty party walking free. His pain must be as great as mine."

He lowered his face and added, "Yet his expression of grief put me into a towering rage, if only for a short time. I must, when the opportunity presents itself, try to make it up to him. He's no more an evil man than you or I."

It was at about that moment that a knock sounded. Hamlet indicated with a gesture that I should answer, so I got to my feet, and straightening my robe, went to the door.

It was Osric. He stood stiffly, then removed his hat and bowed with a flourish. "Is the lord Hamlet present, sir?" he asked. "I have a message for him."

"Enter," Hamlet commanded in a loud voice from behind me. I opened the door wider and showed Osric into the room. He bowed once more, even more deeply, to Hamlet.

Osric is another ambitious man, a weak, contemptible man. *Will he ever show some spine? And he's a knight!"* I thought to myself at the time. I knew him as a minor country aristocrat (knighted at some stage for service to Claudius), one with courtly manners and a heart and mind tuned to intrigue and gossip.

"Your lordship is right welcome back to Denmark," Osric said with a forced smile.

"Do you know this gentleman?" Hamlet asked me.

"His name is *Sir* Osric," I informed Hamlet, and Osric lowered his head slightly in assent, eyes on the prince. "He lives about the court in the service of the king."

"Cool weather this time of year," Hamlet said to Osric. "Might you not wish to keep your hat on?"

"My lord, it seems quite warm to me, thank you."

"Oh, no, the wind is northerly. Please, for your health?" Hamlet waited.

Osric looked at me, as if expecting some kind of help, then swept his hat back onto his head, adjusting it rakishly.

"Thank you for your concern, my lord," he said to Hamlet.

"Yet there truly is a sultriness in the air," Hamlet added, and waited again.

In relief, Osric removed his hat once more, murmuring, "Oh, yes, my lord. A cool, northerly sultriness, perhaps?" and he giggled politely. Hamlet looked at me and raised his eyes. It was obvious that he already had the correct measure of this water-fly.

"What is the message you have for me?" Hamlet demanded.

"Ah, yes, my lord. There is a gentleman newly returned to court named Laertes, a fine man, truly the epitome of gentry, also a fine swordsman, one of the fairest men of noble rank in all of Denmark, refined of manner and person."

Hamlet overrode him. "Yes, yes, that shining angel recently arrived from Paris, showing the ordinary Dane the sensibilities of true civility and fashion as only the French understand, a man whose only rival for perfection is his shadow. Is he the one?"

"Your lordship speaks most infallibly of him," Osric gushed. "Perhaps you swell his virtues with oratory, but I know you are not ignorant of his many qualities..."

"Oh, you know that, do you?" interrupted Hamlet.

"My lord?"

"Well, I suppose my inner thoughts may be just that transparent, although that supposition does not much appeal to me." Hamlet's voice had sharpened. "I scarcely know him, but I recognize the gentleman of whom you speak. Perhaps one might even say that *what* I know about him, I know well, and after all, to know a man well is to know oneself, is that not true?" He directed this last rhetorical stab at me, although he continued to speak to Osric. "What of this 'epitome of gentry,' as you call him?"

"Of...of...Laertes?"

"Yes, sir, what of him?"

Osric's purse full of golden words had already all been spilled on the table.

"You will get to it soon, will you not?" Hamlet said.

"Why have you raised this gentleman to our attention?" I asked.

Osric looked uncertainly at me, then back at Hamlet.

"My lord, the king, your father, has suggested that perhaps you and Laertes might entertain the court with a friendly fencing match, tomorrow or the day after. The king feels that your skills are too often overlooked..." At this Hamlet perked up slightly. "He would like to create a wager on your skills against those of Laertes."

"What's his favored weapon?" Hamlet asked, now genuinely interested.

"Rapier and dagger," Osric pronounced dramatically.

"That's *two* of his weapons," Hamlet answered in mock protest. Then he raised his hand before Osric could reply again.

"How if I answer, 'no?'" Hamlet asked.

"The king and the court will surely be disappointed." Osric tried again. "His majesty wishes to wager on *your* success, that despite Laertes' reputation, in twelve passes he will not exceed you by three hits."

Hamlet thought a moment, then replied, "Tell the king that tomorrow, at the eleventh hour, I will win for him, if I can. The worst that might befall is my shame—or the odd hit." It was the expression 'odd hit' that leapt out at me.

"Shall I answer him thus?"

"Do so...with whatever flourish you will."

Osric bowed. Hamlet held out the hat that Osric had somehow deposited on the table before him. Osric accepted it, blushing slightly, and placed it on his head. Then he turned and let himself out the door.

I looked at Hamlet. "You will lose this wager, my lord," I said.

"I do not think so. I have been in continual practice. I shall win at the odds." He looked wistfully toward the window. "But something feels wrong. My uncle is too friendly. At least Laertes is honest in his anger."

"My lord, please indulge your misgivings. I shall send the news that you are ill or otherwise unfit. If something is troubling your judgment, obey it."

"No," he said emphatically. Then more quietly, "No. After all, there is providence in the fall of a sparrow. We are all in God's eye, are we not? If it be now, it is not to come. If it be not now, it is to come some time. For oh, yes, it is certain that at some time it will come. The readiness is all. No man knows when he will die, neither you nor I nor anyone. Let be."

He smiled at me, perhaps more calmly than I had seen him smile since Wittenberg. I felt an involuntary shiver of anxiety once more.

"Tomorrow it will be, then," he said.

Chapter 54

The Unwinding

In the scriptorium, Horatio sat unmoving at his table, his quill in his hand, staring unseeing at the wall opposite. Despite his immobility, his heart raced. He knew what he was about to write, knew it all—the excitement, the despair, the treachery, the exaltation. How many times could he review such things in his mind without going mad? Others had succumbed to madness on such provocation. How many times? Again and again, apparently.

Finally he bent over the sheet and attempted to write, but his quill was already dry. He swore softly, chose another quill, dipped it in the inkpot, and began.

I called for the prince at his apartments, and he emerged in high spirits. Hamlet knew where to go, and though I had been with him to the training room on numerous occasions, I had always followed his lead. This time was no different, and I hastened to remain near his side.

The training room was a section of the palace structure devoted to combat drill for those of noble birth. Located behind the stables and above the jails, and with a separate entrance leading to apartments for the nobility, it was easy to overlook.

It was here I had often observed Hamlet and his instructor going through their routines.

Hamlet was whistling on the way, when he wasn't smiling. He was almost jaunty of pace. It was as if he had spat out any misgivings and was ready for anything. Just as I was about to take a wrong turn he clutched me by the arm and pulled me to the left with him. I smelled perfume—that of the queen, I thought. She must have walked this way.

We turned into another corridor where, only a few paces away, two armed guards stood beside the entrance we both recognized. One smiled at Hamlet and Hamlet greeted him easily.

"Anton!" he said to the man, who nodded smiling. "So—practice makes perfect, does it not?"

"I am sure, my liege," he said, and he stepped aside for the two of us.

I followed Hamlet through the door. We entered the large, high-ceilinged room lit by four great windows facing a southern sunny exposure. It was floored with narrow planks of some pale, hard wood, polished and gleaming. Along the walls were racks of weapons—épées, halberds, partisans, and great broadswords in leather scabbards, blades enough to skewer any number of foes. They glistened in the sunlight. Displayed above them were numerous shields that displayed the arms of famous Danish heroes. Between each shield was a nocked crossbow, its arrow pointing toward Heaven.

Heaven help us, I thought.

At least forty people were in the room, and many began to applaud as Hamlet entered. He nodded in appreciation. I noticed the king (who frowned at the applause) and the queen beside two plush chairs alongside the north wall.

Several servants, at least two with wine in decanters on platters, were in attendance. At the east end of the windowed wall Laertes stood, speaking to a servant, who looked at him earnestly and nodded. Laertes glanced up at the applause. He, too, frowned.

Osric was also present, examining some swords in a glass-fronted cabinet, and looking over upon our entrance applauded politely.

Claudius came toward us, smiling with that unctuous expression he usually reserved for foreign diplomats.

"Hamlet!" he exclaimed, with a kind of bonhomie that raised my hackles. "You shall yet be my rescuer!" he said. "I have always argued that no one can fence with more skill and finesse than a native Dane, and most especially, one of royal blood. I am determined that you shall prove my argument true." He put his hand on Hamlet's arm.

Hamlet's contentment seemed to evaporate for a moment. Then he recovered his mood (or so it seemed), as he said, "I am afraid your majesty has laid his wager on the weaker side."

"I do not fear it," Claudius answered. "I have seen you both, and we have the odds," he finished, as if some numerical guess can outmaneuver fate. Hamlet gave a wan smile and nodded.

I stayed near the entrance, watching. If anything untoward was going to happen, I was determined to ferret it out before any damage could be done.

The nobles in attendance turned their attention toward the principals—Hamlet, Claudius, Queen Gertrude, and to one side, Laertes.

The king steered Hamlet toward Laertes, who turned again to them, a serious expression on his face. Claudius grasped each of them by the right wrist and pulled them, not completely unwillingly, I thought, face to face.

"Come, Hamlet, take this hand from mine. It is time two such gentlemen as yourselves were able to forge the kind of accord that is becoming to members of the Danish royal court." He thrust their hands toward one another.

Hamlet did not hesitate, though I could see some misgivings in Laertes' expression. They clasped their right hands, like friends.

"Come, sir, and allow me in this public forum to extend to you my sincerest apology" Hamlet said, loudly and clearly, both for Laertes and for the assembled audience, who were now fully attentive. Laertes looked down, then met Hamlet's gaze. Hamlet continued.

"I recognize that I have done you wrong," Hamlet said, "but I must make clear that what I did, *I* did not do. You have surely heard that I suffer a sore affliction, a kind of intermittent madness. In the throes of such distress, I confess, this machine I call my body killed your father. Yet who truly committed this crime? Hamlet's madness did, never Hamlet. I beg you to give me your most generous thoughts, as only a gentleman such as yourself might find himself able to do, and to understand that, in my madness, I shot my arrow o'er the house and hurt my brother. For in my love for your family I regard you thus."

Laertes looked suspiciously at him for a long half minute, as if unaccustomed to such rhetoric. In the suspended moment there was a hush among the spectators, who watched the pair as if with bated breath.

Laertes finally replied, "Your words are clean and bright, and I would be a churl to tarnish them with untoward thoughts or imaginings. Yet, you must understand as well as any of us the weight of filial obligation and devotion." (At this, the king raised his head and looked most pointedly at the pair of them.) "And most surely I cannot ignore such calamities as a murdered father without taking every measure to ensure my family name shall not be sullied. And yet I am drawn to your intentions with a strong measure of compassion and at least some trust. Insofar as known masters of honor and civility can instruct me on how to proceed, I shall accept your apology, with the provision that I understand the debts a son owes a murdered father. Until such instruction I shall accept your brother's love like love, and not wrong it."

Hamlet looked at him a long moment, then smiled and said, "If that be so, then I embrace it freely. Let us play this brother's wager, and let sport dominate duty for this interval of pleasure and entertainment."

"Done," Laertes said, and he turned toward a rack of weapons where Osric seemed to be waiting. Osric hastened forward with a handful of foils, half a dozen or so. Hamlet accepted one and asked, "Are these foils all of similar length?"

"Of course, my liege," said Osric.

Laertes, who had drawn one and swept it back and forth in mock combat, handed it back to Osric saying, "This one is too heavy." He walked over to another quiver-like container beneath the weapons display and from it withdrew another, which seemed to satisfy him.

I looked around the room. The queen, attended by a young blond woman, moved to her seat and arranged herself carefully. The king snapped his fingers and a page appeared carrying a tray that supported a decanter and a pair of goblets. The king poured wine into one of the goblets, and he raised it toward Hamlet.

"Hamlet, I drink to thy health!" He raised the cup and swallowed some wine. Then, before restoring the cup to the tray, he drew a large pearl from the pocket of his damask robe. He raised it to Hamlet and before the audience.

"He who gains the first hit shall gain, as well, this pearl!" He returned it to his pocket, and smiling, made his way to his seat beside Gertrude, who took his hand, and kissed him on the cheek when he sat. Hamlet looked at them with a vacant expression for a moment, then turned to the open floor where Osric and Laertes stood waiting.

"Judges!" Claudius called. "Bear a wary eye."

Osric nodded, as did his fellow judge, who had stationed himself to one side. Hamlet and Laertes approached one another, and took their opening stance, swords crossed with Osric's foil between them. Osric swept his foil upward, separating their swords momentarily, and stepped rapidly backward. The bout was on!

If only I had noticed the swords. I should have seen the swords.

Truth be told, I was startled by Hamlet's skill. Although Laertes was known to be a sparkling swordsman, Hamlet easily bested him to the first hit, a light tap past Laertes' forearm against his rib cage.

"One!" cried Hamlet, and Osric confirmed it, as did his second judge, a gaunt-looking man in dark hose and a velvet jerkin, who nodded his agreement.

Laertes appeared momentarily surprised by the talent of his adversary. He backed away to a corner of the playing surface and eyed Hamlet, more warily this time, as if he suddenly realized that his confidence, which can sometimes reinforce skill, might in fact be overconfidence, which can sometimes betray it.

"Come, again!" he cried, and was about to move forward when the king intervened.

Claudius had gotten to his feet and moved to the tiny side table where the wine sat. He picked up one of the goblets, poured some wine into it, and after holding up the pearl for the inspection of the assembly, dropped it into the goblet saying, "Hamlet! This pearl belongs to you, now." He offered the goblet to Hamlet, who was not yet even perspiring.

"Not yet. I shall drink by and by." Hamlet looked carefully at Laertes, who suddenly grinned, saluted Hamlet with his foil (a cavalier gesture), and crouched, once again ready to fence.

Claudius set the cup back onto the tray and moved back to his seat, where Gertrude sat waiting, a puzzled expression on her face.

"Then commence once more," Claudius pronounced. Osric resumed his stance between the two men, swept his foil upward, and once again the two began.

The nobility among the crowd were riveted, including the ladies. Hamlet and Laertes fairly danced back and forth across the hardwood, rapiers flashing and clattering. At one point Laertes seemed to have Hamlet's foil disabled with a true 'tour-de-force' manoeuver, yet instead of backing away as one might expect, Hamlet closed with his opponent, rotated his body while sliding his left arm under Laerte's sword arm, spun his opponent around and away, all while slipping his own foil free and tapping Laertes on his left shoulder. What a move!

"Two!" Hamlet said, and even Laertes gazed at him in grudging admiration.

"A touch, a touch, I must confess it," he admitted.

At this moment the queen got to her feet, and pulling a soft kerchief from her sleeve approached Hamlet. She dabbed his forehead and muttered something in his ear, but Hamlet shook his head. "Not yet, Madam. I dare not drink yet. By and by."

She smiled at him indulgently, and said, "Oh, you men...so strong and noble," and she picked up Hamlet's goblet from the tray, raising it to her lips.

"Gertrude!" The king's voice was unusually loud, and everyone turned to look at him. He flushed self-consciously, but raised his hand, palm toward her, and said in a lower tone, "Do not drink yet. We will have ample wine to celebrate Hamlet's victory!"

"But I thirst, my lord. I pray you pardon me," she said with a saucy air, and she took several swallows, then set the goblet back on the tray.

The king stared blankly at her. Laertes looked at Claudius apprehensively and moved to him to whisper something in his ear. Claudius turned to him, some muscle in his jaw twitching. Then he said, "No. Not yet!" I was truly puzzled by this exchange, and the audience seemed nonplussed, as well.

"I fear you but dally, Laertes," Hamlet said cheerfully. "Come, pass with your best violence. It seems you're only playing with me."

"Say you so?" cried Laertes, and without waiting for Osric's commencement, strode toward Hamlet, rapier raised.

Yes. I should have noticed the swords, the moment when Laertes chose another foil.

The combat was furious, as if lives truly were at stake (and indeed, they were, although I did not realize this at the time). The room rang with steel blade on steel blade, and the shouts of encouragement or dismay from the audience.

I was captivated by the action, and yet, for a brief moment I looked back at the king. He, too, was not watching the fight. His eyes were on Gertrude, and the expression on his face was one of a mixture of despair and acquiescence. For her part, Gertrude was watching the fencing sequence keenly, wincing in fear at moments, then expressing relief. I, too, returned my concentration to the sport.

Finally, Laertes scored his first hit, but the shock of it was astonishing, for his blade sank into Hamlet's left forearm, and blood rapidly began seeping into the white sleeve. Hamlet looked at Laertes in disbelief.

Laertes stepped backward, and sneered, "Have at you now!" A rumbling murmur came from the audience, as watchers expressed their shock and horror to one another. A commoner attacking a prince! It was unthinkable.

Laertes must have seen the expression on Hamlet's face, for suddenly his own blanched. Hamlet took a rapid two steps, struck Laertes in the face with the hilt of his rapier, and pried Laertes' sword from his hand. Hamlet backed away, holding a rapier in each hand.

His nose bleeding, the scarlet runnel dripping over his lips, Laertes looked at him in sudden terror. He spat some blood and began to back away.

Hamlet smiled, the kind of smile a gambler exhibits when scooping up his winnings, the hint of amusement that might appear when some lesser opponent has been utterly destroyed. In what must have been a twitch of generosity, Hamlet tossed Laertes his own blunted sword and kept Laertes' sharpened blade.

"Have at *you*," Hamlet said quietly, yet all the room heard him. He advanced upon Laertes, who reflexively raised his blade.

Once more the two men attacked one another ferociously. Thrust, parry, thrust, parry, riposte, parry, thrust... Then it was suddenly finished. Hamlet slid the sharpened blade past Laertes' defensive move, slicing the forearm and sticking the point deep into Laertes' right bicep. The forearm bled forcefully. Laertes dropped the foil and gripped his arm hard. Scarlet blood leaked between his fingers and ran down his arm from his punctured bicep. He was pale with shock. He locked his eye on Hamlet and was about to speak when Osric shouted, "Look to the queen!"

Gertrude had risen from her chair and moved a few steps into the room, then sunk to her knees and vomited. She collapsed onto her back, gaping at the ceiling, her body twitching. She rolled half sideways, accusing eyes fixed on king Claudius, and raised her hand to point at him before collapsing backward once more.

"She swoons to see them bleed!" Claudius cried, but few heard him. He stood before his chair, swaying slightly. He looked at Laertes, who had sunk groaning to the floor, his hand on his wound. Gertrude's lady-in-waiting was at her side, wiping the queen's forehead with a silk kerchief.

Hamlet stepped quickly to her side and knelt. He cradled her head gently in his hands. She turned, and retched violently. "Mother?" he said plaintively.

"The drink...the drink..." she muttered, almost inaudibly. "I am poisoned...poisoned..." A tremor passed through her body, her eyes closed, and she relaxed into her death, an expression of resignation on her face, which still twitched every second or so, then became still.

"Poisoned?" Hamlet said softly.

Laertes, who held himself semi-erect only with great effort, interrupted.

"Hamlet! Hamlet. You, too, are as good as dead. The blade you hold was poisoned, as well. No medicine in the world can do thee good. And the foul practice has turned itself on me."

He looked toward Claudius. "*He* blended the mixture. It is all down to him. The king—the king's to blame!"

Claudius emitted half a chuckle, a snort to indicate how ridiculous such an assertion might be. Then he turned to Osric, as if for some moral support, but even Osric was staring at him blankly.

I stood near the entry, half paralyzed with astonishment and fear. I watched Hamlet struggle to get to his feet. He stood, swaying slightly.

"Poison? Poison again? First my father, then my mother..." he said as he moved across the floor toward the king, who raised his hand half in protest. It was his last significant gesture.

Hamlet drove the poisoned sword into Claudius's midriff at an upward angle, slicing through his diaphragm and up into the heart. Claudius emitted a startled gurgle, collapsed to his knees, whined slightly once, and then fell sideways. His crown toppled onto the floor and rolled with a metallic clatter.

Hamlet looked once more at Laertes, who now lay twisted on his side, straining to speak to the prince. Blood still leaked from one nostril, and he shuddered once, violently.

"Hamlet," he said. Hamlet raised his own head slightly. "Exchange forgiveness with me, Hamlet. Mine nor my father's death on you, nor thine on me..."

"Heaven make thee free of it," Hamlet said softly. Laertes rolled softly onto his back and his head lolled sideways away from us.

I finally found the strength to move and reached Hamlet just as he fell against the queen's table, which collapsed from his weight, the lethal goblet of red wine and the ewer both spilling across the hardwood floor. I caught him as best I could and let him down slowly to the floor, where he slumped, leaning against my chest. He coughed, a kind of sob or hiccup, and he convulsed under my grip.

"My lord," I said ineffectually. "Oh, Hamlet." He looked at me as though I were nearly a stranger. My heart contracted with sorrow.

"There is no king," he whispered to me hoarsely.

Then, more a question than a suggestion, he whispered, "Fortinbras? He has my dying voice."

Then, as if all the voices in the world had suddenly been extinguished, he said, "The rest is silence." He collapsed limply in my arms.

It must have been several minutes before I recovered sufficiently from my shock to get a true sense of what had just occurred.

When I looked around, most of the audience had fled. The king lay in a pool of his own blood, the waxen character of death on his face. Laertes was on his back, his head twisted sideways, his lifeless eyes gazing blankly at the wall. The queen's lady-in-waiting held Gertrude's head in her lap and keened softly to herself. I looked once more at Hamlet, motionless beside me.

"The rest is silence," Hamlet had said. "'Rest' as remainder, or 'rest' as repose, I wonder. I truly hope the latter."

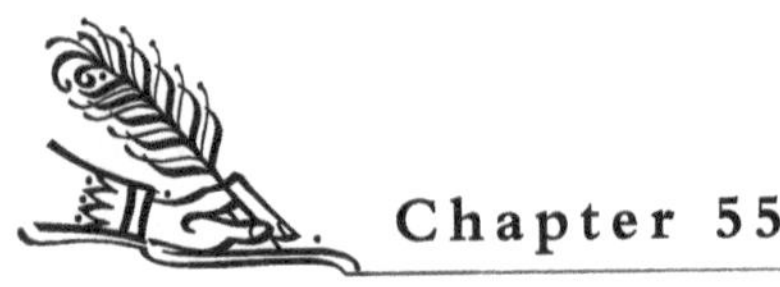

Chapter 55

The Arrival of Fortinbras

Fortinbras felt his belly churn, the kind of tension now familiar from his experience in Poland, the tension one feels when at any moment his life might be at stake.

The Norwegian ships had landed away from settlement, as they had in Poland, more than a dozen miles down the coast from Elsinore. This time in Denmark they weren't coming through the front door.

From horseback Fortinbras and Lars gazed at the city which lay strangely quiet just a few miles off. No flag flew above the palace precincts. Only the odd trail of smoke from a chimney wafted upward into a pale grey sky.

Fortinbras turned to Lars. "Something is wrong," he said. "We should have been challenged by Danish forces miles back. What from our scouts?"

Lars continued staring at the quiet city. It was as if a plague had struck (and indeed, that was not out of the question). A few crows circled overhead, and then cawing, winged away to roost in a copse of trees about fifty yards away. Along a low rise toward the water a pair of dogs appeared, stopped to look at the column of armed men, gave a few half-hearted barks, and then turned and loped away.

"Neither is yet returned, my liege," Lars finally answered.

Then, from the harbor area, a cannon boomed. Fortinbras craned his neck. The sound echoed out over the water, and he and Lars could see the puff of smoke rising from where the gun must have been mounted below. Out on the water a small trading vessel was making its way in toward the docks.

"Bring thirty mounted men," Fortinbras said. "We'll investigate. Ensure that the remainder of our force be kept alert."

Lars gave a half salute, turned his horse and rode back toward Nils, one of the sub-commanders.

Fortinbras continued to watch the harbor. There was still no significant activity at the palace area that he could see. But at a bend in the road perhaps two leagues away a rider on a mule appeared, trotting briskly toward Fortinbras.

As the man came closer, Fortinbras recognized one of the two scouts he had sent to reconnoiter the city. He had dressed as if he were a tradesman, with two panniers containing a variety of tinker's tools hanging over the mule's flanks behind the rudimentary saddle. Fortinbras rode out to meet him. The man pulled up before him and saluted briskly.

"Well, what have you?" Fortinbras asked.

"As you can see from here, the city is deathly quiet. In two of the inns a rumor was circulating that there has been some kind of incident in the palace. No one knows for sure what has happened." The man paused and took several deep breaths.

"Go on, man," said Fortinbras impatiently.

The man continued, measuring his words carefully.

"Jarl, the other scout, and I separated. He headed down toward the harbor and is probably even now investigating the arrival we heard signaled. I went up toward the palace and got within a few hundred yards of the main gates, where palace guards prevented my admittance." He took another deep breath.

"At first they were suspicious, but I told them I was seeking my little daughter who had run off with a friend. I shared with two of them some brandy from my flask, and they agreed with commendable sympathy that they would keep a sharp eye out for her. When I asked why everything was so quiet, they confided in me that access to the palace had been shut down by a king's representative named Sir Osric, and that no one was to be permitted entry. If I might be allowed to say so, sir, it's very eerie."

Fortinbras eyed him a moment, then asked, "Do they appear prepared for any kind of military engagement?"

"Far from it, sir. There was no sign of any sizable force aside from a few dozen guards posted at intervals where gates access the palace precinct."

"Hasten back to Lars. Tell him to bring sixty more mounted warriors. He will know what I mean. Well done."

The scout saluted again, kicked the mule, and headed back toward the main column.

Within minutes, Fortinbras and Lars were leading their extended line of crack troopers on into the outskirts of Elsinore. The streets were nearly deserted. An old priest standing on the steps of a small church crossed himself as they passed, then retreated into the building, closing the door behind him. Above the clatter of their hoofbeats the Norwegians heard the heavy thump of its locking crossbar falling into place.

A few minutes later they were heading up the low, cobbled hill road toward the palace. Their lances and other weapons at the ready, a dozen guards formed up at their approach, looking nervously at the Norwegian troopers.

Fortinbras raised his arm as he slowed to a stop, and his troops stopped behind him. The Danish guards were perhaps fifteen paces away. One of them came gingerly forward, sword sheathed but at the ready, and greeted Fortinbras carefully.

"I am Karl of the king's Swiss guard," he said in halting Danish.

Fortinbras studied the man for a moment. Then he said, loudly enough to be heard by all the Danish guards, "Sir. Kindly inform the

Danish king that Fortinbras of Norway is returned from conquest in Poland. By agreement and with the king's express approval we passed through Elsinore only a few weeks ago. I would parley with him to report the outcome of our expedition and to continue to cement the growing cooperation between our peoples."

The guard recognized Fortinbras and his men. He gave no answer, but bowed low to Fortinbras, and then turned and made his way past his own comrades to the closed gate. At their guard line, he paused and whispered a word or two to a burly man who appeared to be more senior than the others. The man nodded and grunted something to the other guards, who remained standing motionless in the roadway, hands on the hilts of their swords. At some indeterminate signal from Karl, the smaller portal within the gate swung open to admit him; he stepped through, and the portal closed behind him.

"Well?" said Lars.

"We wait," answered Fortinbras.

The town was still quiet. Fortinbras's men remained mounted. Occasionally a horse nickered or stepped sideways, only to be brought back into line and stillness by the pressure of a knee or a light tug on a rein. A few gulls squawked as they sailed up the street from the harbor, then lighted on the crown of an inn roof a hundred feet away. A ragged grey cat looked at them from an alley, then turned and disappeared between two wooden kegs.

After about twelve minutes one of the troopers trotted up from the rear to his commander. "Lord prince," he said. At Fortinbras' nod, he said, "There is a group of eight or so well-dressed men approaching from the harbor."

"Bring them to me," Fortinbras commanded.

The younger man nodded and wheeled his horse around to canter down along the men. He selected ten troopers from the back of the line and they trotted into the side street that led to the harbor. Four or five minutes later four of the troopers escorted two lavishly dressed gentlemen riding mules up to Fortinbras. The Swiss guards looked on with interest but did not interfere.

"And you are?" asked Fortinbras.

One of the men swung off his mule and straightened his cloak and doublet. The other remained mounted. The first gave Fortinbras an ironic smile and said, "I might ask the same of you, do you not think?"

Fortinbras smiled despite himself. He looked the man over, obviously a gentleman, a man accustomed to power and deference, both given and received.

"I am Prince Fortinbras of Norway, sir, at your service…in a manner of speaking, that is. And you?"

The man removed his hat and gave Fortinbras a sweeping bow.

"Lord prince, I am Sir Reginald, envoy of the governor of England in York to his majesty King Claudius of Denmark. I have important news for him."

Fortinbras nodded. "Well, Sir Reginald, it appears we shall both have to wait."

But at that moment the larger gate in the wall began to swing inward. Karl, the guard commander, emerged beside a haggard looking gentleman wearing a blue felt hat with a wide brim. Behind them walked a bearded young man who appeared to be wearing the robes of a scholar.

They made their way past the guards' small line and came to within five paces of Fortinbras and Sir Reginald, who looked at them expectantly. The three men bowed low, and upon straightening up, the gentleman said in a quavering voice, "Welcome, gentlemen, welcome to Elsinore."

At a signal from Karl, the line of Swiss guards parted to form a short corridor leading to the gate. The scholar moved out of the way, but never took his eyes off Fortinbras, who, for a moment, returned his gaze. Then Fortinbras, Sir Reginald and the others trotted slowly into the palace grounds.

Chapter 56

A New Beginning

How can it be so cold? Horatio thought to himself. He wore fisherman's gloves and had even managed to get an extra bundle of firewood from brother Henrik, at least half of which was already blazing in the small fireplace. The cat paced back and forth in front of the flames a few times, then curled up in some sawdust as near the fire as it dared.

Horatio selected a new quill and dipped it into the ink, which looked distinctly frosty on its surface. But the quill came up dripping, and Horatio wiped its sides before moving it to the paper before him.

I first saw our noble King Fortinbras the day he returned to Elsinore from Poland, strangely coincident to the day of Hamlet's murder, directly after the disastrous fencing tourney.

Events threatened to become quite chaotic in the fencing hall after the multiple deaths. I was in personal shock of some kind. When I became myself once more, I noticed Sir Osric holding a flask of brandy before me. I recall taking a large swallow.

Hamlet lay on the floor before me, glassy-eyed, staring at God's eternity for all I knew. My heart contracted in pain when I saw him.

Beyond Hamlet was Laertes, face averted as if in shame, a sticky pool of his own blood spread beneath his forearm.

When I turned, I could see the queen, rigid on the floor behind me, a strangely frustrated expression on her face, as if in her final moments she had seen one of life's supreme disappointments.

A few feet from her the king lay, waxen and unmoving, his countenance displaying a kind of sneering confidence, except that it was utterly still.

"You're awake!" Osric said.

"Yes, I'm awake, you fool," I recall answering. Then I regretted it, for however vain or ambitious he might have been, he is not a fool. He knows where and how his bread, however rough the flour might have been milled, is buttered.

Despite my insult, he helped me to my feet. The courtiers who had been present for the fencing match had long since fled, to whatever safe warren they imagined they might find within the palace precincts.

"I have already ordered the gates locked down," said Osric, apologetically. "I used the king's name." He paused. "I don't think he'll mind," he added as a kind of ironic afterthought. I merely stared at him.

It was then that a breathless servant appeared in the doorway. He stared, dumbfounded, for a few moments. Finally I found my own voice.

"What do you want?" I asked him, in a tone that I imagined might fit an officer or aristocratic superior. I remember Osric's looking at me with a kind of new respect in his expression.

"My lord," the servant said, and from his head movements it was not clear whether he was answering me or addressing the more suitably costumed Osric. "There is a group of armed men at the east gate. Karl from the Swiss guard is outside, awaiting instruction.

Osric and I looked at one another, before Osric took control.

"We will come to meet them," he said, and indicated that the man should precede us. The man took another gawk at the room and its macabre decoration of extraordinary corpses. He blanched.

"You will not speak of this!" Osric said emphatically. The servant nervously swallowed and nodded. We left the room and closed the door behind us. He turned, indicating that we should follow him.

"Is there a guard nearby?" Osric asked him, and then, noticing a group of three guards led by Anton approaching along the corridor, snapped his fingers imperiously for them to come quickly.

"Ensure that no one, I repeat, no one opens this door until I return," Osric said to the man on their approach. "On pain of death, probably yours, if this command is not obeyed," Osric added for emphasis.

Anton straightened to attention, and he stammered, "I will, my lord."

Karl was waiting for us, as the servant had said. He rapidly summarized what he had seen, and he was clearly expecting some kind of instruction, although this usually came from the king.

"We must open the gate and invite and escort them inside," I quickly asserted. I remembered vividly what Hamlet had said, just before his death. "There is no king," and, "Fortinbras--he has my dying voice."

"And his majesty will approve?" he queried, regarding our decision to meet these foreigners in such a trusting way.

"Undoubtedly," I said, and Osric nodded emphatically.

Within minutes we were at the gate. Karl indicated to the gatekeeper that the larger gate was to be opened.

Although momentarily taken aback, the gatekeeper did not say anything. He and a younger assistant lifted the great bar that held the gate closed, and deposited it with a 'thunk' to rest against the gatehouse wall. Then the man lifted the smaller latch and began to swing the great gate inward. I recall watching its shadow sweep across the courtyard, and to my surprise hearing no squeal or screech. *Someone must have recently oiled the hinges*, I thought.

Karl and Osric moved through the gate ahead of me, but I was not averse to following. Had I not been something of a follower for most of my life, reading others' thoughts, squatting in Hamlet's magnificent shadow? Still, I followed closely, for who knew what foolishness these two might commit in the dead king's name?

I had never seen prince (now king) Fortinbras before. He was in the rough gear of a common soldier, yet it was obvious at first glance that he held the power in this gathering. When Osric invited him and his troopers into the palace grounds he looked at me closely as they rode past.

One always wonders what is in a look. Judgment? Mirth? Offence? So much can be read into the focus of another's eyes.

I remember Hamlet's eyes, sparkling in jest as he was so prone to do, clouded in puzzlement over some philosophical conundrum, the kind of preoccupation that filled our youthful lives with meaning in Wittenberg.

I remember, too, the dark eyes of the young, beautiful Ophelia, doleful yet shining with hope, wells of mystery, and savage sorrow.

Then Fortinbras was past, and I followed them all into the palace grounds.

Fortinbras' second-in-command (a man I was later introduced to as Lars) stationed his troopers in tight formation between a large well and one of the king's stables. The men looked around in measured apprehension.

Fortinbras himself dismounted and said to Sir Osric, "Take me to the king."

At this point I felt compelled to interrupt. "That won't be possible, I'm afraid."

He stared at me so darkly that I quickly added, "The king is dead." I paused, then said, "We can take you to him, but I fear your intercourse will be rather limited."

He scowled at me. "Prince Hamlet? He is still in England?"

"No," I answered. "He is here. But he, too, is dead."

"Dead?"

"And the queen, too." I took a deep breath and looked away to gather my thoughts. A horse nickered nearby, and some harness rattled.

"I have a long story to tell you," I finally said in a low voice. "Much has happened since you passed this way weeks ago, and indeed, the tale goes much further back than that. But some of those details are for another day."

"Show me," he said.

It was a simple command. It was not its meaning that struck me, but its tone. This was a prince speaking, a man not only accustomed to command but born to it. I nodded slowly, twice.

He selected six men from the troopers to accompany us. Osric, Karl and I escorted them. We scarcely spoke except to say, "This way," or "Turn left here."

The guard Anton at the fencing hall seemed grateful to see us and readily unlocked the door. Osric eyed him carefully, but I am sure the man had not entered in our brief absence.

Nothing had been moved. The king's face was grey, as if some contagion belonging to him alone ate at him from within. The crown still lay gleaming on the bloody hardwood between Hamlet's and Claudius' bodies.

"This quarry suggests havoc!" Fortinbras exclaimed to no one in particular, as we stood together at the entrance, staring at the bodies.

He turned to the man called Lars and said, "Everything I was ever told of Hamlet suggested that, had he been crowned, he would have proven most royal...an opponent, perhaps, but most royal."

Lars raised his eyes, but did not reply. The group seemed transfixed by the grotesque postures in disarray on the floor before them.

A moment or so later Fortinbras said, "Take Hamlet's body. Prepare it appropriately that it might be displayed upon a public stage. The people here must learn of what has happened, yet must hear it in a manner and milieu that suggests no need for fear. And this must happen quickly, while others' minds are wild, before such wildness might infect the people of Elsinore, and Denmark as a whole. Fire cannon to alert the population, and prepare messengers to disperse the news throughout the town."

He looked at me, somehow expectantly.

"I have many things to tell you," I said, "not the least important of which is something Hamlet said to me only minutes before he died."

He eyed me critically. "Go on," he said.

"Hamlet, my prince, said that you have his dying voice, that you should become king of the Danes."

He looked at me for a long moment, then at the others, who seemed almost suspended in time in their stillness.

Then he drew himself up and said, "I have some rights of memory in this kingdom, and although the Danes and my personal forebears have not always been generous or amicable one to the other, the practicalities provided us all by Fortune seem to indicate that your prince was both wise and prescient. But indeed, as you say, you have much to tell me."

He gave me a rather severe look of appraisal, then turned to the others. "We must call an assembly of the noblest among the Danes. Messengers must be sent throughout the kingdom. Meanwhile, these deaths must be explained, not only to me, but to the people at large."

Osric had been gazing at the floor, but he looked up quickly and nodded his agreement. Karl appeared wan but equable.

I said, "I am at your disposal, Prince Fortinbras."

He looked at me as if to say, 'I know.'

Epilogue

Horatio blew on his hands and selected a quill. He was thoughtful for a moment or two before he began to write. He stared at the familiar table top, now stained here and there with ink drops. He glanced at the black window. Not even a star showed light without.

He thought a moment. He had been working on this report for the better part of two months. He lowered his head again and began.

Resolved that he should come to understand the downfall of the Danish royal house, king Fortinbras commanded that I create this history. I have reread its contents over the past few days, and I could argue before the strongest court to avouch its accuracy. However, in many aspects its choice of details and narrative style are, in my judgment, too personal and informal to serve. I shall have to risk the 'tsk-tsk' disapproval of brother Henrik and the impatience of the king himself before I shall have a document suitable to serve as the kind of report he requires. There exist details in the present copy that may not serve anyone's memory or interests well. Given that knowledge, I have decided to rewrite the report more formally and to present it as a Christmas gift to king Fortinbras himself.

Although this story recounts much evil, I believe it will suitably bolster our new king's position. I recall a chilly night when Hamlet had disappeared with the ghost of his father: "Something is rotten in the state of Denmark," Marcellus had cried. Yes, rotten it was. Now, with God's help, the decay in the apple of Denmark has been cut away. (True, the good fruit—Hamlet—was cut away, too; but Providence has a way of turning our lives to unknown ends. This was one such time, I believe.)

Among Hamlet's papers I salvaged this bit of reflection that I believe lends perspective to his state of mind a scant few weeks before his death. It was dated the night before the play, the night before he killed Polonius. I shall quote it directly, for it eloquently addresses an ongoing problem for all of us—how we should live, how we should act, in a world that often constitutes itself as an obstacle to our interests or as a danger to both ourselves and to our friends and neighbors.

What is a man, if the sum total of his virtues consists merely of sleeping and feeding? A beast, no more. Surely the God that we fear and love, and credit with our creation, having given us the immeasurable gifts of love, reason and idealism, intends that we use our powers toward the betterment of His world. I have tested the king. He has failed. Surely this rancid sore of a man must be removed from the body politic before he corrupts us all. I have waited too long to act on my father's dread command. But if vengeance be bloody, it may also be the hot iron needed to cauterize the wound that infects my family and my nation. I am shamed by my delay. It is time to act.

He knew, of course. There are times to think, times to act. Hamlet succeeded, yet at great cost.

Now we have a new king.

King Fortinbras has not made dramatic changes to the structure of Denmark—yet. Perhaps now that he has power, he, too, is considering how to act. New acts for a new year, after Christmas?

The time of our Savior's birth should be one of rejoicing, or at the very least, one of acceptance. Did not Marcus Aurelius himself say that we should live in hope and gratitude that things turn out exactly the way they do?

Fortune's wheel is ours to cope with and accept, not something it is profitable to question. And certainly the new king, and even in large measure the people of Denmark, have much to be grateful for.

As Hamlet so simply and wisely advised only hours before his death, "Let be."

Horatio looked up from his manuscript. He thought a moment, then set down his quill. The cat stared at him sideways from its cushion, and reaching to rub its head, Horatio gave a brief smile. Then he bent forward and blew out the candle.

The End

Acknowledgements

This book would have been impossible were it not for the contributions of numerous colleagues, friends, and family.

The staff members at Lulu Publishing, including Kevin Foran, Danny Hale, Adriane Pontecorvo, Mandy Tancak, and presumably other members of their team, were unfailingly professional and supportive in their directions and advice.

Teachers from my own adolescence, however distant now in time, helped in numerous positive ways. Mr. Melvin Coates was my own English teacher when I was young, a man who skillfully introduced me to the value of Shakespeare's plays. Through his compassionate understanding of the wayward but impressionable attention of adolescents, and through his knowledge and personal enthusiasm, he first brought them to life for me.

Colleagues from my own staff at Caledonia Senior Secondary School were also helpful. Ian Jordan, a close friend for many years, helped keep my own interest in these works alive through his many insights into English history and language, as well as the classics.

Thank you to another friend and colleague, Bruce Chapman, for being the first guinea pig to read the initial manuscript, and to my sister, Elizabeth Greenwall for being the second. Their encouragement gave me the impetus to rework the book for publication.

Finally, I'd like to express my continual love and gratitude to my wife and partner, Elaine Fleischmann, who not only designed the cover, but who also spent countless hours editing out inconsistencies and contradictions that lay somehow invisible to me in the initial text, but readily observable by a percipient mind such as she.

As always, any errors or artistic blemishes that remain are fully the fault of the author, who has developed a new appreciation for the creative chore that is all writing.

Questions for Study

If *Hamlet: the Novel* has served to enrich classroom study of Shakespeare's story, the following questions might assist students and their teachers to dissect its larger themes. Even a casual reader may enjoy considering these puzzling problems.

1. Horatio, the narrator of the report that makes up a large portion of this book, clearly loves and admires Hamlet. Based on your knowledge of Hamlet from the larger story, does Hamlet deserve Horatio's nearly unreserved approval, or does he fail to live up to Horatio's assessment?
2. *Hamlet* is a story with many victims, some more or less innocent, and some guilty of heinous crimes. Select any two of these victims and compare their moral culpabilities.
3. A common literary 'trick' used by authors to enhance our understanding of main characters (protagonists, such as Hamlet) is to provide them with one or more character foils, characters who are superficially similar to the protagonist but who also have striking differences to him, differences that serve to sharpen our perception of the main character through comparison and contrast. From the other characters in the novel, select a character foil for Hamlet and through reference to your choice's personality and behavior in the story, show both his similarities and differences to the prince.

4. There are numerous references to fate in this story. Locate (and quote) two such references and discuss the attitude toward fate's power expressed in each. Is there any sense in which the culture's dominant religious beliefs contributed to this attitude? Explain.
5. Madness or insanity is an elusive concept. In contemporary society we have tended to 'medicalize' it, speaking of 'mental illness.' In earlier societies it was often attributed to demons or to the actions of the gods.
   Two of the characters in Hamlet putatively suffer from madness: Hamlet and Ophelia. (Curious, is it not, how they should be attracted to one another?) What are some of the features of their maladies, both common and different? Discuss, with reference to speeches and behaviors in the story. Is it possible that Hamlet was not mad at all?
6. How do honesty and deceit contribute to the unfolding of this story? (Consider its various plots and counterplots, and characters' assertions, both true and counterfeit.) Is Hamlet's claim true, that an honest man is one to be picked from ten thousand? Discuss, with reference to more than one character, conversation, or event.
7. There are various sources of political power in the world. What sources of such power are evident in *Hamlet*? To what extent are these based on either cooperation or conflict?
8. In conversation with the soldiers on the guard platform (prior to meeting the ghost of his father), Hamlet remarks that in our encounters with other people, "We seem to look always for the evil, never the good, to expect the worst, even to demand it, and to forget that man is at least partly angel." Is his generalization borne out by events in the story? Is it borne out in our own lives and experience? Discuss.
9. During the play, the player king explains (in poetry) that we all too easily abandon our purpose or resolve regarding our own

actions. Select two or three of his arguments. Quote them, interpret them, and evaluate them. How might his argument apply to more than one character in the novel? To us?

10. Horatio often comments upon ironies he observes in the actions and speeches of the people around him. Describe one of these incidents. How does the irony enhance our understanding of the event, situation or dilemma that it describes?
11. Numerous contrasts heighten our understanding of this story. Select one of the following pairs and explain how the pair achieves this in *Hamlet: the Novel.*

    a. thought and action
    b. idealism and practicality
    c. love and hate
    d. power and vulnerability
    e. life and death
    f. guilt and innocence
    g. ambition and contentment
    h. loyalty and treachery

12. Fortinbras concludes that he thought Hamlet, as a king, would have proved "most royal." What do you think? Would Hamlet have made a good king? Why or why not?